MAKE BELIEVE

Teresa Warfield

J

JOVE BOOKS, NEW YORK

MAKE BELIEVE

A Jove Book / published by arrangement with
the author

PRINTING HISTORY
Jove edition / May 1995

ISBN: 0-515-11610-6

A JOVE BOOK®
Jove Books are published by The Berkley Publishing Group,
200 Madison Avenue, New York, New York 10016.
JOVE and the "J" design are trademarks
belonging to Jove Publications, Inc.

PRINTED IN THE UNITED STATES OF AMERICA

10 9 8 7 6 5 4 3 2 1

For Rhonda Hermes,
friend extraordinaire

MAKE BELIEVE

Prologue

"SPLENDID! OH, SHE'LL be splendid!" Margaret Anne Murphy said, bubbling with excitement as she ducked beneath the arm of her stout nursemaid, Mrs. O'Brien, and shot into her father's study. Mrs. O'Brien had appeared in the doorway not a minute before, saying that Miss Margaret was adamantly requesting to see her father. The woman had been employed in the Murphy household for little more than a month, and though she'd been told numerous times by Thomas Murphy himself that Margaret did not need special permission to see or talk to him, Mrs. O'Brien persisted with the propriety.

"I know she will be! I just know it! I've heard the talk and I just know it!"

Hiking one side of her flounced yellow skirt nearly up to her bottom and showing more than the usual amount of pantalets, Margaret fairly flew across the room, almost colliding with a wing-back chair that had been resting peacefully near the fireplace. She had what looked like a newspaper tucked under one arm. A stack of papers, arranged neatly on a side table only a second before, caught the breeze the girl created and blew about, scattering carelessly across the carpeted floor. She collided with a second table, dropped her paper, and paused only long enough to scoop it up. Thomas wasn't sure she even took a breath before tearing his way again, her golden curls bouncing and shimmering in the lamplight.

"Maggie, love, what is it that's got me girl in such a fuss?" he queried, pleasantly surprised, employing the heavy brogue she always found so delightful. There was no finer feeling than the one that came over him when his Margaret was near and happy.

She eased between the large desk and his chair and jumped up onto his lap, knocking the pen from his hand and scattering more papers. Her blue eyes glowed as he hadn't seen them glow in a good long while—since before the death of her mother last year.

"Look, Papa. Oh, look!" the girl exclaimed, pushing the paper beneath his nose. "Katie Farren gave it to me and—"

Mrs. O'Brien sniffed loudly as she approached. "She's been down at the levee again, Dr. Murphy. That is where she spent the afternoon. She returned home with her dress torn and dirty, and when I scolded her, she uttered words she learned from the riffraff with whom she's allowed to associate. It's a disgrace that Miss Katie and Miss Margaret, being from the upper class, are allowed to run with that band." The lines had deepened across the woman's forehead since her employment began here, Thomas thought. She'd developed more of them, too, since taking charge of his daughter. He sighed. Maggie, with all her energy and stubbornness, could tax a person's patience and endurance. There was no denying that.

"They're not riffraff!" Maggie said, glaring at the woman. "They're my friends!"

"Down at the levee with those undesirable children she's befriended," the nursemaid continued, undaunted. "No good'll come of this, I tell you. A child of her position must be watched. She must not be allowed to—"

"Is it not yer task to watch her, Mrs. O'Brien?" Thomas interjected, lifting one brow.

Wincing, the woman clasped her hands, pursed her lips, and withdrew a bit, apparently realizing that she had gone a little too far in her criticism. Thomas turned his attention back to Margaret.

The girl smiled smugly, tilting her chin up at Mrs. O'Brien, then lowering it as she turned the smile on her father. And what a bright, mischievous smile it was. Thomas narrowed one eye. Perhaps people like Mrs. O'Brien were right in their speculations: If he did not stop allowing Maggie to manipulate him and always have her way, she'd come to no good. He gave her most everything she wanted. In fact, he couldn't remember denying her even one request since Abby's death.

"It's her! Her!" Margaret said, thrusting the paper at him again. "And she's coming here to St. Louis! They're fixing up the ballroom in Concert Hall just for her. That's because she's special! A beautiful actress with a wonderful voice is what Jonathan called her. He saw her upriver a bit. She's with the Jefferson Company, and the whole company's good, Jonathan says. But Josephine Gavin . . . he calls her splendid. He stood in the pit and had to strain to see her and hear her at first, but then he got a good look and the noise was less, and he said he couldn't take his eyes off her!"

Thomas, an eye still narrowed, took the paper from Maggie's hand. "That's Jonathan Drury, is it? The lad I met outside the garden gate only last week?"

Maggie nodded earnestly.

"Well, now. I was his age once, and not that long ago, either, mind you. I'd judge him to be near twelve, wouldn't you?"

Another nod. Her cheeks were flushed. Her eyes shimmered prettily. Give the lass another five years, and he'd be fighting the suitors off their doorstep. She was a beauty, his daughter, and she was charming.

"When I was twelve, I was beginnin' to fancy just about every girl who walked by. So it's not surprisin' that Jonathan thinks—"

"Papa," Maggie said sternly, sobering, looking a little wounded that he was making light of all of this. "Jonathan says she's beautiful, so she is."

He grinned. "Well, there you have it. If Jonathan says she is, then she is." The last thing he wanted to do was hurt the girl's feelings by ridiculing her friend. "Let me have a look at what the paper says, at whatever has me girl so excited,"

Thomas said, easing her off of his lap.

She stood nearby as he placed the crumpled copy of the *Missouri Republican* on his desk and attempted to smooth a few wrinkles from it. He did not miss the smile of victory Maggie tossed Mrs. O'Brien. Huffing, the woman turned on her heel and stomped off, saying that he should call her when he was ready for her to take charge of Miss Margaret again.

"Right there," Maggie said, pointing to the part of the paper she wanted him to read. Thomas's gaze fell on a declaration:

> *Messrs. Jefferson and Neville respectfully announce to the citizens of St. Louis that they have fitted up the splendid ballroom in Concert Hall for dramatic representations. On Monday, March 9, will be presented*

THE LADY OF LYONS
or, Love and Pride

Claude Melnotte	Mr. Leicester
Colonel Damas	Mr. Jefferson
Deschapelles	Mr. Sankey
Madame Deschapelles	Miss Gavin
Pauline Deschapelles	Mrs. Ingersoll
Dame Melnotte	Mrs. Edwards

After the Play

Song "The Last of Gowrie"	Miss Gavin
Comic Song	Master Jefferson
Sailor's Hornpipe	Mr. Burke

To Conclude with

An Affair of Honor

Major Limsky	Mr. C.L. Green
Martha	Miss Gavin

"And the actress again yer Jonathan is so taken with?" Thomas inquired, thinking the whole affair looked like quite a production, that he might even consider purchasing box seats and taking Constance, the woman he had been seeing for nearly four months now, the very woman who seemed enthusiastic about mothering Margaret. He glanced at the date of the production. March eleventh. Only a week away. He seemed to remember Constance mentioning their having supper with her parents right around that date.

"How could you forget her name, Papa?" Again, Maggie looked wounded. She was very good at assuming looks like that one, and sometimes—frequently—he thought she used them because she knew they tore at his heart.

"Margaret, love. I was teasin'." He glanced back down at the paper, and his eyes were drawn to the one name that was repeated in the announcement three times, the name of the actress who must be featured. He hoped he was right. "Surely Miss Gavin becomes confused as to who she is, playin' so many different parts an' people."

Maggie giggled, a sound that never failed to warm Thomas's heart. For too long, for months and months after Abby's death, she'd not smiled, much less laughed or giggled.

Thomas pulled his daughter onto his lap again, and now they both glanced at the declaration. "It looks to be a spectacle, love. It surely does. One people will turn up for, that's for certain."

"Papa . . ."

"Hm?"

"I'd like to go see her. I want to hear her sing and I want to meet her. You've taken Constance to the theater before, that one just down the street from Concert Hall—the St. Louis Theater. And you know where Concert Hall is. Even I know that." She wriggled excitedly on his lap, her words coming faster and faster. "I'd dress real pretty and be real well behaved, so behaved even Mrs. O'Brien's sure to like me. I'd—"

"Maggie, I've told you to call Constance Miss Blanche."

"I know, Papa," Margaret said, casting her lashes down, looking meek, calming almost at once.

Maggie? *Meek?* Thomas stifled a bark of laughter at the thought.

He watched her, growing serious, knowing he couldn't possibly grant her latest request. True to what Mrs. O'Brien had implied, he had allowed his daughter many more liberties than a child of her upbringing—especially a girl—would normally be afforded; and in the long run, that would not be good for Margaret.

As a boy he had struggled, the son of poor Irish immigrants. He had wandered the streets of St. Louis, entertaining the dream of someday becoming a doctor and climbing the social ladder, not struggling anymore for a bite to eat and for respect. His father had saved penny after penny and had eventually sent Thomas to medical school in Chicago, and there he had excelled, getting the highest marks in his class. He had returned home shortly afterward, opened a practice, and gained the respect he had always desired. More and more people had grown to know him, and his prominence in the city had grown. He had married Abby, Margaret's mother, the daughter of a colleague. And then last year, right before Abby's death, the board of directors of St. Louis University had asked him to join their staff.

His prominent social position in the city almost guaranteed his daughter a comfortable future. Although he had hired Mrs. O'Brien to replace the nursemaid who had left his service some three months ago, he was guilty of being complacent where Maggie was concerned. She was so dear to him, he allowed her to run wild by not scolding or punishing her when she did things like go to the levee after he had told her not to. He wanted her to have friends; in fact, he thought her newfound friendships had helped bring her happiness again. But this . . . he glanced down at her torn and dirtied dress, the result of her excursion to the levee this afternoon.

He could not continue to allow her to run wild. She was Margaret Anne Murphy, daughter of Dr. Thomas Murphy, and she should not be running the streets, which were crowded with the hundreds of people the steamers brought to port and deposited daily. She had a nice life ahead of her, free of struggle, but not if she earned a poor reputation.

"Maggie, you went to the levee after I forbade it," he scolded gently. He had to take a firm tone with her. He had to.

"But, Papa, that's where my friends are," she objected, her lower lip protruding suddenly.

He cleared his throat. "The levee's no place for you. Yer friends may come here to visit with you."

Her lashes shot up. "Here? Mrs. O'Brien'll run them off! I just know it. Papa, you can't mean it."

"I do, Maggie. I love you, but the levee's no place for you, an' I don't want to hear of you goin' there again. I'll have to punish you if you do, an' that'll break me heart—but I'll do it, Margaret. Yer mother wouldn't have wanted you down there, either, an' if your grandparents ever learn of it, I'll never hear the end of it from them. Runnin' the levee is not somethin' a proper girl like yerself should be doin'."

She studied him, her head tilting back a bit, and he knew he had a battle ahead with his daughter where the levee and her friends there were concerned. He knew Maggie's stubbornness and determination—they were not unlike his own—and though she suddenly dipped her head and tried to look meek again, he'd wager his accounts that Maggie would run off to the docks again, and soon.

"What of the theater performance, Papa?" she asked quietly.

"Maggie, I know you an' yer friends play at actin', that you have for some time now, an' I know by the look you had on yer face when you came runnin' in here that you'd like nothin' better than to go see an' hear this Miss Gavin. But the truth is . . . the truth is, the theater's no place for a child, an' actresses aren't the nicest women." He watched her, wondering how to explain to a nine-year-old child exactly what he meant, that this Miss Gavin was undoubtedly a "woman of the night." He shifted nervously.

She jumped off of his lap, plopped her clenched hands on her hips, and glared at him, thoroughly offended. "You're wrong about that! Jonathan met her, and he says she's beautiful, has a lovely voice, and she's as nice as can be!"

"I'm not talkin' about as a person, Maggie."

"I wanna go to the play. I wanna hear her sing and act! If you don't take me, maybe someone else will!"

Thomas inhaled deeply and straightened in his chair. Yes, indeed, he knew Maggie was stubborn and could be defiant, but he'd never seen this much stubbornness and defiance out of her. Not toward him, anyway.

He rose behind his desk and looked down at her, trying to hold firm in his decision. "Margaret Anne. You asked about goin' to the theater, an' I told you no. No one else will be takin' you. If you leave this house the day of the eleventh, you'll be punished. Is that understood?" He'd never used such a severe tone with her, and doing so pained him more than she could know.

She studied him, measuring whether he was serious, he thought. Then she lowered her chin to her chest, snatched her newspaper from his desk, and shuffled away.

She reached the door without ever looking back, and once she had disappeared into the hall outside the study, Thomas sank down into his chair, propped his chin in his palm, and shook his head. He strongly suspected that he hadn't heard the last from Margaret about Miss Josephine Gavin and her performance at Concert Hall.

One

"THEY BE TRYIN' to get to ya, Miss Gavin. We'd best hurry along now."

One of the Jefferson Company's hired girls, a rather robust Negro girl, had just bustled into Josephine Gavin's dressing room, a lavish red gown tossed over her left forearm. She had fought her way through the crowd gathered outside the door, and now she paused breathlessly beside the actress, who sat before a dressing table. "Lawd, but they be the most worked-up folks ah've seen in a good long while, and they be determined! We'd best get ya dressed fo' supper with Mr. Carlisle 'n' get ya outta here."

Josephine, better known to herself and friends as Josie, wiped the last of the paint from her face and lips. Her gaze fell briefly on the dress Dulcie held, then she closed her eyes for a moment. Mr. Carlisle . . . Mr. Carlisle . . . *Drat that Orson.*

The rowdy gathering bothered her, but not nearly as much as something else; she'd certainly faced crowds before. What bothered her the most of late was her manager. More and more, Orson Neville tried to dictate her life—her dress, her food, her speech, the way she carried herself, how she wore her hair . . . her acquaintances, for the love of God. And this late supper he had concocted was the end. Simply the end. Orson wanted to impress Carlisle because the man was so wealthy, and certainly he might be convinced to become a future sponsor of the troupe. The man was infatuated with her, Orson had explained, and she could not think of turning down the invitation he had issued upon learning of her appearance in the city. Orson had had this red gown made especially for tonight, or so he had said earlier, and by the looks of it—the low-cut neckline, the satin and lace—he meant for her to impress Carlisle very much indeed.

"I'm an actress, not a whore to be peddled out," Josie muttered, opening her eyes. Sometimes she was weary of the life she had made for herself—the everlasting masses, the traveling to a different city every few months, the sense of having no home, of perhaps never having a family to call her own. But Orson . . . oh, yes, Orson and the rendezvous he had arranged this evening troubled her more than anything else.

She picked up a silver-backed brush from the table and began stroking her black hair, vaguely registering the voices, laughter, shouts, and curses outside the dressing room door as she stared into the looking glass. Her dark brown eyes, usually filled with calm gentleness, were lit with shards of orange fire. A natural color, the color of brooding anger and defiance, rose high on her cheeks. She had shed the burgundy gown she had worn for this evening's performance and now sat in nothing more than her drawers, corset, and camisole.

"C'mon now, missy," Dulcie said behind Josie. "It's a real pretty dress. Don' look so upset."

Josie again glanced at the girl in the mirror, albeit briefly. Movement behind and to Dulcie's right caught Josie's eye, and her gaze fell on a trunk just in time to watch a hand retreat and the lid snap shut on a lock of golden hair. Josie blinked, wondering if she was imagining things. She was tired after two performances this evening, which had followed two last evening—and she'd slept little last night, wondering what to do about Orson and the supper with Carlisle.

"Lord!" Dulcie said, spinning around. She had obviously heard the trunk snap shut. She put a hand to her mouth and whispered, "There be somebody in there, Miss Gavin! A thief, mebbe, up from Battle Row."

Josie pulled a small pistol from a drawer in her dressing

table. She had grown up in New York City, after all, and had spent a great deal of time in other big cities; she knew one could never be careful enough. When the steamer transporting the company had docked at the St. Louis levee, she had been told by one of the ship's crew that the crowd milling about the dock was really nothing—that most days the steamers brought hundreds upon hundreds of newcomers to the city, people who hoped to prosper here. Many of the newcomers Josie saw looked half-starved, and her heart went out to them—so much so that she disembarked, stopped at a nearby market, bought up all the bread there, and passed it around.

But . . . while she had a compassionate streak, one for which Orson frequently criticized her, she also knew that desperate people could be dangerous people.

She rose from her chair while Dulcie looked on, her hand still covering her mouth. Approaching the trunk, Josie felt a little fearful herself.

She studied the lock of hair as she drew nearer. So fine in texture . . . so long and curled in sweet ringlets . . . Josie began to feel more at ease. Instinct told her that whoever was in the trunk was not a danger at all, really nothing to fear. Still, in the event she was wrong, she kept the pistol in hand.

She eased to one side of the trunk, tossed the lid up, and pointed the pistol straight at the occupant. She found herself staring into the sparkling blue eyes of a girl who could be no more than ten years old.

Dulcie gasped. Josie stood stock-still, though her brow wrinkled. The girl rose slowly, twisting her lips, glancing up and down repeatedly, looking as though she might burst into tears. She looked pitiful, standing there amongst Josie's carefully packed gowns.

Questions swirled in Josie's head. Why was the girl hiding in the trunk? How had she gotten in here? Josie opened her mouth to demand answers, but stopped when the child's lower lip began to quiver. A prickle of compassion pierced Josie's heart, and she placed the pistol on the floor beside the trunk, thinking it alone probably frightened the girl nearly to death.

"I only . . . I only wanted to meet you, Miss Gavin," the child whispered, stealing a frantic glance at the door, behind

which the crowd still mingled. She was obviously fighting
tears—her eyes had grown red and glazed. "I swear it; though
my papa, he'd scold me for that. Don't tell anyone I'm here,
please? I'd be in trouble forever. I think Papa was serious
when he warned me not to leave the house today. I asked if I
could come'n see you, see, and Papa, he said no, the theater's
no place for me, and well, I just wanted to meet you is all. I
saw the bill in the paper, and my friend Jonathan . . . he saw
you once and said you were beautiful and that you were splendid at singing and acting and all that—all the things I like to
do. But Papa, he says I'm wasting my time, that I'm gonna
grow into a lady and be decently educated, and that no lady
sings and acts on stage, not really." She was twisting the front
of her yellow skirt now, twisting it frantically, and glancing
back and forth between the gowns on which she stood and
Josie.

Josie looked at Dulcie, bewildered and at a loss for what to
do with the girl. Dulcie appeared as bewildered as she; she
shrugged, and her eyes grew wider, if possible.

"Constance, *she* says no decent woman gets up on a stage
dressed like you dress," the child continued, "that the only
women who do are . . . well, you know. . . . She has a name
for it, but I'm not real sure I should say it. I—" The girl
glanced up, her eyes brimming with tears. "You're not like
that, are you? Like Papa and Constance say you are? You're
not like some of the women who walk up and down the levee?
I had to meet you'n find out. I just had to! Bad enough Papa
wouldn't let me come and hear you sing. I sneaked in here
'cause I knew it was the only way I'd get to see you and find
out for myself and . . . oh, don't send me away and tell Papa
what I've done! Please? Don't? He told me not to go out today
at all!"

The girl wrung her hands. Her eyes were filled with fear
that Josie would tattle on her to her ogre of a father. But
beneath the fear lay admiration and awe. The child's excitement and eagerness to meet her was charming.

Oh, but Josie despised judgmental people! What did the
girl's father and this Constance person really know of her?
Because she was an actress, they assumed things about her

that were not true? That she was a loose woman? That she was a whore? My, but Orson would certainly make me into one if he had his way, Josie thought, tossing her head.

But she was not that way; she was not a whore. She had been raised better, and people who assumed she was a loose woman simply because she was an actress offended her. They watched her perform and sing—attending the theater was fashionable, after all—but beyond that, they refused to associate with her. They criticized her to children who admired her.

Josie immediately loved the rebel in the girl. But the child would have to return home sooner or later, and the truth was, ogre or no ogre, her father had told her not to come here; therefore, she shouldn't have. She had to leave.

And yet Josie couldn't bring herself to simply send the girl away. No child should be permitted to wander the streets of a city alone. Besides, risking her father's wrath, the girl had escaped her home and come here. She had somehow weaseled past the men Mr. Jefferson and Orson always placed at the door, and she had hidden in the trunk—all to meet her, Josephine Gavin. Knowing all of that, Josie thought she owed her a visit, although that certainly could not be accomplished here. They would have no peace as long as the crowd milled outside the door and as long as Josie knew that Orson awaited.

"Dulcie, that will be all," Josie said, her gaze never leaving the girl as she spoke the words.

"B–but, Miss Gavin! You ain't got very long b'fore you got to be dressed and—"

"I'll manage alone. Thank you."

Dulcie hesitated a moment more. Then she carefully draped the gown over the back of Josie's dressing table chair and walked toward the door, a pout on her face.

"And Dulcie . . . ," Josie said.

The girl glanced over her shoulder.

Josie looked her straight in the eye. "You saw and heard nothing. There was no one but you with me in here this evening."

Dulcie nodded unhappily, knowing that with a word to Mr. Jefferson, perhaps a little something about how unhappy Josie was with the girl's services, Josie could have her dismissed.

She opened the door that led to the hall where the crowd mingled, and closed it after exiting.

Josie hurried to bolt the door. Then she turned back to the child, her mind set. "There's another way out." She jerked her head toward a second door that she knew led to an alleyway. "I was trying to dream up a reason to escape an . . . affair this evening when I saw you in the glass. You're a fine reason! Tell me your name," Josie said excitedly, rushing to another trunk that sat in a far corner. She flung the lid open and rummaged through the gowns there, searching for a specific one, one that would help her blend into a crowd. And perhaps a cloak to match, with a hood to throw over her head.

"M—my name?" the girl sputtered.

"But of course. You have one, do you not?"

"I'm not in trouble? You're not angry?"

From the trunk Josie pulled a modest dress of brown-checkered cotton with puffed undersleeves, and smoothed it quickly. She also found a brown cloak and quickly decided that it would hide the few wrinkles in the dress.

"Now why would I be angry?" she asked, stepping into the garment. In her haste she had no time for petticoats, and the truth be known, she hardly cared at the moment. What mattered more was that she and the girl escape the Hall as soon as possible, she so she wouldn't have to endure the rendezvous Orson had arranged, and the girl so she wouldn't be discovered by anyone else and dragged home to her father. When Josie met the man, she planned to defend the girl. Then she planned to look the ogre right in the eye and tell him she was a fine model for any child to look up to. That he was wrong about her.

The girl shrugged, tipping her head sheepishly. "I just thought you would be, is all. Me sneaking in here . . . hiding. Anybody else would be angry. Papa will be furious."

Josie did not miss the tears that swelled in the child's eyes, or the way the girl twisted her hands as she fretted over having to face her father. Feeling a stab of compassion, Josie placed a hand over the child's and dipped her head to have a better look at the sweet face. "Well, then . . . we won't tell him. No one will tell him. He need never know."

The girl glanced up at her in surprise. "Really?"

"Really."

A charming smile was Josie's reward.

Josie pulled the dress up over her hips and pushed her arms into the sleeves, feeling more lighthearted at the moment than she had in days, perhaps in months. All in one evening she was about to thrill the child and escape Orson's well-laid plans.

"You haven't told me your name," she said. "And do step out of that trunk. You risked your father's wrath to meet me, and I could not possibly ignore someone who went to such extremes, particularly a child. But if you don't leave that trunk, someone might close the lid. Then you'll either starve to death or someone will ship you downriver in a matter of weeks when the company heads that way," she teased. "Perhaps you could help me with the laces on this dress." Bending slightly at the waist, she lowered her voice to a conspiratorial whisper. "We'll escape out a back way, dash off down the alley, and find a quiet place to talk."

The girl's eyes grew wide as saucers. "Really?"

Josie laughed. "I don't say things I don't mean. Now come here."

The child stepped out of the trunk just as someone pounded on the door. Voices rose to shouts on the other side. Josie heard Orson telling her that a carriage awaited her out front. She thought about not responding, then thought better and called, "A moment more!"

More voices: "She's coming out soon!" "A kiss from her is all I want, a kiss on the cheek!" said one man. Another responded that he'd like a bit more than that, and Josie rolled her eyes. She loved the praise her voice had brought her, and certainly in the last five years she had received the highest due for her acting ability. But the many lewd and scurrilous comments . . . she had no tolerance for them.

"You're sure we can get out of here?" the girl queried, glancing around fearfully.

Josie tilted her head and grinned, slipping the dress over her shoulders. "My mother always told me that my stubbornness would enable me to do anything I wanted to do. She was right. We *will* escape.''

The girl approached, timidly, shyly, as Josie struggled with the clasps on the back of the dress. "You were going to tell me your name," Josie said gently.

The child twisted her lips, clasped her hands properly in front of her, and lowered her lashes. "You're Josephine Gavin. I'm Margaret Murphy, and I'm not sure I should touch you.''

Josie wondered for a second if Margaret thought such a thing because of what her father had told her. In his eyes, as in the eyes of many, Josephine Gavin the actress was no better than a brothel whore. But again, the girl had defied her father to come here, and if she had seen anything that shocked her, surely she would have raced away. So her reason for not wanting to touch Josie was something more. . . . It was awe.

"Margaret, I was once a little girl like you," Josie said softly. "I'm not so different from everyone else, not so different from you, I'm sure. We're both runaways tonight—and you certainly may touch me.''

Slowly Margaret's lashes came up, and after another brief look of uncertainty she broke into a smile.

"Very pretty," Josie said, and she felt then, though she knew little about the girl, that they would be wonderful friends. Margaret admired her, and Josie found the girl adorable, her sweetness and innocence, her trusting nature, charming. Though Josie had her faults—impetuousness, rashness, a flaming temper at times—tonight she would be an angel for this child who idolized her.

Margaret helped with the clasps on Josie's dress. Then Josie tossed the cloak about her shoulders and pulled the hood up over her head, explaining to Margaret that if people saw her, some would undoubtedly recognize her. She fetched a reticule and the pistol she had dropped beside the trunk as the girl looked on. Saying that one never knew what sort of person one might encounter on the streets, Josie placed a hand on Margaret's shoulder to urge her toward the back door.

Seconds later, Josie and her companion fled down the alley, escaping the crowd still lurking within Concert Hall.

Thomas Murphy was furious—and worried nearly out of his mind.

Earlier, while he was at supper with Constance and her parents, Mrs. O'Brien had discovered Margaret missing, and she had fretted for an hour over how angry he would be and that he might even release her from his employment when she told him that Margaret had escaped her watchful gaze; he had, after all, warned her to watch Margaret closely this evening. Finally she had sent him a message, and he had rushed home.

"I was watching her carefully, just as you instructed," Mrs. O'Brien had said. "I left her for a few moments, Dr. Murphy. For only a few moments. Only long enough to attend to personal business. She was seated on a chair in her bedroom with a tablet on her lap, ciphering. When I returned, she was gone, and I discovered the—"

"Rope made of sheets she'd tied together," Thomas responded dryly. "Tell me how a child gathers that many sheets without someone in the household discoverin' them gone, Mrs. O'Brien. Tell me how she manages to tie them all together without anyone knowin'—particularly since she was bein' watched every minute." Just the thought of Maggie easing over the edge of the two-story balcony, gripping the first sheet and starting down, a maze of bricks below her, made nervous perspiration bead on his brow.

Mrs. O'Brien grew pale. "I'll gather my things, Dr. Murphy. I shall gather them and be gone by morning."

Thomas rubbed his forehead. "No, Mrs. O'Brien. Maggie'll be found, an' we'll all take time to sleep an' get in better spirits. Then we'll discuss things. First, we've got to find my daughter."

Margaret Anne . . . He'd find her, and he'd find her safe and sound, and after embracing her, he'd swat her backside. He'd never lifted a hand to her. Never. But she deserved a good swat for worrying him like this.

After the words with Mrs. O'Brien, he had mounted a horse and ridden directly to Concert Hall, the very place he thought Maggie would be. Where he knew, almost without doubt, that she would be.

And now, here he was, flying about frantically, describing her to numerous people, and then searching Concert Hall himself. Most of the audience had gone home, or so he was told by a thin elderly man who was sweeping a hall floor. But the actors and actresses, sometimes they stayed late, the man said. There'd been a crowd around Miss Gavin's dressing room, but finally everyone had left. Still, he'd not seen her come out.

"Would you mind directin' me to her dressing room?" Thomas asked. He was thinking that perhaps Maggie was in there having the visit of her life with a woman he didn't necessarily want wielding any influence over her, and he meant to collect her and take her home.

Jerking a nod, the man led the way to a door just up the hall.

Thomas knocked and waited. Then, hearing no response, he took the liberty of turning the knob, pushing the door open, and stepping into the room.

"Here now, you ain't suppose ta—"

"I'll just be a minute. Stand there an' watch," Thomas advised. "I don't plan to collect anything but my daughter."

The air was heavy with the smell of sweet perfume—but not overwhelmingly heavy. Still, it was more perfume than most women wore, Thomas thought. Painted dressing screens were planted here and there, and lavish gowns, done up in reds, maroons, and deep purples heavily decorated with flounces and lace spilled from a trunk. Another trunk had been left open. Bottles of perfume and small pots cluttered the dressing table, and Thomas soon realized that the pots contained grease for painting one's face. He became more convinced than ever that the Gavin actress was not a woman Maggie should be idolizing. She should look to Constance instead.

Satisfied that neither the actress nor Maggie was here, he backed out of the room, having seen quite enough, and he thanked the man for allowing him a brief search.

For hours he traveled the streets near the levee, stopping to describe Maggie to people and hoping to catch a glimpse of her. If she hadn't gone to Concert Hall and she wasn't at the levee, then where the devil was she? Lying facedown in one of the many sewer-filled gutters? His Maggie . . . his Margaret.

He was nearly sick with worry.

Perhaps she's home by now, he told himself over and over. Perhaps she's home and tucked safely into bed. That was a possibility.

He rode that way, stopping only to alert a constable he spotted, and once in front of his home, he dismounted and couldn't get inside fast enough.

He tore open the front door and skidded to a halt almost as soon as he stepped into the entryway. A voice . . . a velvety female voice drifted from somewhere up the hall, from one of the rooms there, and it was a sound like no other. Someone was singing a slow waltz, caressing the words of the tune: *"Come back, Belinda, oh, come back to me. Your lips are like roses, your eyes like the sea. . . . Our love is greater, than any can be. Oh come back, Belinda, and mar–ry me."*

The actress, the singer, Thomas thought, all painted and wrapped in one of those low-cut gowns. But if she were here, surely that meant Maggie was here, too.

Still, the actress . . . right here in his house, trying to lure his daughter into a world he had decided he didn't want her exposed to. Without even removing his wrap, he rushed up the hall.

He was ready to barrel into whatever room they were in and snatch his Maggie from the evil clutches of Josephine Gavin. He would definitely send Mrs. O'Brien packing this time! Where the devil was the woman? He couldn't believe she'd allowed the painted creature in his house, much less allowed her to make herself comfortable!

He had nearly reached the sitting room door when the sound of the woman's clear voice and then Maggie's laughter touched his ears. But Maggie wasn't just laughing; she was giggling, and that was a sound he always loved to hear.

He slowed his pace, listening to Maggie, relishing the sound of her giggles, and when he reached the doorway, he paused,

standing a little to the left of it. From there he observed a sight
that relieved him and warmed his heart.

Maggie and a woman sat cross-legged on the floor, a black
kitten frolicking between them, batting at the piece of yarn
Maggie held just out of its reach. Maggie swirled the string,
and the kitten leapt at it, making Margaret giggle more. Her
face was bright, brighter than Thomas had seen it in a long
time. "She's cute and funny. I love her! Thank you, thank
you for getting her for me!" she said, obviously talking to her
companion.

The woman couldn't be Josephine Gavin. Her brown-
checkered dress was modest and respectable—high-necked
and buttoned up to nearly beneath her chin with rows of ruffles
forming a vee from her shoulders to her waist. She was beautiful, there was no denying that, black curls arranged and
pinned to the crown of her head, others dangling around her
face, her dark eyes aglow as she smiled brilliantly at Margaret.
Lamplight and firelight flickered around the room, dancing
shadows here and there, on the furnishings and on the woman's remarkable and very distinct features: clear ivory, un-
painted skin; finely arched brows; high defined cheekbones; a
nose that was narrow and came to a point, but looked almost
sculptured. Her lips did, too—they were full, as perfectly
formed as female lips could be, and dusky rose in color.

Obviously the woman wore no petticoats beneath her
dress—with them on, she couldn't have curled her legs beneath her and sat on the floor with Margaret in such a way—
but that hardly mattered. The plain dress and her overall
appearance told Thomas that while she might not be from one
of the finest St. Louis families, she was nonetheless respectable.

She laughed, watching Margaret with the kitten and the
yarn, and what a sound it was! Rich laughter, bubbling up
from within. The kitten lurched, twisting its body, and grabbed
the end of the yarn between its paws, finally coming down
with it. The little creature took the string in its mouth and
shook its head, as if making sure the catch was dead. Maggie
giggled.

"Sing another song now," Maggie said, tilting her head and

clapping her hands together. "Please, oh please!"

The woman laughed again. "You don't have to beg, Margaret," she said, and then launched into a lively tune: *"I'm thinking tonight of my blue eyes, a girl who is sweet as can be . . ."*

"I have blue eyes!" Maggie exclaimed.

Smiling, the woman nodded, then continued: *"Her hair is the color of—"* She glanced at the door, apparently feeling as though she and Maggie were being watched. Thomas's gaze locked with hers, and he was taken aback for a second by the brief look of hostility that flickered in her eyes. But it was gone in a flash, and then her dark, sparkling eyes were pulling him in, their depths tempting him to draw forth. He almost couldn't break their hold.

Where the devil had Maggie found the bewitching creature?

"I believe your father has arrived, Margaret," she said, smiling, one corner of her mouth tipping up as she gripped the sides of her skirt and rose. The curve of her neck, her every fluid movement, her voice and manner of speaking . . . they all indicated an air of refinement. She dipped her head to him in acknowledgment, her lashes lowering briefly, then sweeping up.

Thomas returned the greeting, suddenly realizing he'd been holding his breath.

Maggie glanced up, her mouth forming an *O,* her face reddening. A second later, Mrs. O'Brien scurried up behind Thomas, sputtering, "Oh, Dr. Murphy. You are home at last! Oh! And here is Miss Margaret, brought home safe and sound by this very nice woman who found her wandering the streets and insisted on escorting her here and staying with her until you returned. I tried to tell her that was not necessary, but she held fast. Her name is Julia Goddard, and she wanted to make certain Miss Margaret was safely in her father's care before she left." Mrs. O'Brien clasped her hands before her ample bosom, looking delighted—and perhaps relieved, too, that after she'd let Maggie escape down the balcony by way of the sheet rope, the girl was safe and sound and had been in the care of a respectable person. Not Josephine Gavin.

Maggie was on her feet now. She'd scooped up the kitten

and was holding it close to her breast. "Yes, yes—I know I shouldn't have escaped, Papa, that I should have done what you said and stayed in my room while you were supping with Constance and her parents. But I couldn't bear to not at least try to meet Josephine Gavin. There I was, wandering the streets near Concert Hall, plotting how I was going to get inside and get near her, and then suddenly this man . . . a horrible, horrible bad man jumped out from around the side of a warehouse and—''

"Oh!" Mrs. O'Brien put her hands to her cheeks. "You did not tell me this part, Miss Margaret. How horrid! Indeed you should have minded your father. I do not doubt that in the future—''

"Th–there he was, the bad man," Maggie continued, tears swelling in her eyes now as she clutched the kitten even tighter, "grabbing me, and I couldn't get away. But suddenly Miss Goddard appeared, beating on him with her parasol and trying to pull me away. Just look, we both have dirt on us from the struggle, though we did clean up a bit after she brought me home! Along the way she wanted to make me feel better, so she stopped and picked up this kitty from a friend of hers, and she says I may keep it if I can think of a name for it. Oh, isn't that wonderful? *She's* so wonderful, Papa! You should have seen her, leaping out—''

"Margaret. I did what I hope anyone in my position at the time would have done," Josie said softly, admiring Margaret's acting ability but fearing the girl would end up stretching the tale a little too far. Then her father would become suspicious and question them thoroughly, looking for holes in their story. Josie fluttered her lashes down then up again, and she fidgeted with the sides of her skirt, knowing she appeared embarrassed and uncomfortable with Margaret's praise. This bit of acting was not difficult—she actually *was* nervous under Dr. Murphy's narrowed gaze. The way he was looking at her . . . It was not an offensive look, not at all like the ones given her by men who crowded the parquets of the many theaters in which she performed. And yet it was definitely one of desire. Josie did not have to fake the heat that suddenly colored her cheeks.

He stepped toward them, a rather handsome man in a dignified sort of way, a black cape still thrown over his shoulders, a white neck-cloth tied neatly above it. His blue-green eyes reflected the light of the lamps and the fire, and his wavy hair—it was the exact color of Margaret's—tumbled in disarray to just below his shoulders. He was well put together, standing close to six feet, she would wager, and as he unfastened the cape at his neck, swept it off, and handed it to Margaret's nurse, Josie swallowed.

He wore black trousers and a fine white linen shirt, slightly loose, that flowed with his every movement. His shoulders were broad, his chest and arms solid; she had certainly worked around enough men and with enough costuming that she could recognize such details by simply observing the fit of the shirt. Put a black waistcoat on him and . . . well, if Orson ever arranged a supper with any man who looked even remotely like Margaret Murphy's father, Josie would make no move to escape.

"A parasol, was it?" he queried, his voice deep and somewhat throaty, containing the hint of a brogue. "In the evenin'?"

From the corner of her eye, Josie saw Margaret wince, a little flaw in the acting as she realized her mistake. Though who was she to talk, considering her reaction to Margaret's father? The very man who was so judgmental of her.

"On city streets, a person, particularly a woman, cannot be too careful, Dr. Murphy," Josie responded. "Parasols make fine weapons. I carry one frequently, morning, afternoon, and evening. Think of the point. Why, perhaps *you* should think of carrying one. Margaret says you're often out till all hours of the night."

He lifted a brow and chuckled. "True. But a parasol, Miss Goddard—it is *Miss,* isn't it?"

Josie nodded. Margaret had come up with the name Julia Goddard when they came face to face with the formidable-looking Mrs. O'Brien in the entryway earlier. They had escaped Concert Hall, going from there to a quaint coffee shop on Market Street. There they had had tea, confections, and conversation, and then Josie had hired a cab to bring them here. Margaret had warned her about the nurse, saying that the woman would bear down on them soon after they walked in the door. And so she had. Josie had been a little surprised when Margaret introduced her as Julia Goddard, but being the actress that she was and understanding that it might not be such a good idea to mention her real name in this house just yet, Josie had played along. Once she and Margaret had settled in the sitting room with the kitten, they agreed to use the name when introducing Josie to Margaret's father, too. At least until they made him realize that he was wrong in assuming that Josephine Gavin was not a nice woman simply because she was an actress.

"But wouldn't a man look a bit odd an' suspicious carryin' a parasol about?" Dr. Murphy asked, twinkles lighting his eyes.

Josie could not help but smile. He smiled back, then reached for her hand, bending over it, his gaze never leaving hers. She felt a thrill go through her as his lips brushed her skin, but she quickly reminded herself of his opinion of her. That thought helped calm the thrill. And yet, there was no denying her attraction to him.

She needed to concentrate. She needed to get her mind back where it belonged—on proving him wrong.

"I suppose a man would, Dr. Murphy," she teased right back. "But he'd be well protected."

He straightened, stepping back and glancing at his daughter. "Maggie, me Maggie . . . Margaret Anne," he scolded gently, placing a hand on her shoulder and drawing her to him. "You had me worried nearly out of my mind, lass. I've been up an' down every street, at Concert Hall searchin' the place. I've talked to hundreds of people, describin' you. An' all the while . . . here you are, safe an' sound, thanks to the lovely Miss Goddard, a gem of a woman."

Another thrill. A gem of a woman? Not only was he far too handsome, he also was far too charming—exactly like his daughter. And with the same mischievous streak. He was either a very good actor himself or he truly cherished Margaret.

"But this . . . what's this, Maggie?" He withdrew a bit and looked down at the kitten, who had snuggled contentedly into

Margaret's arms. "A kitten, love? I know you've always liked them, an' yer mother, she'd never let you have one—Maggie's mother didn't take to cats," he said, glancing at Josie.

"Mother . . . Oh, no! She'll miss her mother, too," Margaret said, looking up suddenly, appearing stricken by the revelation. "Oh! We've got to take her back. We've got to! I wasn't thinking! She'll miss her mother! I won't have that. I can't bear the thought! She'll cry'n cry, and she'll have awful, terrible dreams the way I did, and—"

"Margaret, no. She'll be fine, really," Josie tried to assure as she stepped around Dr. Murphy. Earlier, in the coffee shop, Margaret had mentioned that her mother had gone to heaven last year, and a sad look had passed over her face. Then she had gone on to more lighthearted conversation, and the awkward moment had been over. But now thoughts of her mother and her mother's death and apparently remembrances of what must have been a difficult time afterward had obviously returned in force, prompted by the thought of the kitten being without its mother. Josie certainly knew the pain of losing a parent—and more.

Josie kneeled in front of the girl, wanting to be at her level, and she ran her hands up and down Margaret's arms. "I promise—she'll be fine. She might miss her mother for a little while, but she has you now. Animals are different than people. They adapt quickly, and their memories aren't as good as ours." Still, tears welled in Margaret's eyes as she stroked the kitten.

"The girl misses her mother so," Mrs. O'Brien said softly.

Josie felt Dr. Murphy move up beside her and Margaret, and then he was on his knees, too, putting a soothing hand on his daughter's back. "She has you now, Maggie, love, just like Miss Goddard said. You'll be her mother now. She's found someone else . . . like I'm tryin' to find someone else for you—another mother."

He glanced at Josie, and their gazes locked and held, his eyes filled with emotion for his daughter and meaning for Josie.

Startled by the look, Josie stiffened, unbalancing herself. She felt herself sway, and then his warm hand was on the back of her elbow, steadying her.

Josie eased away from the touch. "Thank you. I'm fine, really. Silly me." She uttered a small laugh. "I've not had a bite to eat since this morning. I just remembered."

Dr. Murphy nodded slowly. "Well, then, perhaps there's cold meat an' bread in the kitchen—there usually is. We'll all have a bite to eat together, you, me, an' Maggie. Then we'll talk. Me'n Maggie, I'm sure we're both wantin' to know more about you."

Almost like an interview for a position.

What Josie really wanted to do was go to her hotel room and lie down. She was tired suddenly, weary from the last two days' activities, and she had a full day awaiting her tomorrow.

She made the mistake of glancing again at Margaret, who was just lowering a hand from brushing tears from her face and who gave her a look that said, "Please stay a little longer."

Feeling overwhelmed and not having the heart to say no, she had to be going, Josie settled back on her heels and gently tugged Margaret down onto her lap.

A rush of relief went through Thomas. It was insane, it was madness, the notion he was entertaining—that this woman might possibly make a good mother for Maggie, that he should learn more about her. All he knew about Julia Goddard was her name and that she'd rescued his daughter this evening and that she appeared to have a way with Margaret; she'd certainly brought out the laughter in his daughter. He knew nothing about Miss Goddard's family, nothing about her upbringing. Sweet Mary—he didn't even know her age.

He knew so little . . . but he intended to find out more.

Two

AFTER JOSIE'S GENTLE assurance that the kitten would be fine and soon grow to love her new home and not miss her mother at all, Margaret settled down. A few more sniffles and tears and then the girl dried up, although she still held the animal close, as if to reassure it. The kitten looked perfectly content, though in her sudden distress, Margaret had been oblivious to that fact. Once Josie had pointed it out to her and Margaret glanced down and saw the pet sleeping comfortably, there were no more tears at all.

Moments later, after numerous strokes on the kitten's head and back, Margaret smiled up at Josie, a smile of admiration and gratefulness. Josie smiled back, tugging playfully on a lock of the girl's pretty hair, all the while aware of Dr. Murphy's observation.

Thomas sent Mrs. O'Brien off to see about the meat and bread while he settled in a wing chair before the hearth, where a fire burned low to ward off the evening chill. Earlier in the day, he'd given two lectures at the college. This afternoon he'd seen a host of patients for one ailment or another, everything from what he was certain was a broken foot to a laceration above the eye acquired in a gaming house in a rough section of the city called Battle Row—and indeed the area deserved the name. At least four times a week Thomas stitched, bandaged, or splinted the limbs of people who had been involved in altercations somewhere in Battle Row. He'd come home tired from his office on Olive Street; but knowing he had agreed to have supper with Constance and her parents, he'd dressed and gone out for that affair, confident at the time that Maggie was playing quietly upstairs in her bedroom. It had been a calm supper until the Blanches' butler came into the dining room with a message for him. Then the search for Maggie had begun. Now he was exhausted . . . but very interested in watching the blossoming relationship between his daughter and Julia Goddard.

Maggie's newfound friend began telling her that she'd once had a kitten, ages and ages ago, that her father had brought it home with him one day when she was a few years younger than Margaret. "He walked into the house with a bundle hidden inside his coat, and I knew he had something for me, but I didn't know what," Miss Goddard said, now petting the kitten with Maggie. "I jumped up and down, telling him to please show me, *please* show me. He walked around grinning, teasing me, and I finally began tugging at his coat. Something was moving. I heard a meow and I remember squealing with delight when a little rust-and-white kitten finally had enough of the struggle and jumped out. My mother smiled all the while, telling my father how horrid he was to tease me so."

"That's all true?" Maggie asked. "You really had a kitten? Your papa really teased you?"

Miss Goddard tipped her head and clicked her tongue, the firelight dancing in her eyes. "Now, Margaret, why would I concoct such a story? Of course it's true."

"Oh, I didn't mean that you lied," Maggie said hastily. "I just thought you might've made it up to make me smile."

Julia leaned forward, smiling prettily, almost mischievously, her voice lower this time, as if she shared a secret: "Why, Miss Blue Eyes, perhaps I will make up a few before the night's over—just to see your smile."

Maggie seized the opportunity to plant a kiss on her friend's cheek. "I've never had so much fun as I've had tonight!"

Julia laughed, stroked the kitten's head once more, then started into a lively tune, sung softly and for Maggie's benefit: *"Once I had a kit–ty, a pretty little kit–ty cat. Dress'd him up with boots, and a great, big hat. Took him out–a strollin', on a sum–mer day. Along came a farm–er's dog, and chas'd my kitty away.''* She tipped her head this way and that, sobering with some of the lyrics, smiling with others, pouting with the last. She lifted her brows, then lowered them as she sang, now and then turning her head and glancing at Maggie from the corner of her eye. She thoroughly charmed not only a trans-fixed and obviously delighted Maggie, but also Thomas.

Now Maggie laughed, her sadness over losing her mother forgotten for a time in Julia Goddard's magic. Thomas propped his elbow on an arm of the chair, his chin in his palm, and realized that even he was smiling as he watched them together, wondering again where Maggie had found the woman. Much better that Maggie adore Miss Goddard than the actress Josephine Gavin, whom Thomas doubted would sing such a cute song for a child.

Miss Goddard was swaying now, singing more of the song, employing facial expressions again, and Maggie joined in the motion as the lovely voice, soft as it was, lilted about the room. An outside wind rattled a window, and Thomas nearly turned around and glared at the pane; it made enough noise that for a few seconds he couldn't hear Miss Goddard's voice.

''All day long he chas'd her, ov–er hill and dale. Bow-wow goes old Bowser, on my kit–ty's trail. Down thru Abner's meadow, o'er the hick'ry flats. Please somebody grab him, and save my kit–ty cat!''

Mrs. O'Brien walked into the room carrying a tray of sliced beef and bread, which she placed on the table near Thomas's chair. He absently thanked her, his gaze still on Maggie and Julia Goddard, and he barely registered the nurse's voice when she mentioned something about Miss Margaret needing to be put to bed soon. After all, the hour was well past midnight.

''The kitty, the kitty! What happened to the kitty?'' Maggie wanted to know, needed to know, her brow wrinkled with concern.

Julia Goddard glanced around, looking baffled for a moment, as if she might not know herself—as if she had come to the end of the song. She almost looked alarmed, and Thom-as almost laughed aloud, amused by her expression, wondering how she would appease Maggie this time, if she could.

"My dear Miss Goddard, you can't think of leavin' it with the dog chasin' the poor cat," he teased.

She shot him a playful scowl as Mrs. O'Brien exited the room. Then she twisted her lips thoughtfully and began again, though a little more slowly this time. The pauses here and there made it obvious that she was making up the lyrics as she went: *"He . . . he chased her through the hol–low, and down in–to the lane. My kit–ty, she glanced back, and . . . and saw him start to gain. She ran into a barnyard, and jumped up on a rail. Bowser came a-chargin', but Flinnigan's bull stopped his tail!"*

"Oh, I can see it!" Maggie said, giggling. "That mean ole dog, chasing that kitty, running into the barnyard, and there stands the bull! Papa, can't you just see it?" She glanced at him, her eyes bright and filled with sparkles.

He laughed, too, marveling at Julia Goddard's quick thinking—and quick composing, even if it was a child's song. "I can, I can, Maggie, love," he said, straightening in the chair and reaching for the tray. "An' what a sight it is! Here now, come have a bite to eat, then it's off to bed with you soon. You've had more excitement than a person should have in a week, let alone a day."

Julia took the kitten from Maggie's arms. Margaret stood, and for the first time Thomas realized she was without her shoes and stockings. He started to make light of the trauma she'd gone through earlier and ask if they'd fallen off during the race to get away from that horrible bad man. Then he saw that Miss Goddard was without hers, too, and he lifted a brow in surprise.

"Well, now, it seems we have a thief," he said, affecting a serious expression.

Maggie and her friend both looked puzzled. Julia turned to place the kitten gently to one side of the hearth where it would stay cozy warm, and Margaret, forever inquisitive, asked, "Why do you think that, Papa?"

"Maggie, love, it seems both you an' the delightful Miss Goddard's shoes'n stockings've been stolen. An' right off yer feet, at that. Why, yer toes must be shiverin'!"

Maggie plopped her hands on her hips and gave him a stern look. "Papa! It was Miss Goddard's idea—feet need to breathe, she said. Besides, our stockings were wet. We left them in the kitchen over the back of a chair so they could dry by the coals still glowing there."

"Well, glowin' coals'll surely dry them," he agreed. Then he glanced at Julia. "Feet need to breathe, eh?"

She tipped her head, gave him an utterly devilish grin, then said, "But of course, Dr. Murphy. My grandmother taught me that, and I've always found it to be true. My feet become so warm sometimes, and they're as alive as any other part of the body, after all. You're a doctor—one would assume you would know that."

"Ah! But when the doctor's kept busy stitchin' an' mendin', he hasn't the time to learn much about feet needin' to breathe," he said, slicing bread for Maggie. "This grandmother . . . since she knows so much about feet, I could've used her advice today with a patient. She lives here, in the city, you said?"

"No, I don't believe I said that, Dr. Murphy," she responded, her tone softer this time as she studied him. For a few seconds their gazes held again, and he read suspicion in her eyes. He suddenly wondered if she was hiding something, and he suddenly wondered, too, why a woman like herself had been out alone in the city earlier this evening. There hadn't been a carriage in the drive when he'd arrived home a short time ago, so how had she and Maggie gotten here?

"She's not from the city, then? From St. Louis?" he pressed.

"No, she—"

"They're in Alton, Papa," Maggie chimed in. "Her relatives. That's what she told me earlier."

He looked from Julia Goddard to his daughter and back, searching their faces for guilt. He saw none. Still, something didn't quite ring true here, something was nagging at him, and he meant to ask more questions and get more answers.

"Ah! Alton, is it?" he said, putting a slice of bread and meat on a small plate, standing and handing the plate to Maggie. "Across the river, an' yet there you were, in St. Louis, on the very street as my Maggie when the bad man came along. Ye're in the city alone, Miss Goddard? And Alton— more than a good thirty miles away!"

Her chin went up just a little. "Yes, Dr. Murphy, I am here alone. I'm not one to always adhere to convention, as the absence of my shoes and stockings and my presence in your sitting room barefoot attests."

Thomas couldn't help a chuckle. There was nothing timid about the woman, that was for certain. She wasn't afraid to speak her mind. "So I see," he teased as Maggie took her plate, went to sit in the chair opposite the one in which he'd been sitting, and began eating. "But Alton, Miss Goddard! How did you get here, an' what possessed a lady of yer manners an' intelligence to wander the streets of St. Louis after dark?"

She moved around him, reached for a plate and fork from the tray, and began serving herself. "Perhaps I lost sight of my manners and intelligence for a time. That does happen occasionally. We all have those moments."

Thomas chuckled again. After Abby's quiet ladylike ways and Constance's rather reserved ways, this woman, this Julia Goddard, seemed so . . . alive and full of energy. She possessed a definite sense of humor and a refreshing spark of mischievousness, and Thomas found that to his surprise he enjoyed both.

"Forgive *my* lack of manners, Miss Goddard." He reached to take the fork from her. He smelled her light perfume, as sweet as a meadow of flowers, and the scent tugged at a memory. Now why the devil was it familiar? He shook his head. Every woman he knew wore a bit of perfume; it could remind him of any one of theirs. And yet . . . he didn't think so.

"You ferried over?" he asked, forking a slice of beef and putting it on her plate.

"Mm," she said, giving a vague answer. But was it even an answer?

"And from there you took a cab around the city?"

"Mm."

"And here. That explains why there's not one in the drive now?"

She tipped her head as he put a piece of bread on her plate, then handed her the fork. "It would, yes. My, but you do have a million questions, Dr. Murphy."

Clasping his hands behind his back, he rocked forward on the balls of his feet, narrowing his eyes at her. "I have a scientific mind, Miss Goddard. I work with facts, an' when facts are missin', I gather them an' put them together like a puzzle. I'm a simple man to know an' understand—I like to have all the pieces an' have them in order. In this case, the pieces are not in order."

She nodded slowly, smiling her sly smile again, humoring him, he thought. "I see. Am I a case to be solved, then?"

"That you are."

He waited for her to offer more information about herself. Instead she began to eat her bread and meat, still smiling, glancing up at him from her plate now and then. He suddenly longed to touch one of the shimmering, springing curls framing her lovely face; he suddenly longed to touch her cheek. His gaze fell on her rosy lips, and he shocked himself by wondering at their taste, how sweet they surely were.

He watched her swallow hard, watched the color rise to her cheeks, and he knew the look he was giving her affected her, no matter that she tried to pretend indifference.

When she started to turn in Maggie's direction, he put a hand on her forearm to stop her. A rather presumptuous, forward move—something her lifted brows confirmed—and one not like him at all. But then, he'd never encountered a woman who intrigued him more, and he hadn't been ready for her to turn away from him.

"The pieces of the puzzle, Miss Goddard," he said in low voice. "Yer family, what really brought you to St. Louis tonight. If ye're in some sort of trouble, perhaps Maggie an' I could help, find a way of repayin' you for what you did for her earlier. You can't think of travelin' back to Alton tonight. Why, it would take the rest of the night, and it's already mornin' if the clocks tell the truth. Alton's a good two hours by horse an' ferry. I'm not even sure the ferry runs this late. We've a few guest rooms upstairs. You'll find the—"

Her dark gaze turned cool, almost like a winter draft. She moved her arm away, slowly and deliberately, sending him a silent message. And then she said in a soft but level voice, "You're so critical of others, Dr. Murphy, and yet you yourself continue to forget etiquette and manners . . . *propriety*. An unmarried woman as a guest in the home of a widower? I think not. We'd be the talk of the city. My reputation, Dr. Murphy. People would be assuming things that are not true. Heaven forbid that that should happen."

That said, she swept away and joined Maggie near the hearth.

Thomas rubbed his jaw, feeling as if he'd been slapped. She was right, of course, but where had all that come from—the bitterness and slice of anger in her voice, that look of hostility in her eyes again, the cutting remarks? True, his touch had been forward, and had he been thinking with a clear head, he might not have even considered inviting her to stay here as his guest. But her open hostility was a bit much.

He spun on his heels. "Hospitality, Miss Goddard. 'Tis all it was. I apologize," he said, giving a slight bow. "But a trip back to Alton tonight . . . I've a friend who would give you a room. Please allow me that courtesy. Tomorrow I'll be happy to see you safely home."

"I'll consider it, Dr. Murphy," she responded from near Maggie's chair. The hostile look had faded some, replaced by one of apprehension, as if she were waiting for his next move—so she could then make hers. Thomas resisted the urge to shake his head again. Obviously he had offended her deeply, but he had apologized, and there was no reason they should be at odds with each other now. Of course, she'd not exactly accepted his apology.

The last thing he wished to do was offend her so much that he frightened her off. She was good with Maggie, and he found her lovely, very attractive, and didn't want her storming off angry. He had pressed her too much, asking one too many questions so shortly after meeting her, and he had asked them in a suspicious manner because something troubled him about

her. He didn't know what it was, it was just there, pulling at
the back of his mind, and it had driven him to close in on her,
more or less demanding answers. Then the touch . . . To her
he probably seemed like another male on the prowl, he
thought, stifling a snort of disgust, and what lady wouldn't
dance skittishly away at such a bold approach?

He would keep his distance, asking no more questions for
a time, until she became more comfortable with him. No more
touches, no more softly spoken words. He reminded himself
of the unspoken rules of courtship—one, to proceed slowly
and respectfully.

Thrusting his hands into his trouser pockets, he approached a settee resting a good ten feet from the hearth
chairs where Miss Goddard now sat with Maggie, and settled on it. He again propped his chin in his palm and observed the two of them. Miss Goddard had launched into a
story, something about a monkey and a jungle and a boy
named Brian. Maggie didn't know what a jungle was, and
so Miss Goddard took the time to patiently explain, then she
went on with the story.

Thomas watched, fascinated, intrigued, charmed, curious.
No one had ever been as good with Maggie. No one. Even
Abby had not interacted with their daughter in such a heart-
warming way. And Maggie had surely never adored anyone
as much as she seemed to adore her new friend.

Josie was again aware of him watching her with a tender
and curious look in his eyes, and that he had hardly taken his
eyes off of her from the moment she had looked up and seen
him standing in the doorway. She was growing more and more
uncomfortable with the situation. She hadn't considered that
he might want to know about her family and where they were
from. And while she had been known to tell a good lie or two
before, she was rather amazed and taken aback that Margaret
had not batted a lash at telling that enormous tale about the
horrible bad man and how Josie had rescued her, or when
she'd told her father that ''Miss Goddard'' and her family
were from Alton.

The tale about the rescue had worked, but the bit about her being from Alton . . . Alton was located clear across the river, too far away not to raise the very questions and concerns Dr. Murphy had expressed—she'd come alone to St. Louis, and now, because the hour was so late, she couldn't think of going home tonight. Besides, the ferries might *not* run at night. As Josie had feared she might, Margaret had taken the game a little too far, and her father, intelligent, inquisitive scientist that he was, had quickly found a gray area to investigate.

Faced with his careful questioning, Josie had begun to feel boxed in, and then he had startled her by placing his hand on her arm, in an attempt to stop her from walking away right then. Not far from her mind all evening had been the fact that he thought her a woman of low character simply because of her chosen profession, and yet he indelicately suggested that she stay the night in his home. It seemed that even the most proper of people had their flaws.

So he wanted another mother for Margaret, did he? And judging from the look he'd given her after remarking that he was searching for someone else for Margaret, and his watchful gaze since, he was willing to consider her—Josephine Gavin.

It was ironic. He was willing to consider the very woman he apparently did not think was good enough to wipe his, or anyone else's, boots.

Josie finished telling the story about the monkey and the boy, and Margaret yawned. She had finished her bread and beef and was now curled up snugly in the chair, looking as if she might fall asleep. Her head rested comfortably on an arm of the upholstered chair, and her eyes were glazed and her lids heavy. Josie had returned their plates to the tray on the table. Now she smiled at Margaret and suggested that perhaps she should go up to bed, that maybe her father would not mind taking her up since Mrs. O'Brien had surely turned in by now.

"I'd rather Papa take me up anyway," the girl responded softly, twisting to glance at her father. "You're not angry, are you, Papa, about what happened this evening? I know I shouldn't have sneaked out, and I'll never, never do it again. I really promise.''

As precious as she thought Margaret was, Josie wanted to roll her eyes. Given the chance, the girl would sneak out again tomorrow.

But for some reason, Dr. Murphy either couldn't see the obvious—that his daughter was using feminine wile on him—or didn't want to. He straightened, lowering his arm, and said, ''I believe you, Maggie girl. I'm thinkin' it was enough of a scare that you won't.''

''You'll take me up to bed, Papa?'' she asked, yawning again. ''And pray, like Mama used to, for the angels to watch over me?''

''I surely will, Maggie.'' He rose, walked over to her, and offered his hand.

Margaret moved slowly from the chair, but instead of taking his hand right away, she approached Josie and planted another kiss on her cheek. ''You'll be careful, going out in the night?'' she asked, looking truly concerned.

Josie patted her back, embraced her, then withdrew. ''Of course I will, Margaret. Now you go and sleep well.''

''She can stay with Constance an' her family for the rest of the night, Maggie,'' Dr. Murphy said. ''She'll sleep well, too, an' be safe an' sound. Now come along with you.''

Margaret took her father's hand, and they started from the room. Near the door, the girl glanced over her shoulder at Josie and waved, moving her fingers up and down. Josie copied the movement, waving back.

Minutes after their footsteps faded up the hall, Josie hurried from the sitting room, walking quickly but softly up the passage toward the back of the house where she and Margaret had left their shoes and stockings in the kitchen earlier.

She found them exactly as they'd been left, the stockings draped over the back of a spindle chair, the shoes on the floor beside the chair. Not knowing how long Dr. Murphy would take to make certain his daughter was comfortable for the night, and not wanting to be questioned more, Josie grabbed her stockings and shoes and headed toward a door she suspected led outside. It did.

A slow rain had started, and the ground was damp, but the grass was prickly on the bottoms of Josie's feet as she raced across the lawn. She fled up Washington Avenue and turned the corner at Eleventh Street, knowing she had a good walk ahead of her before she reached the hotel. All lamps had been extinguished—in most large cities they were extinguished at least by midnight. Three blocks later, when she reached Olive and stopped briefly to slip her shoes on, she shivered in the March air, realizing she had left her cloak behind.

Ah, well. She had tossed it over another chair in the kitchen, and there it would stay until morning, when perhaps one of Dr. Murphy's staff either claimed it or brought it to her employer's attention. Without casting another glance over her shoulder, Josie straightened and hurried up the dark street, rolling her stockings into a ball as she went.

Thomas tucked Maggie in safe and sound, and heard her breathing change almost before he reached the door of her bedroom to leave her for the night. He pulled the door, leaving it open part of the way, exactly as Maggie liked it, and once out in the hall, he headed for the stairs, anxious to get back to the sitting room and Julia Goddard.

Excluding the furnishings, the room was empty, the silence broken only by the incessant ticking of the mantel clock. The house . . . this room . . . they were too quiet suddenly. Maggie slept upstairs, and Thomas suspected she might rest more peacefully than she had in a long while, not have nightmares the way she sometimes did. Her dreams this night, if she dreamed, would surely be filled with images of Julia Goddard. Perhaps she would hear her laughter and her voice, and feel her comforting, motherly arms about her.

Thomas frowned, casting another glance around the room. Julia was gone. She had seized the opportunity to flee while he was upstairs putting Maggie to bed. She obviously had not wanted to talk to him further, fearing more questions perhaps, and so she was gone.

She might have just gone to the kitchen for a drink of water, he told himself; but almost as soon as he had the thought, he knew there was no truth to it. He *felt* that she was gone. Julia Goddard had a presence about her, a warmth and a gaiety, and it was no longer here.

Remembering what Maggie had said about them leaving their shoes and stockings to dry before the hearth in the kitchen, he wandered up the hall, his boots thudding on the oak floor. He reached that room, and as soon as he entered it his gaze fell on the chair before the fireplace.

Only one pair of stockings was draped over the back of it, and they were Maggie's—they were too small to belong to a grown woman. Beside the chair, on the floor, sat Maggie's shoes, the straps having been tossed to one side. The coals in the fireplace had burned down to a soft glow, but warmth still rose from them.

Thomas released a long breath as he stood staring at the coals. Had he frightened Julia Goddard so badly that she'd felt it necessary to run away without another word to him? She was from Alton, she and Maggie had said, and surely finding her would not be that difficult—provided she wanted to be found. He'd gotten the distinct feeling that she hadn't wanted him to learn any more about her than what she and Maggie had told him.

Perhaps he should give it up. Forget her. Keep on with his courtship of Constance, who was more the sort of woman he wanted raising Maggie. Constance was very proper and mannered. She would assure that Maggie was raised the same way, into a young lady deserving of respect. She certainly wouldn't allow the girl to do things like relax on the floor in the sitting room—and without her shoes and stockings.

Thomas chuckled to himself, recalling the sight of Maggie's and Julia's bare feet.

It had become obvious to him of late that Maggie merely tolerated Constance for his benefit; she was subdued around Constance, and not once in the months Thomas had been seeing the woman had Maggie ever reached out to her and been affectionate the way she had been affectionate with Miss Goddard. She had surely never giggled with Constance, and her eyes did not light up when she regarded her.

What was more important—that Maggie be groomed into a proper young lady, or that she be happy? That she smile and giggle and have a mother she adored and enjoyed? Certainly Abby would have wanted the proper young lady. In fact, during the last two years of her life, Abby had often expressed concern that Margaret was too headstrong and stubborn and that the child was becoming more and more defiant. But looking back, Thomas wondered if perhaps he and Abby had tried to stifle Maggie's true personality. Some things were not acceptable—Maggie going to the levee, for instance—but what the devil was wrong with relaxing on the floor of a sitting room without one's shoes and stockings?

His hands clasped behind his back, Thomas turned to leave the room, thinking he'd go have a glass of brandy in his study, then try to clear his mind so he could sleep. What was obviously a cloak tossed over the back of another chair to one side of the wide hearth caught his eye, and he paused, then approached it.

It was plain, made of wool, he realized as he lifted it; the material was scratchy, thick, and lined with homespun. It was too large to be Maggie's, and he almost immediately knew it didn't belong to one of the staff because its smell was familiar, sweet but not too sweet, a nice flowery perfume that might just haunt him until he found her again . . . Julia Goddard.

He lifted the garment to his face and inhaled the scent. Images and sounds flooded his mind again—of her with Maggie and the kitten, of her singing, tipping her head this way and that, glancing from the corner of her eye, smiling mischievously, the firelight dancing in her dark eyes. Her voice, velvety soft, drifting around the room, up the hall, making his heart beat a little faster.

This was nonsense. Utter nonsense—him pining over a woman he had met only a few hours ago, him inhaling the scent of a garment she had worn. Inhaling her scent.

And yet . . . as mad as his behavior seemed, he knew it wouldn't end here. In the space of a few hours, she had gotten under his skin, more than any woman ever had. He would search for her. He would locate her, find out if she was in some sort of trouble—that might explain why she had come to the city alone and why she had run off to avoid more questions. He would again offer to help her, and then, when they sorted through the trouble, if there was trouble, he would ask to court her. His nature, his inherent curiosity, never allowed him to walk away from things that intrigued him—and Julia Goddard was a puzzle he intended to solve.

Three

EARLY MORNING HAD already arrived when Josie fled the Murphy home, and by the time she reached the hotel, she was cold, damp, and exhausted. The lobby was empty, thank goodness, since she must look a fright, and she wearily climbed the stairs, wondering if she would ever see Margaret again and if the girl would eventually tell Dr. Murphy who she really was.

That had been the initial plan—for him to see for himself that she was a nice woman, of good character really, then for her and Margaret to tell him her true identity. Josie realized, however, as she climbed the carpeted stairs, that as angry and resentful as his wrongful assumptions made her feel, she was glad she and Margaret had not told him; she was not as eager anymore to see the look on his face when he discovered who she really was.

She had initially thought to get some enjoyment out of what would surely be a look of anger over the knowledge that he had been tricked. But during the walk to the hotel, she had recalled the many emotions on his face as he watched her and Margaret together—amazement, his brow lifted; amusement, his blue-green eyes twinkling with merriment; charm, an admiring glow to his gaze as he looked upon her. Respect that she had such a winning way with his daughter. He had wanted to know more about her, and that had been apparent and had made her feel apprehensive. Because, she now realized, at that point, deep inside, she knew she would find no satisfaction in watching the amazement, amusement, merriment, charm, and respect change to hurtful anger.

She had not expected to be as taken with Margaret's father as she was. She had not expected him to be so charming himself—after all, Margaret had made him out to be an ogre—and now she hoped the girl would leave well enough alone and not take any delight in telling her father that the woman he had met was really Josephine Gavin. The evening was over, and Josie was glad.

She took the room key from her reticule and started to insert it into the lock. She must not have pulled the door completely shut this morning, she realized, as the pressure she exerted to insert the key pushed the portal open. She removed the key, dropped it back into her reticule, then stepped into the room.

She had apparently left a lamp burning, too, or else the cleaning girls had left one lit. The soft light cast a glow on the furnishings: a small secretary, a wardrobe, a large tester bed and its deep maroon covering, a table and several chairs near the room's one window. The carpeting was done up in a gentle floral design, and the soft light rose from flickering flames in wall sconces which flanked the mantel over the small fireplace.

Josie untied the reticule from her wrist and placed it on the secretary, then crossed her arms and rubbed them. The room felt chilly, and she could hardly wait to slip a heavy nightdress over her head and burrow under the bedcovers. She'd be lucky if she did not take ill, if her voice did not suffer.

She struggled with the clasps on the back of her dress, finally succeeded in freeing them, and pushed the damp garment over her shoulders and down her arms.

"You're cold, I see," a voice said, startling Josie. "I would have had the girls light a fire, but no one knew where you were or when you planned to return."

She whirled, clutching the bodice of the dress just above her breasts. Orson's voice. It came from one of the chairs near the window. "What are you doing in here?" Josie demanded.

"This happens to be my room. My private room. You've no business intruding."

"Dear Josephine," he responded, drawing out the syllables of her name as he rose, the fingers of one hand tucked into a black waistcoat pocket. His voice was raspy, as always. He was a thin man, unusually thin of late, with a hacking cough that had become more and more frequent. His bearded chin was tilted in its normal manner.

All in all, Orson Neville was a man who exhibited an air of dignity, and professionalism, which Josie had always found redeeming in him. For all his demanding ways, he was indeed a manager and worthy of some respect. He had invested a great deal of time grooming and nurturing her from the fifteen-year-old aspiring actress he had plucked off of a dirty New York street to what she was today: the actress that crowds flocked to see. Weeks before engagements were scheduled to begin in various cities, he scouted the crowds there, discovering their likes and dislikes, and he always made certain the company played to those likes and dislikes, that Josie did to the best of her ability. Despite still being angry with him over the supper he had tried to involve her in this evening, Josie could not deny that he possessed qualities deserving of respect.

"You are my business," he said, his head wobbling a little as he lifted a box from the table near the chair in which he had been seated. "I made you what you are. You would do well to remember that. Of late, Josephine, you forget." He opened the box, pulled out a cheroot, then placed the box back on the table. Josie stiffened more, if possible, sensing trouble, sensing that he was infuriated with her beneath his calm exterior.

"You're not thinking of lighting that thing," she said. "You know how I detest cigars."

He bit off the tip and soon lit the cheroot anyway. Smoke swirled around his head as he regarded her, his eyes narrowed.

"Orson, if you don't mind . . ."

"Do you remember the day we met, Josephine?" he asked suddenly.

She laughed, a sharp sound. "This is absurd. I'm standing here half-dressed in damp clothes. I'm cold and shivering, and the hour is late—and you want to discuss the day we met! Orson—''

''I've seen you in less. . . .''

She stiffened. So he had. As well as developing her into a poised and graceful actress and nurturing her talents, he had taught her not to be so modest. Many a time Orson had walked into her dressing room while she was clad in nothing more than her undergarments, and he had sat and discussed the evening's performance with her. But this was different. He had never made himself comfortable in her hotel room. He had never waited for her to start undressing before making his presence known.

''Orson, have you been drinking?'' she queried uneasily. In the last two years, he had taken to the bottle more and more. Within the company, people often whispered that he and Mr. Jefferson had fallen heavily into debt, and Josie guessed that was why he had arranged the supper for her—he hoped to recruit a sponsor. The actors, actresses, and stage helpers always saw their pay, of course. After all, there would be no company without them. But that did not mean that Mr. Jefferson and Orson were not overextended with creditors. It certainly was not something either man would even think of talking about openly, however, as neither wished to be known as a ruined man.

Josie sometimes worried about the rumors—what would she do if the company dissolved?—but her mother had often told her not to worry about things she could not fix, to concentrate on the things she could. And that was what she usually did. She concentrated on her rehearsals and performances. She wanted the company to be successful and prosperous, but Orson's supper arrangement was too much.

''Whether or not I've been drinking is irrelevant, Josephine,'' Orson responded. ''What is relevant is the question of where you were for hours and hours after your latest performance.''

''You're my professional manager, not my personal manager,'' she reminded him in a cutting tone as he puffed on the cheroot. She had never spoken to him so coldly. Yet he did not even flinch. More smoke rose, swirling around his head, stinking up the air. "Orson, toss that blasted thing out the window!"

"Ah!" He half grinned. "More rubbish on the street of this great American city! The lion of the valley . . . the gateway to the West, or so many people are calling it. A growing, prosperous place with so many . . ." He swayed, catching himself with a hand on the arm of the chair.

Josie spotted a half-empty whiskey bottle on the floor near one leg of the chair. She glanced at it, then back up at him. He seemed pitiful suddenly, swaying so, still holding onto the arm of the chair, bent at the waist but with his chin still raised. Even in death Orson's chin would be raised, she knew.

". . . so many merchants. Wealthy merchants, Josephine, growing wealthier by the day! Right here under our noses. And one so caught up in your grace and beauty, he wanted to dine with you. But you, Josephine"—he whipped his arm around and she started, feeling certain that glowing ashes from the cigar would fall on the chair and burn the upholstery— "you decided to spend the evening elsewhere. You escaped the Hall right under my nose, didn't you? How clever you are! Indeed how graceful and beautiful and clever! Josephine, most beautiful of all actresses, contributes to the demise of the great Orson Neville, former thespian turned stage manager!" With the last word he erupted into a fit of coughs.

"Orson." Josie had stiffened with shock, embarrassment, and concern for him. She was suddenly thankful he was alone with her, that no one else was witnessing his drunkenness and undignified behavior, the fact that he was making it apparent that he was indeed in a great deal of trouble financially. Obviously even Orson had his moments of weakness; yet, as much time as they had spent together through the years, she had never seen him in such a state.

"Sit down, Orson, before you fall down," she said as gently as possible.

She approached the wardrobe, opened one of the doors, and, standing behind it, she slipped out of the dress. Her underclothes were slightly damp, too, but not so damp that she felt uncomfortable. She grabbed a wrap from the wardrobe and slipped it on, then she approached her manager, who was stubbornly still on his feet.

"Sit down," she said, placing gentle pressure on his forearm with her hand, urging him toward the chair. She turned her head, trying to avoid the smoke from the cigar, but it reached her anyway, making her cough—and oh, the stench of it!

"Josephine, you cannot comprehend how important that supper was. Carlisle, he stood ready to sponsor the company. He stood ready to hand us a draft for—"

"Orson, don't. Please sit down and compose yourself," she urged. "You're sick and you're saying things you would not normally say, behaving in a way you would not normally behave. You've had too much to drink, too. Sit down and compose yourself before you wake others who'll come banging at the door and see you this way."

Still coughing a little, he sat finally, wobbly, as if the drink had only really hit him in the last few minutes. Josie lifted a spittoon, and he flicked ashes into it, then puffed again on the cheroot, though now she watched his hand tremble. She had never seen Orson like this. She had never seen him frightened and looking so pale and sick. A thin sheen of perspiration had broken out all over his face.

"Have you seen a doctor?" she could not help but ask.

"Do you have any idea how much in debt I am, Josephine?" he queried breathlessly, speaking slowly, ignoring her question. "How much in debt the company is? Last season . . . last season was nearly disastrous, with people being scared to spend a penny after financial upheaval had swept the country. But so far this year the turnouts are incredible. We'll recoup our losses, surely, by the end of the season. But for now . . . for now, we struggle. And that"—he raised a hand and let it fall on the arm of the chair—"is the truth of it. For now we struggle. Carlisle might have made it possible for us not to have to struggle so much, for Jefferson and me not to spend so many sleepless nights. But your disappearance this evening . . ." He coughed more, unable to go on for the moment.

Josie sank down onto the opposite chair and rubbed her arms again. She felt sorry for him now and wondered if she couldn't have endured one arranged supper for the sake of helping the company, Orson, and Mr. Jefferson through their financial difficulties.

"It was only a supper?" she asked.

He stared at her blankly for a moment, his eyes glazed. She thought he was more sick than he knew. If not, then the whiskey had worsened his lung illness. "What else would I have arranged, Josephine?"

"People sometimes assume that because I'm an actress, I'm also a whore, Orson; you know that. It's a notion I've worked hard to dispel over the years. It's certainly one I've never appreciated and don't deserve."

"No one in the company has ever assumed that," he assured her weakly.

"I saw the gown you had made."

"One supper. That is all I am asking of you. One evening of your time. Smiles and flattering conversation . . ."

Josie closed her eyes briefly, sighed, then opened them again. She rose from the chair and moved to the window, drawing the lace curtain aside and looking absently down on the street below. *You're not like that, like the women who walk up and down the levee, are you?* Margaret had asked, looking nearly frantic with worry.

"I suppose it's their business," Josie murmured into the night, thinking of the women walking up and down the levee. "But it's one I'll have no part of."

She turned and faced Orson, her jaw tight. "You're not so naive. You know he'll want more than smiles and flattering conversation, and what happens when 'more' is not given— and I assure you, Orson, it will not be. You're grasping, and even if I do sup with the man, there are no guarantees. Besides, I'm well aware of my reputation, which stems from the mere fact that I'm an actress. Do you think he hasn't made assumptions like everyone else? Oh, the day I realized that no decent man would have me!" She waved a hand wildly, feeling a knot rise in her throat, feeling tears burn the backs of her eyes, wishing she could erase certain memories. She was tired, that was all. She'd had so very little sleep lately, and now here he was, putting her in a position she did not wish to be in: she could let the company sink, or she could save it.

"Josephine, what do you—"

"You asked if I remembered the day we met," she said, her voice softer now. She turned back to the window in time to watch a carriage start by on the street. The sound of its wheels grinding on the pavement was muffled through the panes, and glowing lanterns dangled from each of its four upper corners.

"Of course I do. How could I forget? On a New York street. I was fourteen years old. My mother was minding our market booth, and I was singing and performing skits on the street corner. We were so poor, and yet she managed to buy cloth and make me and my brother a new set of clothes twice a year. I knew she always spent her last dollar to do it, and I wanted to help in any way I could. Most people only dropped a penny in my basket after watching me perform. You watched for a long time, then tossed a handful of pennies in the basket and began talking to me, telling me how good I was, how very, very talented I was."

Josie looked over her shoulder at Orson. He was still smoking that blasted cheroot. She gave a little laugh. "Oh, indeed I remember. You were smoking then, too, and I told you I didn't like it. But you persisted, exactly as you persist now. I remember you telling me that I was as good as any actress anywhere, and I told you about the time I had walked by one of the theaters, wondered at the crowd milling around the entrance—why they were all there and talking so excitedly— and curiosity had gotten the better of me. So I sneaked inside and watched the show from between two crates just off the stage. I ran home and told my mother all about it, how wonderful and pretty the actress was and that I wanted to be like her. My mother told me to put the nonsense out of my head, that a girl could ruin herself that way . . ."

Again she turned to stare at the street below. "Children," she said sadly, shaking her head. "My mother . . . she was so right about everything. And yet I thought she was wrong. I knew actresses were not well thought of, but they were so pretty and they seemed so nice—how could they be bad women? They couldn't be, not in their hearts, I decided. And there I was when you came along. Fourteen, naive, and full of energy and eagerness. With your encouragement, I knew I could do it. You convinced me, Orson. But of course I felt pulled then, too—I couldn't leave my mother and brother. I had to help them survive. When they died in that fire months later, there was nothing left for me in New York, and going with you was easy, something I did not think twice about.

"The summer I turned seventeen, when Frank Douglas came along . . ." She spun around, her arms crossed now, both hands rubbing her upper arms as if she had a chill. "Do you remember him, Orson?"

He puffed lazily on the cigar, then again flicked ashes at the spittoon. He was slumped down in the chair. His eyes were half-open. "There have been a number of men who have grown infatuated with you along the way, Josephine," he said wearily.

"But Frank Douglas, Orson. The banker in New Orleans. You do remember him," she insisted.

Another puff. "Very well, I remember him."

"I was so naive," she whispered, "so very, very naive. My mother warned me, but you . . . you developed me. 'Concentrate, Josephine. Head up. Give a smile. Louder. Project.' It was so much fun, Orson, and I had a good time learning it all! Wearing beautiful gowns all the time and learning to act like a lady. Only I wasn't regarded as a lady, I soon found out. Frank came along with his charm and his nice way of putting words together, and I believed he regarded me as a lady. I thought I could have all that I wanted, but—"

"What did you expect, Josephine? That Frank would marry you afterward? Simply because of what had passed between the two of you? Because you shared his bed? Stop this nonsense, Josephine," Orson grated. "Stop blaming me for what you should have known all along. No one . . . no one forced you to leave New York. You should have known better than to allow yourself to be caught up in foolish dreams. You're an actress, for the love of—"

"I'm a woman," Josie retorted. "A woman. And you don't know my dreams anymore. I was a girl when you found me. Now I'm a woman, and my dreams are different."

"I'm almost afraid to ask what they are," he grumbled.

She lifted her chin, displaying defiance, but not feeling so strong inside. Inside she felt as though she might crumble. "You asked where I spent the hours following the performance tonight. I'll tell you. I spent them with a child. I spent them in a home, not a hotel room or a boardinghouse. I spent them in front of a warm fireplace with the child's laughter ringing in my ears and a kitten crawling across our laps. We were up to trickery, the girl and I, but soon her father came home, and then we were there, the three of us, and despite what I know he thinks about me—what the girl told me he thinks about me—it almost felt as if—"

"Who is he, Josephine?" Orson asked gruffly, struggling to straighten as abruptly as a sick, drunken man could, his gray brows drawing together.

"He's a doctor. He lectures at a college here in St. Louis. That's all I—"

"He won't have you. You must know that. Don't be a fool, girl!"

Pain ripped through Josie, tearing at her heart. "Do I look like a girl? Damn you, Orson. Damn *me* for opening my mouth. Take your bottle and go," she ordered, spinning back to face the window, resolving not to care that he was sick. "Go now before I decide to accept the offer Mr. Carson at the St. Louis Theater put to me only this morning. I love our company, but his sum is tempting."

She knew Orson paled more; she didn't need to see him.

"He . . . he—he didn't!" he finally sputtered.

"He did."

"Trying to steal my actress, is he? I'll whap the man with my cane!"

"All challenges are met out on an island in the Mississippi, from what I hear around here," Josie offered. "Tell me who is the bigger fool—a woman who longs for a family, or a sick, drunken man who threatens another man with a cane?"

"Josephine . . . you're not thinking of . . ."

She tossed him a sad smile. "As much as I would like to, Orson, no, I'm not. There are twenty-nine other people in our company, and I care for many of them. What will they do if the troupe dissolves? Where will they go? Like me, Orson, and like you, many of them do not have homes. We're all nothing but glorified gypsies. But at least we have each other. I won't see Lauretta and Stephan and the others lose the only family they know.

"But I will not have supper with Mr. Carlisle. I will not offer myself in that way for a price."

Silence reigned for a time. Finally Orson shifted in the chair. "I've had some interest from a few gaming houses," he began almost cautiously. "You could make an appearance or two on the evenings when there are no performances scheduled. Perhaps sing a few songs. It will pay well. Very well."

"Provided that Andre and one of the other men go along for protection," she agreed, running her fingers along the scalloped edge of the curtain. "Gaming houses can be distasteful, dangerous places."

Another silence ensued, longer than the last.

He exhaled deeply. "Josephine, I sometimes wonder how much longer I shall have you."

She laughed, a sound that was edged with sadness. "Perhaps into eternity, Orson, for no one else will."

Four

"JOHNNY OWENS, YOU'VE got to sit still, my boy. Otherwise we'll never get these wounds cleaned."

Thomas turned from the table on which the twelve-year-old boy sat, and dipped the bloodied cloth in a basin of water that rested on a nearby washstand. Johnny was another victim of Battle Row, and Thomas, feeling grim and angry about the condition of the boy's arm, had little patience at the moment. He almost wished a band of concerned citizens would rise up and demand that that section of the city be cleaned out. But then again, Battle Row certainly helped keep him in business.

"Be still so the doctor can mend you, Johnny," the boy's mother pleaded from nearby. Eveline Owens stood twisting her hands, fretting, worry lines marking her face beneath her gingham bonnet. Thomas had asked her to wait in the next room. She had insisted on being near her Johnny, but now and then she would dare a glance at her son's arm and grow pale behind the handkerchief she kept lifting to her nose. "He'll be fine, won't he, Dr. Murphy?" she asked anxiously for at least the tenth time. "He'll be fine?"

"He surely will," Thomas said, wringing the cloth and turning back to the table. "Unless those wounds aren't cleaned an' they get infected. Then he might not stand a chance. There's some stitchin' that might need to be done, too, but I've no way of knowin' if I don't get a good look." Every time he barely touched what he thought were some fairly deep knife wounds on Johnny's left arm with the cloth, the boy jerked the limb away.

"I don't need no stitches," Johnny growled, though Thomas thought it was more that he was speaking through slightly gritted teeth—his arm had to be throbbing by now. Three lacerations on the forearm, two on the upper arm, and as near as Thomas could tell through the dried mud and grass caked on the boy's shoulder, there was a mighty good one there, too. Johnny sat glaring at him, his blue eyes wild, his blond hair filthy with more dried mud and grass.

Thomas wiped at one of the cuts on the boy's forearm, the same cut he'd been trying to clean for the last ten minutes. Again Johnny jerked the arm away, wincing. "God . . . ! Just give me some of that stuff doctors give people sometimes, some of that laudanum! They don't need cleaned and they don't need stitched!"

"Oh, Johnny!" Mrs. Owens sobbed. She hurried over to the table and put a hand out to touch her son's back. It was a comforting gesture, nothing more, from a mother who wanted to soothe her child.

"Get outta here, Ma!" Johnny flung his arm around and knocked her arm away. She gasped and reeled back.

Thomas nearly dropped the cloth as he reacted instinctively, grabbing the boy by what remained of his shirt and lifting him a good four inches off of the table to bring his face up to his. "See here, lad," Thomas seethed. "You won't sit in my office an' talk to yer mother like that. You damn sure won't strike her. You went wanderin' where you shouldn't have, an' that's no one's fault but yer own."

Johnny's face was twisted with pain. His voice, when it came, was weak and higher than normal: "Please . . . put me down."

Thomas lowered the boy back to the table, shocked at himself that he'd grabbed Johnny like that. He never liked children treating their parents disrespectfully; he was already short-tempered because he'd hardly slept a wink for the last two nights, and Johnny striking his mother had been more than he could stand.

Mrs. Owens was collecting herself, smoothing her skirt, touching the handkerchief to her nose again, sobbing a little more.

Thomas draped the cloth over the edge of the basin, washed his hands and arms up to his elbows—his shirtsleeves were rolled up—then dried them on a cloth hanging from a bar on the edge of the washstand. He went to calm Mrs. Owens, knowing he needed to settle her somewhere. Her fretting was driving him nearly as mad as he knew it was driving Johnny. Still, there was no excuse for the boy striking her.

"There, Mrs. Owens," he said, putting an arm around her shoulders and urging her toward the door. "The next room is the place for you. I even know where there's some sherry that'll help calm you. Yer Johnny will be fine, but lads his age . . . they tend to not want their mothers about when somethin' like this happens."

They walked through the doorway together and down the hall to the next room, which was comfortably furnished with evergreen carpeting, a few cabinets, several settees, and against one wall, facing a window, Thomas's desk, where he often sat to write papers and notes about patients he had treated.

"You see," Thomas said, trying to ease her down onto one of the settees, "Johnny's at the age where he's still a boy, but he wants to be a man."

"But, Dr. Murphy," she objected, stiffening, a flash going off in her blue eyes, "he—he came to me! He came running home—to his mother—holding his arm, telling me he needed a doctor."

"Of course he came to you—have a seat now." She did, finally, and Thomas crossed the room to a small cabinet, opened one of the upper doors, and reached for a tumbler and the bottle of sherry.

"Yer his mother, an' there isn't a person alive who doesn't want to run to his mother when he's first injured," Thomas said. "Even when we're grown up. We all remember our mother's nursin' our cuts an' bruises, or just mendin' us in general by holdin' us or givin' a little kiss to make it better." He crossed the room again, this time to hand her the glass.

She glanced at it, then shakily lifted it to her lips for a sip.

Thomas dropped one hand into a trouser pocket and rubbed his scratchy jaw with the other. "Johnny wants to be a man, like I said, but he was shocked when he was first cut, shocked enough to forget for a bit that he wants to think of himself as a man. An' so he ran home to his mother, because in the back of his mind he has these memories of you always makin' a cut or a scrape or a bruise better, y'see. You knew you couldn't mend him this time, as badly as he's cut, an' so you brought him here . . . to a physician. But to Johnny I'm more than a doctor, I'm a fellow man, an' he doesn't want his mother comfortin' him in front of another man. It's not that he doesn't love you an' doesn't want you about ever again."

Mrs. Owens tossed back the remaining sherry, then sat with the glass in her lap, watching him and listening. "I'll sit here," she said, her voice cracking. "You see if you can fix his arm, Dr. Murphy. I promise to stay here. Right here."

"I'll fix his arm, Mrs. Owens," Thomas assured her. "The sherry's in that cabinet if you decide you want more. Think nothin' of layin' yer head against the arm of that settee if you get sleepy. I'll go back in there with Johnny an' have him mended in a bit."

She nodded quickly, sniffing again, bringing the handkerchief to her nose for at least the twentieth time since she'd entered the office with her son.

Thomas left her there, hoping she would stay put and not decide to join him and Johnny again and try to comfort the boy. How well Thomas remembered his own awkward days. He was only thirty-two years old now, but he sometimes felt older, and twelve years old seemed like a lifetime ago.

He went back in with Johnny, who was looking pretty pitiful by now, and he took care to close the door behind him. Earlier Thomas had ripped the boy's shirtsleeve open clear up past his shoulder, and the cloth hung in tatters from his arms. Johnny sat with his head hanging down, his bottom lip protruding slightly, almost as if he were ready to cry. Thomas returned to the washbasin.

"Where's yer father these days?" he asked, wringing the cloth in the water.

Johnny shrugged his unharmed shoulder. "Gone upriver, last I heard. Had business up that way. We hardly see him anymore, he's so caught up in what he's got to do."

Thomas dropped the cloth, having a better idea. He moved the basin to the table and lifted Johnny's arm over it. He began scooping up water in the palm of one hand and pouring it over the cuts. Johnny winced, but didn't jerk his arm away. He put his other hand up to his eye and made like he was brushing away a piece of grass there. But Thomas knew he was swiping at a tear.

"It hurts, Johnny. I know that," Thomas said gently, lowering the boy's arm to rest on the edge of the basin and stepping away.

From a corner cabinet, Thomas took a bottle of whiskey, uncorked it, and stepped back over to the table. Johnny glanced up at him. As Thomas handed him the bottle, their eyes met briefly. For all his toughness and the way he'd braved Battle Row, the boy had never even had a drink.

"It'll be like fire goin' down at first," Thomas warned, splashing more water up on the cuts. "Have at least three big swallows, though, 'cause you do need stitches, an' there'll be more pain—I'm not lyin' to you. An' I'll tell you something else. These wounds'll hurt for days an' days, more tomorrow than today, an' on an' on for a solid week probably. I'll give you some laudanum to take home with you. You'll have to let yer mother nurse you for the next week or so, an' you need to stay inside, in bed, for the next few days. If you take a notion not to, Johnny, then think about what I'm about to tell you: I remember another arm like this one, all cut an' damaged, an' I remember sawin' it off after it got infected an' swelled up an' turned nearly black. That's the honest truth. So if you want to keep yer arm, Johnny, an' you want to keep it attached to yer body, you'll do as I'm tellin' you. Don't worry about bein' a man so much right now as makin' sure this arm is taken care of."

He felt Johnny tremble and then caught a glimpse of tears flowing down the boy's cheeks, making tracks on Johnny's dirty face. He was almost sorry he'd grabbed the boy like that earlier. Almost.

"You'll be fine, Johnny," Thomas said. "But if you ever get it in yer mind again to wander down to Battle Row lookin' for excitement . . . you remember this pain an' what I said to you about that other arm."

Johnny sniffed. "Yes, sir."

Thomas cleaned the remaining wounds, though he knew the water on the cuts hurt like hell. He bathed Johnny's entire arm, changing the water a few times, tossing the dirty water out a window and pouring clean water from a ewer into the basin. He helped Johnny out of the tattered shirt, urged him to have a few more gulps of whiskey—though by now the boy had had at least five, coughing and sputtering with each gulp—and then Thomas fetched a needle and thread from a cabinet drawer.

He had Johnny, who was now a little groggy, lie back on the table. He poured whiskey over the wounds to clean them more, and then began stitching, talking as he did, asking Johnny what kind of things he liked to do, what his interests were.

Though the stitching hurt—Johnny winced now and then—overall the boy was feeling better since the whiskey had numbed the pain. He told Thomas that he liked to fish and race horses with his friends along the riverbank. The group of them often put bets on how many times they could make a stone skip across the water. Johnny laughed a little bitterly at one point, saying they'd once bet on when his pa would be home the next time, and for how long. Mr. Owens had a lot of merchant dealings going on in some upriver towns and cities, and he was hardly home at all, despite making promises that he'd do this and that with his son. The promises always began with "Someday, Johnny. Just you wait. Someday we'll . . ." The "somedays" had gone on for years, and they continued as Johnny got older and older.

And now here he is, Thomas thought, a boy on the edge of manhood, with a lot of questions and needs. A boy who needs a certain amount of time with his father. Thomas didn't quite know what to do or say.

"I've thought about being a doctor," Johnny announced, almost cheerily. "I think it's great the way you fix everybody up the way you do. The way you mend people."

Thomas looked up from his work and saw admiration and respect in Johnny's eyes. Smiling sadly, he shook his head. "I can't always mend people, Johnny, an' not everyone mends after I put them back together, either. I'm not Christ, travelin' among the sick, layin' on hands and workin' miracles. I use what I've learned an' I've had some luck so far. With every stitch goes a prayer, lad—an' prayers go far."

Johnny smiled back, then winced as Thomas began working on the shoulder wound, pulling the flesh together.

"So Johnny wants to be a doctor. . . ." Thomas said.

"I said I've thought about it."

"You've thought about it. Well, now, if you give it more thought an' you decide you want to do it . . . The truth is, I've been needin' some help around here in the afternoons. Come evenin' and night I get called out on occasion an' I could sometimes use help then, too, if ye're interested. Someone to hand me instruments an' wash them afterward. Someone to help with just about anything I need help with. You'd be learnin' along the way an' makin' some money for yer pockets, an' I'd be happy knowin' you don't have time, between school an' workin' with me, to be wanderin' Battle Row."

Johnny gave him a look of disbelief, his jaw falling open. "You mean that, Dr. Murphy?"

Thomas chuckled. "I don't say things I don't mean, Johnny. Now you'd best lie still an' not move yer head too fast anymore. You might get a needle in the jaw if you do."

"Yes, sir," Johnny said, and throughout the rest of the stitching he lay perfectly still.

Thomas and the boy found Mrs. Owens sleeping when they walked into the next room some time later, Johnny's arm secured by a cloth wrapped around his chest. Johnny walked over, hunched down, grimacing, and gently shook his mother awake just as the sound of a bell indicated that someone else had entered the office.

Thomas rubbed his jaw wearily. It was early evening, and he was exhausted and eager to go home. He had had breakfast with Maggie this morning, but he looked forward to seeing her again before she went to sleep at night. Like Johnny's father, he was sometimes too busy. He hoped he paid enough attention to Maggie, that he pulled her up onto his lap and visited with her enough so that she felt important and secure in the knowledge that he loved her.

Leaving Johnny with his mother for the moment, Thomas headed up the hall, on his way to see who was calling now. He was still drying his clean hands on a cloth as he stepped into the front room of the small house he had converted into his office several years ago.

He spotted the back of a familiar figure who stood looking at a picture on the wall, and he stopped short, blinking.

"My eyes are deceivin' me!" he blurted. "I didn't drink any of that whiskey I poured on Johnny Owens's wounds, but now I'm wonderin' . . . I swear Alan Schuster is standin' in my office."

A chuckle rose from the six-foot, blond-haired figure as he turned and faced Thomas. Alan's brown eyes sparkled with amusement. "I told m'self, as soon as the captain ordered the line dropped and the boat moored, that the good doctor would be here, not at his home. But I went there first, despite my own thinking, and now here I stand. If you haven't had a drink yet this evening, if you're *sure* of that," he teased, "then finish up here and come and share a bottle with me. I've been perfecting my skill at billiards and feel certain I'll beat you this time around."

"Dr. Schuster, tell me how Davenport is survivin' in yer absence," Thomas teased right back. Saints, but seeing Alan was good—like a breath of fresh air had blown into the office! He and Alan had met at the medical college in Chicago. Alan had spent some time here in St. Louis afterward, then had moved on to Davenport, a town that was in need of doctors— or so a friend had told him at the time. Alan and Thomas had kept in touch over the years, and Alan had dropped in like this during the winter thaw last year, too, not only to visit, but also to have a peek at some rental property in which he'd invested. "Are these becomin' annual visits?" Thomas couldn't resist asking.

"Davenport survives with or without me," Alan answered. "There are a dozen doctors with high standards and the utmost regard for the Hippocratic oath."

"Business isn't good anymore, then?"

"Business picks up. Give it a few months, and cholera will be making the rounds again and—" He shook his head, sobering as Thomas felt himself stiffen. "Thomas, I'm sorry. In our river cities, it's getting to be such a common thing, cholera. . . . I should have thought before speaking."

"Abby was one of hundreds, Alan," Thomas said sadly. "An' ye're right. It is becomin' a common thing. I'm dreadin' spring, if the truth be known. I've considered takin' Maggie an' leavin' the city."

Alan nodded slowly, understanding. He swept hair from his brow and squinted an eye, scrutinizing Thomas. "From the looks of you, you have had a day of it, my friend."

Thomas glanced down at his bloodstained shirt. Another one to be thrown out.

"You have a patient in the back still?" Alan asked. "I could help. Two doctors are always better than one."

Thomas grinned. "Only if they agree. About this billiards thing . . ."

Alan's gaze went beyond Thomas, to the hall behind him. "Here comes the patient now, I believe. As usual, it appears as though you've put another body back together, Dr. Murphy."

Johnny and his mother were coming up the hall, Thomas discovered when he glanced over his shoulder. He knew they had a buggy waiting outside, the one in which they had arrived, but he meant to first fetch Johnny a blanket to drape over his bare shoulders, then see them home safely himself. Neither mother nor son was in any condition to be in command of a pair of reins and a horse. Mrs. Owens looked as if she might fall asleep again any moment, and Johnny's eyes were glazed, the result of hours of pain and the whiskey he'd drunk. Besides, he wouldn't let the boy risk tearing those wounds open.

"Ma's tired, Dr. Murphy," Johnny said, grimacing slightly with each movement, "and you look tired yourself.

We'll go home, and I'll take good care of myself, I promise. I'll do what Ma says, I promise that, too, and when I'm all well, if your offer still stands, I'll be here afternoons to help out.''

"You need somethin' over yer upper body, Johnny," Thomas responded. "It's March out there, in case you've forgotten, an' I won't have you gettin' a chill. I promised a bottle of laudanum, too, an' I already told myself I'd be the one takin' the two of you home. Take a seat while I fetch a blanket an'—''

"Thomas, Thomas." Alan stepped up behind Thomas, then around, and dipped his head in greeting to the boy and his mother. "Dr. Alan Schuster's the name," he said, "and it seems I arrived just in time to be of service to a friend and colleague. Dr. Murphy will fetch the blanket and laudanum, then I'll take you home while he jots a few notes and cleans up. Knowing him like I do, I believe he's had an exhausting day, seeing to the sick and injured, and I'm glad to be of service."

Mrs. Owens glanced at Thomas, uncertainty in her expression. Johnny said, "Another doctor!" and Thomas shook his head, grinning. Alan always raced into a situation headfirst, ready to take control and manage things. This time Thomas meant to let him.

"He is indeed a colleague, Mrs. Owens," Thomas assured Johnny's mother. "A friend I attended medical college with an' one I'd trust with my own life. If you don't mind him seein' you home . . .''

"Oh, no!" the woman said. "Oh, not at all, if you trust him so, Dr. Murphy."

Thomas fetched a blanket and a bottle of laudanum from the small cabinet in the room where he'd stitched Johnny's cuts, and when he rejoined the others, he explained the dosage and how often Johnny should take the medication. He had plans to call on Johnny tomorrow and the next day, and every day for a week, to make certain things were going well and Johnny was following his instructions, that the wounds were healing, and that there was no infection. He gave the boy a hard, long look, silently reminding him of what he'd said

about the other arm he'd stitched. Johnny pursed his lips, nodded grimly, and then Thomas knew he had remembered and
that he just might not ever forget. The three of them—Alan,
Johnny, and Mrs. Owens—started for the door.

Once they had left the office, Thomas headed down the hall,
thinking to don a clean shirt from a rack of them he kept in
a small supply room near the back of the house. Clean shirts
were something he had learned to keep in stock. He washed
his hands and arms again over a basin in the same room, then
washed his face, too, and finally slipped the clean shirt on,
enjoying its freshness. He'd planned to get home in time to
kiss Maggie good night, but she would forgive him when she
woke in the morning to a nice surprise—Alan.

By the time Alan returned an hour or so later, Thomas was
feeling much better and eagerly looking forward to billiards,
drinks, and conversation.

The Silver Dollar was one of St. Louis's most popular gaming establishments, complete with not only billiards tables, but
also tables for roulette, cards, and dice. The woodwork was
dark and well polished, from a long bar and its stools to the
shimmering mahogany staircase branching up near the back
of the establishment. Smoke hazed the air, and laughter and
conversation filled the place as people sat or stood, crowding
around tables. Thomas hadn't been inside the Silver Dollar
since Alan's last visit, which had been a month or so before
Abby's death. He wasn't much for cards and dice. He never
had been. But billiards . . . In Chicago, he had mastered the
game, and there hadn't been a person around who could beat
him, including Alan.

Alan went for drinks at the bar while Thomas racked the
balls and tried to ignore the conversation going on between a
group of rather boisterous men at a nearby roulette table. It
was a little hard to ignore, however, because they weren't
discussing their chances as they took turns tossing dice onto
the colorful wheel. They were discussing the actress Josephine
Gavin and an appearance she was apparently scheduled to
make at the Silver Dollar this evening.

"She could sing a man right into his grave," one man joked, thumping his chest.

"Or into her bed," another said.

Laughter went around the table as many of the men tossed back drinks and the wheel was spun again.

"Ain't heard of a man yet who could resist her!"

"Ain't heard of one who's had her in a while," someone responded somberly. "She's got some high-an'-mighty ways about her, from what I hear. She don't let the common man around her too often. Not even the higher man, I reckon. I heard she got her heart broken down'n New Orleans. Took a fancy to a feller who wanted a little something to do with her, if ya catch my meanin', but that was all. He was a little too uppity himself to think about hitchin' up with an actress. Can't figure—"

"I'd hitch up with her all right!" the first voice cut in. But Thomas didn't think the man meant in the marital way. He had the urge to rap one end of the cue stick he'd picked up against the edge of the billiards table, and when the men looked this way, glare at them. No woman deserved to be talked about in such a manner. But then, surely Josephine Gavin had known what sort of life she was getting into before she'd gotten into it.

"Ah, Jim, she surely wouldn't let *you* near her, stinkin' like you do," someone teased.

Jim puffed out his chest. "Wait an' see if I don't!"

Laughter and speculation about whether Jim could get near the actress rose from the small crowd. Alan returned with a bottle and two glasses, which he set on the table he and Thomas had claimed nearby. He popped the cork on the bottle and filled both glasses, and Thomas joined him at the table to have a drink before they began playing.

"Josephine Gavin should be here anytime," Alan said, looking a little excited himself—his eyes were bright.

"So you've fallen victim, too, have you?" Thomas asked. "Seems every man in the place is holdin' his breath, waitin' for the woman."

"She's something to wait for. I saw her perform at a make-shift theater in Davenport."

Thomas tossed back the bourbon, feeling its fire in his throat, its warmth in his belly. "Maggie's taken a likin' to her."

Alan lifted both brows. "Has she? Just where did Maggie meet her? Surely not inside the theater—that's no place for a child—and surely not out in public. Other than immediately after her performances, Josephine Gavin doesn't make herself available to the general population. She keeps to herself most of the time. People have wondered about her and her manager, Orson Neville—if they'll ever marry, that sort of thing. But others who have worked with her say the two of them have a business relationship, more like a father-daughter relationship."

"I had no idea you were so infatuated with the actress, my friend," Thomas said, a slow grin working its way across his face as he studied Alan. "But then, it seems that just about every man is."

"Excluding you? You're indifferent to the woman's beauty and charm onstage?" Alan brought his glass to his mouth and tipped it, his eyes narrowed on Thomas the entire time.

"I've never seen her perform."

"You're far too busy. Snatch the opportunity while she's in St. Louis. You won't regret it."

Thomas laughed. "I've no desire to. I told Maggie the same thing, y'know. That the theater's no place for a child. She hasn't met her, but she's wanted to. I'm rather surprised that I've heard no more about it. We had a quarrel one evenin' over it." He shook his head, remembering Maggie standing there with her fists planted on her hips. "I knew my daughter was a stubborn one with a temper, but I've never seen that much temper from her. Said she'd find someone else to take her an' her friends if I didn't."

Alan coughed. "Maggie?"

"My darlin' Maggie," Thomas said, nodding.

A commotion started over near the front door. People began crowding that way, talking excitedly. Women in bright dresses, laughing, clung to the arms of men as they pressed forth. Jim and his friends deserted the roulette table and joined the mass. A male voice boomed above the din, telling people to clear the way, clear a path—Miss Gavin was coming through, and she didn't intend to fight her way through. She'd be going over to the corner where the piano stood, and she'd sing them a few songs if they minded their manners.

"Providin' we've got manners to mind!" a man shouted. People responded with laughter, agreeing. But they began moving aside to clear the actress a path.

Thomas would have a straight view of the door once the path cleared entirely. Half grinning, thinking this was all a bunch of nonsense—he doubted that an appearance by the president of the United States would create this much of a stir—he leaned across the table toward Alan, whose neck was twisted so he could watch the door. "Yer actress is arrivin', if you didn't already know," he teased.

Alan slanted him a grin. "When you lay eyes on her, Dr. Murphy, you'll be as smitten as every other man in the place."

Thomas grunted, thinking he'd never make a fool of himself over a woman; he'd never nearly mob a doorway just to have a peek at her.

Spasms of excitement went through the crowd, now divided except for a few men who insisted on standing in the path. Apparently the actress was in the establishment now, but getting to the piano in the far corner was going to be a chore. Clapping started somewhere and rose, spreading through the mass of people. Thomas caught a glimpse of burgundy flounces and was reminded of the many extravagant, low-cut gowns he'd seen in her dressing room the night he was looking for Maggie. He poured himself more bourbon while Alan stood transfixed, waiting for a look at the woman. Nonsense, Thomas told himself again as he turned back toward the billiards table.

He drank the bourbon he'd poured, then left the glass on the table and grabbed one of the cue sticks, thinking he'd practice while Alan waited for a glimpse. "Fools," he grumbled as whistles and cheers filled the Silver Dollar. He wasn't thinking of Alan, of course, since Alan might watch the woman, but surely not behave in such a manner.

Thomas began hitting balls into pockets, one after another,

at least six while the actress apparently made her way across the large room. He glanced up once and caught sight of the back of her. Long, wavy black hair cascaded over her shoulders and down her back, ending at her waist. The bodice of the gown clung to her creamy shoulders. Her arms were thin and graceful, bent slightly as she clutched either side of her skirt. She seemed to be talking to people in the crowd as she walked—she wasn't that unfriendly and reclusive after all. But what was the Silver Dollar but a stage, and what was the crowd but her audience?

He hit more balls into pockets, then gathered the balls and reracked them. He heard the tinkling of piano notes just as he lifted the rack. The excited voices died down, then the piano tinkled again, and a moment later her voice joined the notes: *"There's a sweet rose-scented val–ley, in the hills of Tennessee. Where the mockingbirds are sing–ing, and they seem to beck–on me . . ."*

The tune continued, but Thomas was hardly hearing it anymore. He stood frozen near the billiards table, clutching the stick, shock going through him. He'd know that voice anywhere. . . . He'd heard it in his dreams all last night and even some during the day today, between lectures and attending patients.

His mind was playing games with him, that was all. He wanted to hear her voice, Julia Goddard's voice, and so he was imagining the actress's voice to be hers. Yes, that's what it was. That's all it was. His tired mind was playing games with him.

All the same, he had to be sure.

Still clutching the stick, he eased forward, past Alan, past the roulette table, past a small group of men gathered near one edge of the bar. He walked slowly between tables, almost numbly excusing himself past people, edging his way forward to have a look at Josephine Gavin. She continued to sing. He almost wished she would stop. He didn't want the voice to belong to her. He wanted it to belong to sweet, charming Julia Goddard, who had sat on the floor in his sitting room with Maggie and played and interacted with his daughter in an irresistible way. The woman he wanted to find and court.

He had almost worked his way all the way to the corner, and now his gaze fell on her as she stood singing. Her hair was different, loose and waving around her face. But the face itself was the same—dark, haunting eyes lined with thick black lashes; well-defined brows and a sculpted nose and jaw. Her cheekbones were high, her cheeks as dusky tonight as her lips.

Thomas stopped near a table, unconsciously placing a hand on the edge of it to steady himself as he watched her, as he stood transfixed by her. She was still as beautiful, but inside . . . inside, the woman standing near that piano couldn't possibly be the same woman who had told Maggie about the kitten she'd received as a child, who had sung so sweetly to his daughter.

Her gaze met his, and she began stumbling over lyrics, putting a hand to her chest now and then. The shock Thomas had felt earlier burst into anger, and he was suddenly childishly glad to hear the grumbles of disappointment that rose from the crowd. She and Maggie . . . they'd had fun deceiving him, *lying* to him. So many lies . . . Her name, her being from across the river in Alton . . . They'd probably lied about her rescuing Maggie. His daughter had gone to the theater and had succeeded in meeting the actress! She'd somehow convinced Josephine Gavin to come home with her and lie to him—or had that been the woman's idea? Yes, that made more sense! Concocting such a scheme would not have been a difficult task for Josephine Gavin. She was an actress, after all, and a damn good one at that.

Thomas read an apology in her eyes, but he turned away, nearly bumping into Alan.

"Thomas, what is it?" Alan asked. He teased, "So she wouldn't affect you, would she?"

"I'm goin' home, Alan," Thomas responded. "Ye're welcome to stay at the house, you know that, if you care to collect yer things from wherever you've put them."

"Thomas, I wanted to stay and—"

"Stay, then," Thomas snapped. "Stay an' hear the infamous Josephine Gavin. I've heard enough of her. If yer unfortunate enough to speak with her, tell her for me that Dr. Murphy says she's a fine actress. A fine . . . *actress*."

Five

JOSEPHINE STOOD NEAR the piano, not knowing if she could continue singing, if she could finish the tune. It was breaking her heart, the way Dr. Murphy was looking at her, with pain and disbelief in his eyes. Why she had ever thought tricking him was a good plan she couldn't seem to remember now. Something about proving herself, proving that she was not a bad person, a whore, a woman of the night. But tricking him had been the wrong way to go about doing that—and yet she wondered if there had been another way. She doubted it. Just walking up to him and telling him she was virtuous and worthy of respect certainly would not have worked. One had to prove oneself, only one had to find a way to do so in an honest manner. She had been angry with Orson, too, and determined to escape his plan for that evening.

Oh, what did it all matter now? She thought frantically, grasping her skirt. While Dr. Murphy had known her as Julia Goddard, he had gazed upon her with respect and admiration, with affection; now that he knew her as Josephine Gavin, all those emotions had been replaced by others—anger and hurt and disbelief. He was walking toward the door, a man whose touch she had enjoyed, in truth, and wanted to feel again.

There had to be a way to explain. She didn't want him leaving like this.

She bolted from the piano, pushing and pawing her way through the crowd, not bothering to excuse herself, only knowing that she had to reach him. She had to explain why she had lied to him, why she had gone along with Maggie's lies—and she had to apologize for encouraging Maggie. Maggie was a child and she was an adult, and she should never have gone along with the scheme. She would offer no excuse; she would simply apologize. That was all she could do. She hoped he would accept. If not . . . well, that was how she would leave the matter.

The crowd began closing in around her, the men Orson had sent along to protect her apparently lost in the mass of bodies. Women in wide skirts, men with canes and smelly cigars and grasping hands. Arms shooting her way, touching her . . . her arms, her hands, her breasts, her neck. The odor of perspiration mingled with the sickly sweet smell of perfume.

Josie jerked this way and that, trying to avoid being touched at all, trying to concentrate on getting to the door. It was madness, and the noise—shouts, laughter, loud voices—it was all clamor in her ears. Ridiculous, awful clamor.

A hand latched onto her skirt near her knees. Josie jerked the material away, hearing it rip. She pushed her way through the bodies, shoving, hoping she was headed toward the door. She couldn't tell, she was surrounded by so many people.

Finally, the door. And miraculously, it was already open.

More people outside. She glanced around frantically, searching . . . not seeing Dr. Murphy. Carriages and cabs lined both sides of the street. The smell of horse dung drifted her way. The crowd was closing in behind her and around her again. Josie heard another rip, felt a fierce pull, and then her knees began giving way.

A sound of fear tore loose from her throat. She was going down and she would be trampled, and then there would be no way to apologize because she would be dead. She would go into eternity with the trickery, the deceit, on her conscience, and she would leave Dr. Thomas Murphy here on earth with his hurt and disbelief. He would never understand her, what had motivated her.

More hands, grasping, pulling, tearing, ripping. Her head

hit the ground hard, and the world began spinning crazily.

Bodies loomed over her, the faces distorted and hideous as Josie lost her tenacious grip on consciousness. She closed her eyes, weary, so weary, having no choice, no control, and the last thing she felt and heard were strong arms enveloping her, drawing her close, and a deep voice whispering in her ear: "You'll be fine, lass. You'll be fine."

Holding Josephine against his chest, Thomas grabbed a man's sturdy walking stick, raised it, then brought it down hard on the shoulders of some scoundrel who still had hold of what was left of the actress's skirt. The man grunted and let go, then Thomas beat off several more, cursing as he did. No one deserved to be mauled this way, and he feared Josephine Gavin was injured. In fact, he knew she was; seconds before he'd finally grabbed her himself, he'd seen her head hit the ground, and his trained eye had spotted cuts and blood on her chest and arms.

The crowd began backing off some, apparently realizing he meant business—that someone would have to kill him before anyone could put their hands on her again. He was still brandishing the walking stick with one hand like a sword, glaring, his gaze scanning the men who headed the crowd, and he meant to use the stick more if anyone stepped forward.

He shouted at a nearby cabdriver, "Open the door!" When the man stood, wide-eyed and frozen, he shouted again, louder this time, bellowing, *"Open the damn door!"*

The driver sprang into action, grabbing the handle and flinging the door open.

"We're goin' to that cab," Thomas told the men who headed the crowd. Several were rubbing their jaws, watching him from the corners of their eyes, contemplating their next move. "You'd best know that I'll kill the next son of a bitch who touches her," he warned.

He must have looked as if he meant it. At least four of the men stepped back. Several turned and started off, giving up the chase. But three others decided to take their chances; one headed toward Thomas's left, another to his right, and the last began closing in from the front. His jaw set, Thomas held the limp, unconscious actress against his chest, prepared to defend her with his life.

Another man broke through the crowd. At first Thomas thought he was another attacker, then his eyes focused, and he realized it was Alan and that his friend had produced a pistol. He stood at Thomas's side, his arm held close to his ribs as he coolly aimed the weapon at one man, then another and another. "Boys," he drawled, "I suggest that you go home—now. Thomas, go for the cab."

Confident in Alan's ability with the pistol—he and Alan had engaged in shooting competitions in the past—Thomas scooped Josephine Gavin's limp form into his arms and hurried toward the cab. "Get up on the seat," he ordered the driver as he ducked his head and stepped up into the conveyance. He gave the man his address. "When my friend gets in, make those horses move."

The driver scrambled toward the front of the cab. Alan was backing toward him, slowly, calmly, having more of a head about him than Thomas thought he'd have if those three men were still closing in on him. The ruffian in front of Alan took two big steps forward and was promptly greeted by the cold steel of the pistol's barrel on his forehead. Alan had anticipated the move, raised and straightened his arm, and now stood staring into the man's eyes. He muttered something at the scoundrel, and a second later the other two men began backing off. Finally Alan simply lowered the pistol, turned, and approached the cab.

He stepped inside, pulled the door shut, latched it, and an instant later, before he was even settled completely on the seat, the conveyance jolted into motion, creaking and groaning.

Thomas took a few minutes to close his eyes and breathe deeply, trying to calm himself inside. Then he glanced at Alan. "I'm thinkin' you just saved my life."

Alan half grinned. "You were putting me to shame, acting so heroic."

Thomas shook his head in disbelief. He'd never seen people act like that!

He glanced down at Josephine Gavin. Her head hung back

over his arm. She had scratches on her neck and upper chest, and red welts and small cuts all up and down her arms where people had grabbed her. But she was breathing. The bodice of her gown was ripped in a number of places, almost revealing an entire breast. The front of her skirt had been torn at the waist and shredded down the front. Her petticoats were tattered, revealing a chemise that was smudged in places with dirt.

He glanced at her face again, at the blood trickling down from her right temple. He lifted a hand and smoothed back her hair, wanting, needing, to have a look at the injury. He was suddenly aware of the silkiness of her loose hair flowing over his arm, and of how nicely she fit against him. Her dark lashes were smooth feathers resting on her upper cheeks. Her mouth was open, her breath constant and even, thank the good lord. The blood trickled from a laceration half an inch from her hairline near the temple. Easily stitched. But it didn't account for her unconscious state; it seemed too minor.

He felt dampness on his arm where her head rested and he recalled watching her head whip back and hit the pavement hard. Lord . . . Sweet Mary . . . he silently prayed.

He spread the hair near the back of her head and gently probed the area with his fingertips, feeling another laceration, this one worse than the one at the temple. If there was bleeding inside the skull . . . He probed a little more, then cursed.

He dropped his head back against the seat, shut his eyes, and swore under his breath. "Her skull . . . there may be a fracture." Feeling Alan's penetrating gaze on him, he opened his eyes, trying to collect his composure, and did his best to cover Miss Gavin's breast with what was left of the gown's bodice.

"They would've mauled her to death," Thomas said softly, his voice trembling. "What was she doin'? She was singin'. She was in the middle of that song. Then there she was, outside with the crowd all around her. What the devil was she doin'?"

"Going after you, my friend," Alan answered, just as softly.

Thomas glanced up at him, feeling more than a little stunned.

Alan shrugged. "I watched her. She became frantic. Her eyes were wild. She watched you all the way out the door, then she tore off through the crowd after you. I thought you'd never met her."

"I—" This would be so complicated to explain, and Thomas really didn't feel like telling Alan right now that he had met her, that she'd been someone else when he had. That he had never really met Josephine Gavin. "Now this. She hit the street hard," Thomas said instead, inhaling a ragged breath. "If there's a fracture . . ."

"I'm here and I'll take care of her," Alan responded. "That would probably be the best course for everyone involved, with the understanding that I'll do everything in my power to help her."

Thomas nodded, understanding Alan's meaning—that he was a little too personally involved to be her physician, that if he couldn't heal her, then just like with Abby, he would blame himself. He'd be forever asking why, *why*. He was indisputedly one of the best doctors in St. Louis, and yet Abby had died in his arms. He understood, too, that if there was a fracture, and he felt certain that there was, even Alan might not have the knowledge or the power to save her.

He glanced down at her face again. So beautiful. His gaze fell on her parted lips, and he heard her voice in his head as he'd first heard it when he had walked into the house the night Maggie had run off: *Come back, Belinda, oh, come back to me. Your lips are like roses, your eyes like the sea. . . . Our love is greater, than any can be. Oh come back, Belinda, and mar–ry me.*

Torment. It was utter torment, hearing her voice caress the words. Images of her smiling at Maggie, then at him, then embracing Maggie, floated through his head. Her brown eyes twinkled at him, looking playful one moment and devilish the next.

He wanted the woman. He'd been snared in her spell.

But she wasn't the same. . . . This woman he held was not really the same woman he had encountered in his sitting room that night. Just as she apparently charmed many of her audiences, the actress had charmed him. For his and Maggie's sake, he had to keep in mind that she'd been acting that night. She had considered the performance over when he had gone off to put Maggie to bed. She'd probably known that afterward, when he came back downstairs, he would have more questions for her. He wasn't difficult to read, even he knew that, and she must have sensed that he had more questions. She'd known he was interested in her, very interested.

He had to wonder if she enjoyed toying with men's emotions and groins the way she did. Perhaps, if she survived this evening's attack, she'd be a changed woman.

And yet, perhaps he was being a fool to hope.

He was. He fastened his gaze on one of the carriage doors, and there it remained until the cab stopped in front of his home.

Josie regained consciousness briefly and tenaciously. She fought her way upward from what seemed like a black hole, grasping and working her way toward a dim light. She had to find him. She had to . . . She had to explain . . . her feelings . . . why she valued the respect and admiration she'd seen in his eyes that night in his sitting room. She needed to apologize for tricking him, for using a false name and for not being honest. If she died before she had a chance to tell him those things, she would not deserve to go to heaven. Shame and embarrassment would consume her.

The light became brighter; numerous lights, flickering. Shapes and shadows moved around her, leaned over her. Fingertips touched one side of her head, then the back. Sharp pain tore through her skull, then died down to a throb. Agony. Such agony! She heard sounds, whimpers of pain, and realized she was making them, that they rose from her throat.

Hands lifted her head. Something—cloths, perhaps—was slipped under her. She was in a bed, she thought. It was soft, though the pulsing in her head and her extreme drowsiness made concentrating on anything difficult. She heard voices, one more than any other, and hearing them hurt. "I need instruments, Thomas, and I need them now. Good God, get yourself together enough to think! You know what needs done, or she'll die. We may still lose her, but there's the chance that we won't if we work at it. Are you hearing me? Wake up, for the love of God! *Instruments, Dr. Murphy. Now!*"

She tried to mouth his name, and she thought she did a little, though weakly. The shapes fell still for a moment, then the loud male voice said again, only with less force this time, "The instruments, Thomas. If you care and you want me to try to save her, go get them."

Tremendous pressure inside her head. The lights were fading again, growing orange, then reddish-orange, then red; burning down. Finally they went out altogether, like a dying sunset.

Thomas didn't know how he managed to stay on his feet during the next few hours. He functioned in a daze, finally snapping to his senses, pulling himself from the grip of panic and rushing downstairs to his study where he always kept extra surgical instruments. Alan was right. He knew what had to be done if there was to be any hope of saving her life. They had to cut down to the bone, find the fracture, secure her head, remove an adequate amount of scalp and pericranium tissue, then ease the pressure on her brain.

On his flight downstairs, he silently went over the procedure again and again, knowing he could assist and that was all, but also knowing he had to clear his mind of all emotion and be what he had been trained to be and what he was—a physician. Alan needed an assistant, and by God, he would have a worthy one.

He fetched a medical bag and a tray of surgical tools, taking care to make certain the trephine and retractors were there. Then he tore off back upstairs, brushing by Mrs. O'Brien and the housekeeper, Mrs. Reardon, in the upper hall. Both women looked half-asleep, their nightcaps a little askew, their eyes glazed.

"Mrs. Reardon," Thomas said breathlessly, "Dr. Schuster is here. We've brought a patient with us—the house was closer than the office. We'll be needin' clean sheets an' cloths. We'll need more water. Bring them to the guest room at the end of the hall." He said it all without even looking over his shoulder, and he hoped the woman would snap from her sleep-dazed state and gather the things he and Alan needed. He'd never felt in such a rush, in such a panic.

He started to hurry into the room, but Alan met him at the door. Thomas stopped short, certain Alan was about to tell him that she was dead, that there was no need to rush anymore. It was all over even before they had begun to try to save her. Massive bleeding inside the skull.

Alan put a hand on his forearm, and Thomas felt a shiver of anger at fate. Why the hell—? "Before we begin, forget who she is," Alan advised, his voice low. "Whatever she means to you, distance your mind. If you think you can't, then summon another physician to assist. Lecturing at the college, I'm certain you know a few in the city."

Thomas set his jaw. "Is that what you're wantin'? For me to summon someone else?"

"There's really not time, you know that. The sooner the procedure is done, the better her chance of recovery. I need you, Thomas, but if you think you cannot do this with a clear mind . . ."

Thomas inhaled deeply. He couldn't forget who she was. He couldn't. But what he could do was try to forget for a time that he had begun to care about her the night he first laid eyes on her. He'd crumbled emotionally when Abby had taken ill. He would not crumble again.

"Together we'll get it done," he responded, looking Alan straight in the eye, and he meant it.

Alan nodded, then withdrew into the room, stepping aside to allow Thomas to enter.

* * *

Some time later—Thomas wasn't sure if an hour or two hours or more had passed—the procedure was finished. Alan worked at packing the hole with dry lint and preparing a dressing while Thomas washed the instruments in a basin of pink-tinged water. There were two more basins of clean water on a dresser nearby. His hands trembled, and he nicked a fingertip with the scalpel Alan had used. Thomas dipped the injured finger in the water to clean the wound, then he lifted it and put a little pressure on it with his thumb. Seconds later, when he was certain the bleeding had stopped, he continued cleaning the retractors, trephine, and scalpel.

"There was very little blood," Alan said from the bedside. "There still is."

Thomas let the instruments rest in the water. He braced his hands on either side of the washstand and leaned over it as if resting for a moment. Really, he was breathing a sigh of relief. *Very little blood* . . . "A good sign, Dr. Schuster," he said softly. "A very good sign." A little pressure, but not much.

"Mrs. Reardon and Mrs. O'Brien—do you think they went back to bed?" Alan asked.

"I've no idea." Thomas remembered Mrs. O'Brien's shocked expression when she had carried one of the basins into the room and glanced over at the patient lying on the bed. "Miss Goddard!" she'd said, and her hands had flown to her mouth. Thomas had ushered her out of the room, telling her that if all the commotion woke Maggie, he didn't want her told who the patient was, only that her father had had to bring a sick person to the house because it had been closer than his office, and that she should try to go back to sleep.

"I told them both that they should go back to bed, but I doubt that Mrs. O'Brien did," he responded.

"Perhaps you could fetch her to help me cut the remains of these garments away," Alan said, waving a hand to indicate Josephine Gavin's tattered gown. "She should not be moved much at all, but we can at least do away with these and bathe her cuts. I need to take a look at them and see if any need stitches."

Thomas nodded. He had assisted with the procedure, but

he couldn't be in the room when they removed her clothing. Just glancing at her face now, so peaceful yet pale and beautiful, tugged at his heart. He would not be able to separate the doctor and the man if he watched her clothing being peeled away.

There was something else—he despised being attracted to a woman who had intentionally deceived him. He meant to keep his distance, emotionally and physically, for as long as she had to remain here in his home. As a physician, he'd do everything in his power to help heal her; as a man, he'd tolerate her presence until Alan said she could be moved. Then he'd help move her.

He wiped his hands on a cloth, leaving the instruments in the water for now. ''I'll fetch one of the women,'' he said, heading for the door.

Mrs. O'Brien sat in a chair just outside the room, obviously dozing—her head hung limply to one side. She liked the woman in the room, but Thomas wondered if she still would when she was informed that the woman wasn't Julia Goddard, but Josephine Gavin, the actress. Maggie already knew, of course, and when she was told that Miss Gavin was the patient in the room, they'd have to bar the door to keep her out. Perhaps he'd keep the information from Maggie.

Placing a hand on her shoulder, Thomas gently shook Mrs. O'Brien awake, telling her that Dr. Schuster was kindly requesting her assistance now.

She rubbed her eyes, saying that was fine—that they both must be exhausted, him in particular. She knew he'd had a long day, first at the college, then at the office, and that he should consider getting some sleep himself. Finally she hurried off to help Dr. Schuster, and Thomas went downstairs to settle in his study, where someone had lit the lamps.

The mantel clock in the study revealed that it was just after two in the morning. Uncharacteristically, Thomas went for the decanter of brandy that sat on the small sideboard near one of the windows facing the formal garden. He tossed back one glassful, then another, hardly thinking, not really wanting to think. Finally he took the decanter and his tumbler, settled in a nearby wing chair, and placed the container on the table next to him.

Damn fate. Damn circumstances. He hadn't gone to a gaming house in months and months, and the one evening he had chosen to, he'd made the most startling discovery of his life—and he'd been on hand to pull Josephine Gavin away from that mauling crowd. Why him? Cruel, that's how he regarded the entire sequence of events—discovering that Julia Goddard was really Josephine Gavin, rescuing her, then assisting with a procedure that might very well save her life, though he wouldn't have thought of refusing to assist.

He was a mess of conflicting emotions, wanting her but also wanting to wring her neck. She'd made him believe for a little while that the woman of his dreams existed, that she was real and that she had walked into his life. That she'd been sent. That God was real and merciful and good. He'd long ago stopped believing that there was a woman made specifically for him and that she was out there waiting for him to find her. He hadn't had the patience for that nonsense. A man married and then learned to love. And then *she* had walked into his life and changed his thinking. All in one evening. Within the space of a few hours, he'd started to believe that there was a woman meant specifically for him. Fool that he was, in such a short span of time he'd begun to entertain the notion that he might easily fall in love with the charming creature he'd watched interact with his daughter in the sitting room that evening.

But now, he thought, refilling the tumbler and draining it again, he doubted. How could he fall in love with someone who was so full of deceit and who would even stoop so low as to involve a child in her schemes?

Again he refilled the tumbler. But this time he rose, lifting the glass as if in toast, feeling the alcohol warm his blood. He prayed that it would numb him. Now that the procedure was done and he'd lived up to the professional oath he'd taken—he'd certainly done everything within his power to help save her—he wanted to forget for a time what he'd discovered last evening, that the incredible creature he'd met that night in his sitting room didn't exist.

"To Josephine Gavin," he said, his voice a little slurred. "A fine actress. A fine actress indeed! May you recover an' live with yer lies." He lowered the glass to his lips, then laughed bitterly. "If you've a conscience, lass. I rather doubt that."

He drained the glass again, then sank into the chair and rested his head against one of the wings.

Moments later, he fell asleep.

Six

THE LIGHT WAS back. So dim at first, but it was there, in the distance, and Josie imagined her arms stretching toward it, her hands reaching, trying to grab it before it slipped away again. She feared she was dying and she didn't want to die. She wasn't prepared to die. Life had ceased having much meaning of late, but now she had purpose: She very much needed to apologize to Dr. Thomas Murphy for the way she had lied to him, for the way she had deceived him.

She also knew the troupe needed her, that Orson and Mr. Jefferson's financial state was critical and that she was their featured actress, that the crowds flocked to see her. They would have to devise another plan, of course—she couldn't perform in another gaming house. The crowds in gaming houses were rougher than in theaters. She had performed in gaming houses before, and the drinking, carousing crowds had always frightened her a little, and she didn't intend to perform for them ever again.

She wanted to live.

The light became brighter and brighter, harsh yet surrounded by a soft haze, a beacon that warmed and comforted her.

"Dr. Schuster, she's stirring, sir!" someone, a woman, said excitedly. Then a figure appeared to her left, bending over her, tucking a sheet more securely beneath her shoulder. The pain was back, but not nearly as severe this time. She had a head-ache, but it had died down to a low throb.

Another figure appeared, and this one touched her forehead. The hand was cold, and she reacted, jerking her head, wishing she hadn't when a sharp bolt of pain assaulted her. She groaned.

"You'll be fine," the man's voice said. "But you cannot move so fast, Miss Gavin."

"Dr. Murphy," she whispered. She tried to lick her dry lips and found that she couldn't produce enough saliva to moisten them. "Dr. Murphy."

"I'm Dr. Schuster. You're in Dr. Murphy's home. You fractured your skull. We feared hemorrhage so we did surgery. You must be quiet and still. If you do well, we will have you up out of this bed in a few days."

"Dr. Murphy," she repeated. So she still might die. She still could, that was what he was saying in a roundabout way. "I want . . . I want to see him."

A pause ensued. "Miss Gavin . . ."

"She's not Miss Gavin," the woman said. Was it Mrs. O'Brien? Was that her voice? Josie thought she recognized the woman's rather deep tone. "She's Miss Goddard."

"G–gavin," Josie struggled.

The man straightened and turned toward Mrs. O'Brien, telling her that he'd like to speak to the patient alone. Josie heard the rustle of skirts, then, seconds later, a door shut quietly.

"Now then," the man began, bending over her again. He paused a second time, as if weighing what he was about to say. Josie's eyes had focused finally. Soft morning sunlight shone through the room's one window. She lay in a large tester bed which was draped with bright-yellow hangings. The man had the prettiest brown eyes. In fact, everything seemed so bright—the hangings, his eyes, the sunlight . . . she wondered how long she had been cast in darkness.

"I realize that something passed between you and Dr. Mur-phy," he said hesitantly. "I also realize that you did not choose me as your physician. But there Thomas and I were while you were being attacked. You were badly injured, so we brought you here and performed the surgery we felt was necessary. Thomas—Dr. Murphy—managed to forget his personal feelings for a time and assist. But now he's gone off to be alone. I think he needs to be alone, and you are in no condition to be upsetting yourself. I'll fetch a drink of water, and by this evening, perhaps you could tolerate some food. I will not fetch Dr. Murphy.''

She breathed slowly, trying to stay calm and ignore the pounding in her head. "A message, then?" she whispered.

More hesitancy. Finally he bent close. "What is it?"

She tried licking her lips again. "Tell him . . . tell him I'm sorry. Please. Tell him I tricked him and I apologize. It was wrong of me.''

Something flickered in his gaze. A change of heart, perhaps? He stared down into her eyes, reading her plea, then he gave a quick nod, agreeing to deliver the message.

''Water,'' she requested.

Nodding again, he moved away briefly, then returned with a small glass. He helped her lift her head and he held it steady when she winced with pain. He brought the cup to her lips and tipped it when she was ready to sip. He was patient while she drank the entire cup of water, but when she requested more, he told her to lie back and rest for a moment first. He looked haggard—his hair was in disarray, he was pale, and though his eyes were bright, shadows were visible beneath them. He has not slept in quite some time, Josie thought drowsily. He has hovered near my bed, waiting for me to regain consciousness. He's been busy saving my life.

"I will tell you something about my friend Thomas Murphy," he said slowly and softly after refilling the cup and returning to her side. "Words mean little to him. A person's actions mean more, you see. I cannot pretend to know what's transpired between the two of you, and it's not even my place to guess. You're not asking for my advice, but if you were, I would tell you to show him that you're sorry rather than tell him. Thomas respects honesty and facts. If you've done something to offend him, then regaining his respect and his affection will take time. It will not happen with a simple apology, whether it comes from my lips or yours.''

He offered her another drink of water and helped her lift

her head again. When she carefully lowered it back onto the pillow, she thanked him sincerely for taking the time to provide her with some insight into Dr. Thomas Murphy. Smiling, he raked a hand through his tousled hair, then ran it down over his tired eyes.

"Miss Gavin, I am pleased to make your acquaintance."

As poorly as she felt, Josie managed a smile, too. "Dr. Schuster, believe me, I'm pleased that you became acquainted with me."

He grinned, then tipped his head and laughed. "Now then," he said finally. "Time for you to rest more. I'm off to deliver your message."

Her hand found his, and she gave it a squeeze and thanked him again. He dipped his head in acknowledgment, then moved from the edge of the bed.

Josie closed her eyes, finding that sleep came very easily.

Thomas woke slowly, and as he did, his mind drifted, from the shack and the fields outside of St. Louis in which he'd spent much of his boyhood, to the dissecting rooms at the medical college, to a report by Dr. Ignaz Semmelweis that he'd recently reread for at least the hundredth time. He failed to understand why physicians and medical staff most everywhere were still so skeptical over Semmelweis's findings that women were less inclined to die following childbirth if physicians were as careful about cleanliness as midwives were. The findings were direct and had been taken from experience and observation. In short, Thomas felt that Semmelweis knew what he was talking about. He certainly had the facts to back his findings—a decline in mortality from childbed fever from 9.9 percent to less than 3 within a year after Semmelweis had ordered medical students to wash their hands with a solution of lime chloride before entering the childbirth ward from the autopsy rooms. The following year, the mortality rate had dropped even more—to 1.27 percent. The drop was significant, yet the medical world, filled with more than its share of pompous, stuffy creatures, men who thought they had all the answers and that there was nothing more to learn, scoffed at Semmelweis.

"Ridiculous fools," Thomas muttered, rubbing the sleep from one eye. He often went to sleep pondering such matters and awoke still pondering them. He sometimes wondered if his brain ever truly rested.

He glanced at the glass and the nearly empty decanter resting on the table near his chair. His mouth felt as if it were full of cotton, and his head ached. He never drank to excess. Why he'd thought doing so last night—or early this morning—would make him feel better, he couldn't remember now. In fact, he didn't think he'd considered the matter. He'd simply grabbed the decanter and a glass and had started drinking. Alcohol had a remarkable effect on the brain and the body, going directly to the central nervous system somehow. Like opium . . . laudanum, and the body got to where it needed the liquid to function correctly. Thomas had seen far too many people who couldn't live without drink or laudanum after a time. Amazing. The very things that could soothe could also end up making life meaningless or killing a person.

A quick knock sounded on the study door, then the door opened, and in walked Alan, carrying a service tray.

"What the devil are you doin'?" Thomas grumbled. "I've a houseful of servants to do such things."

"Ah, exactly as I remember in the mornings, Dr. Murphy," Alan said, placing the tray on the table. "A royal grump. Abby was a dutiful wife, suffering through your moodiness and your morning grouchiness. But do you think any other woman will? Not many are as devoted as Abby was."

Thomas rubbed his rough jaw, wondering what all this talk of Abby was about. Why mention her? Why mention any woman at all? He rubbed the other side of his jaw. He must look a fright. "Abby's dead. I'd rather not—"

"Yes, she is, and perhaps you should stop trying so hard to replace her." Alan looked straight at him, his brows slightly lifted. "I've spent a little time with some of the staff, and I've learned what you've been up to. Constance Blanche, Thomas? She's not your type. Stuffy and gangly and full of herself—I met her at a supper party last year. Of course, her father heads the St. Louis Medical College, so—''

''Ye're stickin' yer nose in a bit far, aren't you?'' Thomas reared back a bit. What was this? What the devil was Alan up to? And him, having just awakened. Alan was right, of course—he was a grump in the mornings. What Alan was confronting him with would be difficult to deal with at any time, but even more so at this hour. Whatever the hour was. It was still morning, he knew that much; soft light spilled in through the eastern window. ''You'll pardon my rudeness, Dr. Schuster, but my courtship of Miss Blanche is *my* concern, no one else's.''

''I brought coffee, Dr. Murphy. Would you care for some?'' Alan lifted a silver pitcher and began pouring coffee into one of the two china cups on the tray. The rich odor of the brew drifted Thomas's way and roused his stomach. ''Ah. I hear that you are indeed interested, my friend,'' Alan said, and lifted the cup and saucer, handing them to him.

Thomas muttered a thank-you, feeling rather surprised by all of this. He sipped coffee while Alan began pouring himself a cupful. Thomas watched him, wondering what mischief he was up to. Something, that was for certain. He damn sure had a purpose, bursting in here with coffee, mentioning Abby, then Constance.

''I've a message from Miss Gavin for you.''

And now Josephine Gavin.

''She's conscious?'' Thomas asked. He didn't care. Well, he did. He wanted her recovered enough to leave his home, to walk out without looking back. Still, he felt a surge of relief that she'd regained consciousness. That was a good sign, a positive sign. She'd live.

Alan turned a lifted brow on him. ''You care?''

Thomas shrugged. ''As any physician would. The surgery was a success, doctor.''

''At the moment. You know as well as I do that she's not out of danger and will not be for days.''

Again Thomas shrugged. ''Ye're her doctor. I was the assistant durin' the surgery, an' now that it's over, I've resigned myself from her care. I'll have nothin' more to do with her.''

Alan studied him for a long moment, then took his cup and saucer and went to stand near the window to look out upon the garden. It would come to life soon, the garden. As March gave way to April, it would blossom with color and foliage. Abby had never much cared for it, but when the many flowers made their appearance and the warmth of spring gave birth to new leaves, Thomas enjoyed walking the paths and even gazing upon the garden from the very window before which Alan stood.

Thomas studied Alan's profile, wondering what he was thinking, wondering what questions were swirling in his head. Alan knew something had happened between his friend and the woman upstairs, but unless Alan had cornered Mrs. O'Brien and questioned her, he couldn't know exactly what. Surely Alan respected his privacy enough that he hadn't done that.

"The message," Alan said, the sunlight bringing out the gold in his hair. "Miss Gavin offers you an apology. She's sorry she tricked you—and I believe her." He turned as he said the last, and fastened his gaze on Thomas.

Thomas rubbed his jaw more, then slid his hand down and around to the back of his neck and rubbed it. So she thought that would mend things? A simple apology? For some reason, she'd meant to make a fool of him and she had. Her trickery had been premeditated and calculated and deliberate, and he did not have it in him to accept a simple apology from her.

"I had a little visit with Mrs. O'Brien, then with Maggie, before I fetched the service tray from the kitchen staff," Alan ventured. "Know before you blow steam out of your ears, Thomas Murphy, that I did not set out to meddle. Well, I did, but only because I know how difficult the past year has been for you and Maggie. Because I care. I knew as soon as I saw you approach Josephine Gavin in that gaming house that something was wrong, that something was troubling you about her. That perhaps you had met her before. I'm your friend and I'm proud to say that I'm your friend, and if there's something I might do to help—"

"Nothin'," Thomas responded, wishing Alan would drop the entire matter. "I would've had trouble performin' the surgery. You knew that so you did it, an' I'm grateful. The woman tricked me, an' I consider the trickery unforgivable, but I've no desire to see her dead. I only wish she were in someone else's home recoverin'. I don't want her here.''

"You brought her here."

"What choice did I have? She was bein' attacked."

"I saw the way you looked at her in the carriage."

"Concern for her health."

"I saw the way you held her, the way you cradled her."

Thomas lifted his chin and tightened his jaw. "She's not for me an' Maggie."

"You've become righteous." Alan drained his cup. "God, but I'm tired." He turned back to the window while Thomas's temper stewed. What was so righteous about wanting what was best for himself and Maggie?

"Maggie fashioned the entire scheme," Alan said. "She admits to it."

Thomas scoffed. "Maggie would protect Josephine Gavin. The girl admires her. She wants to be like her."

"Yes, Maggie told me about her friends at the levee, that they all like to play at acting. She told me she asked you to take her to see Miss Gavin and that you refused. Of course, you told me that yourself."

Thomas's ears perked up. "Are you now sayin' that I shouldn't have?"

"Not at all. A parent has to direct a child on what he or she thinks is the right path. But you—and Constance, too, apparently—told Maggie that Miss Gavin was a 'bad' woman."

"No one used that word."

Alan glanced over his shoulder. "A child's perspective, then. Children see and realize more than we do most of the time. As adults, our minds are often too cluttered, so cluttered we cannot see simple things. Josephine Gavin is an actress. Does that make her a 'bad' woman?"

"She was singin' in a gamin' house, for the love of God!" Thomas objected. "You saw her gown."

Now Alan shrugged. "No less—or *more*—than a proper woman would wear to a ball." He gave a little laugh. "I don't know why I'm bothering. You're caught up in appearances, Thomas, because you're caught up in rising above what you were. In medical college, I knew that, but I don't think I realized how important rising above it was to you until you met Abby and married her despite the fact that you didn't love her. God forbid that Thomas Murphy should tarnish the reputation he's built for himself by having anything to do with Josephine Gavin, an actress." He strode back to the tray to pour himself another cup of coffee.

"Are you finished?" Thomas had to ask. His tone was sharp and clipped. He felt insulted and outraged that any man, even Alan, especially Alan, would saunter into his home and attack him verbally. "If you—"

"No," Alan answered, "I'm not. You are my friend, Thomas, but I don't like what I'm seeing and I will not help you hide. As the hours passed and this . . . mystery unraveled more and more, particularly after I spoke to Maggie and Mrs. O'Brien, I believe you have some things to sort through in your mind, some things to face and examine. Now that the surgery has been performed, perhaps the best treatment for both you and Miss Gavin would be to place her in your capable care. I know you'll take good care of her."

Thomas straightened in the chair, his back going rigid. "Alan, she's here because we had to bring her here. I'll have nothin' to do with her beyond toleratin' her presence in my home. I—"

"Then have nothing to do with her beyond tolerating her presence, my friend. Be her physician and nothing more."

"Alan, I'll find another doctor for her," Thomas warned. "I'll contact her manager an'—"

"Or you could gather your courage, Thomas, and go see her. You don't fool me. What I'm seeing is more than anger over being deceived. For the first time, you may be encountering something more. Deeper feelings. Perhaps love. The woman touched you somehow."

Thomas glared at him. "What do you know about love, Alan?"

Alan drained his cup again, then brought it down hard on his saucer. He placed the cup and saucer back on the tray and shoved his hands into his trouser pockets. "I know much more than you know, Thomas. I had it and I let it slip away. Damn if I'll help you make the same mistake."

"I spent part of an evening with her—that was all. She was singin' to Maggie. She gave her a kitten. She was good with the girl. She was beautiful. But she was someone else, Alan. She was actin'."

Alan stood firm. "Miss Gavin is now your patient, Dr. Murphy. I know no other physicians in the city of St. Louis, therefore I know no one I would trust with her care."

He started off toward the door, and Thomas tried one last thing, feeling desperate. "I wouldn't think of involvin' myself with a patient! It goes against every professional standard, against the oath itself. Leave her in my care an' you'll damn the relationship for sure. If there's any possibility of one developin'. Which there isn't."

Alan hesitated. A few seconds later, he chuckled. "True. But then again, perhaps you'll realize that oath or no oath, you're mortal. You have not ascended to any throne that I can see, Thomas. Do you think no one else can rise above his or her beginnings? In caring for her day after day, you'll come to know Josephine Gavin. If she's the 'bad' woman you've condemned her to be, then once she recovers, she can go her way and you can go yours."

"I'll have her recovered so quickly there won't be time for more," Thomas grumbled, not believing this. Alan was walking out. Walking out and leaving the woman in his care! What kind of friend did such a thing?

"I'll call again soon," Alan promised. "For now, I'm off to find a hotel room and sleep."

"I offered accommodations," Thomas shot at his back.

Alan grinned over his shoulder. "Me staying here would change everything, wouldn't it? I would be too easily accessible."

"Alan."

"Good day, Dr. Murphy. I shall see you soon."

With that, Alan slipped through the doorway.

Thomas listened to the fading clomp of his boots in the hall. Then the sound was gone altogether, and Thomas sat back in his chair, suddenly wanting to fling the cup and saucer he held across the room. He was behaving like a child, and he despised feeling so short-tempered and at a loss as to what to do. He felt indignant—how dare Alan resign himself from Josephine Gavin's care?—and he despised that feeling, too.

He should enlist the services of another doctor; in fact, he thought he would consider doing exactly that as soon as he could think of someone and get a missive off. He not only didn't want Josephine Gavin in his home, but he also didn't want to be the one responsible for her care and treatment. He didn't want to have to be near her. He didn't want to have to touch her.

He wanted as little contact with her as possible.

Maggie lay in her bed upstairs, still sniffling after her confession to Dr. Schuster, holding the kitten Josephine had given her close to her breast. She wanted to tear out of her room and down the hall and peek in on Miss Gavin. Oh, she couldn't be so sick. She just couldn't be!

Papa's friend, Dr. Schuster, had come to her first thing this morning, before her eyes had even opened all the way, and questioned her about the Miss Goddard that Mrs. O'Brien had told him had brought her home the evening she had run off. Who was Miss Goddard, really? Dr. Schuster had wanted to know, though Maggie saw in his eyes that he thought he already knew, that he was highly suspicious.

She wondered why he needed to know. Was something the matter? Had Papa discovered her plot and sent Dr. Schuster to question her and see if she would tell the truth? But where was Papa right now, and why would he do such a thing? Where was Mrs. O'Brien—she usually woke her by opening the curtains and letting the sun spill into the room. She usually helped her dress, then hurried her off downstairs for a bite to eat, then off to the little building out back of the house where Maggie spent many an hour with the servants' children and with the tutor Papa had employed.

Dr. Schuster had had a serious look in his eye, and he surely hadn't greeted her the way he usually did whenever he visited—with an embrace and a twirl and some playful tussling about. His tone was serious, too, as if something were wrong . . . as if he knew part of the truth and he expected to hear the rest of it from her.

"Miss Goddard?" she'd said, swallowing and sitting up in the bed. She'd rubbed her eyes, hoping she looked as if she were still half-asleep and that he might at least walk away from the bed so she would have some time to decide exactly what and how much she should tell him.

She hadn't told Papa the truth about Miss Goddard. Tricking him had been great fun, but the next day when she'd done some thinking about whether she should tell him who Miss Goddard really was and when she'd considered that she might really be punished this time—Papa would be furious—she had elected not to. Josephine Gavin was not a bad woman, she knew that in her heart, and that would have to be enough. She didn't want to have her window boarded or some other awful punishment issued and carried out. She didn't want to not ever be able to leave the house again. Not that Papa had ever threatened that. But Jonathan, one of her friends at the levee, had told her that his mother had locked him away in their shed for nearly a week one time after he'd gone out when she'd told him not to, and he'd only seen daylight during that time when she'd brought him food and water. Maggie realized that she had a better life than her friends at the levee did, and after considering the way she'd tricked Papa, she had wondered that God himself didn't punish her by having Papa turn as mean as Jonathan's mother. Perhaps she deserved some punishment, but she couldn't stand the thought of being locked away.

"That's what I said, Maggie," Dr. Schuster responded. "Miss Goddard. The woman who brought you home that evening. The woman who sang to you. Mrs. O'Brien says you fell in love with her, that she thought everyone who witnessed the events in the sitting room that evening did—including your father."

Blinking, Maggie had glanced up at him. "Papa? Oh, he'd never love an actress. He'd—" She'd slapped both hands over her mouth at that point, realizing that she'd let the truth slip, that she'd just let him know who Julia Goddard really was.

"We didn't mean to trick him, not really!" she cried, making sure her eyes filled with tears. "I knew he wouldn't like me bringing her home. He wouldn't take me and my friends to see her. He said she was a bad woman. I couldn't—"

"You brought her here, Maggie?" he queried, his eyes narrowing. "Mrs. O'Brien said Miss Goddard rescued you from a man who was attacking you and that she brought you home and refused to leave until your father arrived."

Oh, faith! Why, oh, why had he, not Mrs. O'Brien, awakened her? Her mind was so fuzzy in the mornings. Half the time she would put her dress on backwards if Mrs. O'Brien weren't there to help her! He'd come here suspicious and she was half-asleep and the story wasn't coming out as she'd originally told it. She wanted the scheme to stay exactly the size it was and not grow any more. She wanted to leave it alone now because if people discovered the truth, she'd have to face some sort of punishment and she didn't want to. But she surely didn't want to have to lie more to avoid that.

"I meant to say she brought me here," Maggie said, glancing down at the sheet. She tried to summon a brilliant smile for him from beneath her lashes. "Papa didn't tell me you were coming, Dr. Schuster. We'll go to Chouteau's Pond and picnic and—"

He lowered a stern look on her. Maggie scooted back against the headboard, clutching the sheet around her knees, knowing he wouldn't be put off.

"Maggie, you have been up to no good," he accused.

She sucked in her bottom lip. She hated his disapproving look more than she hated receiving a stern look from Papa. Dr. Schuster had held her in his lap the night she had realized that Mama was dying, and she loved him almost as much as she loved Papa. She knew that if anything ever happened to Papa the way something had happened to her mother, Dr. Schuster would take care of her. She wouldn't be alone like Eliza down at the levee. She wouldn't be an orphan scrapping for food and water and a place to sleep. But his look made her feel . . . guilty.

"I want the truth, Maggie," he said. "I want the entire truth and nothing less."

She swallowed hard, wondering how she could avoid punishment now. If she told him the truth, he would go to Papa with it, and then she would be doomed.

"Your father loves you, Maggie—more than anything in the world. But he's a confused man right now. Josephine Gavin is lying in a bed just up the hall. She was injured last night, and your father and I worked half the night performing surgery we hope will help keep her alive."

Maggie's eyes had widened. Her heart had seemed to leap up into her throat. Josephine Gavin, in a bed just up the hall? Injured last night? They'd worked to keep her alive? What had happened? Maggie opened her mouth to ask questions, but no sounds emerged.

"Your father is in a state right now, I think, full of confusion and anger," Dr. Schuster said. "If you're scared of being punished, well, I think you should consider that you and Miss Gavin obviously tricked him and that Miss Gavin may still pay the price with her life. I think your father does love her, Maggie, and she nearly died trying to get to him to tell him the truth. Both of them are having to sort through the mess, and if you had a hand in creating it . . . Don't lie more, Maggie. You'll only make the situation worse for everyone."

Maggie tried to scramble off of the bed then and tear toward the door, but Dr. Schuster caught her around the waist and tugged her back. "You can't see her right now, Maggie. She needs her rest if she's to live. Right now, what you need to do is tell me the truth. Tell me the entire story, from beginning to end. How you came to meet up with Miss Gavin that evening and how she really came to be here at the house with you. Then I think you should give thought to telling your father the truth—and you should realize that he's entitled to his anger. Miss Gavin has already offered him an apology. Perhaps you should consider doing the same."

Maggie had burst into tears and sobs at that point—real tears and sobs this time, not willed in order to manipulate anyone and get her way. She felt so awful about what she'd done, about tricking her father. He was feeling terrible, angry and confused. And Josephine . . . she might be dying. This was surely God punishing her. Oh, it surely was! If Papa really did love Josephine and she died . . . Maggie remembered the pain in his eyes the morning after Mama had died, and she didn't want him to have such pain again. She would pray to God and promise to do anything, *anything*, if he would only spare Josephine—for Papa, not for her. Then, if Josephine survived, she would pray as hard as she could for Papa to find it in his heart to forgive them both.

Between sobs and through tears, the true story of how things had happened had come out. Maggie told it willingly, filling in every little detail even down to how pretty Josephine Gavin's gowns had smelled while she had been hiding in the trunk. The silk and satin had felt so soft, and Maggie had nestled against the gowns while waiting, her ears perking up when she'd heard the dressing room door open. Then voices had followed, and she'd realized that the actress was in the room. She'd been so excited to see and hear Josephine Gavin, and she'd been so angry with her father—she'd only meant to show him that the actress wasn't the awful woman he and Constance both thought she was. Constance had laughed absurdly only the day before after Papa had told her that Maggie wanted to meet the actress. Maggie had thought that cruel, and when Constance had bent before her, taken her by the shoulders, and told her that an actress was hardly the sort of woman a girl of her position should think of associating with, Maggie's anger had deepened. All she'd been able to think of at that point was showing them. Showing them both—Papa and Constance—that they were wrong about Josephine Gavin.

Dr. Schuster had held her until her sobs died down and she seemed to have no more tears to cry. He had made her promise to consider telling her father the truth—he'd not do it for her. This was something she must do alone. He had a little thinking of his own to do, he said, and then he had left her there on the bed.

And now, here she was, still feeling miserable, knowing Josephine lay down the hall, very ill.

Maggie somehow collected herself enough to put the kitten aside, leave the bed, wash her face, and dress herself. Mrs. O'Brien came into the room just as she finished. Maggie expected an incriminating look from her, a judgmental, disapproving look, and she thought she would burst into tears again if she received one. Instead, Mrs. O'Brien gently brushed her hair and fixed it in a smooth braid and told Maggie that breakfast was waiting downstairs. As usual, the tutor, Mr. Ackerman, would be waiting for her and the other children in the little schoolhouse. Just before leaving the bedroom, Maggie turned back to Mrs. O'Brien, who was now fixing the sheet and coverlet on the bed.

"I lied to you, Mrs. O'Brien," she said timidly at first. Then she forced herself to be courageous. She had lied to everyone and people were suffering and she now meant to face what she'd done. So she raised her voice so that Mrs. O'Brien was sure to hear her. "I lied to you about Miss Goddard. She's really the actress, Josephine Gavin. I wanted to trick Papa by pretending she was someone else because he thought she was a bad woman and she's not. I tricked you, too. I lied to you and I'm sorry. I really am sorry. I'm sorry for making the sheet rope and I'm sorry for all the trouble I am sometimes."

Mrs. O'Brien stared at her for a long moment, holding an edge of the sheet in her hand, looking as if she weren't quite sure what to say or do next. She glanced down at the floor, then up. "I believe you, Miss Margaret. Now run along downstairs."

Relief washed through Maggie. She hadn't thought she would care whether or not Mrs. O'Brien ever forgave her for anything, but she did. "Is Papa gone to the college already?"

"It's not his morning to lecture. He's in his study. But I hope you will heed my words this morning and not trouble him, Miss Margaret. He's not in the best of spirits, it seems."

Maggie didn't imagine he was. She knew she must face him sooner or later, but perhaps if she let the day slip by, his temper would cool and he would be more willing to listen to her. After she spilled the truth about all the trickery, then she would stand before his desk and take whatever punishment he chose to give her—even if it meant being locked away in her room for a week.

On her way to the staircase, she glanced down the hall, wondering which guest room Miss Gavin occupied. She wanted to have a look. She so *badly* wanted to have a look.

And yet she knew she shouldn't.

She continued on downstairs. In the dining room, she nibbled at a muffin, wishing her father would come and have breakfast with her the way he sometimes did. They talked and laughed together, and she really loved him so, despite having been so angry with him.

Not feeling especially hungry, she dropped the muffin on her plate, forced herself to drink her milk the way she knew Mrs. O'Brien, if she were here, would insist that she should, then trudged off toward the little schoolhouse.

And there she spent the better part of the day, not really concentrating on her ciphering, unable to read correctly when called upon. When the day was half over, she remembered that this was Thursday, the day for her music lessons, and that after schoolwork, she would be expected to tidy up, eat, and wait patiently for her music teacher.

She sighed and placed her head in her hands for a moment, wondering if the day would keep insisting on dragging on so, if there would not be one moment when she might have a simple peek at Josephine Gavin and then a peek at Papa. She wondered if he was still squirreled away in his study, if perhaps his head was in his hands. So much to worry about . . . She felt overwhelmed.

She ate, picking at her food again. But Mrs. O'Brien was there this time, looking worried—lines wrinkled her brow—and Maggie made herself do more than nibble. It was work, behaving oneself, she decided with a sigh. The house seemed too quiet, almost as if a dark cloud had settled over it. Like when Mama had died.

As soon as that thought occurred to Maggie, she knew she could bear it no longer. Mama had taken ill, and that had been the last Maggie had seen of her. She hadn't been permitted in the death room—Papa had been so afraid that she would contract cholera, too. This time, she didn't mean to have someone she loved taken away without having a last look at her.

She shoved herself away from the table and tore from the dining room. She scrambled up the big dark staircase. To an adult it probably didn't seem big at all, but to Maggie sometimes it seemed monstrous. She heard Mrs. O'Brien calling

behind her, and then somehow the woman moved fast enough
to beat Maggie upstairs and plant herself in front of the very
door behind which Miss Gavin must lie.

Mrs. O'Brien stood looking down on her, breathlessly barring the door, her chest heaving. Maggie, not quite as breathless, felt tears burn the backs of her eyes again.

"Please, Mrs. O'Brien, please? You can't imagine how I
love her, and Dr. Schuster . . . he sat on my bed this morning
and said she was nearly dying because she'd tried so hard to
get to Papa to explain and apologize. Papa loves her, too, and
. . . Don't you see, Mrs. O'Brien? Don't you understand? I did
this! It's my fault, and I've just got to see her. I've got to pray
over her that God will forgive us both and please let her live."
She was crying now, tears streaming down her face. She
swiped at them because she didn't want them there. Most of
the time when she cried she did so to affect people, but this
time she had no control over the tears. She felt as if she had
no control over anything right now. Things had gone horribly
wrong, and people were suffering because of her lies.

Mrs. O'Brien stared down at her, and for a second Maggie
thought she saw tears in her eyes, too. But she couldn't be
sure because her vision was so blurred.

Maggie heard footsteps behind her, but she didn't turn. She
didn't care who was behind her right now. All that mattered
was being able to pray over Josephine Gavin. She would ask
for forgiveness and plead with God to let Miss Gavin live.

Mrs. O'Brien stepped aside, and Maggie went for the door,
twisting the knob and pushing the portal open. She was petrified suddenly that if she approached the big bed too quickly
and startled Josephine, that would be the end for certain. So
she took tiny steps, being careful that her shoes did not make
too much noise on the wooden floor.

She reached the bed and walked around to the left side of
it, tears still blurring her vision somewhat.

A white cloth was wrapped around part of Miss Gavin's
head, which was turned toward Maggie. Her face was
scratched in places, and her shoulders and arms were, too. A
sheet covered her to just above her breasts, and Maggie almost
couldn't tell where it ended and where she began—she was

that white. Her black hair spilled everywhere, all over the pillow and some over her shoulders and down her arms. She was so pretty, and remembering the way Miss Gavin had sung to her about her blue eyes, Maggie thought she would start sobbing again. She sucked in several deep breaths to keep from doing that, then she dropped to her knees beside the bed, folded her hands together tightly, and squeezed her eyes shut.

Seven

"I DREAMED UP the name, God. I wasn't supposed to leave the house that day, but I made a rope from sheets and I climbed down and ran off to Concert Hall when I shouldn't have. I'm little for my age, people tell me, and I don't always like being so little—it seems everyone's bigger than me most of the time—but that night, being little worked. I sneaked between people and I went all over Concert Hall, except for the theater area where I figured someone would spot me. Children aren't allowed in there—neither are ladies without escorts, a sign said. That means that they have to have someone with them, a man told me. I found my way to the back of the theater and I went from room to room until I found the room I thought was hers, and it *was* hers. I'm the one who sneaked in and hid in the trunk and thought up the name and that she was from Alton and everything! I did it all, but Miss Gavin and Papa, they're the ones suffering for what I did, for all the lies I told and for the way I didn't mind Papa. She might die, and Papa's brokenhearted, and oh, God! Please don't let this happen. Don't punish them for what I did, God, punish me!"

Thomas stood just outside the doorway and closed his eyes as he listened to his daughter's desperate prayer. Some of her words were broken, she sobbed and sniffed now and then, and the panic and fear in her voice were unmistakable. Alan was right—according to Maggie, she'd concocted the entire scheme that evening. And yet Miss Gavin had not had to go along with it. She might have been a responsible adult and told Maggie no, that what she was doing was deceitful and wrong. Mrs. O'Brien stood on the opposite side of the doorway, and her troubled gaze mirrored his, Thomas was certain.

"She doesn't even look like herself right now, God," Maggie said, and Thomas glanced into the room and saw his daughter twist her lips and heard her sniff as she stared up at Josephine Gavin. "She's all scratched and she's so still. Is she even still alive? Oh, please let her be. Oh, please! Please let her heart still be beating. If she's still alive, then do what Papa always says you do—work through him to heal her. I know you can. I know he can! My papa, he heals everyone with your help. Amen."

Thomas's heart had never felt so heavy. *Except for yer mother, Maggie. I couldn't heal yer mother. Ye're forgettin' that.* There had been others, too, patients he had lost along the way, people who had died of infection or heart failure or disease. Maggie never knew about those patients because he saw no need to tell her. He realized the mistake in that; his daughter obviously thought him an angel who carried divine power. Her papa had the power to heal, God often worked through him, and there was no reason why God couldn't and wouldn't tonight if only He would forgive what she had done.

Thomas had been coming out of his study when Maggie had raced from the dining room and Mrs. O'Brien had torn off after her, running faster than he would have guessed the woman could. It hadn't taken him but a few seconds to realize where Maggie was headed—she'd somehow learned that a very ill Josephine Gavin lay upstairs and she meant to see her. He'd never expected to witness such a touching scene when he climbed the stairs and saw Maggie pleading desperately with Mrs. O'Brien. He'd listened for a moment, then a quick jerk of his head, an indication that Mrs. O'Brien should let Maggie pass, was all that was needed for the woman to step out of the way.

"Mrs. O'Brien, how has Miss Gavin fared today? You've roused her a few times an' given her water an' food as I requested earlier? Did Dr. Durham call?" Thomas asked softly, so as not to disturb Maggie, who was now holding Josephine Gavin's hand. He had gone out for a bit this afternoon to call on Johnny Owens and to see a few patients at the office. Before that, he'd sent a missive to Dr. Ezekiel Durham, requesting that he call on a patient who was presently laid up at his home, namely, the actress Josephine Gavin.

"She took water, sir, and then she took a little stock, which she promptly vomited up," Mrs. O'Brien answered, her hands clasped properly near her thighs. "Mrs. Durham sent a message back. Her husband's gone off to see an ailing brother in Philadelphia for a time. He's not expected back in St. Louis for at least a month. She sent her apologies. Is there another physician we could send for, Dr. Murphy?"

Heaving a sigh, Thomas rubbed his jaw, then shook his head. He didn't want to take Josephine Gavin on as a patient, but he would for Maggie. He would because Maggie believed that through him, God would heal the woman. He wondered if he would ever have the heart to tell Maggie that he'd been such a mess of emotions last evening he hadn't even been able to perform the surgery—that Alan had done it. He wondered if Maggie would believe that. He'd never known that his daughter put such confidence in him.

"I suppose I'm a doctor, Mrs. O'Brien," he responded. "What you can do is fetch more stock an' my medical bag from the study. My daughter places a lot of faith in me, doesn't she? She seems to think I'm the hand of God."

"Aren't you?" the woman asked quietly. Then she walked away, toward the staircase and, Thomas assumed, his study downstairs.

"A weary hand of God, I suppose," he mumbled, and strode into the room.

Maggie glanced up as he approached the bed, and she scrambled to her feet, swiping at the tears on her cheeks. She twisted her fingers in front of her waist, her gaze fixed on the floor. "Hello, Papa," she greeted timidly.

"Maggie, love." He whispered her name. "Never be afraid to look at me, girl."

She raised her wet lashes, and emotion took his breath, clenching his chest so he thought his heart might burst. For days after Abby's death, he'd hidden himself away, consumed by grief, not caring to comfort anyone but himself, not even his daughter. And though he was gripped by the same fear for Josephine Gavin's life that had seized him when he'd discovered that Abby had cholera, this time he would not hide from his daughter or anyone else. He'd started to this morning, when he secluded himself in his study and drank nearly the entire decanter of brandy. He had allowed emotion and fear to control him, but for Maggie's sake, this afternoon he'd pulled himself out of the gutter he'd fallen into, one that felt all too familiar. He would not allow himself to slip into it again.

Thomas held forth his hand. After a few seconds of hesitation, Maggie took it, and he drew her to him, embracing her, then leading the way to a chair near the hearth.

He sat, then tugged Maggie down onto his lap and cradled her against him. She buried her face in his chest and sobbed quietly. Thomas rubbed her back and rested his chin on her head.

"It all went so wrong, Papa," she cried.

"I know, Maggie girl," he whispered. "I know."

"I prayed. I prayed really hard!"

"You've got to realize, love, that I can't save everyone. Some of my patients die, Maggie. That's the truth of it. I can only—"

"But I prayed so hard!" Maggie lifted her head and sniffed, wiping at her wet face. "She won't die. You'll take care of her, and she won't die!"

Thomas released a long breath. "We'll cling to your faith, girl, an' now an' then we'll say another prayer. Mrs. O'Brien's bringin' soup an' my bag. We'll see if Miss Gavin'll take more water."

"You won't send me away, Papa? Like you did when Mama took ill?"

Managing a weak smile, he brushed hair from her face. "No, Maggie. That was a mistake. I never should've, an' I won't again."

She laid her head against his chest again, and he held her just so for a bit longer, until Mrs. O'Brien returned with a tray and his medical bag. Then he eased Maggie from his lap and, holding hands, they approached the bed and Josephine Gavin.

"Mrs. O'Brien, you'll tell Maggie's music instructor that she won't be available for her lesson this evenin'?" Thomas requested, watching Miss Gavin's chest rise and fall. Her breathing was steady and fairly even.

"I will, Dr. Murphy." Mrs. O'Brien's boots touched lightly on the floor as she left the room.

He lifted Maggie under the arms and sat her on the edge of the bed. She gave him a wide-eyed look, an uncertain look, but he smiled, saying that if she was still, she wouldn't hurt a thing. Crossing back to the chair where they had sat, he retrieved his bag from where Mrs. O'Brien had placed it and the tray on a small table, then returned to the bedside.

He sat beside Maggie and opened the bag, removing two wooden tubes, each about four and one-half inches in length and one and one-half inches in diameter. He screwed the two pieces together, then reached into the bag and quickly found the chest piece. It was shaped like a bell but was also made of wood, and at one end was a small metal tube that fit down into a hole in one end of the wooden tube. Once the chest piece was in place, Thomas leaned over Josephine Gavin, placed the bell of the stethoscope on the center of her chest, the open end of the tube against his left ear, and listened.

He heard a steady beat, strong, without any of the sounds associated with a dying or diseased heart. At least for now . . .

Telling himself to stop being such a pessimist, Thomas waved his hand a bit to indicate that Maggie should scoot closer. When she did, he removed his ear from the tube and with a slight jerk of his head and a smile, indicated that she should place hers against it and listen. She did.

"It's her heart!" she whispered in amazement.

He nodded. "Strong an' steady, Maggie me girl."

She lifted her head, and he took the stethoscope away and placed it on the table beside the bed. "Fetch the tray Mrs. O'Brien brought," he said. "We've got to rouse Miss Gavin an' replace what she vomited earlier. Restorative drink will surely help her right along."

Maggie took great care to move slowly from the bed so as

not to cause too much motion. During the brief moment that it took her to fetch the tray from the table across the room, Thomas took time to observe his patient.

Her face and skin had little color, but he'd seen worse. There was no sign of the grayish-blue coloring around her lips and on her fingertips that he had associated with a dying patient many times. Her lips appeared dry, but water and other drink would help that. She was sleeping a lot, rousing only when awakened, he thought, or so Mrs. O'Brien had indicated. But that wasn't unusual in a patient who had suffered a skull fracture. He should have stayed by her side most of the day, urging her to drink and eat. Instead he'd been pouting over the fact that Alan had left her in his care, and he'd tried to go about business this afternoon as usual. Damn irresponsible, and behavior that went against the oath itself. If she did perish, he'd blame himself a little for her death, for the way he'd ignored her because he hadn't wanted to care for her.

He leaned over her to peek at the amount of drainage on the dressing wrapped around her head. Very little. He'd change the bandage in a bit, after he and Maggie got some water and broth in her. He thought he'd let Maggie wake her with soft words in her ear.

Maggie had just placed the tray on the table near the bed and he'd just started to withdraw from the patient when Josephine Gavin's eyelids began fluttering. Oh, for another look into her dark eyes! Oh, to see them sparkling and laughing again, lit with amusement as they had been when he'd teased her about the parasol that night. Thomas found himself frozen, unable to withdraw more, waiting, holding his breath to see if her lids would open and she would gaze up at him.

They did. She did.

Her eyes were just as beautiful as they'd been that night, just as dark and mysterious, though without the sparkles. They were deep, lined with black lashes. They tempted him, pulled him in. . . . He became painfully aware of the fact that she was naked beneath the sheet that ended just above her breasts. He'd tried to ignore the feel of one of those soft but firm breasts as he'd placed the belled end of the stethoscope on her chest. He'd succeeded then. But now . . . now that her eyes aroused his every nerve, as his heartbeat quickened, he remembered the exquisite feel of her breast against the side of his hand.

"Dr. Murphy," she whispered, and as relief and weakness over seeing her awaken on her own washed through him, he had the unsettling urge to lower his head to her breast, to rest it there, to press his ear directly to her chest and listen and listen to that strong, steady heartbeat. He wanted her to live as much as Maggie wanted her to live.

"Thank God," he whispered back as a little hand touched his shoulder from behind.

"She's awake!" Maggie said, her voice a soft exclamation.

That snapped him out of the trance. He blinked several times, then slowly withdrew from his patient and managed to smile at Maggie over his shoulder.   .

"She surely is, love. Perhaps she'll take some water. Perhaps you might offer her some."

Maggie's mouth formed an *O.* "Me, Papa?"

"That's right, lass," he responded, his smile widening. "God needs even the smallest hand."

With that, he moved away from the bed and gave Josephine Gavin up to Maggie's care for a time.

Josie smiled weakly as Margaret's trembling hand brought a cup of water to her lips and tipped it. Her stomach felt like it was in knots one minute, like a big open hole the next, and the next, like a huge lead ball. Her head no longer hurt as much as it had earlier. Honestly, she didn't know if she could take water or anything else and keep it down. But because she saw in the girl's eyes how heartbroken Maggie would be if she died, Josie was determined to drink and try to retain whatever liquid they gave her.

"I need to sit up a little," she told Margaret. She might be able to take the water better and hold it down if she sat up.

The girl hesitated, then glanced at her father. "She wants to sit up a little."

Nodding, he drew forth and around Maggie to help Josie ease up against the headboard of the bed. His hands were large, warm, and comforting. Josie held the sheet up over her breasts, feeling her face warm at the realization that her clothing had been removed. By whom? she wondered, and immediately hoped it had been Mrs. O'Brien or the other woman she vaguely remembered from one of the times when Mrs. O'Brien had awakened her. Dr. Murphy situated the pillows behind Josie's back, obviously taking care not to meet her gaze; his eyes strayed everywhere but to her face. She closed her eyes, fighting dizziness, and she breathed slowly and deeply. She could do this . . . she could and she would.

Josie wondered why Dr. Murphy, not Dr. Schuster, was here taking care of her. Of course it was the former's home, and perhaps Dr. Schuster had merely gone out for a time. She wondered how long she had lain in this bed, how many days had passed since the evening at the gaming house. She wondered if Dr. Schuster had delivered her apology. She wondered what Dr. Murphy was thinking and she wondered at the fact that Margaret was here, helping to nurse her. She had been certain that he would never again allow his daughter near her.

So many things cluttering her mind . . . so many questions. But for now, she would ask none of them. He was here, and Margaret was here; the three of them were together again, and that fact alone gave Josie's heart and body more strength and will than they had had when Mrs. O'Brien and the other woman had awakened her and given her water and broth.

Moments later, she opened her eyes, slowly, hoping the room would not be spinning. It was fuzzy at first, and then everything came into focus again—the upholstered chairs near the small fireplace, the tall armoire, a table and wooden chair near the right wall, a chest of drawers, the yellow hangings on the bedposts . . . Dr. Murphy, who wore dark trousers and a white shirt with the sleeves rolled up to the middle of his forearms, and Maggie, who now sat near the foot of the bed, holding the cup of water in her lap, her sweet brow wrinkled as she watched Josie, her blue eyes filled with concern and worry.

Josie managed another smile, though her head had begun to throb some. She stretched an arm toward Margaret and said, "Now we can try. Bring the water."

Margaret did, looking unsure at first and then hopeful when

Josie sipped from the glass. Dr. Murphy went to stand near the fireplace, one hand on the mantel and the other on his jaw. Josie admired his profile. He looked thoughtful.

Handsome, too. The flickering light from a nearby lamp enhanced the copper in his hair, making it shimmer as it waved softly over his collar. The shadow of an early growth of beard peppered his slightly tilted jaw. The tilt was one of confidence, not arrogance; it was one of the things Josie realized she found attractive about him. And yet, based on what Margaret had told her about him the evening she had discovered the girl in her dressing room, she had assumed that he would be arrogant. She had assumed he would be full of himself and his world. She had seen Margaret manipulate him that evening. Had the girl also manipulated her? Had Maggie concocted the story about how her father had refused to take her to the theater to meet Josephine Gavin? What had really gone on between father and daughter? Josie wasn't sure anymore that she was in possession of the facts. Surely he had questioned Margaret by now. Remembering his expression at the gaming house, Josie couldn't imagine that he hadn't.

His eyes caught the light, too, and reflected a soft yellow-orange, though Josie remembered their color well. A deep blue-green, though tonight they held little of the sparkle they had possessed the evening she had met him. His brow was strong, jutting forth slightly, half hidden by the hair that spilled down upon it. Josie averted her gaze just as he turned her way.

He wandered back over to the side of the bed and told her and Margaret that they should now wait a bit to see if she could keep the water down. Remembering the way her stomach had rebelled the few times Mrs. O'Brien and the other woman had urged her to drink water and broth, Josie agreed.

"How long have I been here?" she asked.

"Not quite a day," he responded.

"I was to perform this evening—at Concert Hall. People are wondering where I am, I'm certain."

He opened his mouth to speak again, then snapped his jaw shut. What had he been about to say? Josie again recalled his look of anger, hurt, and outrage in the gaming house, and wondered if a sharp comment about her performances in general had been about to roll off his tongue. He was helping to nurse her back to health, he was even allowing Margaret to help, but he in no way approved of her profession. That was apparent.

"I need to send my manager, Orson Neville, a message," she said. "He should be informed of where I am and that I am well."

Clasping his hands behind his back, Thomas Murphy slanted her a look of warning. "He'll be informed of where you are, dear lady, but he'll not be informed that ye're well. You can hardly sit up in the bed. You'll damn—" He caught himself, casting a quick glance at his daughter, obviously realizing that he'd just cursed in front of her. "You'll not be returnin' to the stage anytime soon. For a good week, you'll be right here in this bed. After that, you'll get around slowly, givin' yerself time to heal properly."

"Are you this strict with all of your patients, Dr. Murphy?" she inquired, feeling a prickle of irritation. She had been fighting Orson for months now, fighting against his telling her what to do all the time, how to dress, think, act, walk, talk. . . . She wouldn't have another man slipping in beside Orson, thinking to be in even partial control of her life.

Thomas Murphy's look never wavered. "As yer physician, that is my recommendation, Miss Gavin—that you remain on or near this bed for the next seven days at least. After that, you should regain yer health slowly."

"Papa is the best doctor in all of St. Louis," Margaret said in earnest, trying to convince Josie that she should do as he said—and perhaps calm the tense moment.

Josie smiled at the girl, remembering how angry Margaret had been with her father the night she had hidden in the trunk. Angry enough to want to trick him. And yet her look was sincere right now. She really did believe him to be the best doctor in St. Louis.

"He helped bring Katie Farren's baby brother into the world," Maggie continued, looking serious. "He didn't breathe at first, not very good anyway, Katie said her mother told her. But Papa, he was there. He cleared the baby's throat. Charlie was nearly blue and cold by that time, but Papa fixed him. He did! And now Charlie just started walking the other day and you'd never know he nearly died at first. Mrs. Farren was sick afterward, too, with the fever, and Papa was there for her, too. All that's no lie, really." Margaret ended by jerking a nod, very content with and proud of herself that she could relate the events and relate them in an honest manner.

"Settle down now, Maggie, love," Dr. Murphy said. "Ye're gettin' a bit excited there, an' excitement's the last thing our patient needs right now."

Josie thought she glimpsed a slight blush steal up over his face just before he turned to walk back toward the fireplace. "Mrs. Farren must feel indebted to you, Dr. Murphy. It all sounds very gallant."

Near the mantel he paused again, turning back slightly to give her a quick but meaningful look. "Nothin' gallant, I assure you. It's medicine. My vow to prescribe treatment to the best of my ability. What I did for Mrs. Farren an' her babe, what I do for you, I'd do for anyone."

He was assuring her that no personal feelings were involved and that they would not become involved, no matter that the first thing that had greeted her when she had awakened was a tender look in his eyes, a desperate plea for her not to die. He confused her, not approving of her profession, being angry and hurt that he'd been so deceived, looking at her so tenderly, and yet now more or less telling her that it wasn't her he would work hard to save. It was her life.

"Personal sentiments never become involved, Dr. Murphy?" Josie could not help asking, though her voice still sounded weak to her. "Was there not a moment when the mother wanted to see her baby and your heart ached because you didn't know if you could hand him to her alive?"

He rocked on his heels, giving her a penetrating look. Finally he said, "I believe ye're holdin' the water fine. You might try the broth now, Maggie. Then we'll go an' let Miss Gavin rest until mornin'."

"Yes, Papa," Maggie responded. She moved to place the glass back on the tray and lift a small china bowl and a silver spoon. "You're getting better already," she whispered to Josie with a big smile. "I can tell. My prayer's being answered."

Though Josie's head was aching worse now—she thought from sitting up—she placed her hand on Maggie's arm and gave the girl a slight squeeze. "I'll be fine, I promise. I'm very glad to see you."

That made Margaret beam. Josie felt Dr. Murphy watching them, and she wondered again what was circling inside the man's head.

He and Margaret soon left Josie, but not before Maggie carefully crawled up to Josie and planted a kiss on her cheek. The girl could be so sweet, Josie almost couldn't believe the fact that she could also be so manipulative. Margaret and her father left, taking the tray with them.

Moments later, Josie closed her eyes, feeling drowsy. Just then there was a knock on the door. The portal opened a second later, and Mrs. O'Brien and her companion, a tall, thin woman with silvery hair, entered the room.

Josie couldn't imagine why the women were here, but having perceived Mrs. O'Brien as prim and proper, she expected cold looks and sharp words. Surely Mrs. O'Brien knew by now that she and Margaret had lied about her real identity, and surely Mrs. O'Brien had been told by now exactly who she was.

The nursemaid introduced her companion as Mrs. Reardon, Dr. Murphy's housekeeper. They'd brought a shift, Mrs. O'Brien said, holding forth a folded cotton garment, and if Miss Gavin was interested in wearing it, they would dress her in it. Josie hated feeling so helpless, but she wasn't comfortable with the knowledge that she was naked beneath the sheet. She consented, and gave herself over to the women's care.

"Mrs. O'Brien . . . ," she ventured, slipping an arm into a sleeve.

"Now, Miss Gavin, there's no need to fret," the woman assured her in a soft voice. "I believe you had a reason for doing what you did, perhaps a good reason, and I'm still grateful that you brought Miss Margaret home safe and sound that evening. If you're thinking to apologize, don't."

Josie had expected Mrs. O'Brien to think poorly of her, because of the deceit in which she had involved herself, and to silently demand an apology. She didn't expect the tender smiles that greeted her when the two women pulled the shift down over her head, or the twinkles of amusement in the housekeeper's and nursemaid's eyes. She was so tired that perhaps she was imagining them.

The two women glanced at each other, their smiles persisting. "The truth is, Miss Gavin, Miss Margaret was at the root of the trickery," Mrs. Reardon said. "While it wasn't right for either of you to deceive Dr. Murphy so, there are a few lessons in this for all three of you."

"Miss Margaret adores you and she adores her father, though she knows how to work him to fit her design," Mrs. O'Brien added with a heavy sigh. "I've chased that child and tried to discipline that child. She's a difficult one, that Margaret Murphy. But she does so admire you. We see nothing evil about you, Miss Gavin."

Mrs. Reardon nodded, agreeing. "She'll stay close to the house while you're here."

"Oh, yes!" Mrs. O'Brien concurred. "No running off to the levee. The girl will be killed there someday, whether it be by accident or intentional. The levee is a terrible place for a child."

"We're very sorry that an injury brought you here," the housekeeper said, straightening the lace near one of Josie's wrists. "But sometimes the strangest things happen when something is meant to be."

Nodding, Mrs. O'Brien smoothed a few wrinkles in the shift near Josie's stomach. "Now then, you lie down and get your rest. Dr. Murphy will look in on you during the night, I'm certain. He's very attentive to his patients that way."

"When he decides to take on their care." Mrs. Reardon's smile widened as she glanced at her companion.

"Usually he doesn't think twice about it."

"Well, perhaps he had a little more to consider this time, Florence."

Like the fact that I'm an actress, Josie thought, frowning. No doubt he detested her presence in his home.

How she had come to be here, she wasn't sure. She remembered his strong arms around her outside the gaming house, and she remembered the comforting sound of his voice in her ear. He was a compassionate man and he had reacted instinctively to the attack. But the fact remained that somehow she had wound up in Dr. Schuster's care. Now that Dr. Schuster was gone, Dr. Murphy had probably consented to caring for her at Maggie's request. Surely no one else could have convinced him.

The women finished fussing over her. Mrs. Reardon put another log on the flames in the fireplace, then extinguished all but one lamp—the one on the table near the bed—while Mrs. O'Brien arranged the sheet and coverlet around Josie, then gathered the tray from which Margaret had taken the bowl of soup. Moments later both women slipped out of the room, leaving the door open.

Josie snuggled beneath the warm covers, watching the lamp flicker shadows on the walls and listening to the fire hiss and pop. She felt wanted and loved by Maggie and accepted by the two women in the household. Too, the knowledge that she could not be in the hands of a more capable physician comforted her as far as her health and recovery were concerned. And yet, despite the fact that she was being so well taken care of, Josie found her mind straying, entertaining thoughts she shouldn't permit.

She was attracted to Dr. Murphy—she could not and would not deny that. After learning the truth about who she was, he had distanced himself from her emotionally—or tried to. But she could not forget the worry in his eyes that had greeted her when she had first awakened. So gentle, his eyes. So sincere. She could almost believe he really cared—and not just as a physician concerned for his patient.

What if he does, Josie? she asked herself. He was obviously a well-to-do citizen, doubtless respected by a great number of people in and around St. Louis. And she, after all, knew her place. How well she knew that if he had anything to do with her beyond the doctor-patient relationship, it would certainly not be anything respectable. He would not offer her what her heart longed for, what her mind dreamed of.

She would not allow herself to dream while she was here in his home. She would not allow the fantasy of one day having a family and a home that emanated warmth like this one to occupy her thoughts while she was here. She would concentrate on recovering. She would cherish her time with Margaret, since she had grown to love the girl. And when she was able, she would walk out and not look back. When the company moved on in a few weeks, she would be right there with them. She would do what she could to help Orson and Mr. Jefferson recover financially, and then one day, in a few years, perhaps, she would settle somewhere. She wasn't sure where yet. But she would buy a small house somewhere and grow lots of flowers and sweet herbs. She would have a few cats and talk to them while tending her gardens, like any spinster would do. She would grow old with them.

A tear spilled onto her pillow. Josie brushed more from her eyes. That was not what she wanted, not really. To grow old surrounded by cats and gardens. She wanted to have people to share her life with . . . a family. She wanted to feel a child growing inside her, a child created in love, and she wanted to bear it and hold it to her breast and nurture it and watch it grow. She wanted to hear children's laughter and watch their mischief, be surrounded by their antics always. She wanted to sing to Margaret for the rest of the girl's childhood and watch Maggie's eyes sparkle and shine with happiness.

"Oh, Josephine," Orson would say. "You think foolish thoughts."

Perhaps she did, but they were there, festering inside her, needs and wants and desires, and she could do nothing to quiet them, it seemed.

Josie turned her head toward the pillow and let her tears flow. A dam broke, one she had held shakily in place for too long. She needed this. She needed to release the fear and frustration and anger she felt. She was what she was, would be what she would be, only she had to learn to release pent-up tears now and then that tore at her heart. Freeing them would make her feel somewhat better; she instinctively knew that.

She didn't know how long she cried quietly, and she didn't know exactly when Dr. Murphy entered the room. All she knew was that he was there suddenly, first near the foot of the bed, watching her, his brow wrinkled as he gripped the bedpost. Emotion skittered in his eyes, and then he rounded the bed, sat on the edge, leaned toward her, and gathered her in his arms.

She tried to push him away, not wanting to be comforted by him, not wanting to give them the chance to grow close emotionally. It had been one thing for him to envelop her in his arms when he had been protecting her from the mad crowd; it was an entirely different matter for him to comfort her while she was crying—all because she did not have a home and a true family.

She pressed her palms against his chest, but the effort was a weak one. His arms felt too good, his breath in her hair felt too warm, his whispers in her ear too comforting: "There now, lass, go ahead an' cry. I don't know what it is, what's got you in such a state, but I heard you from clear down the hall. It can be a good thing, cryin'. I didn't do it last year when I should've. I hid myself away, hid the pain away when I should've let it go."

He understood at least that much—that she had to let the tears go.

She melted against him, it seemed, slipping her arms around him and clinging to him, forgetting the dull throb in her head for a time. She loved Margaret, and Mrs. O'Brien and Mrs. Reardon had been so sweet to her, welcoming her and more or less telling her they were glad she was here. But it might be better if she didn't feel welcome in this house, in this home. She would get more and more attached to everyone here and she might start wishing things she should not wish. Then she would have to leave one day, and the pain would be too much to bear. She knew that in her heart.

"I—I'm frightened, that's all," she managed, her voice sounding muffled against Dr. Murphy's chest.

"You've had a terrible experience. But it's over. There's no one here to grab you now, an' you'll heal just fine."

He thought she was afraid because she almost had been killed, and because she still feared she might die. He didn't know the real reason for her tears. He couldn't know. She wouldn't tell him.

She managed to pull away, and he withdrew his arms, along with their warmth and comfort. She stared up at him, wondering what he was thinking now. A second later he did the most tender thing. He brushed the tears from just beneath her eyes, then slowly ran his fingertips down over her cheek to her lips, brushing the bottom one for a heart-stopping instant.

"I'll fetch somethin' to help you sleep," he said softly. "You'll rest easier, I'm thinkin', an' so will I."

He left the room and returned moments later with a bottle and a spoon. He gave Josie several doses of liquid from the container, and she grimaced, it tasted so awful. Then he put the spoon and bottle on the table beside the bed, brought a chair from across the room, and sat near her.

For a time, silence prevailed. If not for the fire dancing orange shadows about the room, the moonlight shining in through the window would have given the furnishings an almost silvery glow. Josie watched the shadows, unsure of how much time passed and why he was still sitting beside her. Merely to keep a watchful eye on his patient? Was the doctor on duty beside the bed, or was it the man observing her, concern shimmering in his gaze as he rubbed his jaw? She almost wished he would hold her again. She missed the feel of his arms around her. She very much wanted to make him understand her, but she wasn't sure why.

"I meet so many people who think I'm something I'm not, Dr. Murphy," she said. "For that reason, I've distanced myself from everyone but those people closest to me—my manager and some of the other actors and actresses in the company. Because of my chosen profession, because of the life I made for myself after my mother and brother perished in a fire, I must live with vile rumors and assumptions, and I do hear them. They do reach my ears, and now and then my temper flares because of them. When Margaret told me you thought I was a bad woman, I was already irritated at my manager. Something snapped inside of me."

She tried to read his eyes, what he was thinking. But the one lamp gave off so little light. She glanced away for a time, then she looked back at him.

"I've had my fill of people who look down their noses at me. If you wondered for a moment what motivated me to do what I did the evening I met you . . . there, you have it. I'm assuming that Dr. Schuster delivered my apology, so I won't apologize again. I merely wanted to explain." The medication was beginning to work, whatever it was—she was feeling more and more drowsy, and her words sounded slow.

He did not respond. She felt his gaze on her, soft but uncertain.

Her eyelids closed once, then again. The room grew a little fuzzy. "I had the time of my life in New Orleans three summers ago," she said. "But I suppose you've heard all about that by now. Poor, poor Josie Gavin. Took up with a man there, thought he'd want her for life, and she ended up getting her heart crushed down in the magical city. It's ironic—because I'm an actress, the high-and-mighty assume things about me. And yet, if they only knew. I haven't let a man touch me romantically since. I haven't wanted one to."

Until you, she almost said, but stopped herself. She felt drugged and thought she should just shut her mouth and go to sleep. She was telling him entirely too much, entirely more than she would normally tell a person she had met only twice. Other than to Orson a few evenings ago, she never mentioned Frank and what had happened in New Orleans. Yes, she should keep her mouth shut.

"I thought I was good enough for him," she went on, unable to stop her fool tongue. It felt heavy suddenly, drugged. "Make believe, that's what I was caught up in. Fantasy. A fairy tale I thought would come true. I won't make that mistake again. People tell me I'm beautiful." She smiled. "They tell me I have a wonderful voice . . . that I'm a fine actress. No one . . . no one cares to look closer and find out . . . what's inside. So I began singing and acting again after Frank, and for a while I forgot about feeling. Then Orson made me angry and I . . . I met Margaret . . . so charming . . . and you. Dr. Schuster, too. Now Mrs. O'Brien and the other woman . . . cannot remember her name. They dressed me and talked to me. So sweet. Something . . ." Her eyes insisted on closing again, and again she fought, struggling to open them. "Mrs. . . . Mrs. . . ."

He moved to sit on the edge of the bed. He leaned over her again. "Shh. I've seen Maggie do this—fight sleep. Ye're needin' yer rest." He brushed hair from her cheek, then he stroked a strand of it, smoothing it over her shoulder.

"No," she whispered, turning her head. "Don't make me feel desired. It's one thing to feel wanted when I'm onstage. But this . . . Don't make me feel cherished. Don't be tender, then later . . . A lie . . . I won't believe."

"Ye're welcome here. As my patient," he said. And then she thought she heard him say softly: "You are wanted."

Why was he being so tender and caring? She wished he would leave the room. Go away.

And yet with him sitting so close to her, with his hand on her shoulder and him gazing down at her, she tumbled easily into sleep.

Eight

THE NEXT MORNING, Josie awoke to the sight of Margaret standing next to the bed, holding a tray. Morning sunlight poured softly in through the window. Dr. Murphy stood near the fireplace again. Maggie smiled down at Josephine, then did a little curtsey with the tray in hand.

"Miss Gavin, I'm pleased to announce the arrival of breakfast. I helped the cook prepare it, I did, I did," she said, her eyes bright. "Muffins and eggs, if you can stand them—when I'm sick, I usually can't. Juice squeezed from oranges brought up from the steamers. Yum! And look"—she held the tray with one hand while removing the cover of a dish with the other—"we even made Papa's favorite so he might have breakfast with you. Hotcakes! I brought him coffee, too, but it's over there," she said, jerking her head toward the fireplace. "On the table. Mrs. Reardon helped me carry it all up. I think she and Mrs. O'Brien like for me to help take care of you. It keeps me busy. Why, just last week I had nothing to do one evening and I decided to slide clear down the banister! Mrs. Reardon nearly swooned. Mrs. O'Brien charged after me and caught me halfway down—she's the only person who's ever been able to catch me. She said I was gonna hurt myself. I wouldn't have."

"You might have," Josie said, unable to restrain a smile.

"Ye're givin' Miss Gavin her breakfast, Maggie me girl?"

Dr. Murphy said, turning, sounding a little skeptical. He approached another tray which sat on the table near the hearth chairs and proceeded to pour coffee. "She needs food and drink, and you need to be off to the schoolhouse soon."

Margaret turned. "But, Papa, I thought I'd stay and help take care of her!"

"Mrs. Reardon an' Mrs. O'Brien will manage while ye're at the schoolhouse an' I'm off at the college an' at the office for a bit. They'll know how to reach me."

"But, Papa!"

He straightened, clasping his hands behind his back and tilting his chin at his daughter. "Maggie, I've said how things will be."

She sighed. "Yes, Papa."

Josie was amazed. He hadn't let the girl talk her way out of school. She had assumed that Margaret could twist her father whichever way she wanted and most always get her way.

"Good," he said, and Josie wanted to laugh aloud, he looked so relieved suddenly, as if the entire little episode had been a test for him, and a taxing one at that. He went back to pouring his coffee while Margaret placed the tray on the table beside the bed.

Josie worked her way up in the bed, and Margaret propped the pillows behind her, almost having to climb up onto the bed to do it. Dr. Murphy looked on from where he now stood sipping coffee near the fireplace. Recalling a lot of what she had revealed to him last evening and remembering the way he had drawn her to him while she cried, she wondered how he felt this morning—if he thought her silly for going on and on and if he regretted having held her. It hardly mattered, she told herself. She could not take back all that she had told him, and he could not take back drawing her to him. He also could not take back the way he had so gently run his fingertips down her cheek to her lips or his tender touch on her shoulder. She almost wished he could. If the touches had not comforted her so much, she might have wished they had never happened.

Once Josie was situated, Margaret placed the tray on her lap, then climbed up onto the bed beside her, taking care to do so slowly so as not to upset the tray and its contents.

"You look pretty in the night shift," Margaret said, smiling big.

Lifting a fork from the tray, Josie smiled back. "Miss Margaret, you look like a spring flower yourself, all done up in purple. You brighten a room when you walk in."

The girl blushed under the praise as Josie gathered a bite of eggs on the fork. "I'll brush your hair for you later if you're feeling up to it. I'll be real careful so as not to upset your bandage. I'll just brush this part," Margaret said, reaching up to touch the hair that waved over Josie's shoulder and down across her breast to her waist. "You eat now. Please eat. Papa says restorative drink and food and rest are the best things for you right now."

"I'd like that—for you to brush my hair," Josie responded, forcing herself to eat. While Margaret looked on, she ate three small bites of eggs and a fourth of the muffin.

Margaret moved carefully from the bed, saying, "You, too, Papa. I know you love hotcakes. They're what me and Mrs. O'Brien surprise you with sometimes. I know you haven't had breakfast. Come here and eat."

"Maggie, that's Miss Gavin's breakfast."

"No, no. It's for you, too!"

"The eggs and muffin will be enough for me," Josie assured him.

"Don't be afraid, Papa," Margaret said.

He lifted his brows. "I'm hardly afraid, Maggie."

"Then come and have something to eat."

His gaze met Josie's, and she smiled and shrugged as if to say, *How can you resist?*

Resigning himself, he placed his cup of coffee on the table near the trays and walked toward the bed, his gaze never leaving hers, as if he meant to prove that he wasn't afraid.

He stepped around his daughter and was just reaching for the plate of hotcakes when a voice sounded from the doorway: "A cozy scene. Very cozy indeed. Almost a family scene, if that can be believed."

Josie glanced at the door, knowing the cultured voice immediately. "Orson," she said softly.

Attired in his usual somber black, he held a beaver hat in

his hands. His sharp gray eyes were fixed on the bed, on Josie and her companions. He appeared disturbed by the sight that greeted him; his posture was rigid, his chin tilted in his arrogant way.

"Good morning, Josephine," he said softly as he approached the bed. "The housekeeper showed me in. Seeing you alive and well brings me relief."

"She'll be needin' to rest soon," Dr. Murphy said, stepping away from the bed. "She suffered a—"

"Who are you, sir?" Orson's hard, scrutinizing stare had whipped to him.

"Thomas Murphy," came the immediate reply. "This is my home. I'm Miss Gavin's physician. Who are you?"

"Self-appointed physician, no doubt."

"Orson!" Josie whispered. He was always brusque when dealing with new people, but never this rude.

Dr. Murphy clasped his hands behind his back as his eyes locked with Orson's. "By chance, I assure you. Would you care to make yer introduction?" he inquired, his voice and brows rising a little.

Orson stood on the opposite side of the bed now. "Orson Neville. I am Miss Gavin's manager. I've made arrangements to have her moved to the hotel where the rest of the company is—"

"You'd best be cancelin' those arrangements," Thomas Murphy responded coolly. "She suffered a depressed skull fracture, as I said in my missive to you. A colleague an' I performed surgery. She's in no physical condition to travel."

Orson's grip on his hat tightened. A muscle flickered in his jaw. "The hotel, my boy, is perhaps two miles away, if that. Hardly a journey."

The two men stared hard at each other for long seconds. "My recommendation as a physician," the doctor finally responded in a clipped and lower tone, "my *adamant* recommendation, is to not be movin' her for a time any more than she's got to be moved to take care of bodily functions an' needs."

"Orson," Josie said, thinking to intervene, "the crowd at the gaming house where you arranged my appearance . . . the crowd went mad, Orson. People were—''

"At the hotel you can rehearse your lines for next week's production while resting, Josephine. You shall have me and the rest of the cast to care for you.'' Orson had glanced at her, albeit briefly. But now his gaze fastened on Dr. Murphy again, who was beginning to look furious—his eyes had narrowed, his jaw had tightened, his shoulders were squared even more than they had been.

"Ye're a physician, sir?'' Dr. Murphy demanded.

"Hardly,'' came the immediate response. "But I know my actress. She has been ill before. I know her far better than you do. I know that she thrives on being among the members of the company and on being onstage. That is the best course of therapy for her.''

"One might assume ye're a medical doctor.''

"Gentlemen,'' Josie admonished, mustering a harsh tone. "I'll be the one to decide what's best for me.''

The two men continued to stare at each other while Margaret fidgeted on the bed, rearranging dishes on the tray, then her skirt around her. She glanced at Josie and gave a makeshift smile, one that said she sensed trouble and was uncomfortable. Josie lifted the small glass of orange juice and drank about half of it.

"Thank you for the breakfast,'' she told Margaret, rather disappointed that they had been interrupted—and before the girl's father had had his hotcakes. "Take the tray downstairs now,'' she said gently with a smile. "Perhaps the hotcakes might be warmed for your papa in a little while. I imagine you should go on to the schoolhouse, too.'' She wanted Margaret out of the middle of the hostility that had sprung up between the men positioned on opposite sides of the bed.

What little smile Margaret had managed faded as she nodded. She was disappointed, too, at having her time with Josephine interrupted. But she took the tray just as Josie had suggested and moved from the bed, past her father and toward the door.

"I've a class of medical students to attend at the college, then a number of patients to see to,'' Dr. Murphy said, his gaze shifting to Josie. "You've heard my recommendation,

Miss Gavin. I'll say no more. If ye're here later this afternoon when I come home, I'll assume I'm still yer physician.''

And if not, Josie thought, you'll doubtless resign yourself from my care, since I went against your recommendation.

With that, he withdrew from the room, leaving her to her manager.

Orson walked around to the foot of the bed, paced a few times there, coughed—though the cough was now rattly, as if fluid were sitting in his lungs—then traveled to the other side of the bed to the spot where Thomas Murphy had stood moments before. He glanced down at the floor, then around at the general area, then at her. He had won the verbal battle and now looked rather satisfied that he was occupying the space Dr. Murphy had occupied.

"You're happy that you ran him off?" Josie queried, though she knew he was. She clicked her tongue in disgust and quickly glanced off at one corner of the room and back. "Orson."

"Josephine. Is he the one?"

"Whatever do you mean?"

"The one with whom you spent that evening. The evening you disappeared."

"Yes," she answered honestly. "Though I hardly spent it with him. I spent it with him and the little girl, as I told you. Her name is Margaret, and I spent most of it with her."

Orson waved a hand impatiently. "Children. They do nothing but get underfoot. They make messes and they are often defiant. A lot of bother."

Josie sighed. "Or so you think. Perhaps some are a lot of bother. I happen to think Margaret Murphy is a delight."

He scowled. "She's a child." He turned away, coughing again, and approached the fireplace as if needing to cover all the territory Thomas Murphy had occupied. "Your appearance at the gaming house was a disaster."

"There's no need to tell me that," Josie said, laughing sharply as she smoothed the sheet over her thighs. "He was there, and as soon as I laid eyes on him, the words of the song were lost to me. It was as if they were spinning in my head, and now and then I would grab one. But most . . . most were simply lost.''

"Why was that, Josephine?'' he asked, turning back. "Why as soon as you saw him?''

She studied him, then inhaled deeply. "Are you afraid I'm losing my heart again, Orson?''

"You know I am. Your heart and your mind.''

"I told you I was up to trickery the night Margaret brought me here. I deceived Dr. Murphy, led him to believe I was not who I am. He has little respect for actresses, and Margaret and I planned to show him that I was not what he thought I was. Things went a little differently than I thought they would. I didn't want the look of admiration he gave me to change, so I never told him who I really was. Then there he was in the gaming house, watching me sing. Where were the men you sent to protect me, Orson? Where was Andre?''

Orson shook his head. "The crowd was thick and wild, he said. He couldn't get to you. He tried.''

"He tried,'' Josie said caustically.

"You should not have run from where they placed you near the piano.''

No, she supposed she shouldn't have. There she had been within her protectors' line of vision.

"It's not advisable for you to stay here,'' Orson said after a time.

"On the contrary,'' she retorted. "The doctor advises it.''

That made Orson hesitate, but certainly not out of respect for Dr. Murphy's recommendation. "Contrary is certainly what you have become. How convenient that he's become your physician, Josephine. How coincidental that you spent that evening here and then that he was on hand at the gaming house when the trouble happened. How convenient that he rescued you and brought you here. It's all very romantic, but—''

"Orson, whether or not you take it seriously, I'm very ill.'' She had no patience or tolerance for this right now, for his way of picking a situation to death. "Yes, it was coincidental. He happened to be there. He happened to save me from people who surely would have mauled me to death in an effort to be near me. I'm grateful to him, and you should be grateful, too. I believe him to be a good doctor, and I plan to follow his professional advice and stay exactly where I am until he says I can be moved. I'm tired now, Orson. I want to rest. I need to rest. You'll excuse me?"

He inhaled deeply. "Josephine . . ."

"He's genuine, Orson. He's sincere. Perhaps you could call this evening. Or better—tomorrow." As fond of him as she was, as much as she felt she owed him, she refused to be bullied into what he thought was best in her personal life.

Obviously insulted, he made a show of putting his hat on at a slant and dusting off his sleeves as if being in this room and this house had dirtied him. The action was absurd, since there wasn't a speck of dust anywhere that Josie could see.

"You've made your decision, then," he said. "You've pushed me away. Stay in this house, Josephine, and you are certain to find yourself in a predicament again. Keep your perspective. He's your physician, and that is all. And the child—she's his, not yours."

Josie could have done without that reminder. "Good day, Orson."

He inclined his head. "Good day."

With that, he left.

Josie slept off and on most of the morning and the afternoon, into early evening. Now and then either Mrs. Reardon or Mrs. O'Brien would awaken her and give her water, broth, or tea they had brewed from dried herbs. They were always pleasant, almost jovial, nursing her with tender care while talking softly to her, washing her face with a damp cloth, and helping to support her head while she drank.

Finally she awoke to Margaret again, who sat on the bed softly humming a tune Josie didn't recognize.

"A lovely voice, Miss Margaret Murphy," Josie said, smiling, opening her eyes.

"You're awake!" Margaret whispered excitedly. Then, in her usual tone, "I was so good today, so well-behaved, just like Mrs. O'Brien says I should be. I did all my studies and I ate all the food I was given—though I sneaked a piece of bread into my pocket for the birds that gather near the school-house. When Mrs. Reardon's boy, Willie, untied my dress like he sometimes does, I didn't even glare at him and threaten to punch him! I just tied it back. I even asked permission to come up and see you. Most times, I wouldn't ask permission to do something. I'd just do it and hope I didn't get caught.''

"Well, it sounds as though you've had quite a day, young lady."

Margaret's mouth fell open. "No one's ever called me that—young lady."

Josie laughed. "You've behaved like a young lady today."

The girl beamed, smiling brightly, her face reddening a little, her eyes bright. She picked up something from her lap, a silver-backed brush and a white ribbon. "I promised to brush your hair for you."

"You certainly did. I'll sit up, and perhaps we can sweep it to one side."

Margaret nodded. "I'll brush it, then braid it the way Mrs. O'Brien sometimes braids mine. Some days my hair's too curly, like when it's been raining, and it can't be plaited at all. I like it then, but I like it best when it's all neat in one or two braids. I unplait it at night, and it's all wavy instead of curly."

Josie sat up in the bed and swept her hair to one side, exactly as she'd promised she would. Margaret brushed gently, starting at the ends and working her way up, carefully untangling the hair, being just as careful not to pull. "I hope you don't have so much of a headache anymore," she said suddenly, as if the thought had just occurred to her.

"A little, but the brushing doesn't hurt, Margaret. Perhaps when you're done, I could brush yours."

"That would be lovely! I like to have my hair brushed, really. Mrs. O'Brien sometimes scolds me to sit still, but those are the days when I just can't sit still. It's not every day," she assured. "Who was that man this morning? He wasn't very pleasant. I thought he talked rude to Papa."

"That was Mr. Neville, my manager, and you're right—he wasn't very pleasant."

"Oh." Then, as an afterthought, Margaret asked, "What's a manager?"

"The other actresses and actors in the Jefferson Company travel from city to city with me to do performances. Mr. Neville helps us learn our lines—he taught me a lot about acting—and he schedules the performances. In return, he receives a portion of our earnings."

"Oh," the girl said as she placed the brush on the bed. She divided Josie's hair and began to braid. "He was rude," she said again.

"I know." Josie sighed. "I apologize for him. I think Orson sees himself as my father."

That seemed to satisfy the inquisitive Margaret for a time. She was just finishing the braid when Dr. Murphy walked into the room, a black medical bag in hand. Josie did not miss the smile he aimed at his daughter, or the way it faded quickly when he met Josie's gaze.

"Well, ye're still here," he said, and for the life of her she couldn't tell if he was relieved or sorry, his gaze skittered away so fast. "I was expecting Mrs. Reardon or Mrs. O'Brien to tell me you had left with your manager this morning."

"I trust your professional judgment, Dr. Murphy," she responded. But what she really trusted even more was his tender way of caring for her. She didn't think for a second that the way he had held her last night was his usual manner of caring for a patient, but having his arms around her, feeling their warmth and strength, as unwise as she knew exposing herself to such tenderness was, had soothed her. She would retain him as her physician because his compassionate nature comforted her, but she would also take Orson's advice and work hard at keeping her perspective.

"An' I trust the healin' hand of my daughter. Maggie has a way of bringin' light to yer eyes. But then," he said, placing the bag on the nearby table, "you've a way of bringin' light to hers." At least he appeared to be in a much better mood than when Josie had last seen him—this morning when he and Orson had had words. "How is our patient, Maggie me girl? I'm thinkin' she has more color in her face than she had earlier, a healthy look."

Maggie nodded adamantly. "Her hair's softer, too, now that I brushed it so much. Feel, Papa!"

His head drew back, and his face reddened a little. His gaze met Josie's again, then skittered away more quickly than it had the first time. She wondered if he would do as Margaret said.

"Well, now, Maggie, I . . . If you say it's softer, I'm certain it is. There's no reason to . . . An' look there, you've got it almost all the way braided. I'm thinkin'—"

"Papa," Maggie said sternly, pursing her lips, looking put out. "Feel."

Josie frowned. The child could be too headstrong for even her peace of mind sometimes.

Thomas Murphy eased forward and around his daughter. She still held the tapered end of the long braid, since she'd not yet tied it off with the ribbon. Dr. Murphy tried to hide the apprehensive look in his eyes and failed. He and Josie both had the same idea apparently: to make the touch a quick one and to keep their eyes downcast. And yet when he leaned over and drew unnecessarily close—he might have merely extended an arm—she glanced up, startled. His lashes raised and his eyes met hers just as his hand touched the upper part of her braid, which began just below her ear.

Josie's breath lodged in her throat for a few seconds. So deep, his eyes, so rich in spirit and noble devotion. She did not doubt that he would go to no end to satisfy those he loved. She gazed into his eyes and saw that he feared her almost as much as she feared him—the heartache that more intimate involvement with him would surely bring.

"I won't bite you, Miss Gavin," he murmured.

She lowered her lashes, feeling her face warm. "Won't you, Dr. Murphy, if I allow it?"

"Isn't it soft, Papa?" Margaret asked excitedly, seeming to have no idea that she was interrupting a tender moment. It was an interruption for which Josie was grateful. "I brushed it and brushed it!"

"Yes, Maggie, love, it's soft," he answered. Then he withdrew, and a long moment passed before Josie began breathing evenly again.

Dr. Murphy placed a hand on his daughter's back. "The cook has supper waitin' for us downstairs, Maggie, an' Mrs. O'Brien'll be bringin' a tray up for Miss Gavin. After the meal you can come back an' visit with her."

"But, Papa," Margaret objected, "I thought we might bring our food here and eat with her. She might need our help, after all."

"Oh, I'm sure Mrs. O'Brien'll help her. We'll do our best to carry on as usual while Miss Gavin's here. She'll be gone one day, Maggie, an' I don't want adjustin' after she's gone to be hard for you, girl. So we'll keep some things the same."

Josie agreed—and she respected him for having such a level head, for looking ahead for Margaret's sake. If Margaret got into the habit of having supper with her every evening and of coming straight here from her studies, she very well might have a difficult time adjusting once Josie left.

"Go ahead, Margaret," Josie coaxed, thinking the girl looked enormously disappointed and reluctant; her smile had drooped into a frown, and her brow had knotted.

"Oh, all right," the girl huffed, as if she had had enough of being well-behaved for one day. Quite enough, thank you very much. "But first I've got to tie this off."

Josie held the tapered end of the braid while Margaret tied the ribbon. Then she gave Margaret's hand a squeeze, and the girl went off with her father.

Mrs. O'Brien soon came with Josie's meal—slices of baked ham, sweet potatoes, and bread that smelled freshly baked. Dishes of strawberries and cream sat to one side of the tray. Josie found that she had finally regained her appetite. The food looked and smelled sweet and delicious. She bent forward to inhale the fresh scent of the herbs sprinkled on the yams. Her stomach growled.

"I love strawberries," she said, glancing at that dish, hoping she didn't sound too terribly eager.

Mrs. O'Brien gave a big smile. "The steamers that travel up and down the Mississippi bring a lot of things to our city. The ice starts melting in the river at about this time of year, and the ships begin docking, unloading and reloading." She sat in the chair Dr. Murphy had placed beside the bed last evening and smoothed the skirt of her light blue dress. It was rather plain, the dress, having only a snatch of lace around the collar of the prim bodice. But it was pleasant, even cheery, bringing a certain glow to the nursemaid's face.

"I enjoy this time of year," Mrs. O'Brien continued. "You wake in the morning to the birds chirping and you know the buds will open on the trees soon. Spring is like birth. It's new life, and there is something exciting about new life."

Josie nodded, agreeing wholeheartedly, wondering at the way the woman had just started talking and then taken a seat. She still sometimes marveled that Mrs. O'Brien hadn't turned up her nose upon learning who she really was.

"Oh, I do not want to keep you from your meal," the nursemaid fretted, clasping her hands.

"You're not," Josie said quickly, thankful for the company. The room had seemed too quiet after Margaret and her father had stepped out. She began cutting pieces of ham, stopping only to take a bite. "I love spring, too. The flowers. Oh, the flowers! I wait for them, and now and then I wander off, manage to find a field, and I spend an afternoon gathering them. They're pretty and sweet and . . . fresh."

"I know where there is a hothouse," Mrs. O'Brien said. "It does not produce everything, of course, but there are plenty of flowers. We get some of our vegetables from the hothouse when the ground is frozen and nothing grows. I wouldn't mind bringing flowers for your room."

Josie froze with a bite of potato halfway to her mouth. "That's sweet, Mrs. O'Brien. Very sweet. But it's really not my room, and I wouldn't want to get too comfortable here."

The woman's brow wrinkled. "Nonsense. It's your room until the day you leave. Flowers would make you too comfortable?"

"The flowers and your sweetness would. Yours and Mrs. Reardon's and Margaret's. I cannot risk feeling like I belong. I cannot risk becoming attached. I'll be leaving in a few weeks with my company and . . . I've been hurt before, leaving people I loved. It's not a pleasant feeling."

"No, and it is one I'm familiar with. My husband and I left Maryland and came here when I was younger because he had ideas for business. I never thought I would stop missing my family—my brothers and sisters. There were eight of us altogether, you know.''

Josie managed a smile, forcing politeness, as she began eating more. Why did the woman insist on chatting with her as if she were a friend? ''No, I didn't know.''

Mrs. O'Brien nodded. ''Eight of us, and we were all very close. But you grow up, and it becomes time to go separate ways, as sad as doing that is. I lost a girl, too, right after her eighth birthday,'' the nursemaid said, lowering her gaze to her lap for a few seconds, ''so I know how unpleasant leaving someone is. I almost could not stand it when they put her box in that grave and I had to walk away and leave her there. My little girl, in the ground. It still pains me to this day. She died down at the wharf. Her father insisted on taking her there with him some days. Rosabelle stepped under a heavy crate some men had just raised and taken off one of the ships. They were getting ready to lower it when one of the ropes broke.''

Josie had stopped eating again, feeling shocked at the revelation. ''Mrs. O'Brien,'' she whispered, her breath catching.

The nursemaid wiped at a tear and blinked others back, then forced a smile. ''Oh, getting through the days now is much easier than at first, when I wanted to be dead with her. But I found other things to live for. My husband, for one, though he died a few years later of disease. I had Rosabelle and my husband for such a short time, it seemed, and I would have given anything to have them longer. I sure would not have passed up the opportunity to have them, knowing how much I grew to love them. Love and family . . . they bring us our share of troubles, but the joys outweigh everything. That is the way I feel.'' Her gaze went back to her lap, fastening on her folded hands. A few seconds later, she looked up at Josie again. ''Miss Gavin, if you were presented with the opportunity to have a family, what would you do?''

Josie stared at her for a long moment. Then she swallowed and finally laughed a little in disbelief. ''Well, Mrs. O'Brien, I . . . I would love to have a family. If one was offered, or if the opportunity for one was offered, I . . .'' Oh, the woman couldn't imagine how talking about this pained her! ''If the offer was sincere and made in a respectful fashion and I thought I either loved the man or could love him, I suppose I might consider it.''

Now it was Josie's turn to glance down at her hands.

''At the very least, calm yourself and enjoy what makes you happy while you're here,'' Mrs. O'Brien said softly, leaning forward as if her words were for Josie's ears only. But that was absurd—there was no one else in the room. ''I've a feeling you're not happy, and I see the way the two of you look at each other, you and Dr. Murphy. You wouldn't want to leave in a few weeks wondering if you could have enjoyed your stay here more.''

What was the nursemaid suggesting? Josie stared at her. Mrs. O'Brien shrugged nonchalantly.

Mrs. Reardon bustled in right at that moment with an armful of fresh linen in her arms, saying she thought they might change the bedding after Miss Gavin finished eating. They hadn't wanted to disturb her rest earlier in the day, which was why they hadn't changed the bedding before now.

Josie finished her food, enjoying the strawberries immensely, and when Mrs. O'Brien helped her to sit in the chair while the women changed the sheets, Josie issued a soft ''thank-you.'' It prompted a smile and a quick nod from Mrs. O'Brien, who was apparently not as prim and proper as Josie had thought when she'd met her the night Margaret had brought her to the house.

Nine

JOSEPHINE GAVIN HAD felt exquisite in his arms. Oh, Thomas had held and comforted people before, but he'd never felt such a need to do it, such a strong sense of being able to make the situation better, at least for the moment, as he'd felt last evening when he'd found her crying. If she hadn't pulled away after only a few moments, he would have held her for a lot longer. He knew he would have. He would have held her for a long, long time, inhaling the sweet scent of her skin, and then he would have stared down into her haunting eyes for hours.

The feel of her silken skin still made his fingertips prickle; the fullness of her lips still burned in his memory. She lay all the way upstairs and yet, even with distance between them, he knew exactly what she smelled like, exactly how her body felt pressed against his.

And her hair. Oh, her hair! Yes indeed, it was soft, spilling over his arm in the carriage the night he'd pulled her from the mauling crowd, last night when he'd drawn her so close, and then today . . .

What had he been thinking when he'd approached to touch her braid only a short time ago? That he hadn't wanted to, because he shouldn't be having such a physical response to a patient. No, he shouldn't. Not to mention the fact that he still didn't quite trust her because she'd tricked him. Also, any relationship he began with her would be brief and have no future, since she clearly would be leaving with her company when it departed St. Louis.

His emotions were becoming too involved, far too involved. He couldn't believe the relief that had swept through him when he'd returned home this evening, mounted the staircase, approached her bedroom door and heard her and Maggie's voices. She was still here, he'd thought. She hadn't left with her manager. The relief had stemmed from more than mere concern for a patient; he had been relieved because he'd gone the entire day wanting to hear her voice again, really wanting to feel her hair again, no matter what he told himself. He wanted to smell her skin, look into her beautiful brown eyes, and be near her. He hadn't been able to resist drawing closer than was necessary to touch her braid. Neither had he been able to resist meeting her gaze when he knew he shouldn't.

Sweet Mary, he was falling in love with an actress—when what he really wanted was a proper, decent woman. One who wouldn't enjoy tricking him. One who was genuine and didn't pretend to be something she wasn't.

She was so damn good with Maggie. If she was putting on an act for his daughter, she was doing a mighty fine job of it, a barrel of a job, as his father would've said. And if she was putting on an act for Maggie, he'd consider that the most cruel behavior in the world. His daughter adored the actress.

And Josephine Gavin adored Maggie. It wasn't an act. It couldn't be.

The more Thomas considered the matter as he watched Maggie dig into her food in an attempt to finish and get back upstairs, no doubt, the more he thought Josephine Gavin's affection for Maggie just couldn't be an act. Maggie's role in helping to nurse the actress had been what had put color back in Josephine Gavin's face. Maggie made the woman smile and laugh. Thomas also remembered Miss Gavin's protective behavior with Maggie this morning when he and that Neville creature were having words across the bed. Josephine had told Maggie to take her breakfast tray downstairs—a clear attempt to remove the child from the middle of two hostile people.

So her interaction with and love for Maggie were not contrived. But what about her response to him?

Why would she need to act where he was concerned? She wouldn't, unless she was a woman who enjoyed toying with men's emotions and groins, then leaving them like lapping dogs.

He recalled the comments he'd overheard from those men in the gaming house—that she'd gotten her heart broken down in New Orleans by someone who thought that because she was an actress, she wasn't good enough for him, and he recalled her own comments about the man after he'd given her the laudanum and she'd bared some of her soul. She'd been hurt, deeply hurt.

Was that it, then? Did she want to capture the interest of a socially prominent man, then hurt him the way she'd been hurt?

Crazy thoughts reeled around in his head. So much uncertainty. He needed to not worry about it. He needed to concentrate on getting her well and out of here before he totally lost his head and heart. He thought he would feel much better once Josephine Gavin and her troupe left St. Louis.

"Slow down, Maggie me girl," he advised, watching his daughter take another bite of bread—when she still had two in her mouth that she'd not swallowed. She had nearly finished her meal, while he'd eaten only half of his.

"Dr. Schuster came by the office this afternoon," he said. "He told me to tell you he said hello."

"Hello," she responded. "If he's still in St. Louis, why hasn't he come back to see me? Is he angry that I lied and lied? Does he never want to see me again?"

Thomas leaned over to tap his daughter's arm. "Now, Maggie, you know how he loves you. People get angry all the time, ev'ryday, but they still see each other an' stay friendly. I remember how angry you were that I wouldn't take you to the theater." He raised an arm and twirled his hand to illustrate his point. "Smoke comin' right out of yer ears an' fillin' the room."

She giggled. "Papa, that's not so!"

"Oh, but it is, me darlin' Maggie. Mrs. O'Brien came runnin' back into the study after you blazed off, wonderin' if the room was on fire. She came with a bucket o' water, ready to toss it at the flames. I said, oh, Mrs. O'Brien, it's smoke from Maggie's ears, 'tis all. But, Maggie, she might could use the water. Careful there, lest you burn yerself!''

Still smiling, Maggie plopped her elbow on the table, her chin in her cupped palm, and fixed her sweet gaze on him. "I love you, Papa. You're so funny sometimes. I really don't need another mother, only you. But if you've just got to pick one for me, I'd rather have Miss Gavin than Miss Blanche. You would, too. You liked touching her braid."

Thomas had just lifted his water glass and taken a drink. He coughed, putting a hand over his mouth to keep the water from spraying out. Precocious, that's what the child was. Far too precocious. She'd rather have . . . Well, he'd never asked her opinion. Maybe he should have.

Maggie gasped suddenly, her arm plopping down on the table, and she sat straight up in her chair. "Katie Farren! Katie Farren and her mother and baby brother just passed the window!"

She was off and running from the dining room before Thomas had a chance to even think about putting an arm out to slow her down a bit. He heard her little shoes clipping up the hall and then he heard squeals of delight as the two girls apparently found each other. Someone—Mrs. Reardon, perhaps—must have just let Katie and her mother and brother in.

Thomas rose from his place at the table and went to join Maggie and her friends in the entryway.

"Charlie's walkin', I hear," he said, approaching. He dipped his head to the bright-eyed Mrs. Farren, who held her baby son on one hip. Blond curls spilled from beneath the rim of her rose-colored bonnet, which was tied beneath her chin. She wore a light cape, Thomas noted, and he stepped forth to lift the wrap from her shoulders.

"Take Katie Farren's, too, Papa!" Maggie chimed as he placed the cape over Mrs. Reardon's outstretched forearm. "You know it's the gentlemanly thing to do." She and her pretty blond friend shared another giggle as Thomas playfully squinted one eye at his daughter.

"Katie Farren's come to see Miss Gavin, Papa! Me, too, of

course. She's come to see me, too! I gave the gardener's boy a few pennies to deliver her a message, and now here she is!''

"Why don't you call me Katie?" little Miss Farren asked Maggie, sounding altogether too grown up.

Maggie plopped her hands on her hips. "Because. Katie Farren sounds like a song if I keep saying it over 'n' over. I really could sing it. That's what I'll do, I'll think of a tune to go with it and I'll sing your name every time I see you!''

Mrs. Farren laughed. So did Charlie, as if he knew what the girls were saying. He waved a chubby arm and babbled.

"Oh, what a sight those teeth are, Master Charles," Thomas teased the boy, hunching a bit to bring his face into line with the baby's. To his surprise, Charlie shot a hand out and grabbed the end of his nose, squeezing hard.

"Oh, Charlie!" Mrs. Farren objected. "Let go now. Let go of the doctor's nose.'' She tried twisting away, thinking her son would let go if she did. He held fast, emitting a shrill sound of delight.

The girls erupted into giggles again, but harder this time. By the time Thomas pried the baby's hand from his nose, gently so as not to hurt the tiny fingers, Maggie was holding her stomach and laughing so hard Thomas wondered how she was still standing.

"Sorry, Dr. Murphy," Katie said, "but it *is* funny!''

"Until someone grabs yer unfortunate nose," he said, scowling playfully, reaching out to tweak hers. She jerked back, laughing more. "So you've come to see the famous actress, have you?''

The girl glanced at her mother, as if they'd already had a discussion and an understanding about the matter, then back at him. "Yes, sir, Dr. Murphy! If she can be seen, that is. Maggie says she's been real sick, and I know you're her doctor and that she probably needs her rest. . . .''

"I told Katie it would all depend on what you said," Mrs. Farren told him as she hoisted the boy up a little higher on her hip. "That if Miss Gavin was resting and you felt she should not have company, we'd be off and I'd have no pouting about it, either. None at all.''

Thomas placed his arm around Katie's shoulders, drawing

her closer to him. "Well, now, Maggie'n I, we left Miss Gavin only a bit ago. She was just about to have supper, then we planned to visit a little more. Maggie's been helpin' me to nurse her—an' what a fine nurse me daughter is. All she's got to do is smile at Miss Gavin the right way, an' color blooms all over the woman's face. I believe our Maggie's found a friend for life."

"Maybe even another mother!" Maggie announced, skipping off up the hall, her curls and flounced skirt bouncing. "Come on, Katie Farren. I'll take you to see her."

Thomas blushed to his roots, feeling Mrs. Farren's surprised gaze on him. "Really, Dr. Murphy? Another mother? She means Miss Gavin, I assume."

"Oh, my Maggie," he said. "She gets a notion in her head, an' there's no stoppin' her. But I'll be havin' a talk with her about this one."

"Oh, my Papa," Maggie mimicked, stopping at the staircase and turning back for just a moment to give him a mischievous look from the corner of her eye. "He gets a notion in *his* head, and there's no stopping *him*. She's an actress, so he doesn't think very good of her. But she *is* good. She loves me and I love her, and that's the truth. That's what should matter. I don't want a mother who doesn't love me, who only wants my papa."

"Maggie," Thomas said sternly. "We won't be airin'—"

"You may boot me out of your home for saying so, Dr. Murphy," Mrs. Farren said, smiling a bit, stepping around him and heading for the staircase. "But I feel Maggie's right—about the actress and about what should matter."

Thomas stood stunned for a few seconds, until Katie gave his arm a jerk, urging him forward. "You're her doctor, and Maggie says you've got to be there in case we tire her," she said. "You've always got to be there."

He went, but grumbling all the way. "Maggie's got a lot to say, it seems," he muttered. "Twists me around her fingers, she does, the sprite. Knows how to get what she wants out of me. Knows how to use her eyes an' even lift her shoulder the right way. Knows just what sort of look to put on her sweet, ever-lovin' face. . . ."

He grumbled all the way upstairs, with Mrs. Farren occasionally glancing over her shoulder at him, a hand to her mouth in an attempt to hide her smile, and with Katie tugging on his hand, leading him up to who knew what fate. Leading him to Josephine Gavin. He wondered what Maggie had put in that note to Katie. He wondered if the three of them—Maggie, Katie, and Mrs. Farren—had hatched some conspiracy. No, he didn't have to wonder. They had.

They entered the room, and there was Mrs. O'Brien, seated by the bed, conversing pleasantly with Miss Gavin. What the devil had gotten into Mrs. O'Brien of late? he wondered. He'd expected her to be put out that the woman had lied not only to him, but also to her. Instead she'd been nothing but friendly with the actress since he'd brought her here.

They were all in on it, he thought, retreating to the fireplace while they gathered around the bed—Maggie, Katie, Mrs. Farren with Charlie on her hip, and Mrs. O'Brien. A big smile on her face, Mrs. Reardon breezed into the room, minus Mrs. Farren's cape. She joined the group near the bed, and all the giggling, talking, and commotion became too much for Thomas.

"I trust you'll send them all away in no more than half an hour, Miss Gavin," he said loudly. When no one turned his way, he cleared his throat and repeated what he'd just said.

The group quieted. "Of course, Dr. Murphy," the actress responded.

He jerked a nod. "I have notes downstairs to look over."

"But you can't think of leaving," Katie objected. "You've got to—"

"I can an' I will," he snapped, passing a stern look over the entire group. "And *no* plotting. None."

"Dr. Murphy, why would we be plotting?" Mrs. Farren asked, trying to look innocent.

He furrowed his brows, then hurried toward the door, escaping them all. He shouldn't leave them. He should stay and make sure they didn't scheme more. But he was annoyed and wanted to be alone. He had no patience for their matchmaking.

"Why is he in such a foul mood?" he heard Miss Gavin ask, just as he stepped back out into the hall.

"Oh, it's nothing, really," Mrs. Farren said. "Katie and I and Charlie want to welcome you to St. Louis. The girls adore you so. . . . I was thinking that when you're recovered completely, we could take them for an outing at Chouteau's Pond. We could picnic and turn a rope for them. You're welcome at our home anytime, too. In fact, I've a supper party planned soon. . . ."

Welcoming her, were they? Thomas thought to himself. And Mrs. Farren more or less issuing her an invitation to a supper that would surely be attended by St. Louis's finest citizens, including the mayor himself. The woman was bold— and she was forgetting the fact that Miss Gavin was an actress and wouldn't be well received by many in the socially prominent crowd. He'd already responded positively to the invitation he'd received, and he'd be escorting Constance. The thought of showing up at the Farrens' home and spending the evening watching Josephine Gavin's character be shredded by others was a thought that unnerved him. He shouldn't care, but he did, and that fact alone annoyed him more than all the plotting and conniving by the group of females.

But it wasn't just the women. He wouldn't have found himself in the uncomfortable position of having to care for the actress day after day if Alan hadn't done his share of plotting—after talking to Maggie and Mrs. O'Brien. Who the devil did everyone think they were, meddling in his life and with his emotions? Today at the office Alan had even asked subtle questions about Miss Gavin and how things were progressing.

Damn them all, he thought sourly. He could get in a mighty foul mood sometimes, and this seemed to be one of those times.

He settled in his study, a pile of notes from the college on the desk before him. He glanced through them, not really reading, his mind still stewing over all the mischief he was sure was going on upstairs. Was Miss Gavin in on it? Was she plotting with them? Only her plan might be to reel him in like a fish and then let him go, injured. Surely they didn't realize that.

He heard them all shuffle out after a bit, Katie and her mother and brother, with Mrs. O'Brien, Mrs. Reardon, and

Maggie saying good-bye to them out in the hall. He knew he needed to change the bandage on his patient's head—he should have done it this morning—and yet he really didn't want to.

This was ridiculous. He should hire another doctor. He wasn't being much of one himself, and he half thought that he'd been manipulated into caring for Miss Gavin by his darling daughter, whose touching prayer and belief in him had seemed sincere at the time. Had it been really? But Maggie couldn't have known that he was overhearing. She hadn't seen him at the door; she hadn't seen him come upstairs that night.

Maggie had gone on to bed because she was tired, Mrs. O'Brien told Thomas when he went upstairs. He was hoping his daughter would have gone up to visit with the actress for a bit longer so he wouldn't find himself alone with her. But then, he'd said half an hour. He opened his mouth and started to ask Mrs. O'Brien to assist him in changing Miss Gavin's bandage, but she yawned and said something about turning in early tonight herself. He asked where Mrs. Reardon was, and was told that her boy, Willie, had a stomachache and that she was seeing to him. Then Mrs. O'Brien wandered off.

It's definitely a conspiracy, Thomas decided, stewing more. Blast them all! He'd decide for himself who to match himself up with, and it would make no difference that they all concocted reasons to make themselves absent so he might be caught alone with Josephine Gavin. It would make no difference at all.

Medical bag and bandages in hand, Thomas knocked lightly on Miss Gavin's partially opened bedroom door. Her voice came softly, bidding him to enter. He did, almost wishing he didn't have to.

He found her still sitting up, a book positioned on her lap. She was not very far into it—only a few pages had been turned.

"I should've changed yer bandage this mornin'," he said, approaching the bed. "I'll do it now, then leave you to yer readin'." He placed his bag on the table near the bed, rolled up his shirtsleeves—he had left his waistcoat down in the study—and moved to the washstand, which stood against the eastern wall.

"You're too critical of yourself, Dr. Murphy," she said, watching him. "You're a busy man. I'm certain that having me here has been a distraction, one you've hardly needed."

Thomas lifted the towel from the bar on the washstand and began drying his hands on it as he walked toward the bed. He leaned over the bed slightly, untucked a corner of the bandage and began unwinding it.

"Did Dr. Schuster tell you we had to clip some of yer hair before the surgery?"

"No," she said, keeping her eyes on her book. Her lashes were beautiful, splaying softly on her upper cheeks. "But I rather thought you did. How could you not? You had to be able to get to the wound."

"The top layer of hair'll cover the place."

"I'm hardly vain, Dr. Murphy. If I have to make a choice between my looks or my health, I'll take my health."

He had the entire bandage unwound now and he tossed it on the table near his bag. Now to have a look at the wound to see how it was healing . . .

She flinched when he lifted a section of her hair and pushed it back, trying to ignore the soft feel of it.

"That hurts?" he asked.

"No." She laughed a little. "I'm protective of my head right now, I suppose."

"Do you trust me?" he queried, surveying the fairly clean wound.

"You're my doctor . . . yes," she answered without hesitation.

Thomas withdrew from the bed to go wet a corner of the drying cloth in the basin. When he returned, she glanced at him briefly, then returned her gaze to the book.

"*Last of the Mohicans,*" she commented as he began dabbing dried blood from the wound and from her hair.

"Ah. Cooper."

"Mrs. O'Brien brought it to me. We began talking about how much we liked novels, and she asked me if I'd read it. I have; I've read all of the *Leatherstocking Tales,* but this was my favorite.''

''Mine, too,'' he said, and Mrs. O'Brien damn well knew it because *they'd* discussed the series of novels, too.

''It's very romantic. I suppose that's why I like it. Mrs. O'Brien thought I might become bored whenever Margaret's not about.''

He would wager that wasn't the only thing Mrs. O'Brien had thought when she'd brought the actress the book. She'd probably expected him to strike up a conversation with Miss Gavin about the novel.

''Miss Gavin, I'm thinkin' I need to be direct about somethin','' he ventured, wondering if she would act surprised. ''There's schemin' an' plottin' goin' on against me in my own home, under my own roof, an' now probably in the Farren household, too. Maggie, Katie, Mrs. Reardon, Mrs. O'Brien . . . the mess of them—Mrs. Farren herself, even— have it in their heads to make a match of us.''

''I know.''

He stopped dabbing and studied her. ''You know?''

''It's very apparent, Dr. Murphy. The way Margaret insisted that you should touch my braid this morning, a conversation I had with Mrs. O'Brien earlier this evening, Katie's insistence that you stay in the room while everyone visited. Margaret told me that she was going to bed early, but that you would surely look in on me before turning in yourself to make sure everyone's visit hadn't tired me too much.''

Thomas grunted his disapproval. That Maggie . . . What was he ever going to do with the girl? She never turned in early. She was always up to something, some sort of mischief.

Josephine Gavin's honesty about recognizing the scheme put a prickle of doubt in his mind that she was involved in it.

''Look at me,'' he said suddenly, and she glanced up, a question in her eyes. He studied them, then went back to dabbing.

''Is something else wrong?'' she queried. ''Something besides the place on my head? Something with my eyes?''

''Dear lady, there's nothin' wrong with yer eyes.'' His voice was thick suddenly. No, nothing was wrong with her eyes.

They were beautiful. "I can usually tell if someone's lyin' by lookin' into their eyes."

She jerked away from his touch, fastening a glare on him. "I lied to you several times the first night I met you, but I've not lied to you since. That insinuation . . . the suspicion is inappropriate."

He went back to cleaning her wound. "I realize you've apologized for yer behavior that evenin'. I was the victim of a cruel joke. How can I not distrust—"

"Feeling sorry for yourself, Dr. Murphy?" she asked sharply. "My conscience drove me to apologize. But I've done some thinking since. Consider my motivation as I explained it to you. You were the victim of a cruel joke, you say. I was the victim of misconception who felt compelled to play the joke. Who is at fault, really? And now . . . now you insinuate that I've lied to you again."

"Ye're an actress, Miss Gavin. Perhaps you don't think of it as lyin'."

She jerked away again. "You flatter yourself, Dr. Murphy—and far too much. You think I'm in on the plotting? If I were lying about knowing what Maggie and her friends and the housekeeper and nursemaid were up to, that would mean I wanted their efforts at creating a liaison between us to work. I do not. I have no desire to try to snare the heart ever again of any man who thinks he's too good for me. I'll grow old in a cottage with cats and plants first. I prefer them!" Obviously riled, she slammed the book shut with her last word and crossed her arms, having no problem looking at him now.

They sat staring stubbornly at each other for a good minute. Thomas grumbled inside. Damn if he would apologize! He was entitled to his suspicions, considering the way he'd first been introduced to the woman.

"Finish the bandage, Dr. Murphy," she said coolly, "then be on your way."

Finish the . . . ? *Be on his way?* She was forgetting whose home this was! He'd never had a woman talk to him so, order him to do something, take such a . . . such a tone of voice with him! He remembered admiring her spunkiness that first evening, her quick thinking, that there was nothing timid about her. But she wasn't that woman. She wasn't Julia Goddard, the woman who had charmed him in his sitting room, the woman whose cloak he still had in his study. Constance would certainly never take such a tone with him.

"You'll be paid well for your services," Miss Gavin said, as if her previous words hadn't been enough. "How well you must have known *that* when you decided to save me from those people—I'm a valuable asset to my company. And I'll be gone from your home as soon as you give the word."

Thomas drew back, feeling as though he'd been slapped. "Dear lady, are you implyin' that that's why I snatched you from that pawin' crowd? I would have done the same for anyone—I'm a doctor!"

She tipped her head, her eyes shimmering fiercely. "I've insulted you, I see. I've insulted your sense of integrity, your sense of professionalism. I've insulted your pride and I've dirtied the image of all that I'm sure you've worked so hard to be. Dr. Murphy, is that not what your assumptions do to me?" She asked the last slowly, and in a lighter tone, lifting her chin a little as she did.

The woman infuriated him. He was stunned, and very much at a loss for what to say back, how to respond. "Ye're not the woman I met that evenin'. Ye're not Julia Goddard!"

She waved her hand. "A name Margaret created. But, oh, sir, I do beg your royal pardon . . . my grandmother *always* told me that feet need to breathe."

He blinked, momentarily confused. Then he remembered that feet needing to breathe was what she'd told Maggie that evening, the reason she'd given for them removing their shoes and stockings.

Damn, if he didn't admire her. She incensed him with her boldness, sharp words, and tone of voice, and yet her forthright nature was one of the things that attracted him to her. He took the clean bandage from the table, unrolled it, and began wrapping it around her head. "A few more days an' you won't be needin' to wear this anymore," he said.

"And a few more days after that, I hope I can leave—at your recommendation, of course," she responded, her voice much lower and a little more civil.

Nodding, he wondered for the first time if he would miss her when she was gone, if he would miss watching her interact with Maggie and miss hearing her voice as he had today. She'd been here only three days and she'd not left this room. But somehow, in those three days, the house had become different. Mrs. O'Brien and Mrs. Reardon were both more pleasant, Maggie wasn't always running off or terrorizing the staff; overall, he thought everyone was more pleasant, whistling or humming as they worked.

"Yer wound's healin' good," Thomas said, tucking the end of the bandage under the whole of it. "Three or four more days an' then I'll be satisfied, if I get a promise from you that you won't let that manager of yers drive you into an early grave."

She opened her book again, not responding, treating him as if he'd already gone.

He gathered his medical bag and the dirty bandage. "Good night, Miss Gavin."

He left the room feeling rather meek and thinking she'd made her point: that he should no more make the assumption that she was a woman of the night just because she was an actress than she should assume he'd rescued her because he'd known he'd be paid well. She was devoted to her profession, he was devoted to his, and they each had their share of pride and integrity that should be respected.

Ten

A SOUND LIKE a child crying jolted Josie from a deep sleep. She sat straight up in bed, then thinking it might be Margaret, she tossed back the sheet and coverlet, scrambled off of the bed, and fairly flew from the room.

Out in the hall where one lamp in a wall sconce still burned, she paused, but only momentarily. She had no idea which room belonged to Margaret, but as soon as she heard the girl cry again, she raced off in the direction of the sound, lifting her shift off the floor slightly to avoid tripping over it. Her heart seemed to be pounding in her head. She knew she shouldn't be racing around like this, that she shouldn't even be out of bed. But something was wrong with Margaret and she felt frantic with the need to protect the girl.

She reached for the knob on a door behind which she heard Margaret crying, turned it, and pushed the door open.

Near darkness greeted her. The bed and other furnishings were shadows in the night. The curtains had been drawn most of the way, letting in only a sliver of moonlight. Margaret's white shift illuminated her as she sat rubbing her eyes and crying in the middle of the bed. Josie heard other people racing up the hall, two sets of feet scrambling along, but before anyone else could even reach the door, she was on the bed, gathering Margaret close to her breast and smoothing the girl's tousled hair.

"No light," Margaret cried. "No light! Mrs. O'Brien or Papa always leave a lamp burning and the door open part of the way. The door was shut!"

"Sh. It's all right now, Margaret, I promise," Josie soothed, rocking slightly. "I'll light a lamp and leave the door open. You'll be all right, I promise. I'm here."

She felt Margaret's little arms slide around her and she rested her chin on the girl's head and closed her eyes momentarily. Her heart was still beating so fast, and she was just beginning to catch her breath. That feeling . . . that awful, frantic feeling of hearing Margaret crying and not being able to get to her fast enough . . . it must be what a mother felt when she thought something was wrong with her child. A horrible feeling.

"Miss Margaret," Mrs. O'Brien said from nearby. "There's nothing in the darkness, girl. We've talked about that before."

"Maggie," Dr. Murphy said softly, just as Josie felt someone sit on the bed.

"I was so scared! I don't wanna play the game that much, Mrs. O'Brien. I don't want to!"

"Miss Margaret, whatever are you talking about?" the nursemaid asked.

"Josephine—she shouldn't be out of bed, she's so sick, but she loves me. And Papa, he hates to hear me cry. You knew they'd come running!"

All eyes were on Mrs. O'Brien now as she stood in her nightcap and shift. She put a hand to her throat and stepped back in disbelief. "You're saying I extinguished the lamp and closed the door? Miss Margaret, I know how you're afraid of the dark and do not like to have your door closed. I would do no such thing."

"That'll be all, Mrs. O'Brien," Thomas Murphy said gruffly.

The woman stared at him. "Dr. Murphy, I did not—"

"That'll be all."

Mrs. O'Brien turned and walked meekly from the room, her shoulders slumped.

"There now, Maggie girl," Dr. Murphy said, stroking his daughter's back. "We're here now, me'n Miss Gavin. I'll light the lamp while she's holdin' you, then we'll tuck you back under the sheet, an' off you'll go to sleep again in no time at all. You'll be dreamin' sweet dreams.''

He left the bed while Josie continued to cradle Margaret to her and rock. Within seconds, light rose from one corner of the room where a table sat, then an orange-red glow spread, comforting Margaret even more. Josie began humming a tune she'd known for years, a slow, soothing song. Dr. Murphy returned to sit on the edge of the bed.

''No, no—sing, Josephine,'' Margaret pleaded, and Josie did just that.

''There's a long, nar–row trail that's a–winding . . . to a cabin that stands all alone . . . in the foothills of my moun-tains . . . just a place that I long to call home. Where the bright moon is shin–ing . . . back where sor–rows and cares are un-known. I know there are loved ones still wait–ing . . . in that vine-cover'd cabin call'd home. . . .''

Margaret began to relax, nestled against her, her head pressed between her breasts. Even her arms relaxed, dropping down to Josie's hips. Josie launched into the next verse of the song, closing her eyes and singing softly from the soul . . . about whippoorwills calling from the wildwood, the echo of love's sweet refrain, and a mother's prayer for her boy to come home again. When she'd sung all three verses of that song, she went right into another tune: *''I've found the girl of my golden dreams . . . her love is worth all that I've lost. She was waiting for me at the end of the trail, and to me she's worth more than the cost. . . .''*

Josie heard Dr. Murphy inhale sharply, and she glanced at him, still singing. He had apparently thrown on a shirt and trousers upon hearing Margaret cry. His shirt was not tucked in, and it lacked cuff links, a collar, and a cravat. His hair was a little tousled, but then it usually was, so that was not sur-prising. She found him watching her with the same depth of intensity and admiration with which he'd gazed upon her that night in the sitting room, only this time there was more to the look. She was singing his song, or so his eyes said, singing words he found meaningful.

''Her lips, her eyes are sweet–ness, her voice like a cool

sum–mer breeze. The girl of my dreams is a vision . . . worth more . . . than any–thing. . . ."

His eyes sparkled with emotion as he sat frozen to the spot, watching her cradle and sing to his daughter, seeming to relish her voice almost as much as Margaret did.

Presently Josie moved, drawing Margaret with her to the head of the bed. She laid the drowsy girl's head on the pillows there, then lay beside her and rubbed her back while still singing. Her head was beginning to pound a little; her left temple was beginning to throb. She had to go back to bed herself soon. Although . . . she could lie right here and sleep soundly, she thought.

"She's a restless one at night," Thomas Murphy said softly, as if reading her mind. "I wouldn't want her accidentally catchin' you in the head with a flyin' arm."

Josie smiled. "I must go back to bed, Margaret," she whispered near the child's ear. "The lamp's on now, and you know your father and I will leave the door open. No more darkness."

"No more darkness," Margaret murmured, drifting. Josie pulled the sheet up over her shoulders and tucked it beneath her chin.

Josie left her like that, satisfied that she would fall asleep within moments. She heard Dr. Murphy follow her from the room. After their earlier words, she had nothing more to say to him. She wished to go back to bed and lie down.

"Miss Gavin," he said, catching up with her near her door. "I'm thinkin' I've a cloak downstairs that belongs to you. You left it in the kitchen the night Maggie led you here."

Josie almost laughed aloud. She turned on him. "The cloak, Dr. Murphy, belongs to Julia Goddard, the woman who lives in Alton—across the river. The woman who ferried over and wandered the city alone for hours. The woman you've separated from me in your mind." She turned, thinking to go into her room, lie down, and ease back into sleep.

"No," he said, stepping forward, barring her way into the room. "The cloak belongs to you . . . Josephine Gavin. Josie, or so I hear yer friends call you."

"I don't believe you're my friend," she retorted. She almost told him to get out of her way, but for some reason she held her tongue.

He was far too close, breathing a little faster than normal, gazing intensely down at her, his spicy scent ribboning around her. She unconsciously gathered a portion of her shift in her hands and lifted it to cover her breasts with an extra layer of material. She thought to lower her gaze from his, but when she did, it fell on his chest, on the open part of his shirt that dipped, revealing curly chest hairs that appeared dark in the dim light given off by one lamp.

"Exactly what . . ." She swallowed. "What made you decide that the cloak belonged to me?" Her heart was racing again, again partly from fear—why was he barring her way into the room?—and partly from excitement at having him so near, at being more aware of him as a man than she thought she'd ever been. She should tell him to move, and she should go into the room right now and shut the door against him.

"Yer grandmother tellin' you feet need to breathe," he murmured. "You . . . sittin' on the bed with Maggie, singin' to her the same way you sang to her downstairs that night. Even better. Comfortin' her so."

"I sang different songs that evening."

"Diff'rent, but the same. The same voice that's haunted me every night an' day since. I came downstairs after puttin' Maggie to bed that night, an' you were gone. *Gone.*" He dipped slightly, trying to look her in the eye, but Josie had fastened her gaze on the floor, and there it would remain. "Yer eyes, yer hair, yer lips, yer voice . . . you. I've seen an' heard it all since I met you that evenin'."

He boldly stroked a loose strand of hair near her ear, the light touch of the back of his fingertips on her face torturing her, tempting her. She couldn't possibly withdraw, his touch felt so good. His fingers slipped down to her neck, and their warmth felt so wonderful she wanted to let her head drop back as she enjoyed, as she relished. They paused on the throbbing pulse in her neck, then eased up to her chin, applying the slightest pressure to lift her face to his.

She should resist. She knew she should resist. One kiss, one touch of his tongue on hers, and she would be damned. She would melt.

"Josie," he whispered huskily as if trying out the name, coaxing her with his touch and voice. With his nearness. "Lass . . . as lovely as a wild Irish rose . . ." His fingers strayed to her lips, one running between them.

That was it. She could bear no more.

She tasted his fingers with her tongue, their saltiness, then raised her lashes and lifted her chin, offering her lips, forgetting her earlier anger, forgetting everything.

He took her lips sweetly, slowly, as if they were a delicacy to be savored. He traced them with his tongue, licked lightly at them, kissed first the top one, then the bottom one, then both corners of her mouth. He nipped at them, then licked again. . . . And finally, when Josie wondered dizzily how much more of the sweet torture she could endure before her legs gave way, he slipped his tongue between them and tasted her fully, gathering her close against his body.

He kissed her, gently and tenderly exploring her mouth with his tongue, and as he kissed her, time slipped away. Josie had no idea how long they stood tasting each other, her savoring him as much as he savored her. She wasn't really thinking anymore, she was feeling. She was responding. She was encouraging, arching her back, tipping her head more. Wanting . . .

He slipped his arm down to the back of her thighs, lifted her, and carried her into the room. The jolt brought her to her senses a little, enough that she realized how frightened she was, how very, very afraid she was of loving this man, of being hurt so badly again, of being rejected in the end, of walking away with nothing—no promise of marriage, just more shattered dreams.

But, oh, how she wanted him! How she wanted to feel his nakedness against hers, his lips pressed to her breasts! How she wanted him to whisper more endearments to her and slip inside her. How she wanted him to fill her with a warmth like no other, with his warmth. But then . . . she wouldn't want him to snatch it away.

She would give herself to him in a heartbeat, she knew that.

There would be no more coaxing, no asking, no seducing. She needed loving and she would give herself to him, then brave the hurt that surely would come.

She withdrew her lips from his as he carried her across the room. She buried her face in his shirt, unable to help the tears that slipped from her eyes or the tremble that claimed her body.

He laid her gently on the bed, then he sat on the edge and gazed down at her. He brought a hand up to her face, and his fingers brushed a tear from her temple. But despite the tenderness that he showed, she knew he might have her in a little while, then be done with her. As Frank had. Which was why she had built a wall around her heart. A wall he had nearly completely dismantled.

"Ye're afraid of me, Josie," he said, his voice low and thick. "Maybe as afraid of me as I am of you. You could make me forget every oath I ever took, every vow I've made. Moments like these, you could make me tell myself they don't matter. You make me realize how human I am."

He bent to kiss her again, so tenderly despite his last exclamation, then he inhaled deeply, withdrew, and pulled the sheet and coverlet over her. She wondered why. He was fighting the desire that could easily rage out of control between them. She was glad, and yet . . . she wanted him here beside her. She wanted to touch him more. She wanted him to touch her more.

"Sleep, Josie," he said. "Ye're not recovered yet, though ye're gettin' stronger. Knowing that, I wouldn't make love to you."

She didn't want him to go, but she knew him leaving was for the best. She didn't want to give herself to him in a few passionate moments, then wake in the morning, regretting her decision.

Margaret woke Josie with breakfast again the following morning, saying that her papa had gone off to the college already. Willie Reardon had been the one who'd snuffed her lamp and closed her door last evening. After Dr. Murphy had carefully questioned everyone in the household this morning, Willie finally admitted to it, saying that Maggie had told him that she was trying to find reasons to make sure her father and Miss Gavin spent a lot of time together. They'd surely both come running if they heard Maggie cry, or so Willie figured because Maggie had told him about her and Miss Gavin's friendship, and he'd already known how much her father loved her. To Josephine, Margaret admitted rather meekly to telling Willie she wanted to find reasons to make sure she and Papa spent a lot of time together.

"If a relationship is going to happen between your father and me, Margaret, it will happen because we want it to—not because a group of people force us together," Josephine scolded gently.

Margaret scowled but nodded.

Presently, after they shared the breakfast she'd brought, she took the tray back downstairs and went off to the schoolhouse.

Josie braved crossing the room to the washbasin, where she splashed cool water on her face, then unfastened the buttons on her shift and washed as best she could. She longed to take a bath in a tub of warm water, and she meant to ask Dr. Murphy soon if she could as long as Mrs. Reardon and Mrs. O'Brien stayed close by the entire time.

Eleven

JOSIE HAD JUST crawled back onto the bed and was thinking of reading more when Orson came to visit, along with Lauretta and Stephan—a pleasant surprise. Lauretta handed her a small bag of clothes and personal items.

"She's taken your role in the company's latest production and is doing quite well, drawing the crowds," Orson said proudly.

Bringing in the funds he badly needed, no doubt. Lauretta was all of eighteen years old, with clear blue eyes and brownish-black hair. There was a shy innocence about her until she took the stage, something Josie had noticed numerous times this past year as Lauretta studied with her.

Josie smiled at the girl now, as proud of her as Orson seemed to be. "Lauretta, that's wonderful! Come here and tell me more," she said, putting the bag aside and patting the bed.

"Well, I'm not you, Josie, that's for certain," Lauretta said. "The audience still lets me know that, too. But we all figured you would be out for some time, and the whole St. Louis trip would be for naught. Mr. Neville and Jefferson, they go to so much trouble, I—"

"Lauretta, I don't feel insulted or threatened. I'm proud of you," Josie assured her. "I'm relieved that you've stepped in and are such a success!"

Lauretta blushed more, if possible. Stephan, nineteen himself, blond and always starry-eyed whenever he gazed at Josephine, urged her toward the bed. Lauretta sat beside Josie and began telling her about the first night, how frightened she'd been, but that she remembered all that Josie had told her about forgetting that the audience was there. She'd taken a number of deep breaths . . . and walked out. She'd thrown herself into the various roles and had had so much fun, and when the applause came, it almost startled her. Josie laughed, squeezing the girl's clasped hands just as Orson began coughing.

He'd had the cough for some time, perhaps for months now, but Josie had never seen him produce a handkerchief, lift it to his mouth, and cough something into it. She knew his pride, so at first, as Lauretta launched into a tale about her second performance in what were usually Josie's roles, Josie thought about not saying anything, not asking questions. Then coughs racked Orson, he stumbled slightly, grabbing hold of a bedpost to steady himself, and she saw blood on the handkerchief and noticed that a thin film of perspiration covered his face. The room was cool—her feet had been cold before she had pulled the sheet and coverlet up to her waist.

"Stephan," Josie whispered loudly, grabbing the coverlet. "Help him sit!"

Stephan hurried over, obviously planning to do exactly as she had requested, but Orson, still coughing, batted his hands away.

"For the love of God, Orson, let him help you!" Josie cried. "Stop being so stubborn."

He staggered against the bed, still refusing Stephan's assistance, coughing still. His eyelids fluttered, and Josie gasped, seeing blood on his lips just before he fell over onto the foot of the bed.

She couldn't scramble his way fast enough. Her heart stopped beating, it seemed, as she lifted his head, placed it on her lap, and held her hand a few inches from his mouth to see if he was still breathing. His face and lips were gray suddenly, his skin clammy and cool. Her heart began thumping with fear. Yes, he was breathing, but his breath was shallow, uneven, and he had lost consciousness.

"Find the housekeeper or Mrs. O'Brien—quick! Find someone to send for Dr. Murphy. Hurry!"

Stephan raced from the room. Josie pulled Orson completely onto the bed, then she used the hem of her shift to wipe the perspiration from his face and the blood from his lips. Orson, who had believed in her and taken her under his wing when she was so alone after her mother's and brother's deaths. She would have survived—she was a survivor at heart—but Orson had helped her find a better life. He had nurtured her, groomed her, helped her become the poised actress she was today. And there were times when Orson had even been a friend. After Frank had crushed her heart, she had knelt beside Orson, placed her head on his knee, and cried for hours.

She cradled his head as Lauretta stood near the bed watching in horror, her hands over her mouth. Mrs. O'Brien came, worry wrinkling her brow. She hurried over to the washstand. Josie heard the sound of water splashing. A moment later, the nursemaid was at the bedside, handing Josie a wet cloth.

Josie softly thanked her. "Perhaps you could take Miss Rimmel downstairs and fix her some tea," she suggested, wanting to spare Lauretta.

"He's been sick for some time," the girl whispered hoarsely. "Coughing a lot. Blood lately, Stephan says. But never this bad. Never like this! Is he dying, Josie? Is he? What'll we do without Mr. Neville?"

"I don't know, Lauretta. Go downstairs with Mrs. O'Brien. She'll fix you a cup of tea. We'll wait for Dr. Murphy to come. Mrs. O'Brien, someone sent for him?"

"Mrs. Reardon sent the gardener, who was clearing paths out back. He and the other gentleman who came with your guests tore off on horses toward the college, so Dr. Murphy is sure to be here soon."

Josie managed another thank-you, though how she didn't know. For Orson's and even for Lauretta's sake, she was forcing herself to keep her head, not cry with fear the way she wanted to, though she felt petrified inside. Life without Orson . . . what would that be like? Oh, there had been times when she had wondered. Times when he had driven her and driven her, when she had rehearsed for hours upon hours. She had been so angry with him the night she had met Maggie, when he had arranged that supper.

She waited until Mrs. O'Brien had placed her arm around Lauretta's shoulders and led the shocked girl from the room. Then Josie bent over Orson and tenderly kissed his forehead. She stroked his hair and waited.

She didn't know how much time passed before Dr. Murphy entered the room, medical bag in hand, as he had so many times now to care for her.

"I asked the others to wait downstairs," he said, meeting her gaze briefly. There must have been a plea in hers. He shook his head as he stepped around the foot of the bed. "I'll do what I can, you know that, Josie. Yer friend Stephan told me what happened, that Mr. Neville's been coughin' up blood for some time now." He placed his bag on the bed, sat, and began opening it.

"Not that I knew! He's had this cough for months. He's thinned over the last year and he's looked almost ashen at times. But I never knew him to look . . . to look gray and to cough up blood."

"Consumption," Dr. Murphy said. "'Tis what it sounds like. 'Tis what it looks like. Tuberculosis. Some people live with it for years. Some people it claims sooner than others."

She stared at him, feeling her eyes burn. She blinked hard. "You're—you're saying he's dying?"

He withdrew the parts of his stethoscope. He glanced up at her, giving her a long look, and nodded slowly. "But it could drag on. I'll not lie to you."

She sucked in a sharp breath, determined to be brave, knowing Stephan and Lauretta waited downstairs. "We'll make him comfortable. We'll take him back to the hotel and make him comfortable. I'll stay by his side, the way he's stayed by mine these past five years. I'll . . . I'll wipe his brow and give him food and water. I'll . . ."

"Josie, you'll kill yourself. Do you think that's what he'd want?" Thomas Murphy asked gruffly, putting the stethoscope together with trembling hands.

"I have to be with him!" she snapped. "I have to be. I won't let him die without me beside him."

"He can stay here. We'll move you to a room down the hall."

He quieted, finishing his task. Then he turned Orson from his side onto his back, pulled his shirt from his trousers and up over his stomach and chest, and placed the bell of the stethoscope on him. As he listened, Josie watched his expression.

He withdrew, grim-faced, and began taking the stethoscope apart. "He won't last the day unless there's a miracle."

Josie closed her eyes, fighting dizziness. This was horrible. It couldn't be. No. . . .

"We'll make him comfortable, then," she said again. "Now. He deserves that. To die with dignity. Help me." She slipped her arms under Orson's, meaning to pull him up to the pillows.

Thomas stopped her by placing a hand on her forearm. "Let me. Don't forget yer own health."

She let him take over, and he soon had Orson's head resting on the pillows.

Dr. Murphy went downstairs for a time, then came back up. He moved one of the wing chairs from the fireplace to the bedside and told Josie that if she had to be up, he'd prefer that she make herself comfortable in the chair. Josie did, trying to keep her eyes on Orson, though she rested her head against one of the wings. Her head hurt a little, but she didn't care. Orson was dying, and his comfort was all that mattered at the moment, for the day.

She drifted at times, aware of Dr. Murphy moving around the room, his black waistcoat now discarded, his shirtsleeves rolled up as he crushed and mixed something using a pestle and mortar he had produced. He bent over Orson, lifted his head, and gave him something. Moments later, he listened to his heart again. Then he wiped his patient's brow and face with the cloth. Though Josie didn't mean to, she dozed.

Thomas was glad to see her fall asleep. He hoped her manager's illness and almost certain impending death wouldn't take her spirit, her will to live. He'd done everything he knew to do for the man, though he rubbed his forehead, wondering if there wasn't something more he could do . . . trying his damnedest to ignore Josie's obvious love for her manager. He remembered Alan saying there had been rumors about the two of them—the actress and her manager—but that other people in the company swore they had only a business relationship, nothing more. Still, the sight of Josie holding the man's head, tears in her eyes, tears of fear over the possibility of losing someone she loved, burned in Thomas's brain and made him doubt. A manager could be replaced. Someone she loved couldn't.

He'd gone downstairs earlier and informed Miss Rimmel and Stephan of his grave diagnosis, that he didn't expect Mr. Neville to last the day, his breathing and heartbeat were so poor. Stephan had decided that he should inform the rest of the company, and by now there were probably several dozen people downstairs awaiting word.

The man stirred on the bed, opening his eyes to mere slits. Thomas approached him, wondering if a miracle was indeed about to happen before his eyes.

"My Josie," the man said weakly, breathlessly. "She's falling in love with you. Do not hurt her. Don't . . ."

"I wouldn't," Thomas responded softly. "I won't."

Orson Neville closed his eyes. Some twenty minutes later, he expelled his last breath.

As much as Josie would have liked to have attended his funeral the next day, she did not, knowing her health might suffer from that much activity. Mr. Jefferson visited before the funeral, however, to give her a package on which Orson had written her name and left with him, and she made him promise to have the procession come up Washington Avenue so she could see it from her window.

As she stood with the curtain drawn back, watching the somber conveyances go by, she soaked an entire handkerchief. She felt gentle hands on her shoulders and she glanced back, finding that Dr. Murphy had entered the room and stepped up behind her. He urged her to lean back against him, then he produced a dry handkerchief for her.

He had given her room to grieve immediately following Orson's death, waking her with softly spoken words, then leaving the room for a time. After a while, people from the company had come through, one by one, to see Orson a final time. Then an undertaker had arrived and taken him away.

Thomas had been walking by the room and had seen her standing at the window, her shoulders trembling with the force of her grief. As much as he didn't want to care, he did. He wanted to hold her and comfort her. He told himself that it was because he was a compassionate person—he would hold and comfort anyone. But he knew that where Josephine Gavin was concerned, more than compassion drove him to walk into the room, approach her where she stood at the window, draw her gently back against him, and offer her another handkerchief.

He didn't understand her obvious love for a man who had been old enough to be her father, and he was maddeningly jealous of that love. Still, he hated seeing her experience such emotional pain. He could no more have walked away from the sight of her grieving at the window than she could have walked away from the sight of Maggie looking so frightened as she'd sat in the middle of her bed.

He held her as she cried, as she sobbed, sinking back against him. After a time, she turned and laid her head against his chest and wrapped her arms around him. They stood that way for the longest time, him simply holding her and stroking her hair.

Hours later, Josie sat with the package in her lap on the bed. It was no more than eleven by nine inches, several inches thick, wrapped in plain brown paper and secured with twine. She pulled one of the strings, and the bow fell apart. She opened the brown wrapping, listening to it crackle, and found a stack of papers. A manuscript. There was a cover page, on which was written: *Josephine Gavin: A Brief But Remarkable Life in the American Theater.*

She turned the page and began reading, more touched than

she would have had words to say if Orson had been standing before her. She read about how they'd met, how he'd perceived her—as a wildly talented, beautiful young girl needing guidance—how admirable he found her devotion to her mother and brother, how tragic it was when they died in the fire. *But I knew she was destined for greatness,* he had written, *and I knew then that her mother's and brother's dying were part of the Maker's plan for her. Life is a progression of events, one thing leading to another, sometimes a search for happiness. I, too, was part of the plan.*

Josie read for hours. Hours and hours and hours. Mrs. Reardon brought food that sat untouched. Dr. Murphy came, sat on the bed, and asked how she was. She glanced up briefly, gave him a sad smile, and said she was fine. Then she went back to reading. Mrs. O'Brien brought tea brewed from dried chamomile flowers, and Josie sipped that, all the while continuing to read the manuscript.

Orson pushed her because he knew she was capable of more . . . more! She could speak her lines with more meaning, she could throw her body into the role more. So many times after a trying performance, when he knew she was drained, he visited her room and sat beside her bed for a time, trying to make sure that he had not driven her too much. And when her heart was broken in New Orleans, part of his ached, too—for her, for the pain he knew she was enduring. He had helped to make her into a grand actress, thinking that was her destiny . . . and yet, was he sure anymore? He was not. He knew she was changing. He had grown to love her in his own way, even knowing that she thought of him as nothing more than a father, and he feared losing her someday to a man worthy of her, to another man who would value her life more than his own, who would cherish her. Frank was not that man, but there would be one someday. Until then, he would do what he could to protect her and guide her. Life would go its way; one had to realize that. A person would have frightening times, times during which he would fight fate itself for a person he loved. And yet, because of an affliction . . . a curse, he could not have loved her, not the way he truly wanted to. Not the way a woman with her passionate nature needed to be loved. And therefore he could not give her the children he knew she desired.

Josie sat with some pages on her lap and others scattered around her for a time as she glanced up, looking at nothing in particular, simply wondering what might have been wrong with Orson. She read the entire last paragraph again, then put the back of her hand to her mouth, realizing. The implication was there, anyway.

She had always seen Orson as a father. He, however, had viewed her in a more romantic light. He had loved her as a man loves a woman—and perhaps he had seen himself as her father, too, in those early days. But Orson had known he'd never be able to make love to her, and so he had never tried to make more of their relationship.

She read on.

She withdrew into herself during the years after New Orleans, and though Orson loved having her practically to himself, he knew she was not happy. They had words at times, sharp words. The company was not doing well financially, perhaps because poor business decisions had been made. He had placed her in a difficult position, knowing she cared about people and cared what they thought of her. She met a little girl one evening, a little girl and her father, a doctor, who both touched her heart in some extraordinary way, more than he had ever been able to. . . .

There was one more page after that one, but it was not a continuation of the story. It was a note from Orson to her: *Josephine, My tribute to a fine actress and woman. I cannot finish it; only you can. The title comes, however, because I do not feel you will remain onstage much longer, that your heart will not allow you to. I wish you the very best. O. Neville*

Josie held the manuscript and cried more, pouring out her grief. He had loved her so much, and in her own way she had loved him, too. His written words were the finest gift he had ever given her. Finer than the belongings she had accumulated over the years.

She cried herself to sleep.

Time passed. Days. Lauretta and Stephan visited, telling her that the performances had been canceled for a time. Mr. Jefferson came again, subtly asking when their prize actress would be able to return to the stage. Weeks ago, Orson had given her several plays to look at and consider. Then she'd become angry with him and hadn't glanced at them. She promised Mr. Jefferson that she would, and soon. Lauretta brought them to her, and she began reading them.

Dr. Murphy and Margaret came and went with food Josie only nibbled at. Mrs. O'Brien and Mrs. Reardon helped her downstairs one afternoon, where she bathed in a tub in a washroom just off the kitchen, sinking down into the warm, soothing water. Mrs. Farren visited an hour or so later, and when Josie greeted her, she asked if Josie would please call her Patricia. With that and a smile, she offered a gift—a shawl she had knitted herself and wanted to give her.

"One of my mother's friends made shawls for people," Josie said, half smiling. "I've done some stitching myself—some of my plainer gowns, when I have time."

"Have you?" Patricia asked, obviously delighted. "I meet with a group of friends weekly. We visit while stitching. I'm sure you'd be welcome."

Josie wondered. Patricia Farren was obviously from the upper crust, and the women in that gathering were more likely to disapprove of an actress's appearance in their sewing group. But Josie thanked Patricia anyway, saying she would consider it.

For the most part, Josie sat in a daze, it seemed, comforted at times only by Thomas Murphy's arms around her, by the strong sound of his heartbeat, and by Margaret's bubbly attempts to cheer her.

"When my mama died," Margaret ventured somberly one morning as her father sat in one of the fireplace chairs, "my heart hurt so bad I thought I'd die, too. But I didn't, 'cause Mama always talked about me growing up and having a little girl of my own and how proud she'd be. I decided I wanted to do that. I wanted to grow up and have a little girl of my own. Don't you want to do that, Josephine? Don't you wanna have a little girl of your own?"

Josie could not help a smile. With tears in her eyes, she

drew Margaret to her and whispered, "Yes, I certainly do." Dr. Murphy was watching them; Josie felt his gaze and turned the smile on him. He remained sober.

She was so grateful for his tender care, for the way he always seemed to know when she needed comforting, for his gentle way of opening his arms and allowing her to nestle against his chest. And yet, there was something so distant about him, something untouchable of late. He would comfort her—in fact, he seemed to be unable to help himself in that regard—but that was all. Sometimes she wished he would not even do that; she was falling in love again and she knew it. She craved knowing him better—the man deep inside, his thoughts and emotions, the things that had molded him into what he was today. And yet, she was afraid to know him better. She was afraid she would grow to love him.

For two nights in a row he sat on the bed with her, and she fell asleep just so, listening to his strong heartbeat, feeling his chest rise and fall, smelling the almost soapy but spicy clean scent of his shirt. She would be leaving his house soon, leaving his care. She knew that, too, and at times she almost couldn't bear the thought of having any distance between them, not even a few streets.

"Sorry I didn't come visit you last evening," Margaret told her the following morning. "We had supper with Constance and her parents. She's too quiet. She hardly ever talks. She tries to play with me, but she's not fun, not even to talk to, not like you, Josie. I don't want her to come and live here. I don't want her to be my mother. She's not mean or anything. She's just always afraid of messing her hair and smudging her dress. . . ." Sighing, Margaret plopped her elbow on her thigh and her chin in her palm. "She's not my friend, not like she thinks she is, and I don't want her to be my mother. She can't be."

Josie summoned a weak smile. "Are you being open where Constance is concerned? You seem to have your mind set on me being your mother, Maggie, and that may not be a possibility. I'll always be your friend, even when your father marries Constance and she's your mother. You and I will be friends always.''

''Don't let him!''

''I have no control over that, Margaret. None. He must do what he feels is best, whatever he feels is right in his heart. He loves you so much and he doesn't take the responsibility of finding you another mother lightly. He must see some good in Constance.''

She hoped there was some good. Maggie didn't like the woman, obviously, and Josie cared about Margaret enough that she was curious about Constance Blanche. She almost wished she could meet her so she could assess whether the woman was right for Maggie. But that would be interfering in Thomas Murphy's very private life—and she would only have considered doing that if Margaret had told her that Constance was mean to her.

Margaret went off to the schoolhouse a short time later, and Thomas entered the room to remove the bandage from Josie's head.

''Tomorrow . . . ,'' he said, and hesitated there. Josie sat in the middle of the bed, facing the window. He sat in front of her, removing the bandage. He had spent another night with her sleeping against him, and she had awakened at sunrise to find him gone. She suddenly wondered if he had gotten any sleep at all these past three nights.

''Tomorrow ye're free to go,'' he said, finishing what he had started to say. He avoided meeting her gaze.

Her breath caught in her throat. ''Do you want me to go?'' she asked, unable to stop the words. Fool . . . She was such a fool for asking that. Setting herself up for sorrow. She had grown too fond of him. She loved the feel of his arms around her, the steady beat of his heart whenever she laid her head against his chest.

He glanced up, a startled look in his eyes. ''When my patients are better, they carry on. Besides, you've been readin' the materials Lauretta and Mr. Jefferson brought you, an' I'm thinkin' you've an itch to get back onstage. I want a promise that you won't tax yer—''

"There's one play . . . I think it was meaningful to Orson. And there's—"

"Orson! You've got to forget him," he said, obviously angry and frustrated; his eyes flashed at her, and he threw the bandage at his bag. "You loved him, but he's gone, Josie, an' dwellin' on the thought of him every day won't help you get through yer grief."

She stared at him, wondering at his thoughts. "That's very easy for you to say. You're not the one who lost someone you cared about, someone who had such a marked effect on your life."

He set his jaw. "About that ye're wrong. There was Maggie's mother. I might not have loved her when I married her, but I grew to care about her. An' she damn sure did have a marked effect on my life. She helped give me Maggie, an' for that an' many other things I loved her an' respected her. But she's dead. Dead an' buried, an' now life goes on for me'n Maggie. Months passed after her death before I finally realized that.

"I understand grief, Josie. What I'm havin' trouble with is hearin' the rumors about you an' yer manager an' puttin' them together with the way I think you loved him an' still love him."

"What do you think went on between Orson and me?" she asked hoarsely. She had been made aware of the rumors over the years. But it was shocking to hear that someone actually believed them. She wasn't sure why she was shocked that Thomas might—he believed her to be a loose woman, after all—but she was. Shocked beyond belief, to the point of slowly becoming furious.

His lips tightened. "I've no idea an' I don't care to know."

"I didn't love him that way," she said angrily.

Sometimes she thought Thomas loved her. He hadn't said it, but sometimes she felt it. She just knew. She saw the emotion in his eyes and she felt the warmth of his arms around her. Other times, he was so distant, so reserved, she wasn't sure. She didn't think his feelings for her were mere desire anymore. She thought they went deeper. But he was obviously still considering Constance—why else would he and Margaret have had supper with her and her parents last evening? And why else would Maggie have sounded so frantic this morning? Children were often smarter and more perceptive than adults gave them credit for being. Margaret knew. If she thought her father was still considering Constance, that meant he was. And now this. He thought she and Orson had been lovers. That was absurd, particularly when she considered what Orson had written in the papers he had left her.

Thomas seized one of Josie's hands and dropped a lingering kiss on the back of it, squeezing his eyes shut as he did. "Damn me for lovin' you the way I do! You loved him an' you still do, whether you realize it or not, Josie."

He had said it—that he loved her. But Frank had said the same thing only days before he had decided he didn't want her near him anymore, that he had tired of her.

Damn *her* for not being able to help herself. Josie slipped her other hand to the back of Thomas's neck, up into the hair at his nape, drawing him closer. How she ached for more of his touch! "You're wrong," she whispered. "I don't love Orson the way I . . ." She squeezed her eyes shut, feeling the same fear that had made her withdraw from so many people these past few years; she didn't want to bare her heart and be hurt again. "No, Thomas. It's you I care so much about, and that frightens me."

He made a sound in the back of his throat, and murmured something. He dipped his head to place a kiss on her neck. Josie cradled his head in her hands, wondering at herself. She *was* baring her heart again and she was bound to be hurt—again. She didn't want to care so much, and letting him know she did was unwise. Like Frank, would he enjoy breaking her heart? She didn't like comparing all men to Frank, but she couldn't seem to help herself.

She was preparing to move away from him when someone whispered a loud "Oh!" from the doorway. The bedroom door was hardly ever shut when Thomas and Margaret visited, or even while Thomas himself visited. Josie glanced that way, over her shoulder, seeing Mrs. Reardon scurry off red-faced just as Thomas jerked his head up and cursed.

Josie scrambled to the opposite side of the bed and worked at composing herself, instinctively grasping the front of her shift just above her breasts, worrying about the blow her reputation would take now. Surely once word of what Mrs. Reardon had seen got out, it would confirm everyone's cruel suspicions about actresses in general. But then, Mrs. Reardon liked her and might say nothing. After all, she and Mrs. O'Brien had been wanting more to come of the relationship between her and Thomas.

She wondered what Thomas was thinking. That after a few more moments of tenderness she might have given herself to him? Surely he was not thinking that. Surely.

But how could she be sure he wasn't? What man wouldn't tell a woman he loved her, knowing the words would make her melt in his arms?

Surely he did not consider his original suspicions about her being a loose woman to be true now.

She closed her eyes, fearing he might.

"I'm sorry," Thomas said, rubbing his mouth and jaw. He grabbed the discarded bandage and balled it. "What sort of physician does such a thing? Lets himself get so damned involved he can't think straight. I knew the door was open!" Obviously furious with himself, he grabbed his bag and started to rise from the bed.

Josie sat, feeling uncertain and awkward, not knowing how to respond. She could only hope he was sincere in his feelings for her. That, like Frank, he had not indicated that he cared when all he might really care about was bedding her, then going his own way. "There's no need to apologize," she said softly.

"I've embarrassed you," he responded, now standing beside the bed.

"Do you think I couldn't have stopped you from kissing me?" She glanced up sharply, wanting him to know that she could have. And that next time—if there was a next time— she very well might.

He stared at her for a long moment, his eyes glazed. "I don't want it to be like this between us, Josie. You bein'

scared of me an' me bein' scared of you. I'm your doctor, an'
for now, till you leave, things are best left at that," he said
gruffly.

Pride and fear drove her; the need to maintain her dignity,
no matter what. She would not be hurt again. She would not.
She laughed, a little bitterly. "Perhaps not only until I leave.
Perhaps afterward, too."

He spent another moment studying her. "If that's how you
want it," he responded. Then he gathered his bag and left the
room.

Josie sank down onto the pillows, resting her head on one,
hugging the other one close. She would not be hurt again. Not
by Thomas Murphy, as much as she admired him . . . not by
any man.

She didn't see him for hours. She assumed he had gone off
to his office, and that was just as well. The less they saw of
each other, the better. Margaret and Mrs. O'Brien came with
supper. Margaret was chatty, saying that Katie would be coming to visit the following day. Josie wondered if Margaret
knew she would be leaving tomorrow, going back to the hotel.

She pulled Margaret onto her lap and told her, but also
promised that she would visit often as long as the company
remained in town, and frequently thereafter. Margaret looked
crestfallen, as if her world were coming apart, but Josie refused to promise her more when she knew she might not be
able to deliver more.

"You'll always be my friend, Margaret," Josie told the girl
again. "Always. I'll write you letters every week."

Margaret managed a smile, albeit a sad one.

She and Josie began singing songs together, then Margaret
hurried off to get a game board, and when she returned, she
and Josie played backgammon for several hours. Mrs. O'Brien
had left the room shortly after helping Maggie bring the supper
trays up. Mrs. Reardon came just as Josie and Margaret were
starting another game, and there was no hint in her eyes that
she thought poorly of Josie because of what she'd witnessed
earlier. She said she thought it was time for Miss Margaret to

be off to bed. Maggie started to object, but Josie stopped her by saying, ''No arguing. Mrs. Reardon is right.'' Josie helped her gather the game pieces, then Mrs. O'Brien appeared to collect Margaret. Mrs. Reardon followed them out, leaving Josie with the quiet again.

Twelve

MRS. O'BRIEN RETURNED presently and asked if she would like to bathe downstairs again. Josie gladly accepted the woman's kindness, and a little while later she sank down into the lavender-scented water Mrs. O'Brien had prepared, and closed her eyes. The sensation of water caressing her, covering her with soothing warmth, was exquisite. She washed her hair with the soap Mrs. O'Brien provided, thinking it smelled so sweet, almost like wild roses in the summertime. After Mrs. O'Brien provided her with a clean shift, one with lace at the neckline and at the wrists, she sat before the fire near the kitchen hearth and dried her hair with a thick cloth. Mrs. O'Brien dabbed ointment Dr. Murphy had given her on the scalp wound and provided her with a brush.

Josie sat brushing her hair for some time, staring into the fire, thinking how different her life would be now. Better, and yet frightening in some ways. She was truly on her own now—Mr. Jefferson valued her but had never sought to nurture her and guide her the way Orson had. The independence felt good, but it was also rather scary. Caring about someone so much again the way she cared about Thomas was scary, too. What did she expect after having spent so many nights sleeping peacefully in his arms after pouring out her grief to him? That she would not grow to love his tenderness and compassion? That she would not miss the feel of his arms around her, the steady sound of his breathing? She missed those things so much she ached inside. Her feelings toward him scared her because she was uncertain of his deepest thoughts about her.

Moments later, she was coming up the hall from the back of the house toward the staircase when she saw him, just entering the front door, his medical bag still in hand, a bundle of papers tucked under one arm, a brown hat sitting at a slant on his head. She paused with her hand on the banister, wondering if he had been busy all day with patients—or if he had stayed away because he hadn't wanted to be near her after what had happened this morning. There was no one else in the hall with her. Mrs. O'Brien had gone up to bed herself in her little room just off of Margaret's. The house was quiet.

He started up the hall, at first not seeing her—only two lamps lit the passage—no doubt heading toward his study. When he glanced up and saw her, his steps slowed, then stopped when he stood some five feet from her, near the sitting room door. He removed his hat, and his jaw seemed to harden as his eyes met hers.

Josie gripped a portion of her shift near her thigh. She would not have believed she could ever look forward to seeing a person so much, that her heart could go from a normal beat to racing in the space of a few seconds. She remembered feeling excited when she was with Frank, but she could not remember feeling so exhilarated.

And yet she didn't know what to make of the look in Thomas's eyes . . . apprehension, almost hostility, if she read it right. Maybe he was back to thinking poorly of her, then—that she was exactly what a lot of people thought and said she was. Those few moments of intimacy this morning had made him doubt her once again.

He cleared his throat as if he were nervous. "This morning . . . what happened won't happen again."

Anger seized her. The walls started up around her heart again. She approached him, the wooden floor cool beneath her bare feet as she swept the length of her hair over her shoulder to her back and tossed her head. "This morning you said you loved me. Has that now changed simply because you think I would have given myself totally to you if we hadn't been interrupted? I wouldn't have—and you do know that. Were you testing me? Both times when you've kissed me and made advances? Have you been testing me, Thomas, to see if I'm a loose woman, as all actresses are assumed to be?''

He stiffened. "Josie, no. The fact o' the matter is—''

"Frank was my first and only. And he was enough hurt for me.''

"I haven't been testin' you. My reluctance has to do with other things. For one, no doctor should become so involved with a patient.''

"Are you throwing blame at me, then? Do remember that I was brought here to your home while I was unconscious,'' Josie went on. "I did not ask to be brought here. I did not ask to be touched or kissed. That sounds cold, but I must make myself clear. Do not assume that I'll give myself to you if you whisper that you love me. I won't. Like any woman, I want a man who wants to court me, who wants to treat me like an absolute queen. I deserve that. I don't want a mere romp on a tick.''

"Josie, I'm not trying to hurt you, an' I'm not blamin' you for a thing.'' He rubbed his jaw, looking weary suddenly. He massaged his temple, then swept his hand down over his eyes. "I took advantage,'' he admitted, "an' for that I apologize. I wasn't thinkin'. I wasn't considerin' the way you were hurt in New Orleans an' I wasn't considerin' the fact that the door was open an' that anyone might walk by an' see us. I wasn't even considerin' the fact that ye're my patient. From the time I brought you here the temptation to touch you an' hold you was great. No excuses, just facts. I'm a man, Josie, but I'm also a physician, yer doctor, an' that's what my reluctance is about. I spent the mornin' discussin' with a few students the morals . . . standards every physician should apply when takin' care of the sick. I almost couldn't speak when it hit me in the chest that I'd violated them m'self. Not that I didn't know before. I did. But today I realized how much I've violated them lately.''

He seemed so sincere, so very, very sincere. He seemed angry with himself, and ashamed. Josie felt a little ashamed

herself suddenly—that she had jumped to conclusions without
giving him a chance to explain himself.

"It makes you angry, the things people assume about you,"
he said softly.

Josie nodded. "Yes. As anyone would be angry. You're
Irish, Thomas, and I know the Irish are not always well
thought of."

He laughed under his breath, dipping his head briefly. "Oh,
but isn't that the truth of it! Indeed it is."

"Do people assume things about you because you're
Irish?"

"Not so much anymore. There was a day when some
wouldn't have minded runnin' me down on the street. But I
was too quick for 'em, see," he said, narrowing one eye, half
grinning. The air seemed to hold a little less tension suddenly.

Josie couldn't help a slight smile despite the seriousness of
their conversation only seconds before. "I imagine you were
a scamp."

"Mm. I could steal money from a pocket, an' the person
wouldn't know it was gone till they reached for it. I could
steal bread from under the baker's nose, an' he wouldn't know
till he counted his loaves. Faith, but I was a slick one on the
streets," he said, laughing reflectively. "Potatoes from the
field was about all me an' my sister an' parents had to eat at
the time. I'd come bringin' home fish an' bread, an' my pa
would ask where an' how I got it."

"And what did you tell him?" Josie said, very interested.

"Well, the truth, of course," he answered, plopping his
hands behind his back and leaning forward on the balls of his
feet. "Dear lady, you surely aren't thinkin' I was such an
ornery child that I lied, are you?"

She laughed softly. "Oh, no, of course not."

"Good. What would people think?"

"Did your father believe you?"

That made him pause. His eyes narrowed playfully. "Believe what?"

"Whatever story you made up—someone gave you the fish
and bread, you caught the fish in the river, bought the bread
with pennies you found on the street. . . ."

He jerked back, pretending to be startled, looking wounded. "You *are* thinkin' I lied."

"Oh, no," she said, shaking her head. "I think you made up stories, like Maggie and that business about Alton."

He chuckled. "Now that I think of it, Maggie's a lot like I was as a boy. Truly an Irish lass. She has a way of findin' mischief."

"She certainly does. Quite an observation you've made, Dr. Murphy." Josie smiled again, the first really warm smile she had given him in days. She loved this playful banter. She thought they might be on the verge of understanding each other better, of holding a decent, civil conversation.

So he had been poor as a child, at least as poor as she had been. And then he had risen above. She understood hunger and poverty and the things it could drive a person to do—to steal, to rise above one's beginning. Her escape had been the theater. His must have been medical school. She wanted to ask him how that had come about, but he spoke again before she could open her mouth.

"My pa always knew about my stories. He'd tell me stealin' was wrong, that I shouldn't do it. He'd take a switch to me, an' when that business was done, he'd say, 'all right now, Thomas m'boy, let's go eat.' Then we'd go off an' eat the fish my mother had already cleaned an' cooked. He couldn't bring himself to steal, but he wouldn't take the food from his family an' throw it to the dogs, either."

"It sounds like you admire your father," Josie commented.

"I did—he's been dead for years now. I still think about him a lot."

She studied him. Then, against her better judgment, she told him, "You're an interesting man, Dr. Murphy."

"Ah! Interestin' enough that you might consider firin' me as yer physician after you go tomorrow an' allowin' me to court you?"

That certainly took her by surprise. He'd said it so light-heartedly—she could only hope he was serious. She stood staring dumbly at him. "I—I don't know."

He nodded. "That is what ye're wantin'—a courtship. An' well you deserve one. Ye're so protective of yer heart, Josie."

He waved the hat he held. "Walls all around it."

"Necessary walls," she said. "Do you know how many men I meet who only want to be able to say they've been intimate with Josephine Gavin?"

"Numbers, no doubt."

"Numbers . . . yes, numbers. I'm told that I'm a wonderful actress," she remarked, glancing away. She gave a little laugh, a sad one, then glanced back at him. "Too wonderful, I think. Few have seen my pain. Few have ever seen me cry."

"Surely even fewer have ever seen you laugh."

Josie considered that. He was right. These past few years she had not been a person who laughed much at all.

"That's what I'd like to do, Josie," he said, his voice rich and deep. "Help you learn to laugh a lot again. Help you realize ev'ry man's not like that one you came across in New Orleans."

She smiled, touched, then slowly sobered as his sparkling gaze held hers.

"Don't be afraid of me," he went on. "I made wrong assumptions about you at first. I've said an' done things I shouldn't have. In truth, I've never met a sweeter woman. So if ye're wonderin' what I really think of you, there you have it. The words to that song . . . *the girl of my golden dreams.* I thought of you. I realize that . . . man in New Orleans must have said all the things a woman likes to hear just to have his way with you, an' that I'm probably sayin' a lot of the same things m'self. Not meanin' to say the same things, understand, I just think I am." He rubbed his mouth and raised and lowered his brows. A second later he turned the hat he held, obviously nervous. "I'm botchin' this, I'd wager. I'm feelin' like a schoolboy again, all jittery inside at havin' you near."

He was trying so hard to let her know he was sincere. One might think Josie Gavin had a heart of rock, as distant and cool as she had become with the majority of people. But the truth was, no matter how much turmoil she had endured and survived, she was still a loving, compassionate person at the core—and Thomas Murphy had tapped that.

"It's all right," she said, smiling, bravely reaching for his hand. "I understand."

So strong and warm, his hand. It could be so comforting at times. She was suddenly ashamed at assuming that he might have had an ulterior motive during all those nights he'd held her, and afterward. She pressed the back of his hand to her cheek and smiled up at him.

He inhaled a deep breath and smiled back tenderly. Then he shook his head and briefly closed his eyes, obviously relishing her touch.

Josie lowered and released his hand, not wanting to make things difficult for him. He took his role as her doctor very seriously, and she respected him for that. She would not compromise his morals or his profound regard for the rules governing his profession.

She stepped away, still smiling. She approached the staircase and paused at the foot of it. With her hand on the railing, she glanced at him over her shoulder. "Good night, Thomas," she said, her voice low. "I'll see you in the morning."

He nodded, his eyes glowing in the dim lamplight. How easy running back to him and throwing herself into his arms would be!

Instead Josie fled up the stairs, her heart pounding, the smile fixed on her lips.

Thirteen

THE FOLLOWING MORNING, Thomas slept much later than he normally did, then woke to thoughts of Josie.

She planned to leave today to go back to the hotel where the company was staying. He remembered the way she'd fled upstairs last evening. He still wasn't sure he'd convinced her he wasn't like that scum down in New Orleans. During his ramblings, in his efforts to convince her, had he said something that scared her? Had she maybe left already without saying good-bye? He prayed not. He wanted to see her this morning—her freshness, her beautiful eyes and smile. He wanted to be the one to take her to her hotel.

What did it really mean—if she'd left without saying good-bye? That she wanted to make the parting less difficult for him and Maggie—and herself? Or perhaps that she didn't believe all the things he'd said last night. Maybe she didn't believe he wanted to court her. That he really loved her.

What if she decided to allow him to court her and yet she also decided to leave St. Louis when her company moved on? That hadn't occurred to him before now. But what if?

Life would go on if she left the city, he supposed. It would have to. He had Maggie to think about, his patients, and his students at the college. Yes, life would go on, but it would be difficult. He wondered if he'd always think of Josie, if he'd always see her face and form, her dancing smile, in his mind.

He wondered if he'd always hear her laughter in his ears, the way she'd laughed that evening in the parlor with Maggie. He wondered if any other woman could make him feel so alive.

He was thinking crazy things. He really had no idea if she'd left already.

God, how he loved her. But he suspected her acting called her. Then there was still the lingering question in his mind: If she really loved him, did both he and Orson Neville have her heart? He'd told her he loved her, but she hadn't told him the same.

It's ludicrous, he told himself. *You're jealous of a dead man.* But he didn't want thoughts of another man in Josie's head whenever they were together. He would give her time to put Neville completely from her mind, except in the role the man had occupied as her manager. He'd give her as much time as she needed.

"Josie, m'love," Thomas whispered to himself. "I don't believe it was an accident that you walked into my life that evenin'. I don't believe it at all. I don't believe it because there's a good an' kind Father watchin' over me'n Maggie— an' yerself."

He collected himself, washing his face and what he could of his body over the washstand positioned against the far wall. He shaved, cutting himself once on the right jaw, wincing, then going on. He soon dressed and headed downstairs, wondering if Maggie had already gone to the schoolhouse.

"Breakfast awaits in the dining room, Dr. Murphy," Mrs. O'Brien said cheerily, passing him near the foot of the stairs. She continued on, humming to herself, clicking her heels together once before turning into the dining room, acting as bubbly as he'd ever seen the woman act.

Actually she was unusually bubbly, he thought as he headed up the hall.

He turned into the dining room a moment behind her, stopping short when he spotted Josie seated at the table beside Maggie. She leaned toward his daughter, laughing at something Maggie said, and Thomas held his breath, drawing the sound close to him.

Josie was still here.

She hadn't gone back to the hotel yet. She hadn't left without saying good-bye. He hated not knowing exactly what she had planned in the future—whether she planned to leave with her company. He hated the uncertainty of it all. And yet he wouldn't close in on her with questions.

The length of her hair had been pulled to one side and braided, and the braid hung down, tapering at her waist. She wore the same dress she'd worn the night they'd met—the brown-checkered dress buttoned up nearly to her chin, the pretty dress with the dainty rows of ruffles forming a vee from her shoulders to her waist. Her hair had been curled and pinned that night, arranged in an elegant style. But he liked the braid—it suited her well.

"I should tickle you for that!" she told Maggie, sobering, and all too quickly, too. "Margaret Murphy, he will not have trouble biting into them. He will *not* think they're as chewy as rawhide! That's an insult, and perhaps one that will drive me to tears." Huffing, Josie sat back in her chair, folded her arms, and sniffed.

Margaret giggled. "I know when someone's acting!"

Josie shot her a pouting smile. "Because you do so much of it yourself."

More giggles. Maggie nodded adamantly, agreeing.

"Oh, look, Miss Margaret," Mrs. O'Brien said, glancing at Thomas, then stretching to open a shutter. "Your father's arrived to join you for breakfast."

"Papa!" Maggie twisted in her chair, sounding delighted. "Good morning, Papa. Josephine's here, though she's leaving in a bit for the hotel. But she promises to visit almost every day. She's agreed to a picnic soon with me and Katie Farren and her mother and Charlie, and she's promised to come have supper here with us soon. And you'll never believe what else—the things we did this morning. Oh, Papa, you'll never believe what we *did*!"

Grinning, trying to act normal though his heart was racing with excitement and relief over seeing that Josie was still here, he strode toward the sideboard, where candles beneath silver dishes warmed the food. "I'd wager ye're about to tell me, Maggie girl, an' I look forward to hearin'." He turned a cup over, lifted a nearby pitcher, and poured coffee.

"We played in the garden without our shoes and stockings, hiding from each other. Then we went to the kitchen, and Josie asked the cook if she could make you more hotcakes." She twisted in her chair again, this time toward the sideboard, and pointed to a certain dish. "And there they are! Only . . ." She lowered her voiced and giggled. "I love Josephine, but the hotcakes really are chewy!"

"Did she now?" Thomas asked. "Asked if she could cook me hotcakes?"

"Oh, Miss Margaret, they are not," Josie said, jabbing the girl in the ribs with her pointed forefinger. "I'll have you know I ate several, and they are *not* chewy."

"Mm–hm. We'll see what Papa says. Yes, Papa, she did."

"Am I to be the mediator in this difference of opinion?" he queried, turning a lifted brow on them.

Josie tipped her head and pursed her lips, trying to look put out. Instead she looked cute. Thomas chuckled. His gaze met hers, and he sobered, looking deep though he knew he shouldn't, again wondering what her plans might be. Unwisely he dropped his gaze to her lips, suddenly wanting to taste them.

Her breath quickened. Seconds later a blush surfaced on her cheeks, and she lowered her lashes. He wanted to cup her chin in his palm, lift her jaw, look down into her eyes, and tell her not to be embarrassed because he wanted to kiss her. He couldn't imagine anyone thinking of her as a loose woman and he was ashamed that he had, and determined to rectify the mistake.

"I . . ." She glanced up quickly and back down just as quickly, ducking her head and giving him an embarrassed smile. "It's been years since I made hotcakes. They're the simplest thing to make. I don't know how I could have—"

"I'm sure they're delicious," he responded.

"They've been sitting there warming for an hour."

"Surely they're just as appetizin' as they were before, maybe more so."

She laughed nervously. "Oh, Thomas."

"Oh, Josie." Chuckling, he turned back to the dishes, lifted the lid on the one Maggie had indicated, and forked several hotcakes. He put them on the plate he'd lifted from a nearby stack. The hotcakes were a bit thin and looked browner than they should have, as if they'd been cooked too long. They probably would be a little difficult to chew. But just knowing that Josie had been thoughtful enough to make them for him warmed him inside. He already knew what his verdict would be: delicious. No matter how they tasted in the mouth, the sweetness behind them was delicious.

"No shoes an' stockin's while you ran around in the garden?" he asked, turning. "It's only the end of March, Maggie girl. An' you, Josephine . . ." He tried to sound stern as he took his seat at the end of the table. Maggie sat to his left. Josie was situated next to her. Thomas furrowed his brows at them, trying to level a severe look on Josie. "You . . . barely outta yer bed an' barefoot on the cold garden paths."

He poured maple syrup over the hotcakes, then cut a bite, using a knife and fork.

"Do you really need a knife?" Josie asked rather anxiously.

He narrowed one eye. "Why, what'n the blazes am I thinkin'? I should drink my coffee first. It has a way of wakin' me, of bringin' me to my senses. Why, for a minute there I thought a cut of beef sat before me an'—"

"A cut of beef?" she spouted incredulously. Any second now, he expected her to wring her hands.

Saints. He'd said the wrong thing when he'd been trying to say the right thing.

"A tender cut of beef, that is. One that melts in the mouth. I always use a knife to cut beef. A habit, you see."

"He does," Maggie chimed in, apparently reading Josie's expression and deciding to go along with him so her feelings wouldn't be hurt. "That's it—he got mixed up. He's so sleepy in the morning!"

"It's true," Mrs. O'Brien said, finally getting the other shutter to cooperate. "Mrs. Reardon and I rarely discuss any of the household business with him in the mornings until after he has two cups of coffee. Dr. Murphy probably did think he was sitting down to supper."

Josie rolled her eyes toward one corner of the ceiling. "We

were discussing the hotcakes. Maggie told him we cooked them for him. The three of you . . . my feelings are not so fragile.''

Thomas popped a bite into his mouth. Definitely chewy. Definitely too thin and cooked too long.

''They're delicious!'' he announced. He stole a glance at the dish from which he'd taken the hotcake. He'd replaced the cover. Damn. How many were still left in there? Six? Seven? Too many. If they weren't all gone by the time breakfast ended, Josie's feelings just might be hurt. He wouldn't have that.

''Come, Mrs. O'Brien, have some hotcakes!'' He shot the woman a look that said, Don't think of declining, though he was almost certain she'd eaten earlier in the kitchen with Mrs. Reardon; that was the women's habit.

Mrs. O'Brien gave him a startled look, then approached the sideboard, shuffling her feet a bit. ''Why, thank you, Dr. Murphy,'' she said, trying hard to still be as jovial as she'd been when he had encountered her at the foot of the stairs.

''Ye're welcome, Mrs. O'Brien. I know you've a tremendous appetite—Mrs. Reardon shared that secret with me—so—''

''She what?'' Mrs. O'Brien looked appalled, her mouth dropping open, her face going white.

''—feed yourself well. Two or three, if you'd like. Go right ahead. An' Maggie girl, surely you've enough room in yer belly for one more!''

Maggie winced as Mrs. O'Brien served herself. ''I didn't even eat one. I only had a few bites.''

''Well, there you have it! How's a girl like yerself s'posed to grow on two bites of hotcakes for breakfast? I hear yer stomach growlin'. Have another, made by the hand of yer favorite actress, Josephine Gavin. Syrup, Mrs. O'Brien?''

''I think so, Dr. Murphy,'' Mrs. O'Brien said, taking the seat near Josie.

Maggie spoke up. ''Papa, it's time for me to go to the school—''

''Not on an empty belly, Maggie. Yer favorite actress, remember that. Yer friend.'' He cut his hotcakes with the side of his fork, pressing down harder than normal. But at least the syrup seemed to have softened them somewhat by now.

Josie sat, looking stunned, her gaze moving between the three of them as Maggie dutifully took her plate and went for another hotcake. She returned to the table moments later, and asked if Mrs. Reardon would pass her the syrup, please.

"You don't have to eat them!" Josie said suddenly. "Don't force yourselves. Thomas, this is ridiculous!"

"Nonsense, Miss Gavin," Mrs. O'Brien said, swallowing. "I happen to be hungry, and these are wonderful."

"I had a bad taste in my mouth earlier, that's all, Josephine," Maggie said, pouring a small pond of syrup over her hotcake.

"Delicious," Thomas said through another bite, thinking he should change the subject now. "Now then, Josie, about you runnin' through the garden barefoot in March when ye're just out of bed an'—"

"Not at all strenuous exercise, Dr. Murphy," she retorted. "Besides, you're no longer my physician. I came to that decision this morning."

He froze with his fork halfway to his mouth. Her eyes sparkled at him as she sent him a silent message: that she'd agreed to the courtship.

"I've a sudden urge to dance an Irish jig on the table," he said.

She brought her hand to her mouth and laughed behind it.

"No longer your physician?" Maggie objected. "But, Papa!"

"Now, Maggie, before you go gettin' upset, the worst is over with her health, an' it's not right for a doctor to be courtin' a woman who's also his patient," he responded brightly.

"Courtin'?" Maggie blurted.

Mrs. O'Brien coughed, nearly choking. She flattened her hand just above her bosom. "Courting?"

"Well, I . . ." Thomas felt his face heat. "Courtin', yes. Is there an objection? Maybe several?"

"No, no!" Maggie said, bouncing up and down twice.

"Why, of course not," Mrs. O'Brien responded, breaking out in a grin from ear to ear. Thomas knew she couldn't wait to tell Mrs. Reardon that a courtship was on, and that dear lady would spread the word from there. But none of them should get their hopes up too high. There was always the chance that nothing would come of the courtship.

"Since there are no objections, I believe it's official," Josie said. "We're courting."

Mrs. O'Brien tossed her arm in the air, saying "Praise the lord," but quickly composed herself, smiled nicely, blushed profusely, then returned to eating her second breakfast. Maggie squeezed between Josie and the table and wrapped her arms around her adoring friend. Josie kissed the girl's cheek.

Grinning, wondering if he was the happiest man in the world right now, Thomas stabbed a big bite of hotcakes.

Maggie soon went off to the schoolhouse, and after finishing her third hotcake, Mrs. O'Brien wished Thomas and Josie a good day, telling Josie that she'd very much enjoyed her stay. Then she left the dining room, leaving Thomas and Josie alone.

"How were you plannin' to get to the hotel?" he asked, thinking again how relieved he had been to come downstairs and find her still in the house.

"It's not very far, not really," she said, drawing circles on her plate with her fork.

"I'm off to the college soon. I'd be glad to take you in the buggy."

"All right," she said, glancing up. "I have to collect the things Laurette brought me. I wonder what everyone is saying and thinking about me staying here. Surely nothing worse than other vile gossip I've encountered over the years. Still, I hate gossip. You don't know how many newspaper accounts I've read over the years in which only a partial truth is told, or no truth at all. Many people believe what they read or what they're told. Or they believe what their minds tell them and take no time to examine the facts. No doubt people know that I'm here, and some have already reached conclusions. I know you're an upstanding citizen—that was not hard to guess— and I don't want your name sullied, Thomas. I don't know how much you've thought about that, if you've considered it at all. This courtship thing is admirable, and it certainly makes me feel wanted. It's what I want. But . . . I've lived with gossip and criticism for years now, and know how vile it can be. The culture in New Orleans is more accepting, though the higher classes insist on marrying well. I learned that by being so hurt there were times I thought death would be more pleasant. I believe it's that way most everywhere— in the higher classes. Even here. To go against the unspoken rules of upper society can often bring ruin. I don't want that for you and Maggie. I won't have it. If I think for a moment that that might happen—''

''I love you, Josie,'' Thomas responded simply and evenly. *And that's all that matters,* he hoped his look told her.

She shook her head, smiling hopelessly. ''I'm not sure what will happen with the company. I . . . Mr. Jefferson had planned . . . I want to . . .'' She glanced down at her hands. ''The other plays. I won't leave the company in financial straits.''

''I fixed a bird's broken wing once,'' Thomas said. ''Maggie wanted to keep the bird, even after it was mended. She wanted to cage it. I wouldn't allow it. I let it fly, then Maggie an' I . . . we went on.''

She studied him for a long moment, understanding his meaning. Finally she moved from the table, saying she was off to collect her things.

In front of the three-story National Hotel on the busy corner of Market and Third, Thomas kissed her in the morning sunlight. He smoothed the hair back from one side of her face, then touched her lips with his fingertips. Josie kissed them, feeling proud, feeling cherished, feeling caught up in the moment. Frank would never have kissed her in broad daylight in front of a busy hotel. He would have been concerned about who might see. Thomas didn't care who saw; he loved her and wanted to show the world. Suddenly Josie's heart felt so large she thought it would burst.

''Tomorrow evenin' I'd like to have supper with you,'' he whispered against her lips.

"What time?" she asked, smiling.

"Seven? The hotel here has a nice restaurant, I hear."

"It does."

"I'll see you then."

She nodded.

Thomas withdrew, and she watched him climb back up into his buggy. He smiled at her, she smiled back, waved, and then he was off. Josie watched him until the buggy disappeared around a corner some distance up the street.

Because of Orson's death and Josie's illness, Mr. Jefferson had canceled a number of engagements upriver. Miss Gavin would have time to recuperate, he had told the others in the company, or so Lauretta revealed shortly after Josie arrived at the hotel. Josie wondered aloud that there hadn't been grumbles of discontent, since the troupe never stayed very long in one place.

"There have been. A few," Lauretta said in a timid voice. Then she hurriedly added, "But everyone understands, really."

"I'll do my best to get back onstage as quickly as possible," Josie assured her.

Lauretta nodded, and Josie did not miss the flash of disappointment in her eyes. Lauretta had progressed into feature roles and would have to fade back to minor ones with Josie's return. Though Lauretta would never dream of giving voice to her disappointment, Josie's return to the company deflated her, taking some of the spirit Josie had seen emerge in her this past week.

As Josie sat on the middle of the bed in her hotel room that afternoon with scripts and Orson's account of their relationship spread around her, thoughts about what she wanted now and what Lauretta wanted turned in her head. Lauretta had grown comfortable within the Jefferson Company, though now that Josie was back she was uncomfortable. She loved her advancement, loved traveling from city to city and town to town, loved the success she'd tasted lately. Josie, on the other hand, would now rather stay in one place. She had been offered a role in the St. Louis Theater by an eager Mr. Carson down the way, as she had told Orson, and she just might have to give the matter of declining the offer more thought. She might have to see if Mr. Carson still wanted her.

"Lauretta is doing a grand job, I hear," she ventured to Mr. Jefferson over a late supper in the hotel dining room that evening.

"She's a spring rose," he said. "Fresh and eager. The audiences love her."

"So you're doing well, too?" she queried, needing to know.

"But of course, Josie. Always doing well." He sipped wine nonchalantly, glancing around the room, sweeping aside a lock of his brown hair, not meeting her gaze.

"You'll forgive me for being forward, Mr. Jefferson. I mean no harm, but I know that Orson was greatly concerned about the financial state of the company, that it was an extreme worry of his. I'm not as eager an actress anymore as Lauretta is—surely you've noticed that. I'm not as eager to travel. But if my performing with our troupe means the difference between the company surviving or dissolving, I would devote myself to helping keep it together."

He smoothed a hand down over his cravat. "I've noticed that Lauretta is bright onstage. She has the charisma and talent every actor and actress must have to be successful. But you will always have a place in the company if you desire it, Josie, because you have a devoted following that will write you into books about the American theater. I won't lie—you draw more of an audience than Lauretta does. The company would benefit more financially from your appearances."

She glanced away, feeling ambivalent. She wanted to stay here in St. Louis with Thomas if he asked her to. But if her performances meant the difference between the company sinking or surviving, she would do what she could to help. She watched two young men, a redhead and a blond, both probably only eighteen or nineteen, rapidly approach the table.

"You're Josephine Gavin," said the taller of the two, the blond.

"We saw you one night at Concert Hall!" the other added, his gaze dropping to her neckline. She'd chosen an elegant but modest gown, one of rich burgundy satin that dipped very little at her breasts. Josie smiled politely, having encountered eager male followers such as these two a number of times, and knowing that after a few smiles and polite words from her, they would wander off, rather disappointed but no doubt eager to tell their friends they'd at least met her.

"I'll never forget one of the songs you sang," the blond said. *"In the hills of—"*

"Miss Gavin! Oh, you look even more beautiful this evening than the evening *I* saw you perform," a young woman said, approaching from Josie's right. "My husband agreed to escort me. It was my birthday and it was the most wonderful present he could have given me. We live a ways outside the city, but we come in now and then. I knew you were staying here. I stopped by to see if I could catch a glimpse of you, and here you sit! I sketched this," she said, laying a piece of paper on the table near Josie's arm. It was a drawing of Josie singing, in one of her theater gowns, her hair flowing around her shoulders and arms. "It's for you. I have others. I want to thank you for your beautiful singing. I loved seeing you onstage."

Josie smiled. If only every follower had such a polite, sincere way of approaching her. She thanked the two young men for their compliments, then, as they wandered off, she asked the woman's name—Dolores. She introduced Dolores to Mr. Jefferson and asked if she would like to join them for a few moments. Dolores declined, gushing the entire time, saying she wouldn't dream of interrupting their meal any more than she already had. Josie sincerely told her how beautiful she thought the sketch was, that she had a talent of her own. After a few more exchanges of dialogue, Dolores wandered away, too, leaving Josie and Mr. Jefferson at the table alone.

He grinned at her. "As I said, a devoted following. That woman was one of many, and there seems to be a flock of them right here in St. Louis. They like Lauretta, but they ask after you."

"Do they?"

"They do indeed."

"The sketch is beautiful, isn't it?" she asked, wanting to change the subject. Would Thomas wait for her? If she moved on with the company for a time, would he move on, too—to another woman? Or perhaps he would simply go back to the woman he had been seeing before she had come along and disrupted his life. She almost couldn't bear that thought.

"It is."

Josie studied it for a time, marveling at how much it resembled her. The woman definitely had a talent.

"You've extended the company's engagement here in St. Louis. I'll be happy to help finish the roles and perhaps help the company through one or two other engagements in towns not far from St. Louis," Josie said, looking up at Mr. Jefferson. "After that, I'd like for Lauretta to take over my appearances. The gift Orson left me . . . it's a manuscript, an account of our first meeting and how our relationship progressed after that. I believe he finished it very close to the time of his death. I would like to see it done onstage as a tribute to him someday. I would like to see it done by our company. I'm willing to portray myself if you want to consider it. After that, I plan to consider Mr. Carson's offer at the St. Louis Theater. I may settle here, you see, and accepting the offer seems a logical choice."

This was difficult. She had had very little business dealings with Mr. Jefferson over the years—Orson had always taken care of business with him—and she didn't quite know what to expect. Her palms and the back of her neck were damp, she was so nervous. It was frightening, being completely independent suddenly.

Mr. Jefferson studied her, finally looking her in the eye. "Has Dr. Murphy asked you to marry him?"

That question took her by surprise. "No, but—"

"You expect that he will."

"I didn't say that."

"You're thinking it. On the basis of an expectation, you're making arrangements to leave the company?"

It did sound like a ludicrous thing to do.

"Mr. Jefferson, I—"

He held up a hand, palm out, to silence her. "You're being

hasty. Have you mingled with his friends? Have you even met his friends? Have you tried living in his social world? Do you know anyone else in St. Louis, Josie? You need to think more," he said coolly.

What had she expected? That he would be happy with what she had to tell him? That he would agree to it outright?

And yet, when she made herself stop and consider the questions he asked, she found that he made a lot of sense, that she was operating on emotion, already missing Thomas and Maggie and wanting to be with them no matter what. While talking with Thomas this morning, she had sounded so logical; now she was thinking with her heart and not her head.

But the way he had kissed her in front of the hotel . . .

She did feel almost certain he would ask her to marry him.

"I don't want animosity between us, Mr. Jefferson," she said, looking him in the eye.

"Mr. Carson is having his own share of financial problems," Mr. Jefferson informed her. "Last season was good for no one. Everyone lowered ticket prices to draw more people, and still the crowds were small. This year they're large, but we'll need the full season to recoup."

He wasn't happy. In fact, she thought he was alarmed.

"The manuscript Orson left . . . ," she said, trying to change the subject a little.

"I want to read it. I want to see if it can be adapted to fit the stage. If it can, of course I want you to be featured in it. You wouldn't even have to act, I imagine. It would draw the crowds. But, Josie, I will take it up and down the river, not just to places around here."

Josie managed a smile. Always the businessman, Mr. Jefferson. "You're right. I wouldn't have to act, and it would draw the crowds." She didn't especially want to spend another entire season traveling up and down the river. But she did feel a little of the old excitement of being onstage again, though she knew the role would be the most difficult one she had ever undertaken. Going through it all over again: her mother and brother dying, meeting Orson, working so hard, meeting Frank and getting through that horrible heartbreak, learning a valuable lesson, but one that had made her somewhat cynical . . . Orson being there to comfort her when she cried. Orson, loving her so much, nurturing her.

The following evening she was dressed and downstairs seated in the hotel lobby by a quarter to seven. After four different people approached her, wanting to meet the famous Josephine Gavin, she gave Thomas a doubtful smile when he arrived.

"Have another place in mind besides the hotel restaurant?" she asked. "I'm not sure we'll be left alone here. People seem to be watching and waiting for me."

"Half a dozen other places," he said.

She went off upstairs for a wrap, returning only moments later. He wore a suit of black with a white shirt and neckcloth. His hair waved to just below the cravat, shimmering in the softly lit lobby. People milled here and there, some waiting to be seated in the restaurant. Thomas settled Josie's pelisse on her shoulders just as two women approached, their eyes bright at having spotted Josie.

"A hasty escape," Thomas said over Josie's shoulder.

"Thomas, I shouldn't."

Josie greeted the women with a smile and took a few moments to converse with them. They wondered when she would be back onstage, and she told them that truthfully she wasn't sure. Soon, they hoped. After they wandered off, Josie and Thomas made for the front doors of the hotel before anyone else could stop them.

They ended up in a relatively quiet restaurant on Market, seated in a far corner. The tables were covered with white linen, gentle light flickered from wall sconces and from candles placed on the tables, and a violinist wandered here and there, making the atmosphere all the more romantic. Josie and Thomas were served strips of chicken on beds of rice, and vegetables cooked in just the right amount of butter. They started out talking about Maggie, with Thomas remarking that she was much happier since she had met Josie, and ended up talking about Josie and her girlhood in New York, her mother and brother, and how she'd started spending a great deal of time around the theaters about the time she turned twelve. Maggie's idolization of her as an actress reminded her of herself, and that was one reason why, when she'd found Maggie in her dressing room that night, she'd taken the girl under her wing. Josie told Thomas how she had discovered Maggie in the trunk after spotting a lock of her hair hanging out.

"She looked so afraid—and she *was* so afraid that I would be angry," Josie said. "She was able to get inside the theater, but she couldn't think of another way to get close to me. It was so sweet."

Thomas smiled, then chuckled at the thought of Maggie hiding in the trunk, her eyes undoubtedly wide with apprehension when Josie discovered her.

"The two of you looked cute together in the parlor that night," Thomas remarked. "I was angry when I found out I'd been tricked, very angry, but now that I think back on it, yer mischievousness was cute."

Josie smiled, thinking back on the events of that evening. "Maggie's a little actress herself. I know that may not be what you want to hear, but she is. She needs no instruction."

"Oh, no. If she had instruction, she'd always get the better of me!"

"Yes, I'm afraid she would. For the most part, she does a wonderful job of it now."

The violinist drew near, playing a slow waltz. Thomas held out his hand to Josie and asked if she'd like to dance. She laughed, thinking he was crazy—this was a restaurant—but a smile and a slight nod from the violinist prompted her to take Thomas's hand and let him lead her to a small open area nearby.

Even with a respectful distance between them during the dance, Josie felt the heat of his body, the intensity of his eyes as he gazed down at her. Earlier they had shared light-hearted conversation; now their time together turned serious. The flickering lamplight, the wine they'd shared during supper, the smooth, enchanting chords of the violin . . . the entire atmosphere exuded romance. And so the desire that sparked between her and Thomas did not surprise Josie. Her every sense seemed acute suddenly. His light touch on her waist seemed to burn through the material of her dress, camisole, and corset. His cologne . . . rich, but like a pleasant spice. His eyes glowed, sparking with orange now and then as he turned just so and they caught the light. The sound of his voice, lower now than earlier, and thicker . . . the way he cradled her hand so tenderly in his—everything combined made her want to draw closer.

Josie swallowed hard, hoping no one else in the restaurant took much notice of them.

Later he walked her up to her hotel room, pausing in the hall before her door. She stood facing him, wondering if he expected her to invite him in. Surely not. She twisted the drawstring of her reticule more tightly around her wrist and glanced down at the red carpet.

"I should go in now," she said a little nervously. "I—I plan to make an appearance at rehearsal tomorrow, so I—"

"Could I call in the afternoon?"

"I may be at the theater. I'll leave word at the desk."

He glanced up and down the deserted hallway as if nervous himself; Josie watched him from beneath her lashes.

"Could I kiss you, Josie?" he asked softly, as if afraid to try this time without her permission. The front of the hotel had been such a public place that there was no danger of more than a kiss happening. But here . . . with her room only steps away . . . the desire they felt for each other was more intense than it had been yesterday morning when he left her at the hotel.

She couldn't help but smile up at him. She nodded, and he stepped closer.

When his lips brushed hers, Josie thought she would die with wanting him to deepen the kiss, to draw her closer and touch her more. She could step closer and deepen the kiss herself, but she wouldn't—she didn't want him thinking poorly of her. She didn't really think he would at this point, but it was not a chance she was willing to take.

"Have you seen another physician to check yer head wound yet?" he asked, twirling a lock of her hair around one of his fingers.

She shook her head. "I haven't thought about it."

"Alan's still in St. Louis. I'll be sendin' him by. Sleep now, sweet Josie,'' he said, touching the back of his hand to one side of her face. "I've tired you. I shouldn't have."

Her voice was soft. "I had a wonderful time. Wonderful! The music, the food, the dancing, the conversation. Thank you, Thomas."

He inclined his head, withdrew, and stuffed his hands into his trouser pockets, as if needing a place to put them to keep from touching her more. Josie smiled again—it seemed she had done a lot of smiling this evening, feeling almost sorry she had lectured him so about taking advantage of her while she was at his home. He was guarded when with her now, maintaining careful control, being much more respectful. She didn't like the guarded part, but she deserved the respect as much as any woman did.

Josie took the key from her reticule and put it into the lock. Thomas said good night and headed down the hall, walking backward at first. When Josie glanced up from the door, she saw another man coming up the hall right behind him. She opened her mouth to warn Thomas, but she was too late. The man tried sidestepping just as Thomas walked into him.

Thomas laughed at himself and reddened. Josie couldn't help the grin she tried to hide behind her hand. She waved her fingers at him, then slipped into the room, shut the door, and lay down on her back on the bed.

She stared dreamily up at the tester for the longest time, thinking about the evening, how wonderfully romantic it had been . . . how much she loved him.

She'd let it happen again. She had fallen in love. She was baring her heart. But this time it felt so right, so beautiful. Still, it was a frightening thing.

Later, after changing into a shift and washing her face, she lay in bed, missing the sights and sounds of the Murphy household. How familiar the room she had been in had become to her. How she had started looking forward to Mrs. O'Brien's and Mrs. Reardon's cheerfulness, their motherliness. How she missed the sound of Thomas coming up the stairs at night, walking down the hall, the thud of his boots fading. Already she missed the feel of his hand on her waist as they'd danced;

his grin, the way he had of narrowing one eye sometimes, his rich laughter, his brogue . . . other things.

She fell asleep thinking about the kiss they'd shared out in the hallway.

Fourteen

He SHOWED UP at Concert Hall the next morning with a bundle of colorful flowers in his arms. Josie saw him from where she stood talking with Lauretta in one of the wings. He stood on the otherwise empty parquet, glancing around. Lauretta nudged her and smiled knowingly. Josie felt her face warm as she grinned back.

"I certainly hope it's me you're looking for," she said, approaching.

He grinned. "An' who else would I be lookin' for?"

"I've no idea, but I'm glad you found me first."

He handed her the flowers, not at all gracefully, dropping several in the process. "Sorry, they're—ouch!"

Josie laughed as he shook his hand, pressing a thumb to a finger where he'd been poked by something. "A few rose thorns lurking in the crowd?" she asked. "Where did you find flowers in March?"

"Conservatory," he answered, scowling at his finger. "But next time I'll remember to leave out the roses."

"Oh, but I love roses." She was teasing. She didn't really have a favorite flower, she just loved flowers. "Come," she said, turning her head slightly to the right. "We'll go put them in water."

She led the way to her dressing room, where she searched around for a vase. Not finding one, she elected to go to the prop and costume room, where she would surely find something.

She was rummaging through a shelf of odds and ends when Thomas began looking around at the racks and trunks of clothing and other items as if he had never seen a costume room before. Well, most people hadn't, Josie reminded herself.

"Margaret would have fun in here," Josie commented.

"That she would," he agreed, then gave her a crooked grin. "Do you?"

Josie lifted her brows at him playfully, finally finding a cream-colored vase that would hold the flowers nicely. She placed them in it and set it on the floor nearby, then approached an open trunk of items.

"Oh . . . occasionally. I used to sneak into the costume rooms of theaters in New York. One minute I'd be Cleopatra," she said, fitting a gold band onto her arm and slowly moving her limp hand, making a figure eight. She grabbed an elegantly painted ivory fan and began fluttering it gracefully just beneath her chin, tipping her head as she did. "And the next I'd be a grand French lady or a queen holding court."

Grinning, Thomas drew forth from where he had been standing near the doorway. "Is that what little girls dream of? Bein' Cleopatra? Holdin' court?"

Josie dropped the fan on a trunk of clothing and lifted a colorful masquerade mask. She was feeling quite playful suddenly, quite full of antics. "Oh, no, sir. Most girls have no idea who Cleopatra is. I, however, read everything I could get my hands on when I was a child. Most girls simply dream of balls and dancing," she said, holding the mask before her face. "And young ladies . . . they dream of being kissed in the moonlight by some dashing man who sweeps in from the shadows."

"Dashing?" he queried, amused.

"Of course." She lowered the mask to smile at him, feeling her heart quicken at the playfulness. "You're dashing."

He paused with his hand resting on a small Greek column. "But I didn't sweep in from the shadows. You did. I came home one evenin' to find the most enchantin' creature in my parlor charmin' my daughter."

She tipped her head, looking at him from the corner of her eye. "Did you?"

He laughed. "Indeed I did. I thought surely the Father opened the heavens an' dropped her down. Have you any notion how beautiful you are right now, playin' an' lookin' at me like that? If there was moonlight, I'd be the one kissin' you."

"I might have some—Oh, don't do that!" She tried to warn him about the column, not to lean against it, that it might seem sturdy but that it surely wouldn't hold his weight. It toppled, and he went with it, sprawling on the floor while Josie stood with her hand over her mouth, trying to stifle laughter.

He scowled playfully at her, then lay back and stared up at the ceiling, mumbling, "This mornin' excursion's goin' poorly so far. First the thorn. Now this."

"Ah . . . ," Josie said. She dropped the mask onto the fan and approached him. "Would you like a hand up?"

He didn't answer. He was still pouting, feeling sorry for himself.

"Oh, now. I tried to warn you about the pillar." She lifted her skirts slightly and settled on the floor beside him. "I did try. Here, did you hurt yourself? Did you bump your head on the floor?"

He narrowed his eyes. "You plan to have a look at it?"

"If there's a bump to have a look at."

She bent over him and smoothed the hair from his brow, then pushed her fingers into it as if searching for a wound. She was being playful, not provocative. But when she looked from his hair to his face she saw that he'd grown serious suddenly, that the color of his eyes had deepened, that he was now staring up at her with an intensity that burned into her soul and made her breath catch in her throat.

"Don't forget my finger," he said, playing this to the hilt.

Josie tipped her head and smiled. "Of course not."

She stared down into his eyes for a moment longer, suddenly wanting to kiss him. The temptation was so great she almost did—almost. Instead she lifted his hand, turning it over and inspecting the fingers.

"Which one?" she asked. Now why couldn't she remember? Her heart had begun drumming in her chest, and she felt light-headed.

He pressed his thumb to the injured finger, then pulled it back. Josie lowered her head and kissed the small wound, closing her eyes as she did, inhaling his scent. She heard him draw a sharp breath, and a second later he sat up beside her.

He stroked a curl near one side of her face, touching her cheek as he did. "You have the most beautiful hair," he said, his voice low. "That mornin' Maggie had me touch yer braid, I thought I'd never felt anything so soft in my life. Days when it was unpinned an' I was tryin' to take care of you . . . it nearly drove me mad."

Her thoughts became clouded. Somewhere in the back of her mind Josie knew she should get up, smooth her skirts, retrieve the vase and flowers, and finish that task. But she ached for more of his touch, and she loved his sweet adoration. She reached back and pulled the two pins that bound her hair, shaking it loose to flow down over her shoulders and back.

He gathered a section of it into his hands and brought it to his face, letting it slip a little at a time between his fingers. Smiling at him, Josie took his jaw in her hands and kissed his lips, praying like mad that he wouldn't think her too forward.

He returned the kiss, sweeping his arm around her and drawing her closer. He smoothed the hair back from her face and stared down at her.

"Where's this goin', Josie?" he murmured. "What happens when you leave St. Louis? I worry about that. I can hardly think straight whenever ye're near. I don't think past the moment, past holdin' you like this. But I've got to think past it."

She swallowed. "Where do you want it to go?"

A muscle flickered in his jaw. His eyes were like a cloudy sky, so filled with emotion and desire Josie wanted to melt against him.

"In truth, I think about marryin' you."

Josie opened her mouth, thinking to ask if he was being serious, but footsteps out in the hallway brought them both to their senses. Thomas kissed her once more, a mere brush of a kiss, then released her. Josie stood, smoothed her skirts, and hurried to where she had left the flowers and the vase.

Stephan entered the room just as Josie turned toward the door and Thomas was getting to his feet. "A little encounter with the pillar," Thomas explained when Stephan halted just inside the doorway, his curious look shifting between Thomas and Josie. Stephan burst out laughing. Josie giggled. Thomas couldn't seem to help a chuckle himself.

"Mr. Jefferson's looking for you," Stephan told Josie. "He sent me for some things and told me to look for you along the way."

Josie frowned, shrugging a shoulder at Thomas. "The manager calls. . . ."

He dusted off his waistcoat. "Could I call on you at the hotel tomorrow evenin'?" he asked Josie.

She nodded, feeling elated. He was pursuing her; she certainly wasn't pursuing him as she had Frank after a time. He was even talking about marriage—if he'd been serious about that. The more she thought about it, the more she thought he had been. His attention was flattering—and it was making her believe all over again that love could happen and that it could be good and beautiful.

Hours after his and Josie's antics in the costume room at Concert Hall, Thomas received a surprise visit at his office from Constance's father, Dr. Lucas Blanche, who directed the medical college.

Thomas and Johnny had just finished tending a three-year-old with an earache. Thomas was making notes about the case while Johnny straightened up the office and washed various instruments they had used at different times throughout the afternoon. They had a patient to call on just outside the city, an elderly woman who couldn't make the trip in. Thomas had called on Mrs. Perry twice a week for years to see how she was and to see if he could help her in any way. He sometimes ended up doing more than doctoring—in the spring and summer, he often planted and tended a small kitchen garden for her and harvested what he could during each visit; and during the fall and winter, he made certain she had wood for her stove. Mrs. Perry had no one else, and besides, she had tended him plenty enough times when he'd been a boy. She'd taken a switch to him a time or two, also, but only when he'd deserved it.

The wounds on Johnny's arm were nearly completely healed now, and he had come to the office yesterday afternoon and then today to assist where he could. He was cheerful, good with the patients, and eager to help in any way possible.

"Always busy, Dr. Murphy," Dr. Blanche said from behind Thomas shortly after Thomas heard the little bell over the front door ring. Johnny brought people back to him if they needed to be seen right away. As soon as Dr. Blanche had informed the boy of who he was, Johnny had surely told him where Thomas was.

Thomas twisted in his chair. "Dr. Blanche—a surprise."

Lucas Blanche was a strapping man, standing well over six feet with a gruff, ruddy demeanor about him and piercing gray eyes. His daughter did not resemble him, as she had inherited her mother's fair skin, pretty blue eyes, and soft features. Lucas was known for his fiery temper and unpredictable ways. He'd been involved in his share of St. Louis politics and in the medical society over the years, and more than one duel had resulted from arguments in which he'd embroiled himself. Still, the man was considered an upstanding St. Louis citizen, and he was well respected in the medical field, heading the college and regularly publishing medical reports about one thing or another.

"I was passing," Dr. Blanche said. "Thought I would stop here rather than at your home."

"Has somethin' happened at the college?" Thomas asked. "Have the students decided to play another prank an' steal a few bodies from the dissection room?"

Lucas Blanche laughed, to Thomas's surprise. He rarely did that. "Nothing like that. Nothing at all. You had the actress Josephine Gavin at your house as a patient for a time."

"That's right," Thomas said, feeling the first prickle of apprehension. Lucas knew he'd had Josie as a patient at his home because he and Thomas had discussed her case. "She was gravely ill. She sustained a depressed skull fracture."

"I understand you left her at her hotel the other morning."

Thomas nodded slowly. The man was direct, among other admirable things. He didn't waste a moment.

"I understand there was an . . . interchange in front of the hotel," Lucas said, the muscles around his eyes twitching.

Thomas had felt elated and euphoric that morning, knowing he was in love, and so he'd given in to the urge to kiss Josie in front of the hotel. He didn't regret the kiss, but he was beginning to regret where it had happened. "I made up my mind this mornin' to talk to Constance soon," he said. "I—"

"I make decisions where my daughter is concerned, Thomas. I introduced you to her because I saw promise in you. I still do and I would still like to see you marry Constance.

"I won't take up much more of your time," he said, plopping some papers down on Thomas's desk.

Thomas's jaw hardened. The papers were the findings of a study he had done on body temperature and an accompanying article he'd written. It was the first study Thomas had attempted, and only two weeks ago Lucas Blanche had read it and promised to circulate it among his colleagues and see it published.

"It's good," Dr. Blanche said. "I don't mind telling you that. With my endorsement and the endorsements of several other outstanding physicians, it might get some notice."

Thomas sat in silence, knowing what was coming next. Anger settled in his chest.

"I won't have my daughter subjected to gossip because you cannot seem to keep your hands off of that actress. She's your patient. The medical board at the college would be interested in knowing that one of our staff has violated an unspoken ethic."

Lucas didn't say exactly what he meant, but Thomas knew. He'd involved himself with a patient when he'd known he shouldn't have, and with a few words in the right places, Dr. Blanche could ruin his reputation in the medical society, at least in St. Louis, his home.

"She fired me as her physician the mornin' she left my house," Thomas said evenly. He shouldn't be arguing. He shouldn't be, not with the head of the medical college. But he had such a difficult time groveling at people's feet. Most of the time he refused to do it.

"Thomas, my daughter loves you. If you want to stay on staff at the college and if you want that study circulated and published, stay away from that actress."

Always direct and brief, Lucas Blanche tapped Thomas's desk once, then stood and walked out of the room, leaving Thomas sitting in a cloud of fury, wondering what his next move would be. Wondering what it should be. He couldn't see Josie again until he had this worked out, he knew that. There wasn't just his reputation to consider. If word of that kiss in front of the hotel had reached Lucas, then people were talking, and Josie's reputation might very well be damaged. It was already scrutinized because she was an actress. But this . . . People would wonder what had gone on while she'd been a patient in his home—if they weren't already wondering. He wouldn't see Josie hurt again, not by ugly gossip, not by anything.

He scribbled a note to her, saying something had come up for the following evening, when he had wanted to call on her again at the hotel, and that he would explain more later. He called to Johnny and offered a few dollars if the boy would deliver the message to the desk at the National Hotel and tell the clerk there that it was for Josephine Gavin. He'd take the rest of today and tomorrow to think about what he should do. Lucas Blanche had the power to ruin him. Damn the man anyway.

Johnny delivered the message exactly as he'd been instructed to, telling the clerk it was from Dr. Murphy to Miss Gavin. He turned away from the hotel desk and headed back for the doors, not seeing the clerk narrow one eye and slip the paper into his trouser pocket. Dr. Lucas Blanche had been here this morning, asking lots of questions about Miss Gavin and Dr. Murphy. On the side, he'd offered bills each time to prompt answers. He seemed curious about the actress and his fellow doctor—so curious he'd surely be interested in any messages passing between them.

With a discreet, smug grin, the clerk went back to sorting a stack of invoices.

Fifteen

PATRICIA FARREN VISITED Josie the following morning, looking bright in a cotton dress printed with pretty yellow flowers that enhanced her golden hair. Josie loved the material—in fact, it was similar to material she had purchased in one of the river towns nearly a year ago, though the flowers on her material were purple, she told Patricia. "I wanted to make myself a few cool summer gowns. I did start them."

"You didn't finish them?" Patricia asked, looking surprised.

"My manager and I often disagreed about what I should wear. My enthusiasm waned. It was often easier to go along with what he wanted. I still have them. The pieces of them." Josie went from the chair in which she had been sitting to one of two leather-bound trunks placed near the wardrobe. Patricia joined her as she hunched beside one, lifted the latch, and opened it. Josie dug down and seconds later lifted a pinned and half-stitched bodice. The flowers on the material were the identical shape and size as those on Patricia's dress. "The other pieces are down in there," said Josie.

"Oh, we should finish them," Patricia said excitedly, kneeling beside her. "I'm going home from here. This afternoon I'll be taking Katie and Charlie to visit Maggie—we hardly see her anymore since you settled her down." She smiled. "You could come along if you want. Bring your papers if you need to study them. I'll make sure you find time between us working on the dresses and visiting with the children. You are still considering joining the sewing group one evening?''

"I honestly hadn't thought any more about it. Not that I don't want to.''

"Then do think more about it.''

Josie glanced down at the piece of the bodice she held in her lap. "Are you certain you want to take me into your circle of friends?''

"And why wouldn't I? You're about the nicest person I've met, welcoming the girls into your heart the way you have.''

"I've never had a problem with allowing myself to be close to children.''

Tipping her head, Patricia smiled gently. "You'll be welcome. You are welcome. Believe that.''

Josie smiled back. "I don't think I know how to be a normal person, a normal woman. I've lived a nomadic adulthood so far, wanting to but never engaging in normal everyday activities. Orson thought I was silly, stitching my own dresses—and from cotton, at that. I haven't marketed for myself in years. I once knew how to cook, but I ruined the hotcakes I made for Thomas the other morning. He made a grand show of saying how delicious they were and of having Maggie and Mrs. O'Brien join him in eating them. But I knew. . . .'' She giggled—something else that she'd not done in years. "He was trying to get rid of them, I think. He feared he might have to eat them all himself so my feelings wouldn't be hurt.''

Patricia laughed with her. "We'll have you cooking again within days. Stitching, too. I do the marketing for my household, so you can join me if you want. I promise to remind you to rest now and then. I know you're still recovering. Fetch your papers now, and if you don't mind, I'll pull the other pieces of the dresses from the trunk.''

Josie handed her the half-stitched bodice, then rose and hurried off to gather Orson's manuscript.

Katie was still with her tutor when Josie and Patricia arrived at the Farrens' home. They settled in the upstairs parlor on matching red velvet settees, the pieces of material spread around them. Josie worked on the partially finished bodice while Patricia stitched the pieces of the second one. Patricia named the women in her group—Claudia, May, Lilian, Hetty, and Eleanor—though she was really close to only Claudia and Lilian. The three of them went for tea often at a café on Market Street, and they spent many an afternoon browsing in the numerous shops in and around St. Louis.

"I believe we're all rather unconventional," Patricia said with a mischievous smile, "but we do have fun. Our many activities and general busyness become a little much for our husbands sometimes, though Michael says he'd rather have me full of spirit, fun, and life than sitting at home doing nothing but running the household—though running the household can be quite a chore. Many chores rolled into one."

"I'm certain," Josie agreed. "But I'm also certain it would become monotonous after a time."

Patricia nodded. "I'll have the baby brought in soon, if you don't mind; maybe after we've picked up the pins and shears."

"Why would I mind? He's precious, Patricia, really."

"Yes," the other woman agreed, "but he's a bundle of energy, just like his sister lately. Sometimes Charlie wears me out, and he's only a year old! Now that he's walking, an eye has to be kept on him all the time; he's into so many things. Children his age . . . they have no sense of danger."

Patricia soon finished the bodice. She and Josie gathered the pieces of material and the pins and shears they had used, then went off to store them in a small trunk in Patricia's room rather than take them back to the hotel. They collected Charlie from his nursemaid and spent a good hour with him in the sitting room, watching him toddle about, laughing when he laughed, sharing more conversation.

"Oh, how I want a baby someday!" Josie said presently, drawing him onto her lap. He gazed up at her with his wide blue eyes, so innocent and sweet. He was so cute and precious with his round, chubby face, plump arms, six teeth, and his way of reaching up to explore her face.

"You will have," Patricia said, her eyes twinkling.

Josie smiled. "And how do you know?"

"A feeling I have."

"Truthfully?"

"Of course. In no time at all, St. Louis's own Dr. Murphy will propose, and Josephine Gavin will accept."

Josie laughed but shook her head. "Not for a time I won't. Not until I do what I want to do for Orson—my manager. Perform in something he wrote. It's . . . it's an account of our meeting and the years we spent together." She shook her head again, this time with a serious look on her face. "I never knew that he felt so deeply about me, that he cared so much. At times I felt like nothing more than merchandise to Orson. I thought that was how he viewed me, and of course any merchandise must be arranged and displayed in a desirable manner. I now believe he took a gruff position with me most of the time because he needed to distance himself, and that was the only way he knew to do it."

"It sounds as though you had an extraordinary relationship," Patricia commented.

Josie watched Charlie turn over in his hands a small wooden top Patricia had handed him moments before, then bring it to his mouth. "Extraordinary, yes."

"Did you love him?"

Josie glanced up. "That's what Thomas thinks."

"It seems so. The way you speak of him."

"I suppose I did . . . still do. But not in any romantic sense. I loved him as any girl might love her father. I think Thomas has a difficult time understanding our relationship." Fighting tears, Josie glanced back down at Charlie. "Orson was a huge part of my life. In many ways, he *was* my life. I miss him."

"If Thomas misunderstands, perhaps you should let him read what Mr. Neville wrote. Maybe after he reads the papers he'll have a better understanding."

"You may be right," Josie responded, thinking that sounded like a wonderful idea.

They played with Charlie a little more, letting him walk back and forth, laughing, between the two of them. Katie soon came in from her schooling and after visiting with her for a while, Josie thought she should go back to the hotel and rest. Patricia mentioned that she planned to take the children, including Maggie, to Chouteau's Pond in the afternoon day after tomorrow, barring spring rain, and asked if Josie still wanted to go along. Josie agreed to the outing; in fact, she honestly looked forward to it.

"The supper party is tomorrow evening," Patricia said. "Would you like to attend? I should forewarn you—I received notice nearly a month ago that Thomas plans to bring Constance, and I haven't been notified otherwise."

"I shouldn't, then," Josie responded quickly, wondering if Thomas still planned to escort Constance.

"Nonsense. Why deny yourself an evening out simply because he planned something before he met you? He probably feels he shouldn't cancel with Constance."

"Would he tell you if he did?" she asked, suddenly seized by apprehension. "Or would he simply bring someone else?"

"He would tell me. He obviously hasn't asked you, so he must still plan to bring her."

"I don't have an escort," Josie said quickly. "I wouldn't dream of attending alone."

Patricia shrugged. "Choose one of the actors in your troupe."

Josie teased, "My, and I thought you were conventional."

"Me?" Patricia blurted. They laughed together. Katie spun the top for Charlie, who squealed and batted at the toy. She playfully snatched it up before he could grab it.

"What's she like—Constance?" Josie could not help but ask.

"Meet her and see for yourself."

"Patricia."

The other woman laughed. A second later, she sighed. "Not at all like him. Not at all what he needs or deserves. She would bore him, as Maggie's mother often did. But I will say that Dr. Murphy devoted himself to Abby. There's not a disloyal bone in his body. Constance is reserved, very much a lady. Quiet and proper. Her father heads the medical college where Thomas instructs."

"I see."

"There would be security in such an alliance—the Blanches are also wealthy. But Thomas . . . I cannot imagine that he would be happy with Constance. And if he's thinking of finding a proper woman to mother Maggie . . . well, Constance is proper, but she would bore Maggie even more than she would bore Thomas. She does bore Maggie.''

"If he was considering marrying her, he must have wanted the security of the alliance much more than he wanted a companion who is like him,'' Josie said. She suddenly wasn't sure he wasn't still considering Constance. He hadn't said anything about the woman. He was certainly spending time with Josie, and he had mentioned marriage that once. Perhaps because he knew it was what she wanted to hear? She shook her head. All her doubt was returning, and with force.

How could she compete with wealth and alliance? Even if she could, she wouldn't. She had enough money of her own and could live comfortably for quite some time, but she certainly was not wealthy. Her family had been poor, and besides, none of them were alive that she knew of. This all reminded her a lot of the situation with Frank's world. One married within one's class for the sake of profitable alliance, both personal and financial. His was an unpleasant world to which she had once been exposed and never wished to be exposed again. She knew the draw of money and it scared her.

Charlie toddled toward Josie, grinning. She smiled, opened her arms, and he stumbled into them, babbling and resting his head against her breast for a few seconds. Then he began twirling his tiny fingers in her hair.

"Would it be unseemly for him to tell Constance his plans had changed?'' Josie asked aloud, searching for logical answers.

Patricia looked surprised. "If they have, no, not usually. But Thomas himself might consider it unseemly.''

"Or perhaps canceling would put him at a disadvantage with her father?''

Patricia studied her for a moment, then nodded.

Josie glanced away. "I shouldn't assume such a thing. I don't even know these people. But I'm surprised that he's bringing her, since he asked to court me. Since he has been courting me.''

"If he's been courting you, then you have every right to

assume things and to question.''

"I don't want to assume anything where Thomas is concerned. I shouldn't question. We haven't promised ourselves to each other. I may move on with the company in a few weeks, if my plan fails to sign with the St. Louis Theater. I'm still confused about what I want to do exactly, about where my future will be. Perhaps Thomas is thinking he'll carry on as usual unless I indicate that I'm staying in St. Louis.'' When she thought of how loving he'd been at the Hall yesterday morning . . . He surely wasn't still seeing Constance.

She wouldn't be the other woman again, the one who wasn't good enough to marry.

"Ask him what he's thinking, then,'' Patricia advised. "Asking is much better than guessing. It doesn't sound as though either of you knows what the other plans to do. In the meantime, surely you can find someone to escort you to the supper.''

Josie smiled. "We don't know what the other plans to do. We're both frightened, I think.''

"Then talk, Josie. And promise you'll attend the party? I could introduce you to a number of people, a number of my friends.''

Josie rolled her eyes, wondering how comfortable she would be wandering among a roomful of strangers. Onstage there was distance between herself and the strangers, and she dealt well with that. But to be right in the middle of them . . . She almost laughed aloud at a thought: that she'd once been a bubbly, social person. She recalled smiling a lot more during the days before her heart had been crushed, before she'd started hiding herself away. Oh, to emerge from the dark cloud in which she had placed herself! Oh, to learn to trust again, not to feel so apprehensive about people, even as much as she thought she had learned to trust Thomas. If the people attending the party were Patricia's friends, they must be nice, trustworthy people; and she did want to try to start meeting more people in St. Louis.

"I'll consider it,'' Josie responded.

"I'll plan on you being there. The next day, I'll come by the hotel for you at noon. I hope the day will be warm. Saturday afternoons are usually crowded at Chouteau's once the weather starts warming. I'll bring food and a rope for the girls—we'll turn it for them." She laughed. "Maybe I'll bring a rope for Charlie, too, and tie it around his waist. He wanders so much now that he's learned to walk!"

Josie laughed, something she had not done much of for a number of years before she had met Margaret, Thomas, Mrs. O'Brien, Mrs. Reardon, Patricia, Katie, and Charlie.

She smiled at Patricia. "Thank you for becoming my friend. I've never had another woman to talk to."

Patricia smiled back. "We'll be friends forever, I'm certain."

Once back at the hotel, Josie rested for several hours. Then she rose, expecting Thomas. She dressed in a gown of yellow silk, curled and pinned her hair, then sat waiting for his knock on her door.

He never came. She fell asleep in a chair, waiting, and woke at around midnight. Thoughts ran through her head: *What happened? Is everything all right? Has he changed his mind about wanting to court me, about wanting any sort of relationship with me?* She thought about taking a cab to his home to check on him and Maggie, then thought better. If he was having second thoughts, she didn't want him to think she was throwing herself at him. That she was desperate for his attention.

She undressed slowly, wondering if she would sleep. Tomorrow she would at least call on Margaret, since she hadn't seen her in days.

She did manage to fall asleep, though it was a restless sleep, and the following morning she woke to sunshine shimmering in through the open draperies. She rose and dressed, then went off downstairs to have breakfast.

She sent a message to the Murphy house, saying she planned to call on Margaret this evening—if there were no objections. After sending the message on its way, she took a cab to the Hall and spent the better part of the morning and afternoon there, going over lines with other actresses and actors and giving opinions about costumes.

Late in the afternoon, she returned to the hotel and rested, sleeping until early evening. For her visit with Maggie, she dressed in petticoats and a gown of purple and beige silk, and she was still brushing her hair, thinking to pin it up for the evening, when a knock sounded on the door. During the last few years, since her popularity had increased, she had become more and more leery of simply opening the door to a knock.

"Yes?" she called, twisting in her chair.

"Miss Gavin? It's Dr. Schuster."

She raised her brows in surprise. She had been so sick when she'd met him, she only vaguely remembered him. She remembered asking him to deliver her apology to Thomas, and she recalled how nice he had seemed, how sensitive. And then he had just disappeared.

She crossed the room and opened the door, greeting him with a smile. He had blond hair, twinkling green eyes, and he was a good foot taller than she. He grinned at her, holding a hat in his hands, and dipped his head in greeting.

"Ah! So nice to see you up and about, Miss Gavin—and with color in your face!" he said. "I thought we might get acquainted under better circumstances, especially since I'll be leaving St. Louis within the week. Would you care to have supper with me in the hotel dining room?"

"I would love to, but . . . I was going out soon to see Margaret, before she takes a notion to escape Mrs. O'Brien and come here. If she did, Thomas would be furious, and Maggie and I wouldn't have a pleasant visit because I would promptly take her home."

"A few days ago Thomas asked me to call on you. Would you mind if I went along?" he inquired. "Forward of me to ask, but I haven't seen Maggie much lately myself, and I am supposed to be checking on you."

"How is Thomas?" She should have bitten her tongue and not asked that. She wondered if he had seen him before or after Thomas had visited the Hall the other morning.

His grin became a smile, but a rather sad one. "He misses you."

"He knows where I am, Dr. Schuster. He could call. He was supposed to last evening and didn't. I hope nothing is wrong. I could call on him, but if he really cares, if he really misses me and wants to continue our relationship . . . I threw myself at a man once, Dr. Schuster. I threw myself completely at him. I won't do that again."

Alan Schuster's brow wrinkled. "You haven't seen him since when?"

"I saw him the other morning at Concert Hall. He called. Everything was fine. He didn't seem apprehensive at all. There's a supper party at the Farrens' tomorrow evening. He's expected there."

"With you on his arm?"

Josie shook her head. "He hasn't asked me. He may still be planning to escort the woman he's been seeing for some time. And yet, the day I left his home, he asked to court me—and he has been courting me. Her father heads the medical college, I hear. Perhaps Thomas . . . No. Foolish assumptions I shouldn't be making."

"Let's talk more in the dining room downstairs or in a cab going to Thomas's home," Dr. Schuster suggested as a man and woman walked up the hall toward them.

Blushing, Josie leaned against the door frame. "Yes, it hardly seems the thing to discuss in an open passage. I'll be out in a moment. I would invite you in, but I've met you only once and . . . I don't invite men into my hotel rooms."

"Notice I didn't ask to come in," he teased, his eyes twinkling again. "I'm Thomas's friend, therefore I'm your friend. If you'll have me," he added playfully.

She laughed. "A few moments, then. Wait for me downstairs, and we'll get a cab in front of the hotel."

"I'll wait near the front doors."

She watched him walk off whistling, and then she pulled back into the room and hurried over to her dressing table. She would forgo the pins, since curling and pinning her hair would take a good hour. She brushed it to one side the way Margaret had that day and braided it, tying the end off with a black ribbon. Not fashionable but practical—and Maggie would like it.

Dr. Schuster was waiting downstairs exactly as he'd promised, and he already had a cab waiting, too. He handed her up, then he climbed in, sat on the opposite seat, and they were off. The sounds of the busy city drifted through the open windows.

"Do you feel as well as you look?" he asked presently.

She tipped her head and smiled. "I feel well, yes, though at times I tire easily."

"*Very* well. You either feel very well or you don't feel as well as you look."

Smiling, Josie glanced down at the reticule in her lap.

"So what is this about Thomas taking Constance Blanche to supper at the Farrens'?" asked Dr. Schuster.

"I don't know that he's actually planning to do that. I was talking to Patricia Farren, who seems to think he is," she said, looking out the window. She watched two young boys, perhaps only seven or eight years old, as they chased a small dog up the street, dodging carts and people. "It's his prerogative if he does, but he might have mentioned it to me. Regardless, if he's gone back to Constance or feels obligated to take her to the supper, that's not about to change my feelings toward Margaret. I told her we would always be friends and I meant it. I devote myself to the people I love, but I refuse to be dirt under anyone's boots, not even Thomas's. Patricia Farren invited me to the supper, too, but I doubt that I'll go. I won't have fun if Thomas is there with another woman on his arm. He shouldn't have mentioned courting me if he didn't intend to pursue it seriously. I'm frustrated," she said, rubbing her forehead, "and I must sound like a pouting child."

He studied her for a time. She wondered what he was thinking.

"People don't realize there's a person behind the woman onstage, do they?" he asked.

She shook her head. "Many don't." She didn't want him feeling sorry for her. She'd said what she had to say about Thomas and Constance, expressing her concern and worry, and she didn't want to dwell on the subject. "So do you practice here in St. Louis, Dr. Schuster?" she asked, trying to talk about something more pleasant. Her problems were her own, especially where Thomas was concerned.

"I practice in Davenport. Upriver. Thomas and I attended

medical college together in Chicago. I came to visit and to take care of some business interests. I have rental property in St. Louis and I like to have a look at it once a year at least. I'd been in the city all of an afternoon and part of that evening when you were injured at the gaming house. As I said earlier, I plan to leave St. Louis within the week.''

"I'm grateful that you were there. My manager and Mr. Jefferson settled with Thomas for his part in my care. Mr. Jefferson said Thomas gave him the name of the hotel in which you were staying. Did he contact you?''

"It's all settled. You don't need to concern yourself," Dr. Schuster said. He tapped the seat. "Almost there. So . . . while everyone is having fun at the supper party, you plan to sit in your hotel room alone?''

Her lashes flew up. "Well, no, I . . . I haven't decided what I should do yet.''

"I think you should let me escort you to that party. Forget Thomas. Forget Constance. If Thomas is fool enough to let you go so easily, I plan to snatch you up—with your permission, of course.''

His attention was flattering. And perhaps it was exactly what she needed. She had been so taken with Thomas Murphy from the start; she had fallen in love so quickly and so easily. Surely he wasn't thinking of escorting Constance Blanche to that supper. Surely not. She couldn't seem to put the matter from her mind. She had spent the last several days trying to adjust her career so that she could stay in St. Louis if he asked her to, whittling at Mr. Jefferson slowly but surely, and she would be disappointed if her efforts were for nothing.

"Do you love Thomas?" Dr. Schuster asked.

"Too much," she answered almost immediately.

"Is he worth fighting for?"

"I don't want it to come to that. I've never even met Constance Blanche. I have no idea what—"

"That's not what I mean. You'll have to fight Thomas himself, because he rose from poverty, which helped mold his determination and ambition. He has the ludicrous idea in his head that he *needs* that appointment at the college, that he needs to keep Constance's father happy. He's wrong. The job doesn't pay very well, but it's his idea of being prestigious, of gaining respect. He needs a proper wife to help make him respectable, too. At least, those are the things he thinks he needs. Those are the things you'll have to fight.''

Josie dropped her head back against the seat. ''I'm not sure I have the courage to fight those things. I tried to fight respectability and prestige and propriety once. I failed.''

''Did the man love you?''

She closed her eyes, remembering Frank's many cruel words, his way of talking down to her at times as if she had no intelligence at all. He had been caught up in possessing the beautiful actress, and once he had, that had been enough.

''No, he didn't. I was a toy he tired of.''

''Thomas loves you. I watched him hold you the night you were injured. I watched a doctor who's most always calm and composed become distraught that you were injured. There's an indifference a physician must have when taking care of patients, and about the only time he loses it is when he's personally involved.''

''Perhaps he does love me,'' she responded softly, glancing at him. ''Then where was he last evening? I hate feeling that I'm not good enough.''

''Is that love worth fighting for?'' he asked.

She remembered how she had felt being with Thomas the other morning in the costume room, how he had made her feel so cherished. She recalled the way he cherished Margaret. . . . She loved the compassionate, noble man. She loved his sensitive nature.

''Yes.''

''Then a little jealousy won't hurt anything. If he sees you with me, he'll realize he has to make a choice. Otherwise, he'll lose you.''

The cab pulled to a stop before the Murphy home, and Dr. Schuster stepped out, then handed Josie down. ''Your fight starts now, if he's here,'' he said. ''Here we are together. . . . Call me Alan.''

This felt so awkward. Josie had never intentionally set out to make someone jealous.

''You're an actress,'' he said.

"He might draw further away," she argued. "We should wait. Perhaps this evening he plans to ask me to the supper."

"He might. But then, he might not. You're here to visit with Maggie; isn't that what you said?"

She nodded.

"Then visit with Maggie. Don't make any overt attempts to visit with Thomas. Be polite if you're addressed, but that's all. If he asks, he asks. If not, I'll escort you."

He started to pull away, dipping into a pocket to pay the driver.

"Wait," she said, pulling him back. "Why are you doing this? Why do you want to make him jealous?"

"Because Thomas is a friend," he said simply, "and I happen to think you're the right woman for him."

Nodding, she let him go. A moment later he offered his arm, and they approached the brick walkway that led up to the house.

Sixteen

MARGARET NEARLY BARRELED over her, throwing open the front door, shooting out of the house and racing up the walk-way. "Josie, Josie!" she squealed, as Alan laughed and stepped spryly away.

"It's that Maggie hurricane," he joked.

No petticoat was going to keep Margaret away. She did her best to wrap her arms around Josie's legs. Laughing, Josie pushed the petticoats aside as best as she could and hunched to Margaret's level, hugging the girl.

"Days and days since I saw you!" Maggie said. "It's too long!"

"I agree." Josie stroked the girl's back, squeezing again, then she withdrew to have a look at Margaret. "Well, I see you've been washing your face, and your hair is so shimmery in the sunlight—I imagine you brushed it three hundred strokes this morning!"

"Two hundred and sixty this evening. Then my arm got tired."

Josie laughed. "Your eyes are so bright, too. And dressed in yellow again! You look beautiful in yellow, Margaret. How's our kitten?"

"My eyes are bright because you're here! The kitten, she eats and eats all the kitchen scraps the cook tosses at her, and just yesterday she chased a squirrel down one of the garden paths. But she lost it when it scrambled up a tree. Some of my friends came from the levee yesterday, but you weren't here. Do you think we could make a time to be together one day so they could meet you?''

"We will."

"My feelings are hurt," Alan said from nearby. "Margaret is so taken with our actress, she hasn't even said hello to me." He stuck his bottom lip out, giving the girl a pout.

Giggling, Margaret went over to hug him tight around one leg. "I wasn't forgetting you, really!" He hunched, too, just as Josie stood and smoothed her skirt, and he pulled Maggie onto his lap. She whispered something in his ear, and he nodded, saying, "That's right. I'm proud of you." She whispered something else, and the conversation went back and forth like that for several minutes.

Josie felt someone watching her, and she glanced up and saw Thomas standing in the doorway, his eyes glowing. Her heart quickened almost immediately. He wore rust-colored trousers, a white shirt, and a neatly tied and flowing cravat. His hair waved gently around his face, falling back at his ears and flowing to just below his shoulders. She remembered the baby-soft feel of it and she longed to touch it again, to let its coolness slip between her fingers as she drew his head to her breast. She wanted to feel his warm breath on her skin, his lips on hers.

Is he worth fighting for? Alan had asked.

"Yes," she whispered as her gaze held Thomas's.

She started to walk the rest of the path, close the distance between them, but then she remembered Alan's advice not to make any overt attempts to visit with him, and she stopped herself. She also wondered if he would come out to meet her.

He did.

"Josie," he said, halting a distance of several feet in front of her, a look of longing in his eyes.

"Hello, Thomas." She wanted to say, *I waited last evening,* but she held her tongue.

Alan and Margaret had finished their private conversation, it seemed—Maggie slid off of his lap, and Alan stood. Josie held her hand out to Margaret and gave her a mischievous look from the corner of her eye. "Miss Margaret . . . the evening is rather warm for the end of March. Would you like to discard your shoes and stockings and play on the garden paths again?"

"Oh, yes!" Maggie said, clapping her hands. Josie heard Thomas chuckle and Alan mumble a question as to what in the world they were about to do. Margaret seized Josie's hand, and Josie gathered her skirt, suddenly wishing she'd left the petticoats back in the hotel room. Then they were off, running across the neatly kept lawn to the side of the house and around. In the back, they could sweep into the kitchen, leave their shoes and stockings there, then escape to the garden paths.

"I love you, Josie," Margaret said as they entered the kitchen.

Josie tugged on one of the girl's curls. "I love you, too."

They alternated walking and running along the paths, giggling at the feel of the unpaved paths and the cool bricks beneath their feet. They swiped at the low-lying branches of trees, hid from each other behind bushes, tree trunks, and the gardener's shed. They inhaled the earthy, fresh scent of the air and bent to ooh and ah over a patch of bulbs that were pushing their way up through the ground. Spring had arrived, sweeping away winter, and the land would blossom with color and life again soon, Josie marveled aloud. She glanced up to find Thomas and Alan watching the two of them from near one of the low brick walls, talking with each other. Thomas didn't seem his usual good-natured self, and it didn't take Josie long to guess that something was bothering him. Her presence here perhaps? But he grinned at her once, and she almost felt as though his arms were encircling her, his smile was so warm and filled with love and admiration.

"I'm thinkin' that dress might not come clean, Josie Gavin!" he called.

She glanced down at the dirt on the hem. Dirt smudged various places on the skirt, too. Smiling, she brushed at it. "If it doesn't, Patricia Farren and I will make another dress like it."

"Will you?"

"Yes. We spent the afternoon stitching some cotton dresses

I never finished because . . . Well, we had so much fun, I'm certain we'll be doing it again.''

"Josie," he teased, "Mr. Jefferson would have gowns made for you; y'know that. A seamstress could make all the stitches an' do all the work."

She stood, still brushing at a few spots. "I enjoy doing it myself."

"Have yer feet breathed enough for one evenin'?"

She laughed. "Oh, never enough, sir. Never. But I'm afraid they now need a bath." She lifted her skirt to her ankles so he could see her feet, which were coated with brown soil. Margaret's were, too, or so she saw when she looked at the grinning girl.

To the sound of his and Alan's laughter, she and Margaret headed up the path toward the kitchen.

From where they stood, Thomas glanced over at Alan and became serious for the first time since the two of them had watched Maggie and Josie race off around the house. Thomas had thought nothing of Alan and Josie arriving together. But in the hour since, he'd watched Alan warmly observe her playing in the garden with Maggie, and he'd become nervous, watching the way Alan looked at her. Was something going on between the two of them—Alan and Josie? He hadn't called on her at the hotel as he'd promised, but he had sent the message so Josie wouldn't be alarmed. Lucas had forced him into a corner, knowing how much his appointment at the college and the circulation of that paper meant to him.

He had called on Constance last evening, grudgingly, not wanting her to be the recipient of his foul mood but unable to help the fact that he was poor company. Lucas had been pleased to see him. He had asked about the paper, if Thomas wanted to return it to him. Thomas had mumbled something about holding onto it for now. He couldn't even look Dr. Blanche in the eye anymore, he was so furious with the man and had lost so much respect for him.

Josie will find someone else if there's no alternative, Thomas told himself, and as soon as he did he felt his chest knot up. He couldn't stand the thought. With the numbers of men who surely flocked around her much of the time, she was *certain* to find someone else—and quickly, too. He didn't know if he wanted her with Alan or anyone else, however. Alan was his best friend, knew he loved Josie, and he should respect that fact and stay away from her, even if he was attracted to her.

"Takin' her around the city to see the sights?" Thomas wondered aloud.

"Some, yes," Alan answered.

"You've a fondness in yer eyes when you look at her."

"She's a beautiful, charming lady, and I'm not one to let opportunity slide by when there's a rare find."

"She agreed to let me court her."

"I know," Alan said. "Are you doing it?"

Thomas narrowed one eye. "She left the house only days ago. I have—"

"Days . . ." Alan tapped his fingers on the top of the low wall. "I would have closed in already."

"I'm not a wolf after prey."

Alan grinned. "Thomas, every man is. And there's this thing called mating, you see. Male after female. Some males are more aggressive than others."

"Don't speak to me as if I'm an imbecile." The man acted like he was playing a game and that Thomas should be as good-natured about it as he was! Thomas almost spilled everything—he almost told Alan about Lucas's threats. But he wasn't ready to share the humiliation and fear with anyone. He would find a way out. He would, and hopefully, in doing so, he would find a way to preserve both his relationship with Josie and his medical career.

"You're taking Constance to a supper party tomorrow evening," Alan said, catching Thomas by surprise.

"How did you learn that?"

Alan turned a hard look on him. "It's true, then. I heard speculation, and that's all that matters. No, what really matters is that you led Josie to believe you wanted her, but you can't seem to let go of Constance and the respect and advancement you know you'll gain by marrying her. What's the matter with you? Does—"

"You're assumin' that's what I'm doin'," Thomas responded tightly.

"I know you, Thomas Murphy, therefore I know that's what you're doing. Josephine Gavin is not only beautiful, she's devoted, bright, intelligent, and witty—and she has a heart of gold for Maggie. If you think for a moment that Josie doesn't have a variety of men and a number of them to pick from, then you *are* an imbecile."

"I know all those things about her," Thomas responded, smoothing his cravat. Smoothing his feathers. They felt rather ruffled right now. "What are yer plans?"

"To see her as much as possible until I leave St. Louis next week. Good God, you sound like her father, not her suitor."

Thomas breathed deeply. "Don't be insulting. We haven't had much of a visit this spring, you an' I. We've argued more than we ever have. Try to understand. Dr. Blanche came to me yesterday morning. He's not happy, I'll say that. A few words in the right places an' he could discredit me, Alan."

"You have to make a choice," Alan responded gruffly. "If it's Constance, then it's Constance. Let Josie go on not having to wonder whether she's more important or at least as important as your position at that damn college."

Obviously not wanting to hear more, Alan walked off before Thomas could explain further.

Thomas watched Josie the rest of the evening as she laughed and interacted with Mrs. Reardon, Mrs. O'Brien, and Maggie over supper and with Maggie and Alan in the sitting room a little later. They played with the kitten, and Alan joined them, frolicking on the floor. What if he couldn't untangle the mess he'd gotten himself into? What if he couldn't break it off with Constance and somehow preserve his medical career? What if it took him so long to find a way out of the dilemma that Josie ended up marrying Alan—or someone else?

Alan would be the better choice, Thomas told himself. He'd make a devoted husband. If she were truly willing to settle in one place—and he didn't know whether she was because he hadn't asked—Alan would be the best choice. Even if she weren't willing to settle in one place, he didn't know that Alan would mind that. Alan really did look at her as if he'd love to have her, and he was certainly financially secure enough that Josie would never have to worry about money. He'd make a good father, too.

Thomas squeezed his hands together, leaned an elbow on the arm of the chair in which he sat, and pressed his fist to his mouth. He'd never felt such turmoil inside.

The three of them began quieting a little, talking and laughing more softly. Maggie yawned. Thomas glanced off at the fireplace and watched the licking flames. Josie laughed again, and he had the sudden urge to sink to the floor beside her, rest his head on her shoulder, and tell her his fears: He was scared of losing her, but he was also scared of losing his position at the college. He was worried that the study and article wouldn't be circulated if he involved himself with her more right now. He was scared that, despite his feelings for her, she might decide to leave St. Louis with her company. He also wanted Maggie to grow up feeling secure in her position in life and proud of who and what she was—he wanted to make it so she was a class beneath no one. Lucas Blanche had the power to rob sweet Maggie of that security.

"Come along, Maggie, I'll take you up to bed," Josie offered, rising and extending a hand. Maggie took the hand, and they left the room together.

"I'm thinkin' I'll join them for a few moments," Thomas said.

Nodding, Alan settled on an opposite settee. Thomas half expected him to be right on his heels, and he was grateful that Alan was obviously allowing him, Maggie and Josie some time alone.

Upstairs, Thomas and Josie tucked Maggie in together. Thomas tickled her a little, nuzzling her neck with his chin, and then Josie softly sang tunes that lulled her to sleep in just a few minutes.

"She was tired from all that activity," he teased as they walked out of the room. "All that runnin' through the garden an' tusslin' around on the floor."

"Yes, she was," Josie said, smiling and turning to walk off down the dimly lit hall. "She should sleep well tonight. And the lamp is lit and the door open."

As he had been a number of times since meeting Josie, he was seized by the thought that allowing anyone else the opportunity to mother Maggie was ludicrous. Josie had become Maggie's mother; there was no doubt about that. He loved Josie more with each passing day, with each passing moment. Right now he thought he was being a fool for still considering Constance, for allowing her father to force him into still considering her.

"Josie," he said, going after her. She had nearly reached the staircase. She would go down and they would be with Alan again. Thomas wanted to be alone with her for a time where no one could see them, where they could hide from the ugliness in which he'd found himself. What he really wanted to do was sweep her up into his arms, carry her into his bedroom, and make love to her. Sweet, passionate, uninhibited love.

She paused with her back to him. Then she slowly turned and put her back to the railing. The lamplight flickered in her eyes, orange one second, yellow the next, as she turned her head slightly to regard him. Her ivory skin appeared satiny; his gaze swept openly over her face, down to her neck, to the gentle swells of her breasts, then down her arms.

He heard the sharp breath she inhaled; he almost felt her stiffen. Afraid she would bolt, he stepped close and planted his hands on the railing on either side of her.

She lowered her lashes, breathing swiftly. "If you changed your mind about calling . . . about everything, you might have at least sent me a message last evening so I would know you and Maggie were fine. I worried. What are you—?"

He dipped his head and boldly kissed her lips, driven by desperation, frustration, exasperation, and fear. She gasped, and he kissed her chin, then nipped his way to her mouth again, bringing his hand to her jaw, wanting her to open to him as she had the night he'd first kissed her outside her room down the hall. This was insane. He shouldn't be doing this. It was madness. It was professional suicide—if he was caught.

"Thoma—"

He kissed her again, parting her lips with his tongue, hoping to end her objection.

She turned her head away, closing her eyes briefly, pursing her lips and swallowing.

He ran his hand down her arm and enclosed her fingers in his. "Josie."

She snatched her hand away. "You don't know what you want. It's late, and Alan is waiting downstairs. If you want to talk, Thomas, I'll be at the hotel most of tomorrow morning. But that's all it will be—talk."

"I can't be goin' near the—"

"Good night," she said, moving away. She lifted the left side of her skirt and fairly fled down the stairs, leaving Thomas standing on the second-floor landing alone.

He cursed under his breath. He had lectures tomorrow morning. Besides, he wasn't going near that hotel. He'd explain to her tonight, even if Alan was standing right there.

Hearing a sound like Maggie crying out, he strode back to her bedroom door. She was still sleeping soundly. He nearly stepped on the kitten when he turned to leave again. It hissed at him, then raced into the room and leaped up onto the bed.

. . . you might have at least sent a message, Josie had said. But he had. Hadn't she received it?

Downstairs, he strode toward the sitting room, where he felt certain Alan and Josie would be waiting to tell him good night before they left, and where he meant to ask her if she'd received his message last evening. Only Mrs. Reardon was present. She informed him that Miss Gavin and Dr. Schuster had left moments before.

Thomas cursed, rubbed his jaw, then sank down onto one of the settees to watch the dying fire.

Josie was introduced to Patricia's husband shortly after she and Alan arrived at the Farrens'. She could think of no other match for Patricia than Michael Farren. He was tall, with golden hair like Katie's and merry blue eyes. It was apparent right away how much he adored his wife. He was friendly and playful, at times filling a room with laughter and conversation. He offered Josie his arm in the entryway almost as soon as a servant took her pelisse and Alan's coat and hat, and she accepted, allowing him to lead her to the nearby parlor where several couples had already gathered.

"Just as Patricia described you," Michael Farren said. "Quiet, musing, a little fearful, maybe. I don't know too many people in St. Louis who would try to snap your head off. Except the aristocratic Creoles, maybe."

"Michael," Patricia admonished, stepping up behind them with Alan at her side. "They were here first, remember that, and slowly but surely we're all learning to live in harmony."

"Yes, dear. I know, dear," he responded, grinning.

She shot him a severe but playful look. "Heaven help us if our son develops your personality."

"He already has. He likes strong drink, strong women, and he likes to explore."

"Michael Farren, you'd better not be giving him spirits!"

Michael grinned. "He already has spirit, Mrs. Farren."

Another severe look. Alan chuckled. Josie found herself smiling at the playful exchange, but also wondering, like Patricia, if Michael really had given the baby something stronger.

He patted Josie's hand. "My wife is disgruntled. "I'd better do as she requested and introduce you to people."

He whisked her away, leading her toward two couples who stood near a window. Patricia and Alan went back out into the hall, with Patricia shaking her head and Alan still laughing.

Josie met the Haslers—Richard and Claudia—and then Russell and Lilian Doss. She recalled Patricia mentioning both women—they were in her sewing group, and they all shopped together. Patricia had already told them about her, too, and they were friendly right away, both Claudia and Lilian luring her away from Michael. She, Claudia, and Lilian settled on a sofa while the men began socializing near the window.

"You have dresses that need to be finished, Patricia tells us," Lilian said. She was a small woman, tiny almost, with shimmery brown hair arranged in fashionable curls and pinned back from her face. Her eyes were a dark shade of blue, but kind.

"After that, she says you need to see the city," Claudia said. "Well, parts of it. Every city has its bad areas."

Patricia could be overwhelming, Josie thought with a smile.

"There's a traveling show due in next week. Acrobats and equestrians," Lilian said just as more people appeared in the doorway—Thomas, with a woman. Constance.

Elegant, almost stately, refined, and doubtless well-mannered, Constance Blanche was more competition than Josie was prepared to deal with. Swept up, curled, and pinned in layers with a modest amount of bangs curling on her forehead, her reddish-brown hair was stunning. So were her vivid blue eyes, lined with dark lashes, as they surveyed the room, assessing. She wore a rich blue gown, off the shoulder, with tightly fitting long sleeves that were ruffled at the wrists. Her milky white skin appeared unblemished, as if she hadn't spent an hour in the sun in her entire life. She could be no more than seventeen or eighteen, which surprised Josie. But then, it didn't if Thomas wanted someone he could groom into the wife and mother he sought. A younger girl might be more willing to be clay in his hands. Josie was not, no matter how much she loved and wanted him—and she wouldn't hide in the shadows with him. If he wanted to kiss her, he could do it in the open—perhaps in front of the National Hotel again. If she let him.

"Don't compare yourself," Claudia leaned close to whisper. "She's cold, one of the snobbish. You shall see."

"Acrobats," Josie commented, thinking she would take Alan's advice and have fun. She felt more insulted than ever—how dare Thomas kiss her on the landing last night and then today escort another woman to a supper party! Her temper was boiling. The situation was too similar to the one she'd embroiled herself in in New Orleans three years ago, only this time she had at least preserved part of her dignity—she had the satisfaction of knowing that she hadn't slept with Thomas Murphy.

Josie faced Lilian, trying to act nonchalant. "Have you ever watched acrobats?"

"No, but I thought the show might be interesting. The thought of people turning somersaults and flying about on swings in the air and walking ropes . . . it sounds exciting."

"And we do like exciting," Claudia said, smiling mischievously.

"Exciting would be learning to master the swings and ropes," Josie said. "A few people in my company do some acrobatics on stage when the occasion calls."

"Do they?"

Josie nodded. "Have your husbands take you to the theater."

Lilian laughed. "Why do we need them to take us? We would go alone!"

Josie laughed too. "Unfortunately the management wouldn't let you in without a male escort."

"There are times when we need our men and there are times when we don't," Claudia said. "Lilian, I'm sure I could strip off the petticoats, stuff my chest enough, slip on a man's hat, and be your escort."

Both Lilian and Josie laughed again, harder this time.

"Please, oh, please, tell me when the comedy is to take place so I can be on hand to watch." Josie requested.

"We should plan on it, Lilian."

"Claudia," the other woman admonished.

"Good evening, Mrs. Hasler . . . Mrs. Doss," came a soft voice. Constance Blanche had apparently walked up to them while they had their heads together plotting Lilian and Claudia's infiltration of the theater, and now here she stood, looking beautiful and elegant, but also as if she would certainly like to be welcomed into their little gathering. Thomas had gone off toward the group of men, Josie noticed.

"Hello," Claudia said stiffly.

"Good evening," Lilian said. Neither woman looked up at Constance. Certainly neither asked her to sit down. Both had sobered.

Affecting a smile, Josie stood and faced Constance, refusing to be rude, not even to the person she strongly suspected Thomas intended to marry. "I'm assuming you're Miss Blanche?"

"Yes. And you are?"

"Josephine Gavin."

Josie watched the woman's eyes flare and her face pale more, if possible. She was surprised her hand didn't fly up to her throat or her mouth, Constance looked so aghast. "The actress," the woman blurted, discomposed.

"*An* actress, yes."

"You were a patient at Thomas's home for a time."

"Yes, I was. Would you like to sit down?" Josie asked, motioning to the sofa.

She hesitated, and Josie wondered if she meant to refuse. Then Constance smiled a little, though stiffly, and sat.

All four of the women sat just so for a long moment, Claudia and Lilian having suddenly become quiet, Constance fingering a tassel on her reticule, undoubtedly wondering why Patricia Farren had invited an actress into her home. Josie normally was angered by superior attitudes, but Constance didn't have her nose in the air; she didn't have a superior attitude. She simply appeared . . . uncomfortable, as if she had been taught to stay away from actresses, especially this one, and didn't know exactly what to do now that she found herself in Josie's company—and in a respectable home, at that. Perhaps the fact that Josie had spent time in Thomas's home had something to do with her looking so uncomfortable, too.

"Your gown is beautiful," Josie ventured. "The fittings required to stitch those sleeves just so must have been endless."

Constance managed another smile, then a slight laugh. "They were. The bodice, too. Hours."

"One fitting of mine literally went on all day. Well, off and on all day. It was for a gown I wore in . . ." Josie laughed. She was so used to discussing costuming and other things with her thespian peers, she'd forgotten the company she was in for a moment. "One of the many productions I've done."

"I saw a sketch of you in the newspaper recently," Constance said. "There was a piece about your return. I probably shouldn't have read it, but I could not resist. I was curious. You're much more beautiful than the sketch."

"I would love to see you perform," Lilian said.

"Thank you, Constance. Soon, Mrs. Doss. Soon," Josie teased. "If you and Claudia insist on being independent about it, and you can't steal some of your husband's clothes, I'll rummage through my trunks at the theater and see what I can find in the way of men's clothing. Surely we'll come up with a good disguise."

She, Claudia, and Lilian laughed together again. Constance sat staring at them, obviously wondering what Josie was talking about.

"Oh, never mind," Claudia told the girl. Lilian waved her hand, indicating she didn't want to bother with an explanation either.

Josie placed her hand on Constance's arm and lowered her voice. "Claudia and Lilian seem to have a problem getting their husbands to take them to the theater. A woman could not attend a performance without a male escort, so Claudia volunteered to dress like a man and escort Lilian."

Claudia and Lilian had both sobered and were now looking at Josie as if she had lost her mind—what did she mean telling the proper Constance such a thing? What did she mean taking her into their confidence? But Josie wouldn't have dreamed of sharing a secret with Claudia and Lilian and excluding someone who sat close by. That would have been rude.

Again Constance's eyes flared, and she paled more, looking uncomfortable.

Josie leaned toward her, looking at her from the corner of her eye. "Imagine it! Claudia, not exactly proper but at least somewhat ladylike, dressed like a man, Lilian on her arm, and the two of them sneaking in, fooling everyone." She sighed heavily, dramatically. "I would like a ticket, please. I do have an appreciation for theatrics. It must have something to do with my background."

That got a smile out of Constance. A few seconds later the young woman actually laughed, gazing at Josie with a touch of amazement in her eyes.

"You could entertain a roomful of people," Constance said.

Josie grinned. "Why, Miss Blanche, that is usually what I do."

"Yes, it is, isn't it?" Constance laughed again, and her eyes brightened. "You are exactly as Thomas told my father you were a few days after you were injured. You're charming."

Josie sobered a little, and the two women studied each other. Josie wondered why Thomas and Constance's father had been discussing her. It didn't matter; not really. By escorting Constance even after their encounter upstairs at his home last eve-

ning, Thomas had made his choice, and she had to live with
it. She would go on with her life. She was actually excited
about going on with it. She was making friends, good friends,
not just acquaintances. She was meeting genuine, sincere people, women who seemed as spontaneous and fun as she had
wanted to be for a long time. She would marry Thomas in a
heartbeat if he asked her, but he apparently did not intend to.
And though she was sad about that, she had survived heartache
before, even worse things, and she would survive this.

Still, the hard part was not knowing how his change of heart
had come about. That morning in the costume room at the
Hall he had seemed so sincere, so loving. He had made her
feel so special.

She dipped her head, acknowledging Constance's comment,
just as Patricia led two more couples into the parlor.

Thomas had been surprised and even somewhat alarmed
when Patricia led the way into the sitting room and he spotted
Josie on the sofa with Claudia Hasler and Lilian Doss. Either
she or Patricia Farren had mentioned days ago that she'd been
invited, but he hadn't really thought she would show up. And
with Alan. Alan again.

He had expected trouble, a confrontation, maybe heated
words from Josie to Constance. Constance was quiet, but he
knew Josie's temper by now. He'd thought about his forward-
ness of last evening, berating himself that he hadn't had more
control. But then, he never had where she was concerned. He
owed her an apology. He wasn't proud of his actions. He'd
wanted to touch her and kiss her and so he had, being rude
and overbearing.

Instead of the unpleasant scene he expected between Josie
and Constance, he watched Josie welcome Constance when it
became obvious that neither Claudia Hasler nor Lilian Doss
planned to. He watched Josie strike up a conversation with
her, touch her fondly on the arm, and even lean toward her,
smile and speak low, taking her into her confidence about
something. Unbelievable, that's what it was, that Josie was
being so friendly to the woman everyone thought he meant to

marry. And it was unbelievable that his main circle of friends, a fairly prominent circle in St. Louis, had welcomed Josie so easily.

"I hear you thinking, What the devil is she doin'?" Alan whispered loudly over Thomas's shoulder. Richard Hasler turned a grin on them. Paul Christy, who had arrived a short time ago with his companion for the evening, chuckled under his breath. Russell Doss fought a grin and lost.

"We heard you'd developed an interest in the actress," Paul said. "Apparently someone in her company spilled the news."

"And someone saw you with her outside the National Hotel one morning. My, my. People are speculating," Richard commented.

"Women are gossiping," Russell added. "The men . . . we're trying to avoid the Temperance folks and lay down bets."

Thomas glared at the lot of them, then fixed the glare on Alan. "Someone in her company, eh? I trust all of you'll keep yer opinions and bets to yerself tonight. I don't want Constance hurt by them. She wouldn't understand."

"Neither would Dr. Lucas Blanche, I'd venture," Richard remarked. "Slight the man or his kin, and he gets hell-bent on revenge. Remember that fiasco he orchestrated out on Bloody Island some five years back? He and Will Franklin took a disliking to each other, Will insulted him a time or two, and Dr. Blanche challenged him. They each missed the other three times before they gave the matter up as a bad affair."

The entire group of men, excluding Thomas, laughed.

"Oh, but what followed was nothin' to laugh about, gentlemen," Thomas said. "Dr. Blanche led a charge on Franklin after that, discreditin' him everywhere, an' he didn't let up till Franklin was a ruined man."

"You won't have that happen to you, is that what you're saying, Thomas?" Alan queried.

"Would you?" Thomas countered. "Dr. Blanche does pretty much run the medical college."

"Dr. Blanche *is* the medical college," Alan responded. "But that's no reason to marry his daughter."

Thomas set his jaw. No, it probably wasn't, but it was none of Alan's business, either.

"Have a conversation with him, Thomas," Russell advised.

"I did."

"If you're in a predicament, get yourself out of it," Alan said. "If you need help—"

"If ever'one plans to berate me about this all evenin' an' interfere in my affairs, I'll be retirin' early," Thomas growled under his breath. He turned away from the group just as a servant appeared in the doorway to announce that supper was served.

Josie and Constance were seated across the table from each other, and managed to hold a conversation during supper. Constance seemed fascinated with Josie, and Josie was polite and even friendly. They engaged in conversation about music, then reading material, and then a little about the theater, which surprised Thomas since he was certain Constance knew exactly who Josie was by now and knew of his involvement with her. Word of his kissing Josie in front of the hotel had made the rounds if it had reached the ears of his friends, and surely Constance knew about it. In trying to shield her from things, Lucas Blanche often gave his daughter little credit for having a brain.

Patricia Farren was seated to Thomas's right, and though she tried to interest him in conversation, he finally apologized and told her he wasn't feeling too talkative this evening. She gave him a look that said she understood. Alan, on the other hand, tossed him a sharp look or two during the meal. Damn the man anyway. A friend? He'd walked away from him last evening when Thomas had tried to explain why he still planned to escort Constance to the supper. A true friend would listen and try to understand. What would Alan do if he were in the same situation?

Patricia had hired a violinist to play for the gathering in a small but elegant ballroom that extended the length of the back of the house, and after the meal, that was where the group eventually drifted. They engaged in quadrilles for a time, and Thomas found himself close to Josie, unable to avoid her when she passed near him a number of times and also when she placed her hand lightly on his arm and turned with him. He was more aware of her than he was of any other woman in the room—but then he thought just about every man was; she was so bright, bubbly, and full of life, winning everyone's affection with her laughter and wit. He caught whiffs of her perfume and watched the lamplight dance in her dark eyes. He'd been under her spell since the night he had rushed into his sitting room, thinking to save Maggie from the evil clutches of Josephine Gavin. What he'd found was an angel. A blessed angel.

Once when she placed her hand on his arm he dared to glance up, meet and hold her gaze, looking deeply into her eyes, wanting to convey an unspoken request that she please understand. He was more frightened than he had been in a long time, frightened of losing things he'd worked hard to attain, but he was also scared of losing her. He thought he had lost her, and he didn't blame her for pulling away from him last evening, but he was in pain that she had. He wanted to draw her to him so badly, inhale the scent of her hair, inhale her scent . . . tell her he didn't know yet what to do about the situation in which he'd found himself. An alarmed look, a look of question, flashed in her eyes.

"Josie," he whispered, and then she was out of his grasp, moving away, turning and circling and dipping so gracefully, appearing calm. Beautiful, poised Josie.

An hour or so later he walked into the parlor and found her standing near Constance, who was playing the pianoforte. They began singing together as the other women and a few of the men gathered around to listen. Thomas shook his head. Josie . . . befriending the woman whom she must think had been chosen over her. She'd done it because she didn't have it in her to be resentful, mean, or spiteful toward anyone. As much as he loved the woman on the outside, he loved the inner woman more.

She truly possessed a heart of gold.

He went outside after a time to breathe the evening air and try to collect his thoughts. Alan was there, smoking. He stepped from the shadows of a tree, flicking the ashes from the tip of a glowing cheroot.

"So what is it?" he asked. "Something's shaken you up
pretty bad, my friend. Given the way you talked about Lucas
Blanche and his Bloody Island duel earlier, I imagine he has
something to do with it."

"I tried to tell you last night," Thomas grumbled.

"I know. But last night you didn't look scared."

"Lucas got word of the exchange between me'n Josie in
front of the hotel. He's makin' threats—he won't publish my
paper an' findin's, an' he's threatenin' to see me discredited.
Lucas doesn't play little games, Alan. He plays big ones. He'll
do what he's threatenin' if I don't either marry his daughter
or find a way around him."

Alan cursed. "Too bad Will Franklin isn't a better shot. He
might have killed Blanche in that duel. Such a disregard for
a human life—but then I wouldn't call Blanche human right
now. So find another reputable physician to publish your paper
and findings. It might take some time, but you could find another one. As for the college position, well, there are other
colleges. Lucas Blanche needs to remember that. Just about
any would snatch you up, Thomas."

"You make it sound easy."

"I didn't say it would be easy—and there's no guarantee
that Blanche won't muddy your reputation. But you do have
options. In the meantime, Josie deserves an explanation. I'll
tell her a little, enough to let her know why you're hardly
speaking to her in public. The rest is your business."

Thomas nodded. Seconds later, Alan snuffed the cheroot
beneath his shoe and strode back toward the double doors that
led inside.

Seventeen

JOSIE STEPPED INSIDE the hotel lobby, turned, and watched as the cab in which Alan was still riding pulled away from the building and traveled up the street. She gathered her pelisse close at her throat, still chilled from the evening air, still thinking about what he'd just told her inside the cab. How frightened and desperate Thomas must feel. How awful. She wouldn't sleep a minute tonight worrying about him. His involvement with her was causing him a lot of grief that he and Maggie didn't deserve. She should pack her belongings and leave St. Louis tonight so there would be no more suspicion or ugly gossip from Lucas Blanche or anyone else.

The glow of the lanterns on Alan's carriage became distant. Still Josie stood, thoughts circling in her head.

"May I help you with something, Miss Gavin?" Mr. Clarey, the night desk person, asked from behind her.

"Perhaps you could have someone fetch me another cab," she responded, reaching a decision. Probably a hasty, unwise one. But she had to see Thomas—tonight. "I need to go out again, and right away."

"I sure will, Miss Gavin."

Moments later, another clerk scurried by her and outside. Less than five minutes after that, another cab pulled up in front of the hotel, and Josie went out to board it.

It's insane, what I'm doing, she thought, once nestled inside the cab, her back against a corner of the seat. She sometimes had very little self-control where Thomas Murphy was concerned, it seemed. As she had told Alan, she loved him too much. Yes, Thomas was worth fighting for, but now that she'd met Constance, she didn't plan to fight. She was going to him to be his friend, to try to understand him, to talk to him about the fear and desperation he must be feeling, about what Alan had told her. She'd looked into his eyes during that dance earlier and she'd known something was wrong. Last evening she hadn't understood the way he had so aggressively closed in on her after she had come out of Maggie's room, but maybe now she did. Maybe his behavior had something to do with being scared of losing her and of being in a frightening situation with Lucas Blanche.

In front of the Murphy home, she paid the driver, then turned toward the house. It was dark except for the glow emanating from an upstairs window. Thomas's room. He was still awake, then. She hoped. He and Constance had left the Farrens' an hour before she and Alan departed, so he had been home for some time.

She rapped lightly at the door, hoping she wouldn't wake Mrs. O'Brien if she had gone to bed. The hour was late—it was probably after eleven.

The nursemaid answered the door, her wrap clutched tightly around her waist, her nightcap a little askew. "Miss Gavin," she said in surprise.

"Sorry to have awakened you, Mrs. O'Brien. Is Dr. Murphy home? If so, is he awake?" Josie asked.

"Why, yes, he's home. I don't know about awake. . . . Is something wrong?"

"Mrs. O'Brien, who . . . ? Josie," Thomas said, coming up the hall, stopping short near the sitting room door, a lamp dangling from one hand. "Shut the door, Mrs. O'Brien. Quickly."

The woman wrinkled her brow but did as he ordered. Then she bid them good night and went off up the hall, turned up the staircase, and soon disappeared.

"Josie, what are you doing here?" Thomas asked.

"You should tell me. What is happening, Thomas? The

look in your eyes earlier . . . fear. I didn't understand until Alan told me about Dr. Blanche. Now I also understand why you didn't call the other night at the hotel.''

He exhaled heavily, stepping toward her and lowering the lamp. Another still glowed in the entryway. ''I sent a message that night. It obviously didn't arrive. I'm not believin' my eyes. 'Tis a dream an' I'll wake soon. I'll blink an' you won't be here when I open my eyes.''

''Thomas, I don't think you should—''

''Shh,'' he said, drawing two fingers down over her lips. ''I love you, Josie. Know that. An' I plan to work to have you.''

His hand dropped to her neck, to the clasp of her pelisse. She gasped, wondering if she should stop him from touching her, knowing she should.

''I do love you, Josie,'' he whispered, and she shut her eyes as he worked at the clasp. What was he doing? What did he plan to do once he removed her wrap? ''I'm scared of losin' you.''

He set the lamp on the floor to his left, then slid his hand up into the back of her hair. His other hand slid under the pelisse and it slipped from her shoulders, tumbling to the floor. The sleeves of her wine-colored gown barely clung to her shoulders. He ran his hand along her collarbone, up and down her neck, and caressed her jaw. She relished his touch, tipping her head back, only briefly thinking of stopping him.

''Tell me to stop if you don't want me to touch you, Josie,'' he grated. ''I'll respect that. God, you looked so beautiful this evenin' . . . now. Still wearin' the same gown. I couldn't bear not lookin' at you much, not talkin' to you, not introducin' you myself to my friends.''

Josie brought her hands up to stroke his hair, catching her breath when he dipped his head to kiss the upper swells of her breasts. She shouldn't let him do this. She just shouldn't. For his sake, she should stop him.

''I don't know what I'll do about Lucas. But I'll do somethin','' he promised. ''We'll be together, Josie.''

She shook her head. ''Oh, Thomas, you're not thinking

clearly. You're not thinking past what you're feeling right now. Neither am I, really.''

He glanced up at her face, and his eyes glowed like fire. She doubted if he would sleep tonight either; so much troubled him. She would stay with him, the way he had stayed with her those awful nights following Orson's death.

Reaching yet another quick decision, she lowered her head to kiss him. ''Grab the lamp, Thomas,'' she said softly. ''We'll go upstairs.''

When he hesitated, straightening to stare at her, she gave a small, nervous laugh. ''Quickly now, before I change my mind,'' she said.

This time he reached for the lamp at the same time she bent and scooped up her pelisse.

Within seconds of their entering his bedroom and of his shutting the door, he was behind her, running his hands up her arms and over her shoulders. She'd meant only to come up and sit with him, perhaps in front of the fireplace, but she wasn't so naive that she hadn't wondered on the way upstairs if something more might happen. She had sensed something different about him last evening, and this evening she knew it was fierce desperation.

He buried his face in her hair and whispered her name in a way that only he could whisper it. It sounded so different when he said it than when anyone else said it; it sounded so special. She dropped her head back onto his shoulder, melting against him, now needing him almost as much as he seemed to need her.

His lips caressed her jaw, then sought the tenderness of her neck. She bared it to him, trusting him in lovemaking as much as she had trusted him with her life. She listened to the sound of his heavy breathing; her desire fed on it as much as on his touch. Again she thought briefly of putting a stop to this, of not letting anything further develop between them. But the truth was, she wanted him as much as he seemed to want her, and damn anyone who might think poorly of her because of her feelings.

She pressed back against him, wanting to feel him but finding that her skirt and petticoats were in the way. He pulled away slightly and began unfastening the clasps on the back of her gown. He pushed the bodice down her arms, his lips following his hands, ravishing, making her gasp with the urgency she sensed in him.

She had dressed for the evening, but her layers of underclothing created no obstacle for him. He pushed her gown down and off, detached the crinolettes and petticoats she'd donned, expertly stripped away her lace-trimmed chemise, then unlaced the front of her corset.

He freed her from all the garments, peeled her stockings off, then began running his hands up and down her body from behind, over the curves of her breasts, along the sides of her waist, along and around her hips, drawing more gasps and moans from her. He pressed up against her, and now she could feel him, exactly as she had wanted to, hard and hot, wanting her, needing her.

"Thomas," she whispered. "You're on fire."

"I love you, Josie. I love you," he said again near her ear, as if unable to say it enough. He slid his hands down over her stomach and dipped them between her legs, delving in her moistness. "Sweet Josephine. Yer taste, yer smell . . . yer nature. Ever'thing about you, I love."

She whimpered as he caressed her, teasing her swollen bud, urging her thighs apart, pushing one finger, then two, up into her. She wondered how much longer she could stand, if her knees would give way. He moved his fingers, gliding them in and out, supporting her from behind. Every sensation, even her ability to breathe and move, seemed centered between her legs suddenly.

His fingers moved faster and faster. Josie felt an explosion coming, deep and exquisite, and she sucked in her breath, finally releasing it with a shudder and a long moan.

Before she could even think about recovering, she was being lifted and carried to the bed.

He laid her back gently across the tick. He came up to her, kissed her, and stared down at her. She thought he meant to enter her then, to plunge deep into where she wanted him. She longed to hold him inside of her for hours and hours. Forever, though she wasn't sure that was possible. If he couldn't beat Lucas Blanche, they couldn't be together, not really. She knew that—and she wanted to remember the feel of him forever.

"I love the way yer eyes slit when I'm lovin' you," he said, his voice deep and grating. "They have a glow, like flames. Yer face flushes, an' you give yerself completely, without a scrap of reservation. I love yer heart. I love the way you look an' taste, Josie Gavin."

She ran her hands from his waist up to his shoulders, then to his hair. She lifted her head to kiss his lips, but he escaped her, moving down, murmuring about her taste again, his mouth whispering over her skin, his tongue darting out to lick her now and then. His hand slid between her thighs again, gently rubbing her nub, and then his mouth was there, kissing, still murmuring, now tasting.

She thought she would die of pleasure, he made her feel so good. She was still so sensitive from when he had aroused her then pleased her with his fingers, and the feel of his mouth and tongue was exquisite, driving her wild. His hands caressed her thighs, moving to her knees, down her calves, then back up. They slid under her and drew her closer to his mouth, if possible.

He made love to her, coming up, kissing her, caressing her, stroking her. His fingertips played on her hips and waist, then danced their way up to her breasts and nipples. He followed them with his mouth, wherever they went—down her arms, around her fingertips, to the insides of her elbows, along either side of her neck, behind her ear, back down to her breasts, tracing a fiery trail over her belly, hips, and thighs. He nipped at her feet, stroking the insteps, then he drifted up again, consuming her.

Again she thought he would enter her—she ached for him to do so. She arched her back, moved her hips against his, pressed her lips against his shoulders and pleaded, speaking his name over and over, making her need known. His hand slid between her thighs again, and she almost groaned in frustration; a sound emerged, but it was one of pleasure as he began rubbing her swollen bud, massaging it, bringing her quickly to another peak.

He untied his dressing robe, parted it, and sank into her depths. The feeling was torment—but pleasurable torment. He had aroused her as fully as she could possibly be aroused and she was so sensitive inside, she thought she would burst. His every movement, his every deep thrust, took her to a new peak of pleasure. She pushed the robe off of his shoulders and down his arms, then slipped her hands beneath it and ran them down his back to his buttocks, pressing him closer, thrusting up to him, joining with him.

His breathing became swifter, harsher, intermingled with groans from the back of his throat, blending with her cries and moans. Finally he stiffened, began panting, then exploded inside of her, dropping his head to rest between her breasts.

They lay on their sides, watching each other, their bodies still joined as their breathing slowed by degrees.

"Alan asked me if you were worth fighting for," Josie said softly. "I answered yes. You still are, but now I've met Constance and I think she's a nice woman. I don't want to see her hurt. And this business with her father . . ."

"Constance," Thomas muttered, rolling onto his back, separating their bodies. "Ev'ryone wants to protect Constance. Papa, an' now you." He tossed his forearm over his eyes and lay just so for a time, his chest rising and falling more regularly now.

"I'm thinkin', Josie," he said, sitting up and throwing his legs over the side of the bed, "that *ye're* worth fightin' for. I'm thinkin' ye're worth ev'rything."

He moved across the room and sat in a window seat. Moonlight created a silver glow around him as he swept the hair from his brow and stared out the panes.

"I don't know what all Alan told you. Constance's father," Thomas said, "heads the medical college at the university, an' he has just about ev'ry trustee in his pocket. He was trained in Europe an' has extensive influence in the medical community. Publishes papers an' such. Could get a doctor like myself the attention an' respect I need, deserve, an' want. Or he could make certain I'm ruined, which is exactly what he's threatening. When Lucas Blanche is slighted, he goes for revenge.''

''You told him you don't want to marry Constance?'' Josie ventured, sitting up in the bed, her interest and concern growing. She reached down and pulled the sheet up over her, fighting a chill.

''I didn't have a chance. Someone spotted you an' me outside the hotel that mornin'. Lucas came to me.''

''And he actually threatened to ruin you.''

Thomas nodded, then lowered his head and swept the hair from his brow again. ''Actually that'd be kind revenge for Lucas—he prefers an occasional duel out on Bloody Island.''

Josie was quiet for a time. Then she blurted, ''This is unreal! I was angry when Alan told me and I get angrier by the second. He can't treat you like this. He can't threaten to ruin you simply because you don't want to marry his daughter!'' She had upset a few lives, it seemed—Thomas's, Constance's, even Lucas Blanche's. What a horrid man. What a horrid, horrid man.

Thomas laughed bitterly. ''Aside from murderin' an' graverobbin' for the sake of dissection rooms, Lucas Blanche can do damn near anything he chooses.''

They quieted again, both deep in thought, Josie shifting her gaze about the room, her heart aching for him, Thomas still staring out the window.

''Did you want to marry Constance before I came along?'' Josie asked quietly.

''I'd planned to,'' he answered. ''I thought she was what I was lookin' for. I thought she was what I wanted.''

Josie thought a little more. ''She's a very nice girl, Thomas, and she's young and beautiful, undoubtedly without emotional scars.''

''You opened yer heart to her the way you do with ev'ryone. They all loved you. Ev'ryone who gets past the fact that ye're an actress loves you, Josie, because ye're special.''

''I was being polite.''

He fell silent again, now rubbing his jaw.

Josie pulled the coverlet from the bed and went to sit beside him, wrapping a section of it around his shoulders, welcoming him closer, wanting to warm him. She wanted to be as close to him as possible for as long as she could. She had a feeling that might not be much longer. She felt as sad inside and troubled as he looked. She felt she had disrupted his life. Everything would be settled if she just left St. Louis.

They sat snuggled together for a long time, perhaps for an hour, staring out the window, watching the trees sway, hearing the branches whisper. A conveyance rolled by on the street below and pulled up in a drive across the way. They watched four people file out, shadows in the night, and then the conveyance pulled up farther into the carriage house.

"I remember when there wasn't a paved street in all of St. Louis," Thomas said reflectively. "I used to hawk fish down at the levee, after I stopped stealin' 'em an' started catchin' 'em. Made good enough money at it to help keep my family fed. Used to watch people ride by in their fine carriages, goin' to their fine homes, an' I told myself I'd have the same someday. It'd just be a matter of time. Met a Dr. Burke, who had an apothecary beside his office. He let me start workin' for him. He an' my father together saw me educated an' then sent me off to medical college in Chicago. They never once questioned whether I could go. They knew I wanted to an' they put their heads together an' made sure I did. My father used to tease me that the slums weren't good enough for me anymore, that I'd come back to St. Louis an' be the best doctor in the city. Future generations of Murphys wouldn't have to settle for only a potato at supper for nigh on a week sometimes. He died of heart failure durin' my last year of college."

"He never saw all of this?" Josie asked. "He never saw what you became?"

Thomas shook his head. "My mother died the year after of a quick cancer."

Silence again. They listened to and watched the trees more.

"I've been poor, Josie," he said presently. "I've been someone whom the wealthy wouldn't have minded runnin' down in the street, if I'd gotten in their way. I've been cursed just because I was a dirty Irish boy, an' I've been treated no better than some people treat their slaves. I built myself up, but I didn't do it so much for myself as for the future generations my pa teased me about. I've learned what gets respect, an' respect is what I want Maggie an' her children an' grandchildren an' on an' on to have. It's what I aim for them to have—an' I'll be damned if I'll let Lucas Blanche stand in the way of that by tryin' to control my life."

"I think you should marry Constance," Josie said softly, though she felt as if an unseen hand squeezed her heart. Squeezed it to pieces. She didn't want him sacrificing what he had worked for. "I'll always love you."

"I plan to find a way to fight him," Thomas said stubbornly, his chin lifting a few notches. "Even when I was runnin' the streets peddlin' I never let anyone run over me. Some would've liked to, but I didn't let them."

"You plan to find a way. . . . How, Thomas? You're not thinking with a clear head. And what about Constance? While you and her father are battling, what about her feelings and desires? I know what it's like to be turned away for another woman," she said, her voice catching. "I know the pain. I felt it."

It would be much easier for everyone if she went away, if she allowed him and Constance to carry on with their lives as they had been before she had invaded.

He turned his glowing gaze on her. Seconds later he swept the hair from her shoulder and bent to kiss her neck. He slipped his arm under hers and around her waist, drawing her closer. And when he urged her back onto the carpeted floor, Josie again opened to him, loving him.

She wouldn't have dreamed of turning him away.

Eighteen

JOSIE LEFT THE Murphy house before daybreak, while Thomas was still sleeping soundly. She contemplated kissing him good-bye, but she didn't want to wake him. She slipped downstairs, out the back door, trying to be as discreet as possible, and walked the few miles back to the hotel, thinking along the way. She slept, but not well, and later she suspected that even during sleep she had been thinking about his troubles and what a disruption she had been to his life. She had been good for Maggie and Maggie had been good for her, but she had come along at a bad time for Thomas. The price he would pay so they could be together was too high. She loved him too much to contribute to stripping him of the heart and soul that made him what he was.

From the hotel, Josie went to Concert Hall for a time to rehearse some with the others, and there she had a conversation with Mr. Jefferson, who was now a much happier man than he had been the first day she had talked to him about leaving the company. Josie herself had hardly smiled all day. She had made friends in St. Louis. She had been welcomed by a number of people, and she had started to consider settling here and calling the city home. Now she felt she must consider leaving, and she must consider leaving alone. The troupe had another week to play out here, but she thought a week was too long for her to stay. The love and passion she and Thomas felt for each other was a strong force, and it might just drive him to try to see her as long as she remained in St. Louis. No matter how discreet they were, being together would endanger the career and life he had made for himself and Maggie. The spies Dr. Blanche employed might see them and run straight back to the ruffian.

That's what he is, Josie thought later, as she walked along the edge of Chocteau's Pond with Maggie. A ruffian. Nothing but a bully.

Trees and gentle slopes surrounded the pond, which stretched along for two miles. The water sparkled and shimmered in the afternoon sunlight. Set back from the trees and slopes were houses, with a few businesses interspersed here and there. People had small boats out already, and Josie enjoyed watching them row along. There was an old two-story stone mill, its huge wheel silent. Winter was but a memory. Trees whispered in the afternoon breeze, water lapped at the boats, and people laughed and conversed. Josie didn't want to leave this place. She hated what she was about to tell Margaret. She had never wanted this moment to come. She had talked to Patricia earlier, who had tried to change her mind. At the moment Patricia had Katie and Charlie on a blanket some distance off. They had all shared food, then Josie and Maggie had wandered off.

"I have to move on later today," Josie said, closing her eyes for just a second, fighting tears. She breathed deeply. She would not break down and cry. The sight of her tears might make Margaret cry. She would be strong, as she had always been.

"What are you talking about, Josie?" Maggie asked, already sounding a little alarmed.

"That it's time for me to move on. I told you I would always write, and visit now and then. That's a promise, Margaret, and I don't make promises lightly."

Maggie stopped walking to stare up at Josie in utter disbelief. Her little face had gone so pale. "You're leaving? You're—you're really *leaving?* Josie, what'll I do without you? I want you to be my mother. I don't want Constance. She's no fun and . . . Josie, you can't leave!"

Josie hunched down in front of the girl and took her by the shoulders. "Maggie, we must settle for being friends. I didn't come to St. Louis to stay. So much has happened . . . I can't stay. Besides Constance, you'll have Mrs. O'Brien and Mrs. Reardon. There's Katie and her brother and mother. You had your mind set on me from the start, but, Margaret, things don't always happen as we have them worked out in our minds. I met Constance, and she's—"

"She's not you!" Tears had swelled in the girl's pretty blue eyes and threatened to spill over.

"No, she's not. Constance is Constance, her own person, just like Margaret is Margaret and Katie is Katie. You've been comparing me and Constance, and that's not fair to her. She's a nice woman, Margaret, and I think she does know how to laugh and smile and have fun. That part of her simply needs to be drawn out. If anyone can draw it out, you can. I know you can."

"Papa will be sad, Josie. Worse than me! And you never met my other friends at the levee! It's too early. Why do you have to leave today? Don't you love Papa? Don't you love me?" Maggie swiped at her eyes, as if she were angry with herself for crying.

"Margaret, stop that," Josie scolded. "You know I love you and your father. But not everyone likes me, Maggie. Not everyone wants me in their lives. Sometimes when you love a person or persons, you have to let go of them, either a little or all the way."

Sniffling, Margaret twisted her lips and looked down at the ground. "Everyone should like you."

Josie managed a smile. "I think so, too, but not everyone does. It's more than that, too. Your father is so proud of being a doctor. He loves helping sick people get well and he works so hard at what he does. He wants you to be proud and always have everything you need and want, not have to be poor like some children. If I stay, Margaret, he might not be able to continue being a doctor, and that would make him sad. Do you remember the bird you and your father fixed, the one you didn't want to set free?" she asked suddenly, grasping at anything.

Margaret swiped at her eyes again and nodded.

"The bird's wing was broken. You and your father took care of it, and while you were taking care of it, you grew to love it—and I bet it grew to love you, too. But then it recovered, and although it loved you, it wanted to do what it had always done, what it loved doing—flying with the other birds. Not being able to fly probably took some of the bird's spirit, its life. Your father would not be happy if he couldn't be a doctor, Margaret. Not being able to help sick people would take his spirit. I know it."

The girl said nothing. She simply stood sniffling, staring at the ground, looking dejected, looking as though the world were about to come to an end.

Josie drew Margaret into her arms and embraced her. "Friends are always friends. But friends cannot always be together. I've played St. Louis before, Margaret, and I'll be back—if not to perform, then to see you and Katie and Katie's mother and the other friends I've made since I've been here. Maggie, I love you."

Margaret wrapped her arms around Josie's neck and buried her face in her shoulder. "You love Papa, too!" she said in a muffled voice, and then she began sobbing.

Tears burned Josie's eyes. She could no longer fight them. They spilled over as she stood holding Margaret, as she stood stroking her hair and her back, needing to soothe her and not really knowing how.

"Yes, I love him," Josie said in a choked voice, "and that's why I must leave. Because I love him."

She and Margaret cried hard together, oblivious to everything around them, clinging to each other.

After a time, Margaret pulled away and swiped at her face again. Her jaw was set, much like Thomas's set whenever he was angry or determined. Josie felt a prickle of apprehension on top of her extreme sadness. What did it mean, the way Maggie's jaw was set and the way she would no longer look her in the eye? Was Margaret so angry and did she feel so rejected that she would never forgive her?

In time, Josie told herself. In time, when Maggie saw that she was sincere about writing to her and visiting her in St.

Louis often, the anger and feeling of rejection would wear off. Oh, God, how she prayed that Margaret would forgive her for breaking her heart! She hadn't wanted to name Constance's father as the source of her reason for leaving because she didn't want Maggie hating Constance and her family. That would certainly make life harder for Thomas and Constance. And unless Josie had misjudged Constance Blanche, Constance had nothing to do with her father's actions toward Thomas; she hadn't seemed the type to run home to her father and cry on his shoulder about Thomas's actress. In fact, taking a seat on that sofa beside Josie had been an act of courage and daring on Constance's part.

"There has to be a way to fight that man," Patricia said angrily a little while later, after Margaret had gone off walking along the pond alone. Katie was playing with Charlie nearby, enough distance away that she surely couldn't hear her mother's and Josie's words.

"If there is, Thomas should be the one to do it," Josie responded, watching Margaret walk along. The girl's chin was nearly touching her chest. "It's his battle. Besides, think about Constance's feelings."

Patricia laughed under her breath. "You think she loves Thomas? Josie, you don't know that girl as well as you think you do. She's completely dominated—and misunderstood by Claudia and Lilian, in case you hadn't guessed that. As soon as Thomas gave the indication that he was a little interested in her, Lucas Blanche was on him like a dog on scraps. She was seeing someone else at the time, a Creole man, until her parents decided to change directions for her. They decided they wanted her married to an up-and-coming doctor. Lucas Blanche has a plan—and he despises the old Creole families. He thinks they're in the way of St. Louis progress, and he certainly won't see his daughter married to one. If Thomas marries that girl, he may be making the biggest mistake of his life. He might as well be marrying Lucas himself. Lucas has already started controlling him."

Josie sighed heavily. "If you were in Thomas's position—"

"I would fight. So would you. Think about the night you

met Maggie; think about how you were revolting against your manager.''

''Orson wouldn't have threatened to ruin my career. The fight is Thomas's, Patricia, if he wants to fight. I won't ask that of him.''

Patricia stared off at Maggie, tears in her eyes now, her lips drawn tight. ''Look at her. She's brokenhearted, as I'm sure Thomas will be, too, once he learns you've left. There has to be a way.''

''There's not,'' Josie said softly. ''I'll leave, and then their lives will be normal again—Thomas's, Constance's . . . Maggie's.''

Patricia's gaze whipped to her. ''Maggie's won't. You're lying to yourself—and you and Thomas are groveling at that man's feet. *Someone* needs to fight him.''

Maggie was frantic.

Josie couldn't be leaving. She just couldn't be. Maggie hadn't always planned on her staying in St. Louis. When they'd first become friends, she'd figured Josie would have to leave someday. Maggie had talked to her friends enough about acting companies to know that they traveled from city to city, performing in lots of theaters and halls. Josie was an actress, and her job was to travel with her company. But people could change jobs. Maggie's friend Jonathan Drury down at the docks had sold ears of corn on a street corner last fall, but this year he was helping unload dry goods down at Mr. Kovach's wholesale grocery. His mother had been a laundress; now she worked in a nice boardinghouse on Washington Avenue. Josie could change jobs or be an actress somewhere here in St. Louis, and Maggie thought she would if she weren't so worried about Papa.

He'll always be a doctor, Maggie thought. She didn't understand Josie's worry about him, the fact that Josie thought he wouldn't be able to help sick people anymore if she stayed. That wasn't right. As long as there were sick people, he'd help them.

Maybe Josie thought he didn't really want her to stay. Maggie was pretty upset with him right now because he'd taken Constance to that supper last night when he should have taken Josie. That wasn't fair to Josie, and maybe that was really why she wanted to leave. Maggie had had her feelings hurt before, and it was an awful feeling.

She had to talk to Papa. She had to make sure he talked to Josie. She had to tell him that unless he did, Josie would leave and they would all be sad. Everyone. Katie Farren, Katie's mother, Charlie, Mrs. O'Brien, Mrs. Reardon, Papa, herself.

"I wanna go home," she told Josie and Mrs. Farren when she rejoined the gathering.

"We were going to take a boat out, Maggie," Mrs. Farren said.

"Maggie, don't go yet," Katie Farren pleaded, turning over on the blanket. She hadn't been much fun this afternoon. She'd kept saying she was tired and that her stomach didn't feel good.

"I don't feel good either. I want to go home," Maggie said more clearly.

Josie rose from the blanket, brushing her skirt. "All right, Margaret. I'll take you home. You and the children should stay, Patricia. I'll send the cab back."

Mrs. Farren sighed heavily. "We'll go, too. Now both girls aren't feeling well."

Josie offered Maggie her hand, but Maggie walked on by, wanting her to think she was angry. As soon as they all reached her house, she needed them to leave. She intended to run around the back of the house, hopefully not letting anyone know she was home just yet—otherwise they might spoil her plan—then leave again and head straight for Papa's office. She knew patients came in the afternoons. He would be there.

Maggie reached the carriage before the others did, climbed inside, and retreated to a far corner.

"What's wrong, Maggie?" Katie Farren asked once everyone was inside and the conveyance was bumping and bouncing along.

"I said—I don't feel good either."

Katie nodded. Josie and Mrs. Farren exchanged looks. They didn't really think she was sick. She could tell. They knew she was upset because Josie planned to leave St. Louis.

The ride home was a pretty quiet one. Katie Farren didn't say much more, except to ask Maggie if she knew there was a traveling show coming to St. Louis soon. Maggie hadn't known, and at any other time, on a less bothersome day, she would have been glad, even happy, to know. Today she really didn't care. All she could think about was Josie leaving. Katie put her hand over her stomach and grimaced, not looking so good suddenly. She leaned against her mother's side, and Mrs. Farren put one arm around her while holding Charlie on her lap with the other.

By and by the carriage stopped in front of Maggie's home. She scrambled for the door, not saying good-bye to anyone, not caring to. Her mind was on getting to Papa's office straightaway.

She thought Josie might try to follow her at least to the doorstep. But she heard Josie say good-bye very softly, and then Maggie hopped out of the carriage and tore off for the house.

She ran around it, along the side path, as she and Josie had done the evening she and Dr. Schuster had come for supper and she and Josie had played in the garden. She stopped with her back against one of the low brick walls, listening, waiting for the carriage to pull away.

It didn't and didn't, and when it finally did, she heard Mrs. O'Brien's voice moments later, calling to her, wondering where she was—she knew she was home because Miss Gavin had come in and told her.

Drat! Maggie thought. She tore off down one of the garden paths, weaving her way through the maze of bushes and trees, knowing it well. When she came to an iron gate, she lifted the latch and escaped, fleeing through a stand of nearby trees, blazing her own path back toward Washington Avenue.

Papa wasn't in his office. There was only an older boy, cleaning some doctoring tools, as her father called the instruments, in one of the back rooms. He must be Johnny Owens, the boy Papa had said was coming by to help him in the afternoons these days.

"Johnny Owens, you've got to tell me where my papa is,"

she said in a rush, breathless after running nearly all the way here. She'd tired when some distance from the house, and she'd had to stop and walk a little ways. But after that, she'd been running again. Just as Johnny turned, a surprised look on his face, she tore over to him, accidently knocking a tray off the corner of a nearby table.

"You must be Maggie," he said matter-of-factly. "Dr. Schuster calls you the Maggie hurricane."

"Where's Papa? Where? You have to tell me where he is! I've searched every room but this one, and he's not here either. He's always here in the afternoons!"

"He went to meet some other doctor," Johnny told her. "I don't know the name."

"Oh, no!" Maggie plopped down in a nearby chair and slammed her hands down on her knees. "Josie'll leave if he doesn't talk to her, if he doesn't tell her that he can marry her and be a doctor, too."

"Well, why couldn't he marry someone and be a doctor, too?" Johnny sounded completely baffled.

"I don't know," Maggie responded, almost whining. "But she thinks he can't, and that's what matters." She glanced up, looking toward a window and twisting her lips. Her mind was going so fast, around and around, she could almost imagine what a wagon wheel must feel like. "Papa's not here. . . . She came in on a ship, that's what Eliza said, and then Katie Farren saw it in the *Republican* before the bill was there. Jonathan said she does performances in cities all up and down the river. . . . If she came in on a ship and she goes up and down the river doing performances, then she's leaving on a ship!" Maggie jumped up with the last six words, her tone rising with excitement. "I've got to stop her somehow, and Jonathan Drury and Eliza and the others might know how to help! If Papa comes back, you tell him Josie's leaving today on a ship—I don't know which one yet—and that she doesn't think he can still be a doctor if he loves her, so he's got to talk to her."

She tore out of the room, and as she did she heard him mumbling behind her, something about how she really *was* like a bad storm coming through. She really was like a hurricane.

Three-story stone wholesale grocery and commission houses faced the levee and intermingled with saloons, restaurants, and lodging houses all along Front Street. Goods and people crowded the wharf. Bales and hogsheads sat here and there between boxes and uncrated merchandise. Papers in hand, clerks darted between the boxes and crates, checking what was in them, then looking at their papers. There were men stumbling around who liked their whiskey too much, as Jonathan Drury often said, and dirty Indian beggars wandered here and there, hoping for a bite to eat and something to drink. They always looked so lost, some barely speaking English, and Maggie always felt sorry for them. Jonathan said they didn't know what to do with themselves now that a lot of their land had been taken over by people who were strangers to them. Some thought they had a better chance in the white man's cities than in their Indian villages. But surely they wouldn't look so sad and so pitiful if they were with their families, Maggie always thought. She couldn't imagine leaving her home and St. Louis. That would be scary.

Maggie raced down Front Street to a two-story gray building with the words Kovach's Wholesale Grocer stenciled on the side of it. There was Jonathan, his red hair flaming in the late afternoon sunshine as he lifted a crate from the bed of a wagon.

"Jonathan, Jonathan!" Maggie cried, racing up to him. She bumped into a crate that sat on the ground beside the wagon, bounced off, bumped into Jonathan, then into the wagon. A dog that had been sleeping comfortably near one of the wheels yelped and jumped out of the way toward Jonathan. Maggie stepped that way, and the dog yelped again, put its tail between its legs, and ran off.

"You've got to help me, Jonathan!" Maggie insisted. "You know everybody at the levee. You even know most of the ships' captains and the people who work on the boats. Josie's leaving, and I can't let her! I've got to do something so she won't. Papa's not at his office, else he'd be here. I've got to know when she's leaving and what ship she's leaving on. I've got to—''

"Maggie, would ya . . . Maggie, stop!'' Jonathan nearly dropped the crate because Maggie had grabbed hold of his arm and was tugging on it. He yanked his arm away and plopped the crate on the ground, then straightened. "Now, tell me what you're doing. None of us have seen ya in nigh on two weeks, an' now all the sudden here ya stand, spouting about this and that. Josie? Who'n the blazes is Josie?''

"Josephine Gavin. Oh, Jonathan, don't get cross with me. Josie got hurt one night, and my papa brought her to the house. She was real sick but she got better and while she was getting better . . . Well, they love each other and I love Josie and she loves me. She wants to be my mother, I just know it, only she's scared that if she tries to be my mother and if she marries Papa, he won't be able to be a doctor anymore. But maybe she's really angry that Papa took Constance to the supper at the Farrens' last night. He really loves her, not Constance, and I thought I'd run get Papa and have him talk to her—he couldn't know she's leaving, he just couldn't! So I'd get Papa and he'd talk to her and she'd stay. But Papa wasn't at his office, only Johnny Owens was. He's the boy who helps Papa some in the afternoons. And Johnny Owens said Papa was gone meeting some other doctor, he didn't know who. I thought, well, Josie said she's leaving today and she performs in river cities. She came by ship, so she must be leaving by ship, though I know people don't always have to travel by ship. But she's going by ship, I just know it. So then I thought, Jonathan Drury, he knows pretty much what ships go in and out and he knows pretty much everyone on the ships, the people who run the ships, that is, and—''

"Maggie, all right!'' Jonathan said, laughing a little. "We'll find Miss Gavin 'n' we'll try to talk her off whatever ship she's booked passage on. Good Lord, you're like a storm blowing through sometimes! Breathe, please, 'n' have a seat on one of those empty crates over yonder.'' He pointed to a stack of overturned crates near the side of the building. "I've got to talk to Mr. Kovach so someone else can come'n unload the rest of these," he said, pointing to a number of crates still stacked in the back of the wagon. "Then we'll be off."

Maggie took a deep breath, trying to calm herself inside, wishing he was in the same hurry she was in. He sure didn't seem to be. She twisted her mouth unhappily.

Smiling, he reached out to ruffle her hair. "We'll find her, Maggie. Don't worry."

She shuffled toward the overturned crates. "Dr. Schuster and Johnny Owens call me a hurricane," she said a little dejectedly.

Jonathan burst out laughing. "Maggie, that's exactly what ya are—a hurricane."

"Hurricanes mess things up. I've heard people talk about hurricanes. I don't mess things up."

"Or maybe you're more like a twister. They hit all the sudden. Hardly no warning; the sky just darkens up some, turns this greenish color, and then, *boom!* the twister's on ya, and things are flying all over. Yep, I reckon you're more like a twister than a hurricane."

She plopped down on one of the crates and folded her arms. "I am not a storm."

He just grinned, then went off inside the warehouse.

Nineteen

JOSIE STOOD ON the deck of the ship as it began moving away from the wharf. People milled all around her, either waving good-bye to people standing on the dock or talking to others around them. Ordinarily, booking passage so quickly on any steamer leaving St. Louis would have been impossible, but Mr. Jefferson had managed it for her somehow, and now here she stood, watching St. Louis become smaller, the muddy waters of the Mississippi lapping gently at the side of the boat. She heard the grinding and churning of the side-wheels and had to grab on to the railing to keep from swaying along with the ship. The stench of dead fish still drifted from the wharf, she could still hear the hawkers as they wandered up and down, pushing carts and calling out, and she was still close enough to observe a diverse group of people disembark from another side-wheeler.

She heard her name being called in the distance: *"Josephine Gavin! Josephine Gavin!"* She glanced around, then off at the levee again, wondering who in the world it could be. She finally spotted someone, a red-haired boy, standing near the edge of the dock, his hands forming a circle around his mouth as he shouted to her. She didn't remember having met him and she couldn't imagine why anyone would be shouting for her. But she untied her reticule from around her wrist and waved it at him anyway, trying to make sure he saw her.

He shouted something more. "Maggie Murphy's on—" A dog began growling and barking nearby, and the chickens housed in crates not far away began clucking and squawking.

Josie had lowered her arm back to the railing. She felt a tug, a jerk, then she was minus her reticule. She turned around in time to watch a boy who couldn't be more than seven years old, if his size was any indication, dart off, weaving his way between people and animals.

The little thief! Josie thought, and then her temper got the best of her—she raced off after him, determined to catch him and retrieve her reticule. She hadn't placed much money in it; she had stored most of her traveling money in a small locked box down underneath numerous gowns in one of her trunks. Still, no scamp was going to make off with something that belonged to her, and especially not without a fight.

She wove her way between people, trying to keep sight of the head of black curls. She bumped into people, excused or pushed her way past them, and once nearly ran over a woman who sat on the deck holding a baby in her lap. She glanced down at the woman and apologized, and when she glanced back up, searching the crowd, she had lost sight of the reticule-snatcher.

Clicking her tongue in frustration, she wove her way back toward the railing where she had been standing, hoping the red-haired boy was still standing on the dock and would finish what he had been saying about Margaret. She was worried that perhaps something was wrong with Maggie; she hadn't exactly left the girl in a pleasant state of mind. Margaret not even saying good-bye and then running around the side of the house toward the garden like that had disturbed Josie greatly. She had wounded Maggie's little heart and she had cursed herself for doing so. But at the same time, she hadn't known any other way to handle the situation. She still didn't, which was why she was on the ship heading away from St. Louis.

The boy was gone, and even if he hadn't been, Josie doubted whether she could have heard the rest of what he had to say, since the ship had now moved quite some distance from the wharf. She could barely hear the hawkers now, and they knew how to bark words; they could be heard from pretty far away.

She stood near the railing for some time, watching the levee grow smaller and smaller, intermittently watching the adults and children on the deck. The river steamers were always so crowded, but at least they were crowded with a mass of interesting people who were going up or down the river for one reason or another—perhaps to visit relatives or friends, perhaps to move to another city, perhaps to take care of business in another place.

The hawkers' barks soon disappeared altogether, and the buildings fronting the St. Louis levee became smaller and smaller, finally fading altogether when the ship rounded a curve in the river.

Josie stared blankly at trees that lined the bank for a time as sadness settled over her. She had found friends and a family in St. Louis. She had allowed herself to dream and hope— something she knew better than to do. For one reason or another, having a family and a home apparently wasn't part of the plan Orson had spoken of in the beginning of the manuscript he had left for her. *Life is a progression of events, one thing leading to another, sometimes a search for happiness.* He had said he'd known she was destined for greatness, but greatness was no longer what she wanted. It hadn't been for some time now.

Hundreds of people crowded the deck of the ship—mothers with children clinging to their skirts, other children scurrying about or sitting in groups; women, seated in places or with their heads together near the railing, men, smoking as they discussed business; entire families occupying areas. A woman walked by, trying to calm the squealing pig she held, and not far away four men cleared an area and began tossing dice— to the religious objections of several women.

Though Josie didn't exactly want to be alone right now— her mind would stray to Margaret, how much she had hurt her little friend and how much she already missed her—the noise and odor of the people and animals clamoring on the deck were suddenly too much for her. One of her temples had begun to pound. Though her head wound was completely healed, there were still times when too much noise and excitement started a pulsing in her temple, which then led to a headache.

She wove her way through the crowd again, nearly tripping over a large crate of baby pigs. She jerked the hem of her skirt away from a menacing black-and-gray dog that looked akin to one of those pigs.

Two dirty, scraggly-looking girls glanced up at her with big hungry eyes from where they were camped near the railing, and her hands strayed to a pocket sewn into her dress. She pulled out an apple she had stopped and bought at the marketplace on the way to the ship and, managing a smile despite the pain in her head, bent to hand it to one of the girls, telling them to share it. The one girl snatched it up eagerly, thanked her earnestly, then bit into it. Josie stayed for a moment to see if she planned to share.

When the girls had passed the apple back and forth several times and Josie was satisfied, she stood and wandered on. Like those girls, most of the people on deck had no decent place to rest while on the ship, and certainly they might receive nothing to eat until they reached their destinations—and perhaps not even then. She, on the other hand, had a cabin secured, and she had stashed several loaves of bread and some fruit in one of her trunks. She hated seeing people deprived, and if she had had one of the loaves of bread with her, she would have given it out to someone, too.

She opened a door in the main part of the ship and took the narrow stairs leading down to a hall and a number of private rooms, finally opening the door to hers. She could still hear the noise of the deck crowd, and now and then a bang or scrape as if something, a crate or a large trunk perhaps, was being pushed around upstairs. But at least the noise was less, and though the cabin was small, it seemed to have more air. Certainly the stench of the animals and some of the people was absent.

Dark woodwork and polished brass fixtures decorated the room. A small bed, large enough for only one person, had been built against one wall. Josie's three trunks sat nearby, one pushed up against the head of the bed, the other two stacked atop each other in a corner. A small table complete with a lamp sat not far away, and Josie wandered over to light the lamp to brighten the cabin a little.

She unfastened the clasps on the back of her dress and soon had the garment pushed off. She tossed it atop the two stacked trunks, then removed her camisole, corset, the one petticoat she had donned earlier, and her shoes and stockings. She could breathe more easily and felt much more comfortable altogether once clad in nothing but a light chemise and drawers.

She lay down on the bed and closed her eyes, wondering if she might miss Thomas and Maggie less as the days passed. In her mind she saw Thomas hovering over her, concern etched into the lines on his forehead one second, relief smoothing them the next. She felt his arms around her, strong and comforting, tender and compassionate. She heard his deep voice whispering her name. She saw his blue-green eyes twinkling at her, then sparkling with surprise, then blazing with passion, then burning low with fear. She loved him so much and she still felt that leaving was the right choice. Her change in plan had been sudden but right.

She turned onto her side, tired but wondering if she could sleep. Noise drifted from upstairs again, voices, shouting and clamoring, another crate or trunk being shoved around, chickens squawking all of a sudden, pigs squealing.

She saw Maggie running along the garden paths, her little bare feet almost black with dirt. She heard Maggie's sweet, girlish laughter, saw her mischievous, sparkling blue eyes—then saw them fill with tears after Josie told her she was moving on. She saw Margaret laughing as she played with the kitten, then she saw Maggie walking along Chouteau's Pond, looking dejected, her chin nearly touching her breast.

Josie flipped over onto her stomach, sighed, and swiped at a tear that slipped from her eye. She didn't want to spend the rest of the day crying. If she could only fall asleep, then she wouldn't be able to think so much. She wouldn't dwell on thoughts of Thomas and Margaret. She wouldn't miss them so much.

She relaxed eventually, but not before she shed a few more tears. The gentle rocking of the ship finally, mercifully, lulled her to sleep.

* * *

A soft voice waltzed around in her head: *"Come back, Jo-sie . . . come back to me. . . ."*

She stirred. The voice tugged at her brain. It sounded familiar. It sounded so sweet. It sounded like the voice that belonged to the little girl she had come to love and cherish. And she knew the song, or at least the tune, though her name had been substituted for Belinda's. The remaining lyrics ran through her head, though the voice did not sing them: *Your lips are like roses, your eyes like the sea. . . . Our love is greater than any can be. Oh, come back, Josie, and mar–ry me.*

Josie stirred on the bed. Her mind was foggy with sleep—and perhaps she was still dreaming, thinking of Thomas standing near one of the low brick walls in the garden, repeating the lyrics.

The familiar voice came again, soft and sweet, little-girlish: *"I am thinking tonight of my blue eyes . . . a girl who is sweet as can be . . ."*

The voice caught, became choked, and then there was a sob. "Oh, Josie, you've got to come back. Papa, he really does love you and I love you and he'll be a doctor forever, no matter what happens, even if you marry him. I remember all the songs you taught me and I remember running through the garden barefoot with you, but I don't want to just remember. I want to do it again and again and again!"

"Can't go . . . back, Margaret," Josie said groggily, feeling more tears swell in her eyes. Her lids felt so heavy. She was so exhausted. Maybe she was getting sick again, though she prayed not. Still, to hear a voice in her head that sounded as real as the one she was hearing . . . The sadness she felt over having to leave Margaret and Thomas was driving her a little mad, that was all. More rest and time, and she would be fine.

"You don't understand, Josie," the voice said again. "Me and Papa, we really love you. We really, really love you."

"No. . . . Stop."

A soft touch on her brow, a little hand smoothing the hair

back from her temple, a light kiss on her cheek . . . if this was a dream, it was too vivid a dream.

Josie bolted upright, twisted around . . . and came face to face with Maggie.

She blinked hard. Surely this was a dream. Surely. Margaret was not on board the ship with her; she was not in the cabin with her. Maggie was safe at home with Mrs. O'Brien and Mrs. Reardon, who had assured Josie they would fetch her from the garden and keep a close eye on her.

"Margaret!" Josie whispered loudly, not believing her eyes. The trunk that had been placed near the head of the bed was now open, and Maggie stood on the gowns in it, leaning over the head of the bed. She had been singing to Josie and touching her, trying to comfort her. "What are you doing here? How did you get on the ship? What are you thinking? Oh, Margaret, we're miles and miles from St. Louis by now, and your father will be terribly worried! What are you *doing* here? Oh, Maggie!"

The girl twisted her hands and lips, flinching. "Don't be angry, Josie. Please, oh, please don't be angry. Jonathan Drury will tell Papa where I've gone, I'm sure of it. I was running onto the ship. I sneaked past the men watching people get on board, and Jonathan shouted that we needed to wait for you right there, that he'd go tell my father if I didn't come back, if I didn't get off right then. He will, too—Jonathan does whatever he says he's going to do. He told me we'd find you, find out what ship you were on, and then I'd be able to talk to you. He was right, too. Jonathan is always right. He said you were beautiful and had a lovely voice and that you were as nice as could be, too, and he was right. Oh, was he right! He tried to have people search for me. I heard them calling and calling and looking, but I can hide good 'cause I'm little. Then I looked in the cabins, hoping to see you. I finally saw some men bringing your trunks, and I watched where they went, and when they left, here I came. I love the pretty smell of your gowns, so I climbed into the trunk and kept the lid open some with a little pillow I found so I could breathe. Lying on the gowns and smelling you and being close to you felt so good, I fell asleep, and when I woke, here you were. You looked like you were sleeping, but you were saying things and crying. I don't want you to cry, Josie. I don't want you to be sad or scared. So I started singing to you like you did to me the night Willie Reardon put out my lamp and shut my door all the way. Do you remember?''

"Oh, Margaret, of course I remember!"

Josie grabbed Maggie's hand and led her around the bed, then pulled her onto her lap. She pressed the girl's head to her breast and squeezed back more tears. Seeing Margaret was so, so wonderful, and knowing that Maggie didn't hate her for leaving was a relief Josie couldn't put into words. But running off from home, sneaking onto the ship, and hiding out in her cabin . . .

"I love seeing you, Margaret, but I can't believe you've done this," Josie said. "Think of the worry your father is going through! Think of how frantic he must be, not knowing if you found me or if someone accosted you before you could or . . . Maggie, you're a stowaway, and that in itself is wrong. Not to mention that your father is probably going nearly crazy with worry right now!"

"I don't mean to worry him. Honest, I don't! I tried to find him to tell him you were leaving later today. I went to his office. He's always there in the afternoons. But today he wasn't there. Today he was off seeing another doctor. Leastwise, that's what Johnny Owens said. And Johnny didn't know which doctor or nothing! I wanted Papa to talk to you, but I couldn't find him, so I figured I had to stop you myself. You're trying to leave us Josie, and I bet Papa will be even sadder than me when he finds out. We love you this much," she said, stretching her arms out as far as they would go and straining to stretch them even more. "Even more. Papa can still help sick people if he marries you. I don't know why you think he can't. That doesn't make sense. Then I thought, well, maybe she's angry because he took Constance to the supper and not her when he should've taken her. I don't know why he did that, but I know he loves you, Josie. Papa told me so and I believe him. This morning at breakfast, he said he was going to find a way for us three to be together. I don't know why he has to find a way—I keep thinking, well, why can't we all just be together, then?—but if he says he will, he will. Just like Jonathan Drury. He threatened to snitch on me and he probably already has, you wait and see.''

Josie sighed, clutching Margaret against her, so glad to see her—elated to see her—but also filled with dread. Maggie being here meant a trip back to St. Louis. She had to take the girl home. She had no choice in the matter. Going back to St. Louis meant possibly seeing Thomas again, which was something she didn't want to do. It would only cause her and him both more pain, since they couldn't be together without his livelihood being in jeopardy.

''Margaret, you have got to stop doing things like this,'' Josie said sternly. ''Running off and worrying people to death . . .''

''But, Josie, how else could I get you to stay?''

''I have to take you back, Maggie, but that doesn't mean I'll be staying. I have to take you back, then be on the next ship out of St. Louis, traveling downriver. That's the way it is. You stowing away isn't going to change that.'' Josie hated to give her that news, but it was fact, and apparently Margaret had to be told exactly how things were. There could be no frosting on the cake where Maggie was concerned.

''Josie, talk to Papa! Please, oh, please talk to Papa,'' Margaret insisted, twisting in her lap. ''He can be a doctor and be married to you, too. I know he can.''

Josie shook her head and closed her eyes momentarily. Maggie was too young and too innocent to understand many of the evils in the world. Lucas Blanche was Constance's father, and Thomas could very well end up married to Constance; therefore, Josie would do nothing to turn Margaret against Constance's family. Not explaining completely surely made it look to Maggie as if Josie didn't want to stay, perhaps because she didn't want her and her father. But Josie wouldn't explain to Margaret about Constance's father. She just wouldn't.

''We're going back, Maggie,'' she said in an even tone,

though her heart constricted. "I'm taking you to the house, then I'm leaving again."

Margaret glanced up at her, disbelief and pain filling her eyes. A moment later she pulled away, retreated to a far corner of the bed, and sat there, grimacing and fiddling with one of the ruffles on her skirt.

Cholera.

Thomas withdrew from Katie's bed, his brain screaming at him to withdraw from the house altogether. The only thing stopping him was the sight of the little girl—Maggie's best friend, at that—balled up on the bed, clutching her stomach, retching now and then, her body burning with fever.

Dear God. He'd seen cholera enough times that he'd known exactly what was wrong with Katie almost from the moment he had entered the room. It scared him because he knew how quickly it could rage through a city, how quickly it could fill a graveyard. It was a little early in the year for the disease— the first week of April had just passed—but once the weather started warming, cholera sprouted and flourished. The epidemic of '32 had claimed at least twenty lives a day, and it too had started early, if Thomas remembered correctly—and he thought he did.

"She was fine this morning when she woke," Patricia Farren said from near the foot of the bed. "Near noon she began saying her stomach hurt. She wouldn't eat. She played with Charlie some on a coverlet near Chouteau's Pond, but she was quiet and she kept saying her stomach hurt. She didn't even play with Maggie. Usually they run all around the pond when I take them there. Katie didn't feel well enough to leave the coverlet. I brought her home, she fell asleep for several hours, and this is how she woke. I heard her groaning all the way down the hall. What is it, Thomas? What's wrong with her?" With the questions Patricia's voice rose, sounding anxious.

"She has cholera," Thomas responded, not wanting to say the words. But he damn sure wouldn't lie to her.

He heard Patricia take a deep breath. "Oh, God, no."

Thomas had learned that Katie was sick when he'd gone back to his office to make some notes about his meeting this afternoon. He'd found a message left on his desk from Johnny. Mrs. Farren had sent a boy by, wondering if he could call on Katie, who had developed stomach cramps and fever along with a few other symptoms. Instead of making his notes, Thomas packed some things he felt he might need in his medical bag and headed back out straightaway, going directly to the Farrens'. Patricia had met him at the door and brought him straight up to Katie's room.

"Have someone bring more water or tea so I can mix something for her that might help calm her stomach. I'll give her some laudanum, too, for the pain. Has she been vomiting? Had diarrhea?"

"Yes," Patricia answered promptly, having gone white. "Both most of the evening so far."

"Bring clean clothes, too, and if you have a supply of clean linen, bring it."

She nodded, glanced at her daughter, then hurried from the room.

Thomas removed his waistcoat, unbuttoned his shirt at the wrists, and rolled up his sleeves. Katie . . . *Why?* Of all children to contract cholera after Maggie's mother had died of it only last spring, why did it have to be Katie?

"God help us," he whispered as Katie groaned. He pulled a small jar from his medical bag. It was filled with pulverized asafetida, which always seemed to help calm the stomach somewhat. What was so deadly about cholera was the patient's inability to keep down food and drink. Usually the old, the young, and the weak succumbed fast, their bodies not having the strength to keep going for long.

He mixed a little of the asafetida in a glass of water that sat on a table near a window, swishing the water around and around. Then he sat on the edge of the bed, lifted Katie's head, and put the glass to her lips.

"Drink, Katie girl. Ye're a strong one, lass, an' you'll get through this. Think about Maggie an' how she loves you, an' keep fightin'."

Katie looked weakly up at him, her eyes glazed and red,

burning with fever, her little body shaking with chills. She drank some of the water, then he lowered her head. Moments later he lifted it again, urging more water down her. He repeated the process over a period of about five minutes until she'd emptied the glass. Then he wet a cloth he found on the washstand near the table, wrung it, and laid it across Katie's forehead.

Patricia and several servants soon returned with clean linen and two pitchers of water.

"I've sent for Michael," Patricia told Thomas. "He planned to spend the evening with his father, but I doubt that he will once he hears how ill Katie is."

She wandered to the side of the bed, sat on it, and pressed the back of her hand to her daughter's cheek. Though Patricia was pale and concern shimmered in her eyes, she displayed courage before Katie. "Your father's coming home soon; I know he is. Oh, and Jonathan Drury came by while I was downstairs and said to tell you hello, and that he hopes you get well very soon. I know you will, my precious. I know it." She planted a kiss on Katie's cheek, then withdrew from her daughter and from the bed.

She went to stand before the window and looked out blankly, a mother fearing the imminent death of her child and feeling utterly helpless.

Thomas glanced back at Katie just in time to observe her bring up the water and medication he'd managed to get down her only moments ago. The night would be a long one, filled with hour after hour of changing bedding, pouring fluid into her, and hoping she retained at least a little of it. He wouldn't be able to separate himself from the fact that Katie was Maggie's best friend, and so he'd probably be tireless for a while in order to give her the care she needed. Right now, he operated on worry, fear, and the knowledge that the drink had to keep coming.

Together he and Patricia changed the bedding, then began taking turns urging Katie to drink. He mixed more medicine, and she took that. Then she took some laudanum and vomited everything up not ten minutes later. But surely the liquid had been in her belly long enough that at least some of it had been absorbed.

He asked if Patricia would have a message sent to his home stating that Katie was very ill and that he'd be staying at least the night at the Farrens' home. Katie appeared to be resting a little more comfortably now, not clutching her stomach quite as much.

Patricia started toward the bedroom door just as Michael entered, raking back his hair and giving Thomas and Patricia both no more than a quick glance. He headed for the bed and his daughter, his brow a map of worry.

An hour or so later, after Patricia had sent a messenger to Thomas's home, she brought him a note from Mrs. O'Brien. Maggie was missing again. She'd run off shortly after Josie and Patricia had taken her home, and she'd been gone since. Mrs. O'Brien and Mrs. Reardon had searched the garden thoroughly, though why Thomas couldn't understand. Did they think Maggie had hidden somewhere in the trees and paths? Then they had waited and waited, thinking Maggie would come home after a few hours as she always did when she ran off to see her friends at the levee—though it had been weeks since she'd last gone there. A Jonathan Drury had come calling, telling them to inform Dr. Murphy that Maggie had sneaked onto the ship on which Josephine Gavin was leaving. He'd had some of the ship's crew search for her, but they hadn't been able to find her. She was determined to find Miss Gavin, Jonathan had said. She'd said she needed to talk to her, and so he'd found out what ship she planned to be on, and then Maggie had flown off, spotting the vessel and slipping by people almost unnoticed to board the ship. When he saw Miss Gavin standing on the deck, he'd tried shouting to her to tell her about Maggie. She hadn't heard him well, he didn't think, and then something snared her attention and she bolted from the railing. He was sure Maggie was with Miss Gavin, almost to Cape Girardeau by now.

"Where might I find Jonathan Drury?" Thomas asked Katie when he next went to give her water.

Her tongue emerged slowly to lick her lips. "Mr. Kovach's

Wholesale,'' she said slowly, her voice soft and weak.
''There . . . a lot.''

Thomas knew the place. He arranged with Patricia and Michael to have someone sent down to the levee to fetch the lad.
He needed to talk to him, and he needed to talk to him ur-
gently.

Twenty

IN CAPE GIRARDEAU, Josie's original destination, the ship docked to deposit some passengers and pick up others. Through a crew member, Josie managed to locate the captain and explain that Margaret had not wanted her to leave St. Louis so she had stowed away on board the ship. She paid the man for Maggie's passage. She felt Margaret's eyes on her the entire time, but she couldn't tell what Maggie was thinking. Every time she looked at the girl, Margaret glanced away. She was sullen, that was for certain, her bottom lip protruding slightly, her jaw set. She seemed to be going along with Josie because she didn't quite know what else to do at the moment. But as soon as she thought of something, a plan would be put into action. Josie knew Margaret by now, and Maggie without a plan was not Maggie. She would have one soon. Or perhaps this pouting and sullen behavior were part of the plan.

"Do you know if there's another ship going to St. Louis soon?" Josie asked the captain, though he was probably not the right person to ask. The dockhands would surely know, but dockhands were a rough lot, and Josie, traveling alone with a child, was reluctant to approach them.

"The *Missouri*," he suggested, cocking a thumb to the right. "She's tied up three down. She goes between St. Louis and Cape pretty regularly. You might see if there's room."

There was, but only on deck with more crates of chickens

and pigs, along with a cow, several goats this time, too, and a loud, dirty crowd similar to the one on the ship Josie had just left. *Work hard, but do the best with what you have,* her mother had always told her. The *Missouri* was leaving in half an hour, and if she traveled up and down the wharf asking if other ships were bound for St. Louis soon and none were, they would miss the *Missouri.* If they boarded it, she would have Margaret back with Thomas soon. He was surely worried nearly out of his mind, wondering where Maggie was and if she was safe.

She paid the fare and had her trunks brought from the other ship and placed alongside three crates of clucking hens. Then she and Margaret sat atop one of the crates, and Josie began batting at a number of flies that buzzed crazily in the air around their heads.

"You sure do want to take me back," Maggie said after a time. The ship had just left the dock and was now swaying slightly, moving farther out into the water. "You hurried all around, trying to get your trunks moved, trying to get us on a ship."

"Margaret, do you realize how worried your father must be right now?" Josie asked, thoroughly irritated. "I love you and I think the way you love me is sweet, but marriage between your father and me wouldn't work for various reasons, for personal reasons, and I wish you would respect that. He loves you, and you worry him when you run off. I'm sure Mrs. Reardon and Mrs. O'Brien are nearly sick with worry, too. I know you felt you had to run off this time because you couldn't find your father and you thought he could convince me to stay in St. Louis, but you shouldn't have been trying to find him to convince me in the first place. Everyone who wants us to be together, you and Mrs. Reardon and Mrs. O'Brien, Katie and her mother . . . it's all very sweet, but your father and I have to work this out by ourselves—if we want to work it out. I love him very much, Margaret. I love both of you. But I feel your lives might suffer if I stay and he keeps wanting to see me. Especially if we marry.

"I don't want to hear anyone talk bad about your father, because he's not a bad man, he's a wonderful man; and I don't want people to avoid you because you're his daughter,'' Josie continued. ''I want you to have the life he's trying to give you, because it's a good life, Maggie. It's a wonderful life. It's better than the future I dreamed of having when I was your age.'' She laughed a little, reflectively. ''I don't think I dared to dream too much. At times I fantasized about living in a big home like the one in which you live. I fantasized about having a dress decorated with lace and bows. I fantasized about having more food to eat, because we had very little at times, and sometimes I fantasized about having shoes when I knew my mother had no money with which to buy them. Your father grew up with very little to eat at times, too, and probably with no shoes to wear sometimes. He's determined to give you a better life than he had as a boy, and I think that's admirable. I think that's noble. I won't watch his dreams be shattered. I love him too much to watch, to think that I'm the reason.''

She had said so much, but she didn't know if Margaret understood. Before, when trying to explain her reason for leaving to Maggie at Chouteau's Pond, and then trying more in the cabin on the other ship, she had held back a great deal of emotion. This had been more of an outpouring, and maybe it might all be too much for Maggie to grasp—though she was a very intelligent child. It might be too overwhelming. In a desperate effort to help the girl understand why she felt so compelled to leave St. Louis, Josie had revealed some of her childhood fears and some of Thomas's. But Margaret had never wanted for anything, or so it seemed, so Josie doubted that she could grasp what hunger felt like, what freezing feet in the winter snow felt like. . . . She knew she couldn't understand that there were people who would gossip and gossip and wouldn't mind if they destroyed a person physically and emotionally.

''I have a friend, Eliza, at the levee,'' Maggie said in a soft tone. ''I take her food sometimes. Her parents are dead, and she doesn't want to go to an orphanage, so she lives in one of the empty warehouses. Jonathan Drury helps her, too. A lot of us do. I even took her a dress one time. You know, like you said you wanted a dress with lace and bows. Well, Eliza, all she had was a torn-up dress, so some of us decided we were going to bring her better things. I took her my best dress, one Mrs. O'Brien had just had made for me. I had fifteen dresses already! I didn't need another one. So I took the dress to Eliza. She's almost my size. It went lower to the floor on her than my dresses do on me, but she'll grow taller, and then it'll be the same on her as it is on me. And then she'll grow even taller and it won't fit her anymore, like when I grow out of my dresses, and I'll take her another one. I'll take her my best dress again, because just like Katie Farren, she's a best friend. Best friends ought to have the best of what you have if you're going to give them something.''

Josie at first raised her brows at what Margaret related, then she shook her head and smiled. Maggie glanced up at her rather sheepishly from beneath her long lashes, her eyes shining, reflecting the orange sunset.

"Margaret, that is the most touching thing I have ever heard,'' Josie said sincerely. "I wish I had had a friend like you while I was growing up.''

Maggie shrugged one shoulder as if she really had not done anything special. Then she smiled hesitantly, not knowing what to expect from Josie at this point.

Josie kissed her cheek. She put her arm around Margaret and drew the girl close, just as one of the nearby chickens began pecking at the crate in which it was caged.

"I don't run off to worry people,'' Maggie said. "Honest, Josie. I've always run off before to be with my friends at the levee because Papa and Mrs. O'Brien won't let me go there for anything. Papa said they could come to the house to play, but Mrs. O'Brien might not like them, and maybe she'll run them off. They're not always very clean and they don't have pretty clothes like I do. Jonathan, he works at a warehouse, and he most always has dirt on him. It doesn't hurt him, so it won't hurt me. That's what I decided one day.''

"I think Mrs. O'Brien would be more understanding about your visiting with your friends at the house rather than at the levee than you realize. You were dirty the night we walked home all the way from the theater, and your skirt was even torn in a few places from when you caught it on those nails on the side of that building. But Mrs. O'Brien didn't scold you," Josie said. "She was glad to see you, Margaret. She thought it was cute when we took off our shoes and stockings and ran along the garden paths. She didn't tell me that, but I could tell. When we went in to wash our feet, she was there grinning. It's not your feet and your torn clothes she wants to watch after so much, Margaret. It's your safety. There are all sorts of people at the dock, and you're a pretty girl someone might snatch up and hurt in a bad way."

Maggie frowned, nodding after a time.

"*I* wouldn't wander the levee alone," Josie said, "and I'm a grown woman."

The chicken was still pecking at the crate, intermittently stepping away, cocking its head, clucking, then coming back to the one corner to peck some more.

"There must be something tasty there," Margaret said, giggling.

"There must be," Josie agreed, smiling.

"I'm tired. Could I sit on your lap?"

Josie lifted her brows in surprise. "Certainly."

A few seconds later, Maggie was comfortably settled on her lap, her head resting against Josie's breast. Before too long, Margaret was asleep, breathing deeply, and Josie leaned her head back against the wall behind her and closed her eyes, too.

Darkness had fallen long before the ship arrived at the St. Louis levee. Glowing lanterns dangled here and there from the deck railing, spreading yellow light. Other people had fallen asleep, too, and the amount of noise had dropped significantly. Even the animals seemed to have fallen asleep. The levee seemed relatively quiet, with the exception of scattered people walking here and there. But then, the only time Josie had seen the levee had been during daylight. The smell of old fish drifted, and the Mississippi exuded the thick smell of mud.

People began moving about, gathering their belongings, pulling their children close, preparing to leave the ship. Josie woke Margaret by whispering her name in her ear several times. The girl rubbed her eyes sleepily and sat up.

Josie's trunks were unloaded from the ship by several dock-hands and placed atop a cab. She intended to take Maggie home, explain to Thomas what had happened, and probably have the confrontation with him that she had hoped to avoid. She had left without telling him she planned to because he had insisted last evening that he would find a way for them to be together, and she didn't think he could—not a way that would also allow him to continue as a respected doctor in St. Louis and at the college. After explaining to him why she had left without telling him her plans, and being adamant that her leaving was the best thing, she would go back to the hotel, sleep the rest of the night, then worry about passage back to Cape Girardeau tomorrow.

The driver handed Margaret up into the conveyance, then took Josie's hand to help her up. She put her boot on the step just as a boy ran toward the carriage, shouting her name.

"Miss Gavin, Miss Gavin! Have you got Maggie with you?"

She stepped back down. "Yes, but . . . who are you?"

"Jonathan Drury, that's who he is!" Margaret said, poking her head out of the carriage. She gathered her skirt close and glanced at the ground as if anticipating the jump. Josie put her hand out to help her down.

"You're furious because I hid away on the ship, and you've been to see my papa, haven't you?" Maggie asked, once safely on the street, her hands on her hips. "I said to myself and to Josie, Jonathan does whatever he says he's going to do, and since you yelled at me that you'd tell my father, I know you've been to see him. Well, I know I was wrong to hide away on the ship like that, but I don't want you scolding me, Jonathan Drury. Not one bit. I don't want you saying—"

"Maggie, forget that!" He fairly screeched to a halt in front of them, kicking up dust and grabbing the side of the cab to steady himself. "Katie has cholera. She's not doing good, not good at all. There are other people with it, too. It's breaking out like it always does, only earlier this year. I just heard there are about ten people over at that hospital they opened not long ago an' another twenty or so in the city in homes. Miss Gavin,

Dr. Murphy said to keep an eye out for ya an' to ask ya to take Maggie away from here if ya come with her. I know that's asking a lot, to get right back on a ship after ya just got off, but that's what—''

"I'm not leaving Katie Farren!" Maggie blurted, her hands on her hips. She looked like an angry storm cloud. "Papa wouldn't let me see Mama when she was sick, and then she died. He promised he wouldn't do that with you, Josie, but now he's doing it with Katie. I'm not leaving. I'm telling everyone—*I'm not leaving.*"

Josie stood stock-still for a moment, feeling shocked by the news that Katie was so ill and shocked by Maggie's outburst. *Patricia,* she thought. God, how frantic Patricia must be feeling. How she must be praying every moment, every second. Poor Katie. Poor Michael. Josie's heart ached for all of them.

"Josie, please don't make me leave," Margaret pleaded, her face white, her eyes larger than Josie had ever seen them. "Please, oh, please don't make me leave. I want to see Katie. She and Eliza, they're my best friends. I saw Mama one night when she kissed me and told me good night, and then the next day Papa was there, telling me she was real bad sick and that I couldn't see her because she was too sick. I never saw her again, Josie. Never. I saw Katie at Chouteau's Pond and then when she asked me in the carriage if I knew there was a traveling show coming to town. That's all. Don't make me leave. Katie's sick, and I could help take care of her the way I took care of you. I could! Papa's scared of me catching cholera, too, I know. But I can't leave Katie. I just can't!"

"Shh," Josie said, running the back of her hand alongside Margaret's cheek. "We'll stay."

"But, Miss Gavin," Jonathan objected, "Dr. Murphy said—''

"I know what Dr. Murphy said," she snapped, not really meaning to. She apologized to him almost immediately, then said, "This has been a very long day." First her decision this morning to leave, then quarreling with Patricia and Margaret at Chouteau's Pond, then leaving St. Louis, then returning to St. Louis—all in one day.

"We're staying?" Maggie asked, sounding surprised.

"But Dr. Murphy said . . . Maggie'll get cholera if she's with Katie!" Jonathan objected more.

Maggie huffed. "No, I won't, Jonathan Drury! Not everyone gets cholera."

"But, Maggie, ya could."

"Maybe I could. But if I get it, I'll get it taking care of my best friend and trying to help her feel better," Margaret retorted.

"Maggie, your father said for you and Miss Gavin to leave."

"Jonathan," Josie said, stepping between the two of them, "Dr. Murphy's wife died last spring from cholera, and while I understand that he fears the disease, Katie is Maggie's best friend. I know better than anyone what good medicine Maggie can be."

Margaret looked at her and beamed.

"Now perhaps you would like to ride along," Josie continued. "If not, it was nice meeting you. Margaret and I are going directly to the Farrens'."

He glanced from Josie to Maggie and back several times, shuffled his feet, raked a hand through his already tousled red hair, sighed, and said, "Reckon I'll go along then, too."

He helped Margaret up into the carriage, and Josie smiled to herself, thinking he might just be the big brother Maggie had never had. The driver, who had been standing nearby all this time, handed Josie up, then closed the door, and a few minutes later, the three of them were headed for the Farrens'.

Thomas was exactly as Josie expected to find him. He looked scared, worried—and furious that she'd brought Margaret to the Farrens' instead of taking her away from the city, or at least home. It had taken some convincing from Josie before Patricia had finally agreed to allow Josie, Maggie, and Jonathan upstairs to see Katie. When they'd entered the room, Josie spotted Michael and Thomas sitting in chairs near the fireplace. Thomas jumped up and came at them, fear leaping in his eyes.

"Maggie, stay away from the bed," he warned when she

started that way. His eyes flashed at Josie. "I told Jonathan here to ask you to take Maggie away from the city."

Jonathan shifted from one boot to the other, obviously nervous. "I—"

"He told me," Josie said, holding Margaret back for the moment with her arms around her shoulders from behind. She glanced at the bed, where Katie lay curled in a ball, a shift covering her to the shins, the bottoms of her feet almost scarlet. "How is she?"

"Very ill. Contagious. Why didn't you at least take Maggie to the house? Why did you bring her here?"

"Because Katie is her friend, her dear friend, and she wants to help take care of her," Josie said stubbornly.

Thomas drew closer, and Josie immediately recognized the set to his jaw. "This isn't a skull fracture," he rasped. "This is cholera."

"Katie," Maggie whispered, wringing her hands and twisting her lips as she glanced at her friend with great concern. Her eyes filled with tears. "Papa, when I found out that Josie was so sick, you said that keeping me from Mama had been a mistake, that you wished you hadn't kept me from her. Papa, it's Katie! I can help her get well, just like I helped Josie get well."

"Maggie, you could get sick yerself!"

"I won't. I promise I won't!"

"Maggie girl, you've no control over that."

"I know I won't. I just know it!"

"Josie, you shouldn't have brought her here!"

"You can't always protect children from all the ugliness of the world, Thomas," she said softly. "You can't always keep from them things like disease and hurt. Maggie's presence here will be a great comfort to both girls." *And I'd like to comfort you,* she wanted to say. But Michael still sat in the chair, Patricia stood in the doorway, looking exhausted, and Josie knew she had no business offering Thomas even a shoulder on which to lay his head. Though she would love to. . . .

He covered his face with his hands. A few seconds passed, then he lifted his head, offered Maggie a hand, and led the way to the bed.

"Madness," he muttered. "All right. She stopped drinkin' these last few hours. I'm thinkin' you might get her to take more water an' medicine, Maggie me girl. She won't get through this if she doesn't. It's a hard battle, an' she has to have at least water an' medicine."

"I'll do it, Papa," Margaret said, sitting on the bed. "Katie will for me. I know it. And Jonathan can help, too. She'll do it for us."

Josie heard a sound and turned toward the doorway in time to watch Patricia put her hands over her mouth and take a few jerking breaths, fighting sobs though tears already welling in her eyes.

Josie went to her, wrapping her arms around her shoulders and drawing her close. "We'll go fix tea," Josie said, fighting tears herself. "Maggie will get her drinking again, Patricia, and she'll be well soon."

"Oh, God, Josie, I pray that you're right!"

Once downstairs, Josie led Patricia into the kitchen and settled her in a chair near the large oak table in the middle of the room. Patricia told her where she could find matches, and she soon had several lamps lit. Together they worked at starting a fire in the large stove that sat perhaps six feet from the table, then Josie poured water from a pitcher into a small kettle and placed it on the stove to warm.

"Jonathan said Maggie followed you," Patricia said.

"Maggie stowed away on the ship. We had been gone several hours from St. Louis when I learned that she was in my cabin," Josie responded, taking a chair next to Patricia. "I lay down to sleep, and she was singing to me when I woke up."

That brought a smile to Patricia's lips. "Sometimes Maggie can be the most charming little girl in the world."

"And other times she can be the most stubborn."

Patricia nodded. "But . . . that stubbornness can be a good thing, too."

Josie agreed. "Where is Charlie?" she asked.

"With Michael's parents. I thought they would want to be here, but I was relieved that they offered to take the baby instead. Babies don't often live through cholera."

They sat in silence for a few minutes, Patricia running a

finger along a dark vein in the oak.

"Maggie has so much courage," she said after a minute, taking a deep breath. "I could tell she wanted to cry when she saw Katie lying there. But she didn't—she was so brave."

Josie smiled. "She certainly helped me regain my strength and health. She brought me breakfast she'd helped the cook prepare, she brushed my hair, she entertained me with chatter. . . ."

Patricia laughed. "Yes, she can chatter."

"Has Katie ever spoken of a girl named Eliza?"

Patricia glanced off at a corner for a moment, then back. "A few times, perhaps. She's part of their levee group. They like to meet in an old warehouse down there where they've built a stage and where they play. The man who owns the building, Mr. Potts, doesn't mind. He thinks it's cute, so he lets the children play in one area. He owns a grocery about half a mile down Front Street from the warehouse."

"They built a stage?"

Smiling, Patricia nodded. "They have so much fun. I must say, I've never liked Katie running to the levee, either. But what I do, instead of forbidding her to be there, is take her myself and leave her there while I do the marketing. We had to come to an understanding, Katie and I, that she wouldn't leave the warehouse. Jonathan looks after the girls, too. In fact, he looks after most all of the children. The last time I counted when Katie was rattling off names, the group was up to eight or ten, and sadly enough, many are orphans. Jonathan's not, but he has a difficult time with his mother, so he doesn't go home much. Some of the children have been in orphanages and swear they won't go back."

Josie was surprised by all of this, especially by the fact that many, not just one of the children, were orphans. But perhaps Maggie had mentioned only Eliza because Eliza was such a good friend. "That's amazing, Patricia, isn't it? They've all banded together. . . . How did Katie and Maggie meet these children?"

"I took the girls marketing with me one afternoon. Jonathan was there, selling corn. Some of the other children were gathered around. I was looking at fruit when Katie and Maggie

struck up a conversation with the group. Those two will talk
to most anyone, anyway,'' Patricia said, giving a little laugh.
''During the next few days, Katie and Maggie both were missing a few times. I was frantic until Katie returned one day and
I got the truth out of her about where she'd been. The warehouse is not exactly clean, so she came home with her dress
dirty. That isn't a crime, but I was concerned. I was afraid
someone had accosted her and she was scared to tell me the
truth. I took her to the warehouse myself the next day and sat
and observed while the children played with each other. Mr.
Potts came along and I spoke with him, and he seemed nice
enough. I saw nothing wrong with what the children were
doing, so I talked to Katie and agreed to take her sometimes.
I told Thomas I would take Maggie, too, but he said he had
already told her not to go to the levee again and he meant to
stick by his decision. Only, over the winter months, Maggie
ran off to the levee often and nearly drove him mad, as well
as the nursemaids he hired before he found Mrs. O'Brien.''

The water was boiling in the kettle. Patricia fetched tea from
a cabinet while Josie found cups in another. She glanced over
at Patricia, her heart heavy suddenly as she thought of what
was happening upstairs. God would not take Katie from Patricia. He was merciful. He was good. He would not.

Twenty-one

NO ONE IN the Farren house got much sleep that night. Josie and Patricia made themselves comfortable on the settees in the upstairs parlor, feeling they were close enough to Katie's room that if anyone called to them they could be down the hall in a minute. They were comfortable, yes, but they hardly slept, both being so worried about Katie. Every half hour or so they rose and wandered down the hall and into the bedroom, pausing at the side of the bed to speak to Katie and to watch as Maggie bathed her face and urged her to drink either water or some of the herbal tea Patricia had prepared and brought up earlier. By morning they would try other things, Thomas said.

He and Michael sat in the chairs near the fireplace, getting up now and then to walk over to the bed and speak to Katie, too. At some point Jonathan Drury had gone home, telling Thomas and Michael that he would call again tomorrow to see how Katie was.

Near dawn everyone but Thomas fell asleep—the women in the parlor, Michael in his chair, and Maggie beside Katie on the bed.

Thomas sat rubbing his jaw, worried crazy that Maggie would contract cholera and perish the way her mother had. He couldn't stand the thought of possibly losing her, and he was still angry that Josie had brought her here.

Actually he'd been relieved to learn that Maggie had hidden away on the ship. By that time he already knew that Katie had cholera, and he already knew that Josie's ship had left the levee—with Maggie on it. He had silently prayed that Maggie would find Josie, because he knew his daughter would be safe with her. He knew Josie would take care of her. He'd figured that Josie would bring Maggie back once she discovered her, and so he'd sent for Jonathan. He'd asked that the lad please watch for them. If he found them, he was to ask Josie to either keep Maggie with her on the ship she was on or board the next outgoing vessel; he would gladly reimburse her the cost of Maggie's fare. But Maggie and Josie's stubbornness and loyalty prevailed. Thomas shook his head.

Now here he sat, watching his daughter sleep beside Katie, who had cholera. Within less than a week, Maggie would almost surely have it, too—unless God had wrapped an invisible, protective shield around her. By this time, Thomas had said enough silent prayers that the Father had surely heard at least one.

Thomas himself nodded off soon, jerking awake only when people walked in and out of the room. Exhausted, he would fall back to sleep within seconds. He slept off and on for hours, his head propped against one wing of the chair, through the sun rising and beaconing through the window; through Josie, Patricia, and Maggie changing Katie's soiled bedding twice; through Jonathan coming back to call on Katie and the others; through Michael getting up and pacing restlessly; and through Josie walking over to him, placing a hand on his brow, and watching him for a few minutes.

"She'll live," Michael told Josie near noon, after she had brought a fiddleback chair from the parlor, placed it near the foot of the bed, and sat down. Understandably he had not been his usual jovial self. He had been quiet and reserved, deeply worried about his daughter.

Smiling, Josie nodded. "She'll be fine. Margaret has her drinking more, and she doesn't seem to be vomiting as much. She woke up with her stomach hurting an hour or so ago. Maggie gave her some of the medicine Thomas mixed with the water, and now she's resting comfortably again.''

"Where's Patricia?" he asked suddenly, as if just realizing she was gone.

"She and Jonathan went to the market. She won't be gone long.''

He nodded. He looked as exhausted as Thomas did. A small growth of beard peppered both men's jaws.

"Why don't you go lie down, Michael?" she suggested. "Things are somewhat better here now. I'll wake you if anything changes, if there's anything to worry about." When he hesitated, looking at the girls then returning his gaze to her, she smiled. "I promise."

He went, though slowly, looking back at the bed at least three times before he reached the door.

A missive came for Thomas, delivered upstairs by a Negro servant girl. Josie took the message and opened it, though in ordinary circumstances she wouldn't, to see if it was anything urgent. If not, she didn't intend to wake Thomas.

It was from a Dr. Moses Linton, who wished to inform Thomas of the cases of cholera breaking out all over the city. While the disease had certainly not reached epidemic proportions, it could easily. He and a number of other doctors had set up a hospital in a private home near the college and wondered if he might be available to help with the influx of patients. If he knew of another physician who wished to offer his services, too, or any individual who wished to help fight the scourge, he should bring them along.

Josie hated to wake him—and she knew he would not enjoy receiving such a missive. No one would, but particularly not Thomas. As much as he loved being a doctor, she knew he dreaded and hated cholera.

She went over to him and hunched near his knees. She placed a hand over his on his lap. "Thomas," she said softly, not wanting to startle him awake.

He didn't stir.

"Thomas," she said again, and this time he moved, bringing his hand up to scratch his neck. She said his name one more time, and his eyelids fluttered open. He stared down at her in sleepy confusion.

"Josie," he said. He lifted his hand and stroked her hair, then caressed her neck.

Startled by the tender touches, Josie jerked back, unbalancing herself and falling back on her bottom.

Thomas stared down at her, still looking confused, still looking half-asleep.

"I . . . Someone brought a message for you from a Dr. Moses Linton," she said, planting her hands on the floor and pushing herself up. She stood, smoothed her skirt, then handed him the paper. "I didn't want to wake you, but it sounds important."

"Dr. Linton," Thomas said, running a hand down over his eyes, then his nose and jaw. He shook his head, as if shaking off sleep. Then he asked how their patient was.

"She seems to be better. Margaret has her taking more water and tea, and she seems to be holding it down. She's not as chilled as she was and she doesn't feel as hot to the touch."

Raising his brows, he glanced over at the bed. "Maybe she'll be fine, then. Maybe my prayers are bein' heard. Now we wait for Maggie to contract it an' we get her through it."

Josie rolled her eyes. "If you keep thinking she'll contract it, she very well might. Think positively, Thomas, that she won't get it, that none of us will."

He squinted one eye at her. "You shouldn't have brought her here."

She lifted her chin. "I did what I thought was best for Maggie and Katie, and I won't argue with you about the matter. What's done is done."

She started to turn away, but he grabbed her hand, brought it to his mouth, and kissed the back of it. Josie didn't have a chance to jerk it away, and almost as soon as his lips touched her skin, her heart quickened and the resistance she had been determined to keep in place began melting.

"Thomas," she scolded softly.

"You were leavin'," he accused.

"Only going back over to the bed to see how the girls are."

"No. You were leavin' St. Louis. Without tellin' me. Without sayin' good-bye."

She swallowed. "This isn't the time to discuss this."

"Or was yer lovemakin' the last night we were together yer good-bye?"

"Thomas . . ."

"I love you, Josie."

She shook her head. "You're going to kill yourself as a doctor."

"No. I'll survive, an' we'll be together, I promise you. This Dr. Linton . . . he wants to start a medical journal, Josie, an' he wants me to help him do it. We've been talkin' an'—"

"So your paper will be published and circulated. And undoubtedly other papers you write, too. That's wonderful, Thomas, but that does not solve the problem of Dr. Blanche ruining your reputation in the medical field."

"It's a beginnin'. One thing at a time."

"Oh, Thomas." Shaking her head, she went against her better judgment and tenderly touched his cheek. Then she pulled her hand away and headed over to the bed.

Katie was awake and staring up at the tester covering, her eyes glassy but not nearly as red as they had been. Josie smiled at her, and she forced a weak smile back.

"Perhaps it's a good time for more to drink," she suggested to a tired-looking Maggie. "Then I think we'll find you a bed down the hall and put you in it for a while."

Surprisingly, Margaret didn't object. She reached for the water glass while Josie helped Katie sit up a little.

"Ye're right," Thomas said, approaching. "She is lookin' better. Katie Farren, you'll recover yet, you will, you will. If my daughter weren't so dear to me, I'd recommend her healin' touch to all my patients."

She gave him a weak smile, too, and he grinned back.

"As much as I'm not wantin' to, now that our Katie's lookin' better, I'm goin' to the hospital Dr. Linton's set up," Thomas told Josie. "I'll stop and look for Alan along the way. It sounds as though Dr. Linton needs the help. Alan'll soon be havin' his own cases to battle in Davenport, when he returns there. I'll leave this note with you. It has the address of the hospital on it, in case anyone comes lookin' for me. I left the jar of medicine to mix in her water now an' then on the table,'' he said, jerking his head that way. "Try some stock soon an' see if she holds it. If she does, then you might try some food, maybe only bread at first. If she starts feelin' worse or if anyone else gets sick, send for me.''

Josie assured him that she would. He tweaked Maggie's nose and told her he wanted her to sleep for a while this afternoon, then he left.

Patricia returned presently. She swept into the room, making a sound of joy in the back of her throat when she spotted Katie sitting up in bed.

"Hi, precious,'' she greeted, gliding across the room, obviously elated.

"Mommy!'' Katie said, as excitedly as a sick child could. "You're back.''

"And with good things from the market for you to enjoy as soon as you start eating again,'' Patricia said.

"Papa said she could have stock soon, and then if she doesn't vomit that, she can have bread and other food,'' Maggie told Katie's mother. "Katie Farren, you'll be playing with me at Chouteau's Pond again real soon; I just know it!''

Katie playfully wrinkled her nose at Maggie, who began telling her how Jonathan had told her that he planned to add some things to their stage, some surprises, and that she'd better get over her sickness so she could come and see.

Josie let the girls visit for a little while, until Katie started looking tired again. Then she told Maggie that they were going to take a rest in one of the guest rooms. Maggie didn't object; in fact, she yawned. Josie imagined she would be asleep almost before her head hit the pillow.

She was, and Josie followed shortly afterward.

Josie and Margaret both slept the rest of that day and into the night. Josie woke at one point to find Maggie gone and moonlight shining in the window. She rose, left the room, and strode down the hall into Katie's room. There was Maggie, curled up with Katie on the bed, a sheet pulled up over them. Patricia sat in one of the fireplace chairs opposite Michael, her head leaning against one of the wings, her eyes shut. Josie wandered over to her and gently shook her awake.

"Go to bed, Patricia," she said. "I've had hours of sleep now. Michael and I will keep watch."

Patricia nodded, looking groggy. She left the room a few moments later, after a long look at the bed.

Morning brought a visit from an anxious Constance.

Josie was just coming downstairs to see what the cook might have to offer everyone for breakfast when a rap sounded on the door. There seemed to be no one about to answer it, so she headed up the hall and into the entryway. She pulled the door open, and there stood Constance, wide-eyed, looking very innocent and springlike in a soft white bonnet embroidered with colorful flowers. Behind her, in the drive, sat a lacquered carriage.

"Miss Gavin!" she said in surprise. "How nice to see you again. I heard Thomas . . . Dr. Murphy . . . was here caring for little Katie—I hope she's feeling better by now."

"She is, thank goodness. Come in," Josie said, stepping aside. "I know this is odd, me answering the Farrens' door; but everyone is exhausted, so it's whoever happens to be the closest at the time someone knocks."

Constance stepped inside, then stopped short.

"Actually I was hoping to speak to Dr. Murphy and ask him to look in on my father. I think he has the cholera, and he is so cantankerous. He's a physician, too, and he has been treating himself. But he is looking terrible, Miss Gavin. Terrible! Like he has lost pounds and pounds in just the last twenty-four hours. It's horrible. My mother fled the city, as a lot of people are doing. She wanted me to go along, but I would not leave my father alone, with no one to care for him. I need Dr. Murphy. I need help taking care of my father."

"Oh, Constance." Josie pulled out the paper Thomas had given her from a pocket stitched into her dress and handed it to Constance. "There's an address on there of a home near the college that some doctors have made into a hospital for cholera victims. That's where Dr. Murphy is. That's where you'll find him."

Constance seized her hands and bent close. "Thank you. Thank you ever so much!" Then she released Josie's hands and fled back out the door. Josie watched her be handed up into the carriage by her driver, and minutes later the conveyance left the drive and tore off up the street.

Three hours later, Constance returned, twisting her bonnet ribbons, looking nearly frantic now. "He said he would be along but he hasn't turned up. There were sick people everywhere at that house, Miss Gavin. You would not have believed it. Everywhere—on cots, on the floor. Thirty and fifty to a room. I know he is busy, but what will I do? I asked if another doctor could come along if he was too busy, and he said he would send someone if he could not come. But no one has come and . . . All but one of the servants have fled. All but a kitchen girl who will not do a thing I ask her to do and—"

"Wait," Josie said, placing her hand on Constance's arm.

She went off upstairs where Patricia had awakened and a half hour or so ago had brought a backgammon set into the room for the girls, who were also awake now. Katie was looking much better. The chills had gone almost completely, the fever had subsided, and she hadn't vomited in hours.

"Constance's father has cholera, and Thomas can't seem to find time to call on him because there are so many patients at the hospital some of the doctors set up," Josie told Patricia, who was seated on the bed with the girls. Josie opened the bottle of medicine Thomas had left, tapped a good portion of it into an empty tumbler, then recorked the bottle and tucked it into her skirt pocket. "Constance is here for the second time in hours, scared and not knowing what to do. Her mother fled the city, but she refused to leave her father. Katie is feeling better now. I'm going to see if I can help. I'll take some of the medicine Thomas left. It seems to work well, if Katie is any indication.''

Patricia slowly came off the bed and approached her, shaking her head. "You're going to help that man?" she asked in disbelief. "After what he threatened to do to Thomas?"

"Patricia," Josie scolded softly, "he's ill, and I wouldn't dream of not helping him. If he even lets me. He may not, you know. I may be back within the hour."

"Your heart is huge and compassionate, Josie. Sometimes our strengths can also be our weaknesses," Patricia warned, embracing her.

Josie withdrew a few seconds later, smiling as she hurried from the room.

Constance was at first reluctant to have Josie help nurse her father. Josie guessed why: While Lucas Blanche might not have told his daughter about the ultimatum he had given Thomas, he probably had made his dislike for Josephine Gavin known in his home.

"Is there someone else to help you?" Josie asked Constance straightforwardly.

"No, but . . . I do not know if he will let you. Mother will be . . . Mother will be shocked," Constance said, casting her gaze at the floor.

"Is your mother here to help care for him?"

"No, but—"

"Can your father care for himself?"

"No, but—"

"He's your father, but perhaps it's time you stopped allowing him to bully you, Constance."

The girl paled, going nearly as white as fresh snow. "Father would *disown* me!"

Josie huffed defiantly. "If he ever does, you can live with me. Obedience to a parent is an admirable quality, but not if the parent abuses the loyalty by dominating the child. That is unreasonable and intolerable. But then, those are my feelings," she said, smiling nicely as she pulled the door open. "Shall we go?"

Constance balked once more, but only for a few seconds this time. At least she wasn't as pale as she had been when

Josie first told her she planned to go with her to help nurse her father. Giving one more twist of her bonnet ribbons, Constance stepped over the threshold.

Josie followed.

Twenty-two

LUCAS BLANCHE BEGAN grumbling as soon as he saw Josie. Constance didn't even have to introduce her; he knew who she was. That didn't surprise Josie. He had somehow learned of her involvement with Thomas—however he had accomplished that—and since learning of it, he had doubtless kept a close eye on them and made it his business to learn who exactly she was.

He ordered Josie from his house within minutes of her arrival in the room. Josie felt Constance's gaze on her as the girl appeared to huddle near the doorway, her hands clutching her shoulders. The man completely intimidated her. It was one thing to respect a parent, but what Josie saw in Constance was not respect, it was fear.

Spotting a pitcher and a glass of water on a table across the room, Josie ignored his order and walked that way. She took the bottle of medicine from her skirt pocket, tapped some of the powder into the water, and swirled the water around thoroughly in the glass, mixing the medicine as much as possible. The man was lying in his own waste, dark circles had formed beneath his eyes, and his skin was almost ashen in color, parched in places and appearing thin and dry; yet when she neared the bedside, telling him she had just cared for Katie Farren and watched the medicine help her a great deal, he reached up and angrily knocked the glass from her hand. It shattered on the floor.

"Get the hell out of my home!" he bellowed.

Constance gasped.

Josie stared at the man, seething inside.

"Constance, fetch your father some tea," she said tightly, her gaze never leaving his.

"Do not order my daughter about!"

"Constance . . . tea," she said again, not wavering.

She heard skirts rustle, then, from the corner of her eye, watched Constance slip from the room.

"Brazen actress!" Lucas Blanche said, glaring at her, struggling to sit up. "Do not think you can march into my home like you own the place! I'll send someone for a constable and have you tossed out!" He reached for a bell that sat on a table beside his bed, his face going red as if he had to summon a taxing amount of strength.

"It's my understanding that your wife and servants have all fled," Josie said coolly. "Who will you send, Dr. Blanche?"

"Why—I'll send . . . I'll send . . . Constance will go for one!"

He began ringing the bell. With one quick move Josie snatched it from his hand.

"I came to offer you my assistance, despite the fact that I know what you've threatened to do to Thomas if he keeps associating with me," she said. "I came because I care about people, because I believe in my heart that everyone has a little good in them, and because I can't stand to see or hear about pain and suffering. Constance rode all over searching for someone to help you. I was the only person who volunteered, and I didn't have to, Dr. Blanche. Now . . . would you like to lie there and die in your filth, or would you rather I help clean you up and nurse you back to health?"

He glared at her a moment longer, then dropped his head back on the pillow. "I'm too far gone," he said wearily, weakly. "I have lost too much fluid and I cannot hold anything."

"Whatever is in the bottle," Josie said, motioning to the

table, "started helping Katie Farren right away. She still vomited for a time, but then her stomach seemed to calm down, and now she's much better. Isn't it worth a try?"

Dr. Blanche closed his eyes. "It depends on the patient's strength, too. Thomas always has been the sharpest-minded physician I have known. He takes note of everything and writes it all down so he can refer back to it later. He's brilliant."

Josie returned to the table, turned over a second glass that sat there, and poured water from the pitcher into it. "Then why deprive the medical profession of him, Dr. Blanche? Why even threaten to?" she asked, tapping powder into this glass. She lifted the glass and moved her wrist around and around to mix the medicine. She felt his stare on her back, then she turned and met it.

"Poisoning would be merciful, if that is what you are considering doing," he commented.

She glanced down at the glass in her hand, then back at him. "The thought never crossed my mind, Dr. Blanche. But I understand why you fear that it might have."

"My daughter loves him," he said, closing his eyes again.

Josie shook her head as she again approached the bed. "No, she respects him and she fears you. *You* love him. You admire the doctor in him, perhaps his integrity and professionalism. She's going along with what you want."

"Was it professional to become involved with a female patient while he was practically engaged to my daughter?" Lucas Blanche snapped.

Josie hesitated at that. No, she didn't suppose it was. "I believe, Dr. Blanche, that even beneath the yards of cloth a priest wears, there is a man. No matter what vow anyone takes, no human is perfect, no human is without a flaw or weakness. Look at you right now . . . so very human, so very ill."

She slipped her hand beneath his neck and lifted his head, bringing the glass to his lips. His lids fluttered up at her, and a frown creased his brow as he regarded her. A moment later, he sipped.

He took all of the water, finishing it just as Constance

walked into the room, a tray in her hands. She placed it on the table beside the jar of powder, then turned and put her back to the table.

"We'll need fresh linen, Constance," Josie told her. "Plenty of it. Do you know where some is?"

Constance nodded, then hurried out again.

Josie began the same process that she, Patricia, Thomas, and Margaret had begun and kept up for hours. She fetched a basin of water from a washstand in the room and began bathing Lucas Blanche. She expected modesty to get the better of him and that he would start objecting. Instead, he closed his eyes, looking relieved—and even more relieved when Constance returned with fresh linen, and she and Josie changed the bedding and his gown. He vomited up some of the water, as Josie had known he might, and then he vomited up the next glass of water and medicine Josie urged him to drink, too. "Even if he holds a drink or two," she could almost hear Thomas saying in her mind. "A little is better than none."

They changed Dr. Blanche's bedding again after only half an hour, and when they finished, Constance convinced him to drink some of the tea she'd brought. It couldn't possibly be warm anymore, but he didn't seem to care. Now that he had people helping him, he seemed to want to recover.

Constance pulled chairs into the room from another room and placed them near the foot of the bed. Her father drifted to sleep presently, and after touching his brow and leaning close to listen to his breathing, she offered Josie a cup of tea, then settled on the chair opposite her.

"He can be an ogre, I know," she said rather timidly.

"Only if you let him. Ogres are ogres because people allow them to be."

Constance glanced up, giving Josie half a smile. "I know. Perhaps that is why my mother fled. She dreaded the giant of an ogre he would be as a sick man."

"It's admirable that you stayed with him," Josie said.

Another smile, this one a full one. "You really love him, don't you?" the girl queried.

Josie gave her a baffled look. She was so weary after the

last few days, it was a wonder she could think at all, or even move around. Her muscles felt sore. Her head ached a little. She rubbed the back of her neck.

"Thomas," Constance said. "You really love him."

Josie studied her to see if that knowledge upset her, to measure whether she might become distraught if Josie confirmed it.

Constance gave her another weak smile, though her eyes sparkled. "I know you do. I could tell the evening of the supper at the Farrens' . . . the way you looked at him sometimes . . . the way he looked at you when he did not know I was watching. I had heard the rumors, too, about the kiss in front of the National Hotel. A wife or fianceé sometimes must turn her head and ignore . . . indiscretions. I was surprised to find myself in the same room as you, at the same supper." She lowered her lashes, fixing her gaze on her skirt. "But I know I will have to overlook certain things at times. That is how marriage is."

Josie didn't know if Constance had witnessed such a relationship between her parents or if she had been taught that a wife should silently allow her husband "indiscretions." The thought outraged her.

"Constance, a husband and wife should be faithful to each other. The woman should not be the only one exercising fidelity—and she should not *ever* tolerate infidelity." She waited to see how Constance would digest that, and when the girl didn't appear too shocked or outraged herself, she said, "I'm sorry about the kiss in front of the hotel. I had no idea at the time how close the relationship between you and Thomas had become. I had no idea that you were practically engaged."

Constance pursed her lips. "You do not need to apologize. I like Thomas very much. I think he's a wonderful man, so devoted to what he does. And he loves people. But I do not think . . ." She pursed her lips again and, blushing, leaned forward and whispered, "I do not think I excite him the way you do."

"Does he excite you?" Josie asked directly.

Constance's blush deepened. Josie watched her. Sometimes

directness was best, even if it made a person uncomfortable for a time.

Josie leaned forward, too. Their heads nearly touched. Constance's gaze still held fast to her skirt. "Does he make your heart pound when he comes near? Does your breath catch? Can you not wait to see him again? Can you not wait to smell him? To hear his voice? Does the mere thought of him touching you and kissing you make you giddy? Can you not wait to do things for him—to make him tea like this, to surprise him with something you know he truly enjoys? Is he worth fighting for?"

As soon as she asked the last question, she sat back in her chair. Then she leaned forward again, this time placing her hand on Constance's forearm just as the girl glanced up at her, a startled look in her eyes.

"I realize how the last must have sounded," Josie said. "I didn't mean to imply that we should fight over Thomas if we both love him. I was repeating a question someone asked me, a question that made me realize how deeply I love him.

"But Constance," she continued, "I won't fight you for him. I like you a great deal, as a friend, and I don't like to see people hurt. I would rather walk away than hurt anyone. In fact, I left a few days ago without him knowing, and I intend to leave again when all of this is over. I returned only to bring Maggie home—she stowed away on my ship—and then stayed because Katie Farren was so ill. I realize that I'm a distraction and that that distraction could hurt a number of people. I won't have that."

"I do not love him," Constance said softly after a long moment. "I do not feel all that excitement you talk about when I am with him. I—I felt it for someone else." She lowered her voice to a whisper again with the next. "I still think of him, too." She glanced at the bed to make certain her father was not awake.

"Then you should tell your father, and I'm not telling you that so I can find a way to steal Thomas away from you," Josie said. "I believe you should have a say in whom you marry—and I believe you should marry the man you love."

Constance sighed. "I wonder if I can be so brave . . . so courageous as you, Josie." She glanced up, looking Josie straight in the eye finally. "I know you are an actress and I know some people do not think good of you, but I think you are the most wonderful person I have ever met. You have the kindest heart and you aren't afraid of anything or anyone. I think you are extraordinary."

Smiling, Josie hugged her.

"More water," Lucas Blanche grumbled from the bed. Constance gasped, probably wondering, as Josie did, how long he had been awake and how much of their private conversation he had heard.

"Don't be so afraid," Josie whispered in her ear. "And even if you are . . . I know he's your father and you love him in a certain way, but don't let him bully you. Don't let anyone bully you. Be loving but firm—and know that you're plenty grown up enough to make your own decisions, especially one as important as whom you should marry."

"Ladies . . . ," Thomas greeted from the doorway. Both women jumped a little and turned their heads that way, now wondering how much of their conversation *he* had overheard. He had a funny look in his eyes, a combination of surprise and apprehension. "A surprise, findin' you here, Josie," he said softly as he entered the room, his medical bag dangling from one hand. "I let myself in, Constance. I hope you don't mind. The door was partially open, an' no one answered my knocks an' calls. How's yer father?"

"Feeling a bit better after whatever it was your woman friend has been giving me," Dr. Blanche grumbled from the bed.

"Miss Gavin, you mean?"

More grumbling, words Josie couldn't understand. Then: "She's quite a nurse; I'll give her that."

"She's a beautiful person," Thomas said, plopping his bag on the table beside the bed, giving Dr. Blanche a hard look, then opening his bag. "Despite her profession."

Thomas was being quite direct with the man, perhaps too

direct considering how he valued his position at the college.

"Dr. Murphy, things must have been a nightmare at the hospital," Josie said, standing and moving to the table to mix more water and medicine for Dr. Blanche. "Constance said people occupied cots everywhere and nearly every available space on the floor, too. I can't imagine what—"

"There's no need to be formal, Josie," he responded. "No need at all."

She mixed the medicine, spilling some of it and shaking her head—at her sudden nervousness and his carelessness. Or was it outright defiance? She had just more or less told Constance not to let her father dictate her life, that she was old enough to do that herself, and yet she felt that Thomas needed to be somewhat docile in the man's presence. If he wanted to continue practicing medicine in St. Louis, that was. And if he really wanted the recognition from his peers that he felt so certain Dr. Blanche could give him with a few words in the right ears.

"Josie, is it?" Lucas Blanche demanded.

"That's right," Thomas responded, fitting together the pieces of his stethoscope.

"I thought we had an agreement," the older man said as Josie approached the bed with his water. "And you do know what I mean."

Josie stood on the opposite side of the bed from Thomas— a safe distance, she figured—and though she would have liked to toss the water in the man's face for the way she knew he was threatening Thomas even now, she leaned over Dr. Blanche, lifted his head, and helped him drink.

"No more threats, Lucas," Thomas said tightly. "They won't work. You do know Dr. McDowell. Dr. Joseph McDowell?"

Dr. Blanche sputtered, then choked on the water and began coughing.

"You threatened him, Father?" Constance asked, coming out of her chair, her eyes wide.

Thomas held up a hand, palm out, to stop her. She gripped one of the posts and stood watching.

"What are you doing, Thomas?" Josie asked, feeling even more apprehensive now.

"I'm puttin' myself back in control of my life," he stated, giving her a fierce look. "I'm about to ensure yer happiness, mine, an' Maggie's."

"Do not make the mistake of thinking that I will not make it out of this room, Thomas," Lucas Blanche warned. "Do not make the mistake of thinking that I will never again be talking to colleagues. Dr. McDowell? Dr. McDowell?"

"Stop threatening him, Father!" Constance demanded, and her chin tilted up instead of down when she issued the order. Josie almost smiled—and she might have if she weren't so worried about Thomas.

Thomas had his stethoscope together now, and he bent over Lucas Blanche, pressed the bell against his chest and listened for a moment, then withdrew. "My, but you are breathin' hard, Lucas. But yer heart sounds strong anyway. Constance, it would take a cannon to kill yer father, so you can stop worryin', lass. Speakin' of cannons and Dr. McDowell, he runs the medical school on Seventh Street, the one protected by the cannon. Some people don't like the fact that medical students must sometimes learn from cadavers, an' those men make their dislike known by occasionally stormin' the schools," he explained to both Josie and Constance. "So Dr. McDowell protects his school an' students with a cannon an' guns."

"The man is mad!" Dr. Blanche tried to shout. If he had been stronger, it would have been a shout.

Thomas chuckled. " 'Make Rome howl,' " he said, and chuckled more.

Lucas tried to sit up now and failed, then tried again, looking more and more indignant and insulted, though Josie couldn't figure out why. She was baffled, not knowing exactly what they were talking about. Thomas was getting to something surely. He seemed to have entered the room with a plan and he seemed to be putting that plan into motion, carrying it out one step at a time.

"Indeed!" Dr. Blanche objected, still trying to sit up.

"Blasting that cannon every Independence Day, annoying Brother Jasper next door. If you think to gain any notoriety by leaving our college for McDowell's—"

"I'll for sure gain notoriety—an' have a barrel of a time doin' it," Thomas said, chuckling still more. "Dr. McDowell likes his Independence Day celebrations, an' so he puts his cannon an' guns to good use every year challenging Brother Jasper, who heads the Christian Brothers College next door to Dr. McDowell's college. Brother Jasper is a bit more conservative than the notorious Dr. McDowell, an' he always pulls every pupil indoors when Dr. McDowell begins his cannonading. Dr. McDowell is a sight to watch when he runs forth to object to the unpatriotic retirement. 'Brother Jasper, oh Brother Jasper, you run a good school, so fine a school I'd send my own boy to it if I had a boy. But there's somethin' wrong with you. You retire from the celebration of yer country's glories!' Then he runs back to his cannon, gathers his forces around him again, an' the celebration continues. 'Tis a sight to see. It is, indeed. Dr. McDowell, stately lookin' physician that he is, all dandied up in his three-cornered hat an' cavalry saber, directin' the firin'. He certainly enjoys his independence!"

Josie was smiling, despite the seriousness of Thomas's rebellion. She imagined what this Dr. McDowell must look like, dandied up in his three-cornered hat and saber, directing the firing, people scurrying around, the dignified Brother Jasper—though she'd never met or even seen the man, she imagined him dignified; doing so made the image all the funnier—gathering his pupils and getting them indoors. She pictured Dr. McDowell rushing up to the doors of the college and loudly making his objections about the man retiring from the celebration, then rushing back to his cannon.

"Dr. McDowell's school does not have the upstanding reputation that our college does," Dr. Blanche argued.

" 'Upstanding reputation . . . ' " Thomas rubbed his jaw, where he now had two-days' growth of stubble. But he looked rather ruggedly handsome. "I've been caught up in wantin' one of those for years," he said, holding Josie's gaze. "So caught up in it I was willin' for a short time to give up the most remarkable woman I know.''

He glanced back down at Dr. Blanche. ''This dealing with sickness an' death day in an' out, Lucas . . . it doesn't always give us the perspective we should have. But at times it does. When I see life cut short I sometimes wonder if my patients knew happiness. I pray they did. I see the smile on my daughter's face, the glow about her when she looks at Josie here, an' I think, she needs a glow like that. She's happy. I need it, too. Josie needs it, too, an' so does Constance. I'm goin' to work for Dr. McDowell, whose reputation has somehow survived his wild cannonadin' an' the speculations about his school. I'm goin' to trade my upstandin' reputation for that glow because that's what I want. I love you, Josephine Gavin, an' I intend to marry you.''

He said the last with the utmost conviction, meeting her gaze again, more or less telling the world he didn't care what anyone thought about him for loving her, or what anyone might try to do to him.

Josie stood staring at him, speechless, loving him and feeling tremendously touched by the depth of his love for her. From her position at the foot of the bed, Constance clapped her hands together and made a sound of delight.

''Oh, that was beautiful! Absolutely beautiful!''

''What about your paper, Thomas?'' Lucas said, still hanging on by a thread. ''No one will publish it once I—''

''Stop it, Father!'' Constance ordered, rounding the bed. ''No more threats, or I'll go away and never speak to you again! Look at them. They are so much in love they would sacrifice everything for each other. You have to stop trying to dictate people's lives. Bad enough that you dictate mine and Mother's. You cannot dictate Thomas's. You shouldn't try to force him to marry me.''

Her father became sullen, his jaw jutting out, his eyes glowing as he shifted his gaze between the three of them. ''How can I fight the three of you? Here I lay, prostrate; how can I fight the three of you?''

''I hope that when you recover you'll leave the matter alone,

Lucas,'' Thomas advised. ''An' never, ever treat my future bride with disrespect.''

Constance clapped her hands again, laughed, then tore around to Josie's side of the bed to hug her.

Twenty-three

THOMAS SOON RETURNED to the hospital, leaving Lucas in Josie's care.

Lucas's condition worsened during the night, and his breathing became so labored Josie feared he would die no matter how diligently she nursed him. But when morning arrived, he seemed better, looking less pale and prostrate and actually holding down the water and tea she and Constance urged him to drink hour after hour. Both she and Constance were exhausted, and when late afternoon arrived, Josie insisted that Constance go rest. The other woman started to object, then wearily left the sickroom.

Josie wondered what Lucas planned to do if he recovered. Still try to ruin Thomas's reputation as a physician? Thomas had more or less declared war, and surely a man of Lucas's reputation wouldn't lie still for that. No matter what Thomas thought, the matter wasn't settled, Josie thought as she dozed in a chair near the bed.

Constance sat with her father that night while Josie slept in a room down the hall. When Josie entered the sickroom the following morning with a bowl of broth in hand, Lucas Blanche was actually sitting up in the bed, his back propped against pillows.

"We owe you so much," Constance told Josie, looking exhausted but delighted. "It looks as if he will be fine—all because of you."

Josie smiled, though Lucas was almost glaring. "I'm sure he will be. Now that the crisis is over here, I'm going to the hospital some of the doctors set up and see if I can be of help," she said. "Do you still have the paper I gave you? It had the address on it."

Nodding, Constance hurried off to fetch it.

"They might not want you there," Lucas said gruffly from the bed.

Josie tilted her chin defiantly. "But then again, they might want every available hand."

Leaving him with that, she departed, still determined to see if she could help at the hospital.

"You're already exhausted," Thomas objected when she located him in the house that had been converted to a temporary hospital and told him she wanted to help.

"Nonsense. I slept all last night while Constance sat with her father."

"How is Lucas?" He asked the question hesitantly, as if apprehensive.

"Much better. Back to being determined to see you ruined, I think," she warned.

"Then I'll do as much as possible to see that that doesn't happen. I'm only beginnin' to realize how respected I am as a physician in St. Louis, Josie. I've shown my study around some myself, an' it's getting notice. Once it's printed in Dr. Linton's new journal, Lucas Blanche can spout anything he wants. He won't be able to harm me."

"I hope you're right, Thomas," Josie said. Then she hurried off to tend a male patient who was calling for water.

The days began to pass in a slow blur. Josie wiped perspiring faces, lifted heads, urged the sick to drink, and even sang to them. She made broth and tea in the kitchen near the back of the house and mixed medicine in the liquids. She changed bedding and helped other women who had volunteered to scrub the soiled linen in large tin tubs placed out back, and at night she slept off and on on a cot in one of the sickrooms. Many people recognized her and commented about her desire to help. She met a number of Thomas's friends, fellow doctors, who all seemed to admire her, and she even helped nurse several of them when they contracted cholera.

"You're going to work yourself into an early grave," Alan said one afternoon as he approached with a tray of food for her. Josie realized she hadn't eaten since the previous evening and that she was famished. "To the kitchen for nourishment, Miss Gavin, and I'll hear no argument."

She wouldn't have thought to argue.

They shared the food—baked fish, corn, and boiled rice— and conversation.

"It might interest you to know that Lucus Blanche has started talking, trying to discredit Thomas and paint you as a . . . need I say it?"

Josie stopped chewing and closed her eyes. What she had feared for Thomas was happening. "And?"

"And . . . hardly anyone is listening. Those who like juicy gossip always will, of course. But Thomas is respected as a physician, and a lot of people have met you and are refusing to believe Lucas. *He's* looking worse and worse every day. I imagine he'll shut up soon out of fear that he might ruin his own reputation."

Josie became aware that she'd been holding her breath. "Are you sure? Are you being truthful or are you saying these things because you want me to stay with Thomas?"

"I'm being truthful. I don't want to see Thomas hurt either, Josie. But I don't think you should have tried to leave without telling him what you planned to do."

She glanced down at her plate. "You've been out in the city. Have you seen the girls—Katie and Maggie? Maggie hasn't caught the disease, has she?"

"Patricia and Michael took the girls away from the city, which relieved Thomas. He received a message from Patricia yesterday, telling him the girls were fine."

Josie released a breath of relief. "Thank God."

"I'm returning to Davenport tomorrow," Alan said. "We're nearing the time of year when cholera breaks out in most all the river cities, and I imagine my patients there will be needing me. I've stayed in St. Louis longer than I planned to." He placed his hand over hers and smiled. "I hope the next time I visit St. Louis it will be to attend your and Thomas's wedding."

She couldn't help but smile back. "You're a romantic at heart, Dr. Schuster."

He sighed dramatically. "Guilty as charged. So why haven't I met the right woman to romance?"

"Perhaps she's in Davenport waiting for you right now. Or perhaps she'll be along soon."

Alan laughed. "Well, that would be nice."

Thomas and Dr. Linton entered the kitchen, and their gazes went immediately to Alan and Josie. She hoped Thomas wasn't thinking she had any romantic interest in Alan. After that evening at Thomas's home, in which she and Alan had decided to work at making him a little jealous, she couldn't be sure what had passed between the two men. She couldn't be sure what Thomas thought about finding them together like this, sharing a meal.

"I think I'll go to the hotel for the afternoon," Josie said nervously, standing, suddenly self-conscious about the way strands of her hair undoubtedly hung around her face. "After washing over a basin for days, I would love a bath."

"I'll fetch a cab for you," Thomas volunteered, giving her a soft look. "This evening, I'll come for you myself an' see that you get a decent supper."

She lowered her lashes, feeling her face warm. She felt all eyes on her—his, Dr. Linton's, and Alan's—as if all three men wondered if she would object.

"Lucas Blanche is puffed full of air, Miss Gavin," Dr. Linton said. "I hope you aren't offended at my saying so. What minor damage he's doing with his tongue can be undone."

Josie studied him, feeling somewhat comforted.

Instead of objecting to Thomas's offer, she inclined her head to him. "A decent supper would be wonderful," she said softly. Then she strode past him and his companion and started out the kitchen door just as Dr. Linton clapped a hand on Thomas's shoulder, doubtless grinning at him, too.

* * *

They ended up having a quiet supper at Thomas's home, in the sitting room of all places, in front of a low fire that helped remove the evening chill. Josie saw Mrs. Reardon briefly when the woman carried in plates of beef and vegetables, smiled, and said how wonderful it was to see her.

"It's wonderful to see you, too, Mrs. Reardon," Josie said. "Truly. I've missed you and Mrs. O'Brien. Did she go with Maggie to the country?"

"I'm afraid she did. I hope the two of you have a pleasant supper," the housekeeper remarked, with a grin on her face. She was obviously hopeful that much more than just eating would happen between Josie and Thomas tonight. She even went so far as to close the door as she left the room.

Thomas produced a bottle of wine and two glasses from the sideboard, then rejoined Josie in front of the hearth, where a thick bearskin had been spread on the floor.

"Where did you get this?" Josie asked, running her hand over the fur. "Surely you didn't hunt and kill the beast?" She was teasing. For all she knew, he might have.

"Alan did. He has a friend who's a trapper an' he goes off with him now an' then for months at a time. He brought this back a few years ago."

The strips of beef were tender and delicious, having been cooked in a light sauce, and herbs sprinkled on the potatoes and beans enriched their flavor. Josie had just taken a sip of wine when she realized that Thomas was watching her intently. She glanced up to find him chewing slowly, the orange glow from the flames flickering in his eyes.

"Mr. Jefferson fled St. Louis with the troupe a few days after Katie took ill," he informed her.

"Did he?" she asked, truly surprised.

He nodded.

Silenced filled the room. Josie looked down at her plate, running a finger along the rim. "And you're wondering what I plan to do now? If I plan to follow him or stay here in St. Louis?"

Another nod. "I never really asked; I just blurted some

things that day at Dr. Blanche's home,'' he said, his voice low and gentle. "But, Josie, I . . . now I'm thinkin' we're at a point, you'n I, where we either go on from here or we end this. I don't want to spend my days an' nights wonderin' about you, when you might decide to leave again. If yer heart's with the Jefferson Company, then that's where it is, an' I won't speak a word to try to stop you if you decide to board a steamer tomorrow an' set off to find the troupe. I just can't go on not knowin'. So I'm askin' if you'll consider marryin' me an' makin' yer home here with me'n Maggie. This is where I first started thinkin' I loved you—right here in this room. The house has been too quiet since you left. There's no singin', for one. I'd be honored if you'd agree to be my wife, Josie Gavin, an' I know Maggie'd be delighted if you'd agree to be her mother. You were leavin' St. Louis to protect me'n Maggie, but the danger's gone now. Lucas has blown himself out.''

Josie was more touched than she could say. *I'm askin' if you'll consider marryin' me an' makin' yer home here with me'n Maggie.* The sweetness of his proposal . . . the gentleness of his tone and manner . . . She wanted to fall over into his arms. She really had very little desire to return to the stage with the Jefferson Company, and her desire to see Orson's account of their relationship had waned, too. It was so very personal, all that had happened between them, and to bare his sorrows and weaknesses before audiences everywhere . . . She wouldn't do it. She did intend to ask Thomas if he wanted to read the manuscript. She thought he would understand her relationship with Orson better if he did.

"Oh, Thomas," she whispered, placing her open hand on his jaw. "How would you feel about my signing with the St. Louis Theater? Mr. Carson says he rarely takes a production to other cities, but I'd still be on the stage and—"

"I'm thinkin' you should do what makes you happy. Take a few days an' think, Josie. Weigh ev'rything. If stayin' here an' marryin' me doesn't feel right to you, don't do it. The last thing I want is for you to have any more unhappiness in yer life.''

He leaned forward and kissed her, breathing her name as

he did. A second later he withdrew, picked up his plate, and began eating again, urging her to do the same.

Once the food was gone they set the plates aside and shared more wine while stretching out on their backs on the skin and watching the fire. They talked softly about Maggie and Katie and Patricia and Charlie. Then they moved on to Alan, talking about how he planned to leave for Davenport tomorrow and how Josie had told him the right woman was probably there waiting for him, or would be along soon.

"I hope ye're right," Thomas remarked. "He deserves the companionship. He deserves someone like you."

Smiling, Josie turned onto her side and pressed a kiss against his neck. "I don't need a lot of time to think, Thomas. In fact, I don't need any more than I've already taken. More than anything in the world, I want to be your wife and Maggie's mother. I want to have your children and I want to sing to them and to you. I've realized everything that's happened to me—meeting Orson, becoming an actress . . . everything— happened so I could meet you. I know that sounds crazy, but I believe it. So, yes, Thomas, I'll marry you. It will be an honor to marry you."

Thomas placed his hand on her far shoulder, pressed her back onto the rug, and stared down into her eyes. He grinned, tipped his head back and gave a throaty laugh, then grinned down at her again, his eyes sparkling more than she'd ever seen them sparkle.

A second later, he turned serious, lowering his head to kiss her. Josie opened to him, welcoming him, whispering his name just as his hand slid up to caress her breast.

Epilogue

SPRING HAD ARRIVED with the outbreak of cholera that lasted off and on throughout what proved to be a sweltering summer. Within days of the outbreak, Mr. Jefferson had indeed fled St. Louis with the troupe. He had no way of knowing where Josie had gone—she certainly hadn't stayed in Cape Girardeau, the way he had planned, until the company could reach her. But somehow he discovered her whereabouts, and Josie received a note from him in June.

"The company is doing better financially," Mr. Jefferson confided. "Lauretta is an audience-pleaser. They love her most everywhere we go. Stephan says hello. We may play St. Louis again next year. Right now I am not certain."

Nothing about her rejoining the troupe. No animosity. In fact, his comment about the company doing better financially . . . Mr. Jefferson had always been reserved with comments about finances, rarely making them at all. Josie gathered that he meant to reassure her, and she thanked him in a return letter, congratulating him that the troupe was doing so well. She briefly mentioned that she had signed with Mr. Carson's group, then she went on to talk a little about the epidemic.

Patricia, her family, Maggie, and Mrs. O'Brien did not return to St. Louis until late September, when the nights once again grew crisp and the threat of cholera died. At Patricia's insistence, Josie moved from the hotel to the Farrens' house, where she would stay until her wedding in November. An odd month for a wedding, but, as she had told Thomas, she wanted to sleep in his arms every night during the upcoming winter.

"We have a fitting to go to," Patricia said one day in mid-October, approaching where Josie sat in the Farrens' garden—on the edge of a fountain. "After that, we're meeting Thomas and the girls at the traveling show near Chouteau's Pond. You look deep in thought, so deep I doubt you remember any of what we have planned for the day."

Josie smiled. "The fitting is for my wedding gown. Thomas took the girls to the warehouse—I thought you would never convince him that doing that was harmless—and then he's taking them to a café for dinner. After that, we're all meeting at the traveling show that bypassed us during the spring because of the outbreak."

"Very good, Miss Gavin!" Patricia laughed, then sat beside Josie near the trickling fountain. "You'll never believe what I heard from Claudia and Lilian when I saw them outside the market this morning."

"What?" Josie said, her interest piqued. Claudia and Lilian gossiped and gossiped, but at least they usually gossiped about interesting topics and people.

"Constance ran off and married her Creole man," Patricia said, giving Josie a satisfied smile.

"Did she?" Josie almost couldn't believe it. After she and Thomas had left Constance and her father at their home in April, Constance seemed to settle back into her docile ways. Josie had been disappointed, but if Constance wanted to let the man dominate her, then he would, and Josie could do nothing about it. She knew that Constance was really the only one who could do anything about it.

"She did."

Josie laughed in delight. "That's wonderful!"

"Yes, it is, isn't it?"

"Yes!"

Josie had half expected more trouble from Dr. Blanche after Thomas broke off from his college. She had wondered if patients would start shunning Thomas, if colleagues would start avoiding him. None of that had happened, however; in fact,

everything was fine—just as Alan and Dr. Linton had promised. Thomas had more patients than ever, and Dr. Linton was
urging him to do more studies about specific subjects and more
papers that he planned to use in the medical journal he would
soon publish. Thomas had called on Josie only two days ago,
laughing and shaking his head. The medical journal Dr. Linton
had planned was beginning to get quite a bit of notice, and
Dr. Blanche had come to Dr. Linton expressing interest in it
himself.

"Perhaps Dr. Blanche realizes that he needs to be a little
civil. No one likes a bully," Josie had commented.

"The fitting," Patricia said, taking Josie's hand. "You're
full of thoughts these days. Come along."

Laughing, they raced toward the house, Josie fairly bubbling
with excitement and life.

Later in the afternoon, Josie and Maggie stood laughing at
a tiny monkey that was turning flips near the water. A long
red leash dangled from his wrist, and he grinned and winked
at Maggie. His owner pulled a piece of hard candy from his
pocket and held it out to her.

"Ooh!" she said, her eyes growing big. "Yum . . ."

"Come on, Maggie," Katie called from some distance off.
"I thought you wanted to see the e-kestri-ons."

Maggie shook her head back and forth, rolling her eyes
playfully, as she glanced at Josie. "Katie Farren can't say that
word. E-questri-ans." Then she ran off to join her friend.

Josie had met Maggie's other friends in the warehouse only
last week, all eight of them, and their excitement over meeting
her had been priceless. She had plans to find them all good
homes soon. She meant to keep her eyes open for couples
without children, or for couples who wanted more. Thomas
had chuckled when she told him about her plan. Then he had
shaken his head and said that just about the time he thought
her heart couldn't get any larger, it did.

"Let's go with the girls," Patricia said, approaching with
Charlie on her hip.

"Oh, no," Thomas said, approaching from the other side.

"I've had no quiet time with my lady today, an' I have a boat waitin' for the two of us—an' only the two of us." He grabbed Josie's hand and eased her toward him, kissing her gently on the lips, then looking down into her eyes and smoothing the hair back from her cheek.

"I can't compete with that," Patricia said, laughing. "All I have are e-kestri-ons, after all."

Josie laughed, too, then raced off with Thomas.

As promised, he had a boat waiting. He helped her into it, then he climbed in, settled on the opposite end, picked up the oars, and soon had them out in the middle of the shimmering pond. Josie watched him—the way his white shirt billowed, the way his hair waved ever so gently around his face and ended just below his shoulders, the way the sunlight gave a glow to his already handsome face. He smiled at her across the boat, affection brightening his eyes, and she thought her chest would burst, her heart swelled so.

"Thank you for making my dreams come true," she said softly. "For years I waited for you and Maggie. I longed for you and Maggie . . . a family. And now here you are, and I love you more than I can say."

He stopped rowing and moved her way, again sweeping the hair from her cheek and caressing her face. "Josie," he said, dipping his head to kiss her lips. "Josie, m'love . . ."

HISTORICAL NOTE

SELECTING THE HISTORICAL time period in which to set a book, especially down to the exact year, is not always an easy task—particularly when some aspects of the characters' lives fit nicely within the time frame and actual events of the day but others don't. I almost always take a few fictional liberties with the aim of writing an entertaining novel, and then I always take time to explain.

Though the Jefferson Company certainly existed and did include St. Louis in its tour of 1840, it was actually managed by Joseph Jefferson and his brother-in-law, Alexander McKenzie. Obviously I took the liberty of (gulp) removing Mr. McKenzie from the company for a time and inserting in his place Orson Neville—a character conjured by my imagination. I also placed my heroine, Josephine Gavin, into the original bill where other actresses' names appeared. The Jefferson-McKenzie troupe actually left St. Louis at the end of March, though for the sake of this story I extended its stay a few weeks longer than that.

Medically speaking, I jumped ahead a little. Dr. Ignaz Semmelweis did form conclusions about why so many women were dying of childbed fever in the Vienna hospital where he worked as an assistant, but not until 1847. Because I find certain aspects of the history of medicine fascinating, I chose to include Semmelweis's findings in this book, though the dates conflict.

Finally, I pushed the Temperance movement in St. Louis forward. It was alive and flourishing in the community by 1840, and most gaming houses and saloons either had been shut down or were about to be shut down. I always envisioned a scene with Josie and Thomas in a gaming house, and when a scene pops into my head with such force and won't leave me alone, it finds a place in the story.

Teresa Warfield
Alton, Illinois
July 1994

If you enjoyed this book, take advantage of this special offer. Subscribe now and get a

FREE
Historical
Romance

No Obligation (a $4.50 value)

Each month the editors of True Value select the four *very best* novels from America's leading publishers of romantic fiction. Preview them in your home *Free* for 10 days. With the first four books you receive, we'll send you a FREE book as our introductory gift. No Obligation!

    If for any reason you decide not to keep them, just return them and owe nothing. If you like them as much as we think you will, you'll pay just $4.00 each and save at *least* $.50 each off the cover price. (Your savings are *guaranteed* to be at least $2.00 each month.) There is NO postage and handling – or other hidden charges. There are no minimum number of books to buy and you may cancel at any time.

Send in the Coupon Below

To get your FREE historical romance fill out the coupon below and mail it today. As soon as we receive it we'll send you your FREE Book along with your first month's selections.
